First Tango In Paris

By

Emma Styles

COPYRIGHT

©Emma Styles. 2013

Emma Styles asserts the moral right to be identified as the author of this work.

emmajstyles@gmail.com

Chapter One: The Seed Was Sown

Chapter Two: Paris

Chapter Three: First Night

Chapter Four: The Day After

Chapter Five: ChrisetManu2

Chapter Six: Saturday Day Three

Chapter Seven: The Return Home

Chapter Eight: The Sexual Aftermath

Chapter Nine: Paris A Triumphant Return

Chapter Ten: The Dinner Party

Chapter Eleven: On Home Ground

Chapter Twelve: A Taste Of Paris At Home

Chapter Thirteen: Internet…Early Days

Chapter Fourteen: An Unexpected Xmas Present

Chapter Fifteen: New Horizons

Chapter Sixteen: The Move and More

Chapter Eighteen: The Request

Chapter Nineteen: The Instructress

Chapter Twenty: Order Established

Chapter Twenty-One: Spreading My Wings

Chapter Twenty-Two: A Manic Few Months

Chapter Twenty-Three: A Memorable Dinner

Chapter Twenty-Four: Going Global

Chapter Twenty-Five: You May Go To The Ball!

Chapter Twenty-Six: The Ideal Mix

Chapter Twenty-Seven: Playing To The Room!

Chapter Twenty-Eight: Moving Forward

Chapter Twenty-Nine: Horney Common

Chapter Thirty: A Devastating Blow

Chapter Thirty-One: "My Return To Form"

Chapter Thirty-Two: "La Nuit Des Sapeurs-Pompiers"

Chapter Thirty-Three: Sarah's Initiation (Paris Style)

Chapter Thirty-Four: The Aspiring Bitch

Chapter Thirty-Five: Sarah's Grand Finale!

Chapter Thirty-Six: Unexpected Turn Of Events

Chapter Thirty-Seven: A Celebration In Kew

Chapter Thirty-Eight: French Riviera Revelry

Chapter Thirty-Nine: A New Dawn Approaches

Chapter Forty: Two Liberated Ladies

Chapter Forty-One: And There You Have it!

AUTHOR'S NOTE:

This book is a work of memoir. It is a wholly true story based on my best recollections of various events in my life. Where indicated, the names and identifying characteristics of certain people mentioned in the book have been changed in order to protect their privacy. In some instances, I rearranged and/or compressed events and time periods in service of the narrative, and I recreated dialogue to match my best recollection of those exchanges.

DEDICATED TO:

All the Men, Women and Couples encountered along the way, and to those of you reading, who have met me, whether for an intimate fleeting moment, or a lasting friendship! A big hello and thanks for all the memories, making this book possible.

And a huge thank you to my husband for his understanding and total support, and to Yves for your wonderful lust for life and endless surprises (oh and all the outfits!!). Likewise, Frederic and Michel, my friends, lovers and associates. Also, thanks to Michael, the absolute G-spot maestro, who turned my "tap" on all those years ago. The list is endless……….. My gratitude immense!

And finally a massive thanks to "Chris et Manu 2" Paris where it all began on that first freezing Parisian weekend.

PREFACE:

This is a true and accurate account of the wholly unexpected erotic journey my life took from my late twenties onwards. From a dedicated mother and wife, to a confident, outgoing woman, who is comfortable across a wide spectrum of sexual situations, whether it be with a wealthy French fashion executive, my sexual education of his son, being the occasional muse and plaything of a high profile and well connected French Politician/Diplomat, and Master of Ceremonies for many of my sexual dalliances, or simply the unashamed anonymous sexual games, played in the clubs of Paris. I accurately and truthfully recount a choice selection of the numerous erotic and daring sexual exploits I've experienced along the way, with a special section dedicated to the "Les Pompiers de Paris Seine "(Firefighters). All the liaisons took place with my husband, or flying solo, as a fully liberated woman (with his full approval), who knows what she wants and lets nothing stop her from turning her fantasies into reality…. however unattainable they may seem. ,

I hope it inspires women from wherever and whatever age you are, to embrace your sexuality, and explore fully the deep dark erotic side that we all have (some hidden deeper than others). To the men out there, read and enjoy…you may just learn something!

A vast majority of establishments mentioned in the book are still in existence today…. simply "Google" them and explore. I just wish I/we had this facility available to us when I/we started our journey.

slut
(noun)
A Woman With The Morals Of A Man

Chapter One: The Seed Was Sown

It was New Years Eve 1990 when everything started to change for me in the most spectacular and dramatic of ways.

Until that night I was living a relatively normal existence as a married woman with two young children in a small commuter town in Surrey. I was a 29 year old stay at home mum, whose husband Paul worked long and intense hours in the Music Industry, which meant he wasn't around as much as other fathers and do his share of child care, however, the financial rewards were worth it.

The Christmas of 1990 was spent traditionally with the exception that, for two weeks, we had Paul's parents staying with us, enabling us to have some time to ourselves and to catch up with friends at various festive parties, knowing the children were in safe hands with their grand parents.

We had been invited to a New Years Eve party at a friend's house whose husband also worked in the Music Industry, albeit for a different company.

The theme was loosely defined as "fancy dress", which gave many of the ladies scope to reveal far more flesh than normal, and led to many furtive "sneaking's" off to various parts of the house by couples who had arrived with different partners. We both had heard of the wife swapping, car keys in the bowl scenarios that went on in suburbia, but had never witnessed it at such close quarters.

Fuelled by some rather strong punch, we found ourselves in the adjoining garage watching two men we didn't know that well having a very frantic time with Erica the hostess of the party, and wife of my husband's colleague Chris.

We watched them intently, whilst getting very excited at what was unfolding right in front of our eyes. Yes, we'd watched many a porn film together, but this was somehow a whole new ball game, one which I found myself intrigued by and frankly very aroused by. My mind was racing.

Fortunately or unfortunately, I didn't quite know at the time! Our taxi came to pick us up and deliver us safe and sound, if not a bit worse for, wear back home.

The grandparents took the kids out for a long New Years Day walk whilst we cleared our heads and started preparing lunch. High on our topic of subjects was the goings on of the previous night, and to both our surprise how erotic we had found it and that we'd like to explore further.

Part of the deal of entertaining my husbands parents over the festive period was a long weekend away somewhere of my choosing, no expense spared.

A week later the grandparents departed, and we sat down over a Sunday lunch and discussed destinations. Madrid, Amsterdam, Venice, Rome, Paris? all of which we'd been to with my husband's work, with the exception of Paris, (my luggage had once ended up at Charles De Gaulle airport without me, but that's a whole different story). My husband had been several times and also had been to school there in his childhood, but we'd never been together.

So, Paris it was, and this is where the next 21 years get very interesting indeed!

Chapter Two: Paris

After much research of "time out" and Fodor's guide books, (as this was prior to anything "Google") we had flights arranged, hotel booked, friend to look after the kids organized.

We had booked to fly on Thursday 24th January and to return on Monday 28th, the only "hiccup" in our plans, was that we didn't anticipate "Operation Desert Storm" in Iraq commencing a few days before we were due to fly.

We arrived at Heathrow Terminal 2, to be greeted by fully armed soldiers, police and a general high level of security…off to a great start!! Eventually we got checked in and boarded to find a three quarters empty aircraft, apparently there had been an unprecedented level of cancelled seats, as everyone was fearful of flying, and the heightened fear of an imminent terrorist attack.

Luckily, we were seated in the last row and pretty much had the run of the drinks trolley, which very quickly lightened the mood, as we took full advantage of the hospitality.

Upon arrival at CDG we left the terminal to find a taxi, and were met by the coldest day Paris had experienced in forty years…. minus 12 degrees C.

We had booked a very nice hotel right in the heart of Paris, just off Rue du Rivoli, close to the Hotel de Ville. We immediately dumped our bags, freshened up and went exploring, well looking for a nice warm bar in all honesty.

After a few minutes we found ourselves on "Rue Saint Denis", my husband Paul was in his element, sex shop after sex shop, some the size of a small Tesco Express, all crammed with every sex related item imaginable.

Nestled amongst all the sex-shops we found a bar called "Conways" and proceeded to warm up with several large Jack Daniels at

100 francs a throw. My husband Paul kept popping out to explore the adjacent sex shops, and each time returned with a new bag of toys and videos and DVD's. We were rapidly going through our Francs by this stage, fuelled by the JD and the excitement of the street, which made Soho seem incredibly tame.

  Strolling back to the Hotel to plan our first evening, we picked up the local equivalent of London's "Time Out" which was called "Pariscope". At a later date Paul said it was the finest five francs (50p) he'd ever spent. It was our weekend travel bible for many a year to come.

Chapter Three: First Night

We agreed that as it was so cold we would commence our first evening with a few hours in a mixed sauna/hammam, ten minutes from the Hotel. We assumed it would be pretty good, as it was located across the street from the Ritz Hotel, and in a very smart area.

Oh how misguided and naïve we were. Upon entering we were greeted by a very elegant looking receptionist, who took our entrance fee in return for a couple of towels each and a locker key, then proceeded to direct us to the changing areas. We nervously undressed and stored our clothes in the locker provided and made our way to the wet and dry areas. The ambience due in no small part to the lighting, which was strategically placed ultra violet tubes, was one of pure fear, coupled with a definite level of intrigue. We showered in the large communal shower and made our way to the sauna cabin. We still had not seen another soul at this point.

As we entered the cabin, we were met by near pitch darkness, the only form of lighting being the glow from the actual smoldering sauna coals. We stumbled and groped our way to a bench and placed our towels on the nuclear hot wooden slats to be sure we didn't burn the flesh off our bottoms on the first night and end up in a burns unit somewhere!

In those first few moments of blindness, I sensed we were not alone, as there were sounds of breathing all around. We sat for a few minutes, whilst our eyes became accustomed to the low level of light, and, as the shapes became clearer, I could definitely attach the sounds to individual bodies. It wasn't long before I realized that we were in the middle of a sauna cabin, with approximately ten men, all naked and masturbating.... it was a very disconcerting moment. Here I was fresh from being a mum in Surrey, to being surrounded by men of all different shapes and sizes gently fondling themselves, whilst staring intently at me. Disconcerting, but strangely arousing.

We hastily left and went to the steam room and experienced pretty much the same thing, so we decided to have a wander towards the relaxation areas on the lower level, again it was lowly lit but bright enough to discover there was a row of cubicles with mattresses, there were a few grunts and groans emanating from all areas, but on closer inspection to both our horrors we discovered some of the men had long blonde wigs and lipstick on, a couple simply wore nappies and to top it off there was a man fully dressed as a baby sitting in a giant pram suckling on a dummy and gurgling away very happily whilst watching an assortment of very strange creatures engaged in various odd sexual acts, all from the comfort of his extra large "Silver Cross Vintage" stroller.

This was not exactly what we had in mind, and very quickly agreed that a sharp exit was required and to find the nearest bar to plan our next move.

A truly bizarre experience, but no real harm done. The entrance fee as a couple was 100Ffrancs (about ten pounds), so we really should have guessed from the price alone, that on the other side of the reception there was never going to be a gorgeous spa packed with beautiful and elegant naked people all enjoying themselves and each other. We had definitely got what we paid for!

We dressed and shuffled off in to the freezing Parisian night. We hadn't walked for more than a few minutes when we saw a glowing neon sign "Harrys Bar". This was on our "to do" list, as we'd had a very romantic evening at the original bar in Venice a few years earlier.

Settling on the stools at the stunning solid oak bar we ordered our tipple of choice, two Jack Daniels and ice, and set about discussing what we were going to do next. It was around nine thirty, so we decided to get a bite to eat and then head for the "Pigalle", where there seemed to be a vast array of choice for the liberated adult.

Slowly enjoying our drinks and the warmth of the bar, we were approached by a rather good looking man, who asked us, where we were from. When we told him that we were from England and it was our first night in Paris, he became the first in a long line of French people who thanked us for visiting and how brave we must be to travel with all that's happening with Iraq and the terrorist threat. We found this strange, but accepted it graciously. He proceeded to point to a rather attractive lady sat at a corner table and asked would we join him and his wife for a drink and they would give us some pointers on things we may be interested in seeing and doing. Taking our drinks we joined them, explaining where we'd just been, which caused much laughter and guffawing, as only the French can. We explained to them that in England things like adult films were heavily censored, unless bought under the counter in a brown bag for an exorbitant price and live sex clubs simply didn't exist. He then suggested that we should finish our drink and go to their apartment where as he put it in his Frenglish " we will take a drink and then we all fuck each other". Being swinging virgins, we were very taken aback and flustered at such a blatant invitation and bluffed and stumbled our way out of the situation saying that we would like to go and see a live sex show, as we had never been to one, and would take a rain check on their very kind offer! They accepted this and went on to suggest that we go to one of the most famous "live sex-extravaganza" in Paris called "Theatre Loving Chair", which was only a ten minute walk from the bar. We returned the favour and bought fresh drinks and chatted and flirted a little with them over the next hour. We took his card and said we'd call the next day to meet for lunch…events overtook us somewhat, so we never had chance to call, but did meet up with them again by chance on a subsequent trip.

After a brisk walk in the freezing cold we found the "theatre", and upon entering we were blasted with a gust of very welcome hot air, which quickly put some warmth and feeling into our bones, even more so the one thousand franc entrance fee! We walked along a small corridor and through some heavy velvet drapes, into a smallish room, with seating for around a hundred people, all arranged around a small circular stage, finding two free seats we settled down and to my pleasure noticed there was a high percentage of couples in the audience, which reassured me all was fine, however, within a few minutes the act finished and the stage went into darkness and the house lights came on to polite applause…. Bugger was that it? What now? Everyone started to go, leaving the two of us sat alone like a pair of lost souls. We soon realized that we'd caught the tail end of the show, and that the next was due to commence in fifteen minutes. My husband decided a drink was required, so ambled off to reception to be told they only served soft drinks, but he could go to the shop a few doors down if he wanted, which he did appearing five minutes later with a half sized bottle of Pastis and two paper cups.

Suddenly, as if on cue people began arriving for the start of the next show. I was anxiously looking around to see if any couples were entering, when to my horror a touring party of Welsh Rugby players appeared noisily through the drapes and sat in the rows in front and behind us. Paul whispered, "this should be interesting, suggest we don't speak and let on we are English and we'll be fine". Famous last words!!

The house lights dimmed and the show started, taking position centre stage, was a rather exotic redhead, who proceeded to strip erotically and pleasure herself with numerous toys that she had as her props, all the men were very vocal in their support of her behavior! She soon noticed that I was the only female present and immediately focused all her attention on me, trying to incorporate me in to her routine. I felt myself sliding lower and lower in the seat, as all the men were whooping and hollering their encouragement. She was inviting me to join her on stage, and partake in some "games" with her. Luckily, after what seemed like an eternity she realized this wasn't happening and she continued her act alone. By now as the only female in the audience, I was getting furtive glances and stares from all the men, and some very explicit comments especially from the rugby boys, who had most definitely been having a few drinks before they'd arrived for the show.

The music changed tempo and a muscular guy in a loincloth appeared and jumped onto stage to join the redhead, he proceeded to stalk her in the style of a slightly eccentric and perverted Tarzan like character. After a few minutes of this, she submitted to his gesticulating and knelt in front of him and unleashed his rather impressive looking penis, to the cheers of all the men. She made great play with it, showing it off to the audience, licking and sucking noisily on it until he was rock hard.

Now it was Mr. Tarzan's turn to notice the sole female in the audience, and made great overtures offering me his cock from the stage, waving it furiously and slapping it whilst grinning like a crazed maniac. What happened next was all a bit of a blur, he picked up his redhead conquest and carried her off the stage, into the cheering audience, homing in on us like a guided missile [well he most definitely had one], quickly arriving to where we were sat and proceeded to lay the redhead across our laps, inviting us to play with them, she was grabbing Paul's hand encouraging him to play with her nipples, whilst he was grabbing my hand and making me rub his rock hard erection...I was in shock and the rugby players were in raptures! With one swift and very well rehearsed movement he entered her, whilst keeping eye contact with me, encouraging me to help him thrust in and out of her, eventually after much encouragement I gave in, and found myself actively slapping his firm bottom vigorously with each thrust. By the look on his face he'd definitely not bargained on my newfound enthusiasm and vigor. The audience loved it, and the whole public/exhibitionistic scenario strangely turned me on. Show over, it was time to go back to hotel, as it had been a long and adventurous day. As it turned out no chance of that happening anytime soon!!

Once outside we spotted a taxi, a white Mercedes Saloon, we jumped in and asked to be taken to our hotel, however, before setting off he enquired as to whether we enjoyed the show, and when we said that it was O.K he shrugged and said it was for tourists and he would happily take us to where the French people go for "loving"!!

Paul immediately went defensive, saying we only had enough money on us to get back to the Hotel (as we'd read about tourist being taken for a ride, literally), so going anywhere else was not possible, to which Joe le taxi, as we later christened him immediately turned off his meter and grinned and said "welcome to Paris, the night is young, we now go and I show you where it all happens, Oui?". He explained that we were visitors to his country and that now we were his personal guests. He assured us that he would deliver us safe and sound back to our Hotel when we had had enough. Paul seemed very alert, but ready to go with the flow, which made me relax and get a second wind... if truth were known I had a very warm excited glow growing inside me.

We soon pulled up outside a "Club Privé", it was called "Le Triangle" (renamed a few years ago as the Full Moon) in the 1st arrondissement. He seemed to know the receptionist quite well, we checked our coats, and proceeded downstairs to the club.....Wow!, was my immediate reaction as we headed to the bar, where a bottle of Tattinger Champagne in a bucket, complete with three flutes was delivered, I could see Paul say something to Joe le taxi, and then nodded and smiled. Our first steps into a French Swing club, with a guide and free Champers, my second wind was blowing hard as we settled into one of the plush sofas along side the dance floor.

It wasn't long until I noticed several dark passageways leading off from the bar area, and the occasional couple wandering off and re emerging after a while in various states of dishevelment, I caught Paul's eye and gave each other a knowing wink…it was time to explore!!

As we entered one of the passages ways we were passed by a semi naked lady with her husband in tow, who smiled and muttered something to us in French, I had no idea what they said, but it definitely sounded very erotic, especially given the circumstances.

We very soon discovered that the passageways led to various small themed rooms, with one leading to a much larger room with a huge circular raised bed in the centre, and several large screens with hardcore films playing, but with no sound, just the hypnotic music filtering from the dance area. There were comfy armchairs and sofas positioned around the bed, with several couples watching a group of people, in various states of undress enjoying themselves on the bed. Shortly, a couple joined us on the sofa and started to play with each other, soon she had unzipped her partner and started to stroke his rather impressive cock, literally inches from me, she slowly knelt in front of him and started running her tongue up and down his penis, whilst all the time keeping eye contact with me, I could sense Paul was aroused, as well as a bit bewildered, and a bit apprehensive as to what was going to happen next! As since we'd been married we'd never, ever been in such a "full on in your face" multi person sexual encounter, especially in public. Suddenly, the girl put her hand on my leg and offered me her partners penis, my emotions were doing cartwheels…I was definitely tempted, but didn't know what Paul's reaction would have been if I taken her up on the offer, so I politely declined and we adjourned to the bar area. This was our first sojourn into the world of swinging, on a freezing but somewhat steamy Parisian night and I was definitely intrigued and wanted to explore further…much, much further. Joe le taxi appeared and said "O.K, we go now to another club", by this time it was approaching 2.30 in the morning, but he said the night was young…. I was, by this time running on pure adrenalin!!!

After a short drive in his taxi we arrived at another Club Privé, and rang the buzzer and smiled into the overhead security camera, we were swiftly let in and again deposited our coats. We followed Joe and made our way into the inner sanctum of the club, again the décor was very decadent/elegant, with a bar and buffet area and a stone stairway leading downwards, to where there was a fully equipped dungeon and also spiral stairway up to several group play areas.

We were both reticent, and unsure as how each other would react if either had any intimate contact with anyone else, this was after all still our first night, even though it was approaching 5 a.m.!

I sensed that we'd be doing a lot of talking during the following day, after a few hours sleep.

We returned to the bar, where Joe had bought us both a rather large Remy Martin Brandy and explained where we should definitely visit the following evening. He gave us his card with the names of a few clubs we must try before we went back to the U.K.

We finally left the club around dawn after soaking up more of this newfound decadent form of amusement. When he dropped us back at our hotel he said he'd collect us Sunday at 2 o'clock and take us to the airport. He wished us a good rest and hoped we'd had a good evening and to enjoy the next few days…True to his word not a single centime changed hands.

Chapter Four: The Day After

Day two: After a few hours of fitful restless sleep we are awoke slightly hung over, but absolutely starving, as it dawned on us that we'd had nothing to eat but a few nibbles since we'd left Heathrow; we definitely needed to refuel our systems, and soon.

We found a small café-bar near to the hotel and settled down to a Parisian breakfast of strong black coffee, a large shot of cognac and a large platter of sweet and sugary crépes, supplemented by a few Marlboro lights to blend in with the locals, not having the courage to go completely native with a "Gauloise" for fear of choking.

We discussed our first twenty four hours in Paris and decided that we both really enjoyed what we had seen of the clubs, even though at the time we were both unsure as how to react, as neither of us wanted to upset the other, however, it very quickly became clear that we'd both been highly turned on by the atmosphere and the people, many of whom were typically chic and stylishly attractive…. even partially clothed! We decided that, that evening after dinner we would visit one of the clubs Joe le taxi had told us not to miss, it was called "Chris et Manu 2" (there is a Chris et Manu 1, which is a different ball game altogether and will feature later) on Rue St Bon, very close to the Hotel de Ville and a stones throw from our hotel, we got the address and brief details from the afore mentioned "Pariscope", in the section near to the back of the pocket sized magazine, headed "les club de rencontre". We decided to take a stroll and do a daytime recce, and having found it tucked away in a little side street, we were pleasantly surprised at how normal and inviting it appeared from the outside. So off we went excited, and highly charged at what the coming evening might offer….We certainly would not be disappointed!

So after a bit of retail therapy, resulting in, amongst other items, a new pair of sheer black Wolford hold-ups, with intricate lacy tops, to go with my black Sarah Sturgeon slinky figure hugging dress, I was ready for the night ahead…our first venture into a "Club de Rencontre"!

Chapter Five: ChrisetManu2

Scratching the surface: After a few hours rest in our room, and a rather rampant session of love making, it was time to get ready for the evening. I had two hours to soak in the bath and preen and pamper myself, and fantasize as to what lay ahead. It was still in the very early days of that having a "Brazilian" was fashionable and very much de rigueur. However, in anticipation of a the weekend, I had given myself a home styled version a few days prior to flying, so everything was in perfect order and would pass any close inspection with flying colours, coupled with a liberal coating of Chanel No.5 velvet body cream and a few dabs of pure perfume I was set for the evening. Face on…dress on…hold-ups on…heels on…good to go!

We had spotted a really cool and chic looking restaurant earlier in the day called "L'Amazonial", a ten-minute walk from our hotel, situated near Les Halles, in the very aptly named " Rue Sainte-Opportune". It was a great start to the evening; we were seated outside, under cover on the bustling street, with outdoor heaters and excellent mood lighting. We were immediately given a glass of Kir Royale whilst perusing the menu, and simultaneously watching the world and his very strange brothers pass by. Also it quickly became apparent that this was a well known and very popular mixed gay establishment, with an overtly camp atmosphere, the waiters were playing up and pinching each others bottoms and generally misbehaving, all of which added to our sense of anticipation.

During dinner we discussed and set the ground rules that we would adhere to in the club, namely "look but don't touch" was the criteria that we would use. Certainly during this, our first un-chaperoned foray in to the swinging scene!

After a very pleasant meal we made our way towards the club, and as it was still early by Parisian nightlife standards, we found a nice bar close by and ordered our customary Jack Daniel's, large ones, to give us some extra "Dutch courage", and continued discussing the do's and don'ts to adhere to in the club, by this time we were both getting very excited and nervous, so at ten to midnight we decided to wander closer to the club and hide in a doorway like a pair of school kids, watching what kind of people the club attracted, we were freezing cold and after witnessing a few very elegant and respectable couples entering ...we could take the cold no longer and simultaneously we said "fuck it, in for a penny......" so we approached the entrance full of false bravado, rang on the bell and smiled politely into the security camera above the door.

    We were greeted with a smile from a very pleasant blonde lady, who spoke a little English, that combined with Paul's rusty French made for a most amusing conversation to the casual listener. The up shot being, that she asked us "were we lost?", as they got very few English people visiting the club, and with a grin she said, she thought that "Zee" English were a bit prudish and she didn't accept any responsibility if we got shocked or corrupted! The price was to be paid upon leaving, which was 420Francs and included the first two drinks each. She gave us a quick tour of the club, on the ground floor was the reception/coatroom, a small bar area leading to a restaurant, which via a spiral stairway had additional restaurant seating, the lighting and décor was very elegant and stylish, a lot of money had obviously been invested in making this club appeal to the higher echelons of the Parisian "swinging" culture.

    We were then led downstairs, and given a sneak peak at the main club area, after which we were swiftly led back up to the reception and asked "were we happy with what we had seen and did we wish to stay and enjoy a night of fun the French way?"..."absolutely" we both said at once, with a more than obvious glint in our eyes. Jesse the receptionist and "mistress of ceremonies" took our coats and gave us a welcome glass of champagne...this was the start of a long association with the club and its staff.

    We made our way excitedly downstairs, with drink in hand and a small slip of paper with our names on, which we handed to Sylvia, the lady in charge of the superbly stocked bar. And who, in between dispensing drinks doubled as a very skilled DJ, playing wonderful uplifting Euro dance music that kept the dance floor pumping with very erotically dressed people.... We took our drink and made a beeline for one of the small alcoves, located off the dance area and relaxed into the soft luxurious sofa, the whole area looked as if in a previous era it had been a large underground wine cellar, with alcoves and rooms of various themes and sizes scattered throughout. In this particular alcove there was a large, semi circular plush crimson velvet sofa, and a large enclosed hanging wicker swing/chair. We settled back and soaked up this newfound hedonistic atmosphere. Soon we summoned up the courage to venture further, and explore all the other areas. We entered a maze of smaller rooms, with several couples in various states of undress, caressing and intimately fondling each other, and many in intertwined groups of four or more! We made our way into a quiet corner to drink in the sights and sounds in front of us. Often other couples would discreetly sidle up and stand by us, there definitely appeared to be a specific etiquette involved if you wanted to participate further. It quickly became apparent, that the female of the couple would engage with the other female, either by eye contact or by subtle touch, to ascertain if there was any interest in getting more intimate. We wandered from room to room, enjoying the voyeuristic feeling of the environment, and best of all there was no pressure what so ever to join in, it was all very relaxed and civilized.

After a few more drinks at the bar, and some "inappropriate" dancing we found ourselves back in the original alcove with the wicker swing, in which, was now a very pretty girl in the throes of an intense orgasm as a woman who was knelt between her legs was pleasuring her orally, both ladies being vocally encouraged by their respective partners, there were a few other couples casually watching the unfolding scenario. The atmosphere was electric, as people started to play with each other, and soon a very attractive couple came and stood beside us, very quickly it became apparent that they fancied having some fun with us, right there and then! She started to run her hand up and down my thigh and whispered something in my ear, I looked at Paul and he whispered "what about our ground rules?" I grinned and said "I'm about to break them...just a tiny bit?". A look of pure ecstasy instantly crossed his face, and in a blur I found myself being gently kissed by her partner. Paul was pinned against the wall being enthusiastically kissed and stroked by the female. I was really starting to get into the moment, when Paul suddenly whispered to me in a panicked voice "meet me at the bar...now".

Once we'd all untangled and excused ourselves, I went and found Paul, and he explained, that the girl was trying to unzip his trousers and, he'd simply lost his nerve and was unsure as to whether we'd both regret things in the cold light of day! So we decided to just to be eager non-participants for the remainder of the evening, and to debrief over brunch the following morning.

We left the club around four a.m., but not before we agreed that we would return the following evening to sample the restaurant. So much to the amusement of Jesse, Paul immediately booked us a table for ten thirty. On the corner of Rue Victoria, where our Hotel was located (coincidently named the Le Britannique), was a small Jazz bar, which was still full of Friday night revelers, we decided it would be rude not to pop in for a night cap! This did become a bit of a ritual!

Chapter Six: Saturday Day Three

We awoke to yet another freezing Parisian day, and decided that we would take a walk along "Rue Rivoli" to find a nice bar to re-nourish ourselves. We sat and talked avidly about the previous evening, and both agreed that we were exceptionally turned on by the situation, and that we both would liked to have gone further, so we came to the conclusion that as we were in France, completely anonymous, we should indulge our desires a little, and if we disgraced ourselves so be it, nobody would know. After all we were there to enjoy ourselves!

We had so far done not a single thing a tourist would do, Eiffel Tower, Le Louvre, Les Champs Elysees etc etc, but we both agreed that we'd be definitely be coming back, so we'd leave them until the next time. We had an extremely different agenda now!

We took a stroll to one of Paris's finest department stores "Galeries Lafayette" on boulevard Haussmann, one of the finest shopping streets in the city. Wow, what a breath-taking store. First opened in 1893, the "Galeries Lafayette" department store is a Paris fashion tradition.

This is an essential stop for fashion enthusiasts: men and women's designer collections are always kept at the cutting-edge, and the latest trends in jewelry and accessories, home furnishings, or cosmetics can all be a drooled over under one roof and what a spectacular roof it is…has to be seen to be believed.

I did a small amount of damage to our credit card in the lingerie department, I was like the proverbial kid in a sweetshop, with all the wonderful stockings, basques, intricate lace panties…so much choice…. so much anticipation, it was an hour of sexually charged shopping. A wondrously warm tingling feeling was coursing through my body, I was feeling faint and giddy with it all. I signed the credit card receipt with a knowing smile from the obligatory elegant French assistant.

During the casual stroll back towards the hotel, stopping and exploring some of the beautiful boutiques, we found a wonderful old-fashioned Parisian "bar à vins" called Le Rubis, with a traditional zinc counter; we sat and sampled a few wonderful glasses of Beaujolais, courtesy of the wonderfully named "patron" Albert Prat, he told us he'd opened in the early seventies, I would recommend it highly, it is located just off the ultra-fashionable Rue du Faubourg St Honore.

After taking a small nap in the hotel it was time to get ready for the night ahead, this time with much reduced "rules of engagement" and a lot less nerves. So for luck I repeated the previous nights routine of soak, make up, smellies and finally the other LBD I had brought with me, complimented by a stunning new pair of hold-ups and panties, all that was missing was the wonderful new shoes Paul had bought me… they were still in the box, seemingly waiting for this moment!! Paul put on a new pair of Armani trousers and a gorgeous John Smedley Sea Island cotton top. We were ready to party and in the mood to go with whatever Paris could throw at us.

We arrived at the club, where Jesse again greeted us warmly, this time with no look of concern that we were a couple of tourists who were confused and lost. We gratefully took the welcome glass of champagne and were shown to our table, all very stylish, with the ladies menu having no prices on it! There was a mouth-watering choice, and once Paul had translated, as best he could with his rapidly improving childhood French we ordered.

The food was magnificent, however, what lay directly beneath us, in the club area was so hypnotically sensual, it seemed to be playing havoc with my taste buds. By the sound of the discreet entrance buzzer going off regularly in the last half an hour, we assumed that the club was filling up quite swiftly. So it was with huge anticipation, that we slowly consumed our fresh raspberries and desert wine, teasing ourselves as to when to go downstairs, eventually it all got too much and we enthusiastically headed downstairs to the basement.

Being a Saturday night the club was packed with many elegantly dressed men and their provocatively dressed partners….some ladies in full length evening dresses, some simply in heels and sheer skimpy playsuits, basically a wide and varied range of revealingly provocative outfits!

We took our customary Jack Daniels and automatically gravitated to the alcove with the wicker swing and grinned at each other, I think we were both goading each other to be daring, and see where it led! It actually, very quickly led to us being joined by another couple, who spoke good English, they were slightly older than us, but in great shape and very easy on the eye. We chatted and told them about all the things we'd seen and done so far, and in return we gleaned lots of information from them, as they were native Parisians and knew all the hot spots. They gave us a comprehensive list of "must do's", and the places to be avoided.

Paul went to the bar to get us all some drinks, and immediately, the female Claudia jumped up and said she would go with Paul to help. As soon as they had disappeared Olivier moved into Paul's vacated place beside me on the sofa and very casually started to gently and seductively run his fingers up and down my thigh, complimenting me on my choice of hold-ups and whispering softly in my ear. I had no idea what he was saying, but it just sounded so sexy and he smelt divine, a very delicate sandalwood cologne and gorgeous minty breathe. I was in complete ecstasy, not having had this level of close up personal attention from another man in seven years of marriage. I was reaching boiling point as his fingers worked their way to the lacey tops of my hold-ups and the fleeting touches of fingers on flesh…my flesh! I was sure he must have felt the heat emanating from every pore of my body. I tried to pull back from the situation, as I anticipated that Paul and Claudia would be back with the drinks at any moment, and when I half-heartedly mentioned this to him, he simply smiled and said that he'd told Claudia to "take her time!" Which turned out to be their code for getting to know a couple at a slightly more intimate level. My internal organs did somersaults and before I knew it we were locked in a very sensual and passionate kiss, with our tongues doing the most outrageous acrobatics, whilst his fingers continued to stroke their way to my panties….what to do?...when to stop?...my mind said cool it ,but my body screamed…I want more…I need more and I need it now. When suddenly, as if by intuition, he leant back from me and smiled just as Paul and Claudia returned with the drinks. Both of them were beaming, they passed us our drinks and sat down beside each other on the sofa…. Paul leant across to me and hilariously stated the obvious "I think we're being seduced" I grinned and whispered "when in Rome"… but this was

Paris, but who cared.... definitely not me! During the next half hour we all flirted outrageously together, enjoying each other's company in this sex driven atmosphere. I'd never experienced anything remotely like this before... and was keen to take it to the next level...I didn't have to wait long, Olivier said it was time for more drinks, so I took a leaf out of Claudia's book and offered to help him carry them.

Olivier and I headed to the bar, where he ordered a bottle of "House Champagne" and four glasses and winking he asked for them to be ready, and on the bar in ten minutes.... I was confused, until I saw the glint in his eye as he took my hand and led me towards the playrooms, we soon found a secluded area in the nearest alcove, where we resumed the kiss, this time with much more unrestraint on my part, he very skillfully slid my dress up over my hips and started stroking me just above the top of my panties, I was in heaven, but knew we were on a slim time frame, so I subtly, but invitingly parted my legs slightly, as a helpful encouragement for him to continue, he took the hint and deftly slipped his hand down inside my panties and skillfully stroked my, by now soaking pussy.....within seconds I came with a massive shudder over his nimble fingers, whilst sucking on his tongue, as if it were his penis. I calculated that I had only a few minutes to reciprocate my pleasure. A wanton side of me, that had been dormant since the children were born came bursting to the surface as I grasped at his trousers, my hands were shaking as I unzipped him, and released a most spectacular erection, I hastily fell to my knees and proceeded to eat his cock like a sex crazed porn queen....I just couldn't take it all in...both mentally, as well as physically, it was like living through an erotic dream, after much enthusiastic licking and sucking he started to tremble and groan as he ejaculated hard and copiously down my throat....it was pure unadulterated lust. It was, however, all to brief.

As requested the champagne and glasses were waiting for us at the bar, which we duly took back to Paul and Claudia, who appreciatively gave us a small round of applause and a meaningful but humorous smile.

After more flirtatious chat, Claudia asked me if she could take Paul and show him around her "favourite areas" of the club.... who was I to argue! Paul looked very nervous as she led him by the hand to explore the "Magic Kingdom" as we referred to it from then on.

When they returned some twenty minutes later, Paul explained that we were being collected at the hotel at lunchtime, which was now only a few hours away and as it was approaching 3.30 a.m., we should be leaving, much to my pleasure Olivier said they would leave with us and buy us a night cap at a small bar they knew close by. We both readily agreed this would be a pleasant end to the evening, even though I was desperate to know what Paul and Claudia had gotten up to. We paid our bill, a very modest One thousand Francs, which at the time equated to about one hundred pounds, very good value for the most erotic night of both our lives…so far! We said our good byes to the staff and told them we'd see them again soon, little did I know how soon!

We had a quick drink at the little late night café/bar, which was thankfully only a few minutes from the hotel, we swapped telephone numbers and a courteous peck on each others cheeks goodnight, which at the time struck me as so strange, considering what I'd been doing with her husband only moments before, but also seemed the most natural thing in the world to do. They disappeared into the night as we disappeared into our hotel; to get a few hours much needed rest.

Chapter Seven: The Return Home

After having crashed and burned the moment my head hit the pillow, I awoke after about five hours of deep contented sleep. I lay there replaying, in my mind the events of the previous night, and I would swear to this day I could still taste Olivier....what a wonderful way to wake up.

After showering and hastily packing, we had a few hours to find a bar and get a bite to eat; we left our bags at reception and braved the freezing conditions once more. We decided to walk across the Seine and clear our heads. Eventually we found a small café and had a wonderful coffee, cognac along with a delightful bowl of hot French Onion Soup served with warm crusty bread..... the perfect morning after pick me up. We barely spoke, as we were both unsure of what to say, as well as basking in the afterglow of a weekend of increasing sexual discovery and awareness. I could sense neither one of us wanted the adventure to end, and that both of us wanted and strangely needed to continue this exciting journey ....to wherever it may lead.

True to his word, Joe Le Taxi was there to meet us at the hotel, spot on time, he was intrigued to hear what we had got up to since he dropped us back that distant first night. He looked so pleased that we had followed his advice, and had, had a wild time, and even more pleased, when we gave him a bottle of Chateau de Montifaud Cognac, complete with two brandy balloons that we'd bought him, to, in some small part repay all his kindness and advice, we said our goodbyes, and agreed we'd meet up if we returned to Paris.

Whilst waiting in departures for our flight I felt it was time that we compared notes on our seduction at the hands of Olivier and Claudia. Paul gleefully fed me tit-bits of his brief interlude with Claudia, which turned out to be an almost a carbon copy of my encounter with Olivier..... We both agreed this was obviously a well rehearsed seduction technique that they'd used before, on numerous occasions, and one that we were swept up in....with, thankfully, absolutely no regrets whatsoever!

Once on the plane, I settled back with a glass of white wine and drifted into my own private little world, reliving over and over in my mind my time alone with Olivier the previous night, and how I wished we'd had more time together, to explore each other fully. My mind was overloaded with filthy thoughts and scenarios, enhanced by the background vibrations of the planes engines I was experiencing multiple mini orgasms, a feeling I'd never ever had before, it was mind blowing. I felt a whole new world of eroticism had started to unfold, and I was more than willing to be carried along on this new found path, and was excited to see where it would lead, and what future encounters were on the horizon.

Chapter Eight: The Sexual Aftermath

After getting reunited with the children after our first real break from them since they were born, I tried to settle back into the same old routine…. nursery…. coffee mornings…Sainsbury's et al, I frequently found myself daydreaming, and couldn't seem to get Paris out of my head. I also found myself mentally undressing and sizing up any attractive man I saw.

The first few days back seemed very mundane, and didn't have any of the day to day excitement of Paris, however, our personal sex life had become very intense, and experimental, with Paul, who during our lovemaking was very much into having me tell him in detail about my liaison with Olivier, and what else I wished I'd done with him, and would do if the opportunity arose in the future. This very much excited him, whilst I was very much getting off, simply by reliving it verbally! Also fantasizing about the possibilities of what I'd like to happen if there was a next time.

By the Thursday I couldn't keep it to myself any longer… I just had to tell someone, the ideal person being Erica. We met for lunch and I recounted the weekend in detail, her face was a picture, and I could tell she would be angling for a similar trip away.

Sadly, that first weekend back Helen my aunt, who lived in the Cotswold's had been taken ill, and as I was pretty much her only close living relative, I felt I had to go and visit her in hospital and check on the house she'd been living in alone, since the death of her husband eight years previously. So trying to juggle this and home life was a strain, and a good three hours a day driving. She'd had a mini stroke but the prognosis was fairly good that she'd make a good recovery and would be back home in about a week. I continued to visit every other day, and was there on the day she was discharged to take her home and help settle her in. In the meantime with her full blessing we'd arranged with an agency, for her to have a live in carer, initially for a month, just to make sure all was well. This was a weight off my shoulders and she seemed very happy with both the arrangement and Celia the agency/nurse/cook/companion. Thankfully all proceeded as we'd hoped for and things settled down relatively swiftly and on the whole problem free.

Then, out of the blue on the Monday after Helen had been back home for a little over a week, Paul returned home from work grinning and told me to get my naughty head on (it never really went away….lots of daydreaming, whilst driving to and from the Cotswold's!) as he'd re booked for Paris, leaving on Thursday morning. I nearly came on the spot…so much to organize, but oh so worth it!

I called Erica to beg her to look after the children, to which she replied "yes of course you lucky dirty bitch".

Paul suggested we call Olivier and Claudia and gauge their reaction to meeting again, and so soon. Maybe they'd moved on and had forgotten us already, but thankfully, it was like phoning old friends, they said we could stay with them, but fully understood, when we declined, as the hotel was already booked, however, they insisted on picking us up from the airport.

The next couple of days were a blur, getting everything prepared and arranged, I really didn't have time to stop and think about how deliciously decadent we were being.

Before I could blink Thursday morning was upon us. Erica had picked up the children and the taxi arrived to take us the short drive to Heathrow. We had a slightly later flight than a few weeks previously, so after checking in we went through to departures, leaving us time to have a light lunch and a nice chilled bottle of "vin blanc" between us, to take the edge off and get us relaxed and in the mood for Paris and all it's mysteries.

The flight was uneventful, apart from the steward who was looking after our section of the plane had the "hots" for Paul, and kept topping his drink, whilst totally ignoring me, he even gave Paul his number for future reference ….the cheeky git …. Paul was most amused but not in the least tempted!

Chapter Nine: Paris A Triumphant Return

Being met at an airport is the only way to travel, especially if it's by a very horny Frenchman, and his equally attractive wife.

Thankfully the weather was much milder this time, and on the way from the airport we stopped off at a bar to have a welcome back drink! They seemed very pleased to see us and it was completely reciprocated. We had a laugh about our first meeting at "ChrisetManu" and we all were, thankfully, once again very comfortable in each others company…I just had a feeling things were going to go to the next level over the next few days.

They dropped us at our hotel of choice "Le Britannique", and left us to our own devices, but said they'd collect us the following evening, as we were to be guests of theirs for dinner, and to meet a few of their close circle of friends, who they informed us were all "tres sympa!"…We were both intrigued and excited at the prospect.

We soon found ourselves in a nearby bar deciding our plans for the evening, and we both concluded that there was no contest…a return to "ChrisetManu2" it was!

A short while later, after a relaxing soak together with a nice glass of white wine from the mini bar, I was ready for the night ahead. Paul had bought me a nice selection of hold-ups from Liberty in London and half a dozen pairs of gorgeous knickers from the "La Perla" section of Harvey Nichols as a surprise…heavenly.

So off we headed, Paul had brought a selection of the latest CD'S with him ,as a gift for the club and we had planned to drop them off first, then find a nice restaurant before we finished the evening at the club…..they simply wouldn't hear of it, they insisted we dined in the club as their guests, whilst thrusting a glass of champagne in our direction. We were introduced to Chris (the female of the pair) and Manu, who would become very good friends. They explained, that they were one of the first "club de rencontre" in Paris, opening in 1982 and that due to the demand and social change, there were now many clubs opening up, of varying degrees of sophistication, catering to every kink and fetish imaginable….more on these later in the memoir.

    The restaurant was already busy, and we were seated adjacent to a lovely couple, whom were in their late fifties, and had lived and worked in London several years previously. They told us they had been coming to the club at least once a week for many years, and how they felt that we'd been given sound advice by "Joe Le Taxi", as in their opinion, this was one of the most chic clubs of its type in Paris and always attracted a high quality clientele.

    We had a wonderful evening flirting and watching all the hedonistic couples playing, with no pretentions whatsoever, the atmosphere was pure sexual lust. Eventually, Paul and I found our way into the back rooms, and had an amazing "frantic fuck" together whilst being encouraged by the older couple, who were themselves partaking in some heavy foreplay and erotically stroking me, as the tension built towards my second or third orgasm, a very attractive young girl joined us and started to caress my breasts. I was literally screaming, but all the while trying to maintain a British sense of decorum…I failed miserably and was swept away on a tidal wave of pleasure and we both enjoyed a wonderful and erotic climax together as the young girl gently kissed me on the cheek and slipped away to find her partner. We were greeted at the bar by the older couple who simply said "Bravo", they bought us a drink and toasted us as only the French can…loudly! We left reasonably early by French standards, as we were anticipating a long and hopefully exhaustive night with Olivier and Claudia. When we tried to settle our account, we were told we were their guests, we could only assume the selection of CD'S was the reason! As was now rapidly becoming a tradition, we stopped of at the little jazz bar for nightcap or two!

    After a good sleep, we awoke mid morning to the sound of the telephone….it was Claudia confirming the evening arrangements, she informed me that the dinner dress code was to be seductive, but elegant, with a degree of fetish, as there was a chance everyone would end up "en masse" at a club close to their apartment, where Friday night was always fetish night.

    During our last visit we had spotted a small, but rather erotic looking clothes shop called "Phylea" on Rue Quincampoix, and Paul suggested that after lunch I should go and buy an outfit for the evening whilst he went walkabout, his expression for a good rummage around the sex shops!.. It sounded a great idea to me. So after a light lunch in a small bistro near the Pompidou Centre we went our separate ways, agreeing to meet back at the Jazz Bar at around four-thirty…two hours or so later.

    Off I went in the direction of the shop, armed with our credit card and full license from Paul to be decadently outrageous, whatever the cost! On the corner of the street was a small tabac/bar, where I stopped for a small coffee, cigarette and a shot of brandy for "courage". Upon entering the shop I was taken a back by the sheer volume of clothes in such a small shop, and the very erotically adorned mannequins. The walls were covered in wire mesh, with all sorts of fetish goodies artistically displayed on them, from outrageous boots and shoes, to whips and costume masks. I didn't know where to start, and suddenly began to feel very self conscious, as I was stood frozen to the spot, when suddenly, from behind a very heavy set of crimson velvet curtains appeared the shop "proprietor/designer", who welcomed me in French and once he saw my blank look he burst out laughing, and in a very husky French accented voice said "ah you are English Madame?"; he introduced himself as Michel, and when I explained to him the reason behind my visit, he said with a twinkle in his eyes "that I wouldn't leave his shop until we'd found me the perfect look for the evening". I said that I'd be guided by him and open to all suggestions!!

    He chose a most outrageous pair of six-inch red/black and Perspex stilettos with a very high platform, as he said; we start with "zee shooz" and build the look around them. We then, between us picked several dresses in varying styles and degrees of daringness. He led me through the velvet drapes, to what was a changing room, doubling as a stock room; and a small area, displaying some very exquisite hand made sex toys. A striking feature of the room was a beautiful antique mahogany chaise longue. He hung the clothes we'd chosen on a rail, and indicated for me to me to put the shoes on, and to start trying on the outfits. He asked me if I like glass of wine, and said he'd be back in a few moments, as he had to go to the bar upstairs in the design studio to get it.

    He left, and a few moments later I heard him put the catch on the door, which I felt comfortable with, as I didn't fancy being caught in flagrante by any customers coming in while he was upstairs. I was wearing my black Armani trouser suit and boots. Therefore, it was necessary to completely undress first, before getting into the shoes and to try the initial outfit on, which was a very slinky black evening gown, that was completely backless, and only just covered the top of my bottom, and it had two thigh high slits either side, just covering ones modesty, however, wearing panties however small would simply ruin the look. Michel appeared with a bottle of lovely chilled white wine, which he poured in no small measure and complimented me on how the dress fitted my body, and how it showed off my figure! He insisted I should wear my hair up, and in a blur he produced some grips and fashioned a look that he said accentuated my long neck and enhanced the flowing lines of the dress. Next, I tried on a short mini dress, in leather with cut away panel at the buttocks, which he agreed, was maybe a bit too revealing for a dinner party, then on to a body clinging lime green rubber dress, which took some getting into, and to achieve the fit he said "Zee knickers must go..Oui?", by this time with the wine and the decadent ambience I was past caring and riding on a wave of excitement. It proved virtually impossible to get the dress on, until he went and got some special body oil, that was designed and sold specifically to ease the getting in and out of these kinds of tight rubber outfits. So here I was, stood naked, in just the heels, my hair pinned up and a glass of wine in one hand, whilst a charming Frenchman that I'd only known for a maximum of twenty minutes was about to liberally apply oil to my body…not my normal Friday afternoon! He smiled at me whilst he warmed his hands and poured a liberal amount of oil onto them and then he very deftly started to rub it into my shoulders and back, paying a lingering attention to my buttocks. He whispered for me to relax and enjoy, as his hands slowly encircled me and started to softly rub the oil into my breasts, he gently squeezed my nipples, which by now were as hard and erect as they had ever had been. I was being swept away on a surge of pure lust as his hands moved over every part of my stomach and were lingering tantalizingly close to my now very wet and excited vagina. He kept teasing me for a few moments, until my knees buckled slightly with the intense pleasure ripping through my body. He slowly brought me a level of orgasm that I'd never experienced before…I started to climax as his skilled fingers found and gently stroked my clitoris, I thought it was never going to stop. In the background, I heard the shop bell ring but he simply put a finger to my mouth and said "shhhhh". He gently laid me down on the chaise longue, where he let his tongue take over from his fingers. He softly ran his tongue over my inner thighs, slowly making his way to my clitoris, which was on fire with anticipation….I continued to climax as his tongue danced all over my pussy, softly nibbling my lips….never wanting it to end. But then all at once it was over as the door buzzer went and the shop phone started to ring. I swiftly pulled my self together and dressed, as he opened the shop and took the call. I clutched the initial black evening gown and shoes and took them to the small counter and handed over my credit card, he smiled as he wrapped them up, and slipped his business card and a gift of a small pair of crystal earrings into the carrier bag.

As I went to leave he kissed me on both cheeks, and said to call anytime, as we had "unfinished business". That's for sure, I thought to myself!

My legs were still trembling and felt like rubber as I made my way back to meet Paul, whilst all the time my mind was saying…."should I tell him or should this be my secret?"

I decided to come clean, as it had become apparent, from our first encounter with Olivier and Claudia that Paul got really turned on when I would tell him in detail what I'd done with Olivier… I was sure he'd really get off on this new encounter…I was not wrong! When I arrived at the bar Paul was already there and immediately got me a coffee and a brandy…and I simply looked him in the eyes and said, "oh have I got a tale to tell you!" He grinned from ear to ear as I gave him a brief outline of events…. saving all the intimate details for later.

Chapter Ten: The Dinner Party

Getting ready was now turning into a slow seductive ritual, with a lot of attention being paid to all the intimate areas, in anticipation of what the evening may hold!

I was just putting on the finishing touches when reception rang and said our lift was waiting, we rushed downstairs (in my normal heels as the new ones weren't really designed for walking far!, so I thought it best to take them to wear once we'd arrived), to find that Claudia and Olivier had sent a taxi for us.

Their apartment was situated in a small street, near "l'Arc de Triumphe", the driver pointed to the building and said, to simply ask the doorman for Monsieur Gavroche.

Upon entering a very grand marbled lobby the doorman was expecting us, greeting us warmly and enquiring questioningly "Paul and Emma…Oui? Follow me please, once inside the lift he inserted a key and pressed level six, the doors closed and off we went. Upon arriving at the correct floor the doors opened revealing a stunning entrance hallway, with Olivier waiting to greet us…. he took my coat, and I could immediately see his look of complete approval of my dress, that I was almost wearing and barely concealing my modesty. He gratefully accepted the two very expensive bottles of red and white wine, that Paul had bought during his earlier walkabout, and just as Claudia appeared, looking like sex on legs, he unbeknownst to me, produced a beautiful small gift wrapped bottle of Hermes' 24 Faubourg perfume for her…I dreaded to think about how much he'd spent, but was already feeling heady with the days events so far, so really was past caring!

They explained that we were the first to arrive, and their friends would be turning up shortly; they just wanted to put us at ease first over a quiet glass of champagne. Whilst Olivier fixed the drinks Claudia took me to their majestic bedroom, where I could change into my heels. She also told me, that since our first meeting, and subsequent telephone call, Olivier had mentioned on a few occasions, how much he was looking forward to making love to me…this was a little disconcerting, but as I was to discover typically French. She could see I was a little flustered, but put me completely at ease, by saying that she would "make love with Paul…oui?" I just nodded approvingly, and we both burst out laughing.

When we returned to the large lounge area, with stunning views over Paris including, the beautifully lit Eiffel Tower, both Paul and Olivier nearly fell over at the sight of me in my new shoes, I had just gone from five foot five inches in bare feet to nearly six foot…. good job both men were a good six foot or more themselves.

Shortly, the other guests started to arrive and the customary Parisian kisses began, once everyone had their drinks we were toasted and told we had become "Honorary Parisians". The meal was very light and tasteful, consisting of lots of fresh meats and exotic salads, with a wide selection of artisan breads, followed by a gorgeous "death by chocolate" layer cake and cream, which one of the female guests kept putting on her nipples and getting random people to lick off, all done with style and wit. The drinks kept flowing until they decided that as it was approaching midnight we should adjourn to the small club close by, called "Au10Bis", this is also a small swingers hotel, but has a club area on two levels. It has many different areas, ranging from small to large group rooms, where many exhibitionistic couples gravitate to once the party is in full flow, there are also very nice bathroom areas with showers. The subtle difference with this club, is that they also welcome very select extra single men, for the more adventurous and insatiable lady…. which, I felt I could very quickly become at this rate! There was a lovely seating and bar area where we were quickly served with the specially blended club cocktail to begin with. The music was very much background mood enhancing, to instill an atmosphere of relaxed sensual eroticism. This, together with wonderful atmospheric lighting definitely had the effect of lowering people's inhibitions. I was totally chilled and was getting many admiring looks from many of the single men, a few complimenting me on my outfit. People were appearing and disappearing into the maze of rooms and the occasional scream of pleasure was to be heard. After another round of drinks were brought to us Claudia winked at me, grabbed Paul and led him away to explore the club…perfect timing…I immediately thought…my turn now!

Olivier instantly moved beside me, and immediately began to stroke my exposed thighs with his nimble fingers…I was absolutely soaking with pleasure and anticipation. A very attractive single man was sat opposite and was watching intently as Olivier started to slowly tease my pussy, the new admirer simply nodded his head in appreciation, which encouraged me to move the material of my gown completely to one side and seductively open my legs wide, giving Olivier unrestricted access and the admirer an unobstructed view of my open, soaking wet sex….. He was stroking himself seductively through his trousers in appreciation, showing an impressive bulge… within minutes I was climaxing and moaning with complete abandon, soaking Olivier's fingers. He knew exactly what I wanted, and we hastily went upstairs to carry on our sexual indulgence, we found a nice dimly lit area, with a giant cushion along the wall, Olivier continued where he left off downstairs and soon had me on the brink of ecstasy again, I reached behind my neck and unhooked the clasp and let my dress fall to the floor, I swiftly stepped to one side, picked it up and draped it over a strategically placed clothes hook for safe keeping. Olivier stepped back and appreciatively murmured something, as he ran his eyes up and down my naked body. With pure animal lust I slowly knelt in front of him and released his hard and pulsing penis, which was even more gorgeous than I'd remembered it. I gazed at it longingly. He took this as his cue to take of his shirt and step out of his trousers and join me naked…. on equal terms now. He lifted me up and lay me across the giant cushion and started slowly running his tongue up and down the inside of my thighs momentarily stopping to flick at my clitoris before licking his way back down and up the other thigh…. I was shaking, as waves of intense pleasure racked through my whole being. I felt like I was exploding from inside, it was a rush I'd never ever had before… eventually he began to concentrate on my vagina, licking, sucking and probing and occasionally letting his tongue roam to explore my anus…I wanted to scream with the joy of it all. Soon it all became too much, and I subtly indicated I wanted him inside me…and with deft dexterity he entered me slowly, stretching me, until his entire length was embedded inside me, we were both frozen, locked in an intense embrace for a long moment, until he started to fuck me with an intensity and animal passion that I'd dreamt of, his powerful thrusting had me riding the crest of a never ending orgasm…this was good…very good! At one stage I glanced up to see Claudia, who smiled at me and gave me a big thumbs up.... I had to giggle. He kept up a steady rhythm as we intimately enjoyed each other and eventually built into a hard pounding crescendo before he withdrew, covering my stomach, breasts and chin with a huge torrent of hot cum...we held each other for a few moments, getting our breath back before we made ourselves presentable again, and returned to the bar for a much deserved drink.

Paul and Claudia were nowhere to be seen, and most of the people from the dinner party had gone in search of their own fun and intimate forms of entertainment. Eventually, Claudia appeared with Paul in tow, looking a bit disheveled, but with a euphoric look on his face. It was a very surreal situation, with everyone very sexually aroused, but totally relaxed and at ease with each other. I couldn't help but feel that this could never happen back in London, this was pure filth, but on a very sophisticated and elegant level.

Olivier settled the bill and we rounded everyone up and took a leisurely late night stroll back to their apartment for a nightcap. Everybody was happy and buoyant, having had such a superb evening of pure decadence. We all took a final drink on the terrace as everyone talked and laughed happily.... all very civilized! A taxi arrived to return us to our hotel, where we both collapsed exhausted, but looking forward to the following day and swapping our stories and experiences of the previous evening! This became a bit of a ritual, and always a very liberating start to a new day with fresh adventures ahead...always with a customary coffee and cognac to hand.

It turned out Paul and Claudia had pretty much got up to same naughtiness as Olivier and myself, with one big difference, that being, whilst showing Paul around she met a guy she knew and had always fancied and invited him to join them for some fun, Paul said he was initially freaked out by it, but said the guy was completely straight, which was a major relief to him. He said Claudia was a true sexual predator and was very vocal in her instructions to them both. Paul explained that the single guys had to be invited by the female to gain access to any fun areas and the staff strictly observed this rule. I thought back to the guy who was sat opposite Olivier and myself, and realized he must have been waiting for a nod from me...poor guy, I felt a bit guilty that he'd missed out....however, I was not quite that adventurous yet!.... as Olivier was the first man to fully have me intimately since our marriage. It was however, something that was running through my mind more and more as time went on.

We met them again late morning as arranged, and they said that we all needed to detox, before we ate and to shake off an excesses from the night before, and that they knew the perfect spot. After a short walk, we arrived at a wonderful place called "Aqua Saint-Paul", it was a beautiful spa complex, located in a very large old building. Inside there were steam rooms, 2 saunas, small swimming pool and Jacuzzi with hydro showers, also massage rooms in the basement.... just what was needed....by now we were all feeling comfortable as a foursome, so we stripped off openly and showered, Claudia and I went for a sauna (however, I still felt it a bit odd, that only a few hours earlier I'd been well and truly fucked by her husband), whilst Paul and Olivier went to the steam room.....to swap notes I assumed, as Claudia and I did pretty much the same thing, making giggly comparisons, and marveling at her openness and pure lust for sex . We spent a good two hours relaxing, finally ending with Claudia and I having a superb massage at the hands of a very skilled Thai lady. Feeling totally revitalized we headed off to a beautiful square nearby, called "Place Des Vosges", where we sat outside and all shared a large plate of "Choucroute Alsacienne", a real hearty dish of different meats, potatoes and white cabbage, cooked to a traditional recipe from the Alsace region of France, accompanied by a nice bottle of Sancerre. It was a perfect, relaxing afternoon. We went our separate ways, after arranging to meet them again, the following lunchtime, for a drink before they dropped us back to the airport.

We were both running on pure adrenalin, and decided we'd spend our last night at ChrisetManu2.

We skipped dinner, as we were both still stuffed from the late lunch, so we took the opportunity to sneak a few hours sleep before we got ready to enjoy the final evening. Now, equipped with an even more open and adventurous outlook regarding all things "naughty"!

As we'd come to expect, we were greeted warmly and enthusiastically... and when Jesse saw my dress, she called all the staff to take a look...talk about embarrassing.... but boy did it give my ego a huge lift.

We spent a good amount of the evening soaking up the atmosphere, and enjoying letting the voyeuristic side of us take over. We both took turns in wandering into the back rooms and watching some gorgeous people indulging their deepest desires, also having a little bit of anonymous fun in the process. On one visit to the playrooms I was pounced on by an adorable young girl, who led me to a little alcove and quickly knelt in front of me and proceeded to enjoy herself pleasuring me with her tongue, it all happened in the blink of an eye! Shortly a young guy appeared behind her, whispered something, then slid her dress up over her waist and entered her, she stared up into my eyes the whole time, as he rode her vigorously...it was a very erotic interlude...after a few minutes I left them to it, and returned to my drink. We continued in this vein until it was time to go and get a few hours desperately needed sleep before our return home to the U.K.

Claudia and Olivier met us for a quick drink before dropping us off at the airport. We enjoyed the brief and uneventful flight back to Heathrow... to the children and normality!

Chapter Eleven: On Home Ground

    I quickly got back into the daily routine, but I was by now constantly thinking about Paris, and all it had to offer. One day over lunch I told Erica about our latest adventures, she was green with envy and wanted all the details, as she was going to work on her husband Chris again, in the hope he'd be game to follow our lead, she said they'd had a few parties where it all "went on", but nothing even close to what Paul and I had discovered in Paris. I wondered whether Paul had mentioned the escapades to him, but I doubted it!

    That evening Erica rang all excited, she'd told her husband a brief account of what I'd told her, and she said the upshot was that he was absolutely up for a long weekend of fun and debauchery. She invited us over for dinner on the Friday evening, so we could give them the lowdown and all the relevant information we'd gathered along the way.

    One of our ground rules we'd agreed on our first trip, was that "what happened in Paris…stayed in Paris", in short we'd not get up to any extra curricula fun on home soil. However, it soon became apparent that we both wanted the Paris fun to be available a little closer to home and on a more regular basis.

    The only information available at the time for this alternate lifestyle was a "swingers magazine" via mail order only called "Desire". Paul acquired a copy from a friend and we immediately took out a monthly subscription, it featured a contacts section, however, the quality of the advertisers left a lot to be desired, you certainly had to careful! Also there was a reader's stories section, and in the second copy we received there was a very erotic and interesting well written account by a couple, who'd had a very similar experience of Paris as ourselves, and appeared to be a class apart from the majority of other advertisers.

    After reading their story, and frankly very forthright account, we both agreed we'd like to try and meet up with the couple involved, for a drink and to swap experiences. Paul wrote them a letter and sent it to the magazine editors department, asking if they'd please forward it on our behalf to the other couple. After a week or two had passed, we received a very nice informative reply on stylish headed paper, along with a contact phone number and Hampstead address. They seemed totally genuine and said to call anytime to discuss meeting up, and introduced themselves as Mike and Sarah. They'd also enclosed a couple of artistic yet erotic photographs of themselves, which we were more than tempted by.

We called them one evening a few days later, and after a long chat it seemed we had one hell of a lot in common, so we took the obvious next step and agreed to meet them for a drink the following weekend, we decided on a small wine bar in Knightsbridge that both of us knew.

Dinner on the Friday with Chris and Erica was an eye opener to say the least, it turned out that they had aspirations of getting involved in the very small scene that existed in London, but had always come home disappointed at the quality of the people, and the tawdry venues on offer at the time.

After dinner we helped them put together a loose itinerary, based around our knowledge and recent experiences. We agreed that we'd ring "ChrisetManu "and speak to Jesse and let her know to expect them, which we duly did, once Chris had sorted the flights and hotel. I could sense, Erica was beyond excited, and didn't stop talking about what should she wear and was getting it all mapped out in her mind…a mind that was seriously working overtime.

During this period I visited my aunt Helen regularly, to check all was well and that she was happy with her helper/companion Celia. She was still very frail, but enjoying life, reading and generally pottering around the house and garden. Celia had turned out to be a real godsend.

We duly met with Mike and Sarah, and as expected we all hit it off famously, and it still remains that way today as I write this memoir. It transpired that they'd also taken a trip to Paris, but never went to the clubs, but had gone to a well known area of the "bois de Boulogne", where adventurous couples met for outdoor group sex, which these days has turned into a national sport in the U.K…. namely dogging! Sarah was particularly fond of extra well-endowed black men, and informed us that there was a specific area in the "bois" that catered for this obsession, as well as a wide range of other sexual shenanigans. She had spent a good few hours being used in the woods by a group of very well hung black men, always under the watchful eye of Michael. They told us they'd had a great time and were consequently invited to several private house parties in Paris, where Sarah got more than her share of attention...being a blonde with a fabulous pair of breasts she was a prime target, something she fully enjoys being, and performs with great enthusiasm. We arranged for them to come for dinner at our house the following week, as the children were going to be staying with their grandparents for a few days. It would be a good chance to get to know each other a bit more intimately.

    In the meantime, Erica and I had met for coffee, and she informed me that everything was booked for the following Thursday and she had booked a full body pamper session for the Wednesday afternoon, so everything was in pristine condition for the weekend. I had never seen her so animated, and she couldn't stop asking for any tidbits and general information that I thought she might need. I simply suggested they discuss, and laydown their own set of ground rules for the weekend, and then just to go with the flow and enjoy whatever happens. I also went shopping with her early the following week, to buy a selection of lingerie that she should take to Paris, whilst at the same time I bought a revealing, but tasteful new LBD from Harvey Nichols for our forthcoming dinner party with Sarah and Mike.

Chapter Twelve: A Taste Of Paris At Home

I thought I'd try and put on a dinner with a fair amount of French influence, staring with Foie gras on brioche, with fig jam, followed by Pork Loin with Apples and Calvados and finished off with a platter of Croquembouche (Caramel-Glazed Cream Puffs). All accompanied with some select wines. I was a busy bunny for most of Friday; luckily Paul's parents had come and picked the children up on the previous evening. I spent a few hours shopping, followed by a good while prepping the food and all the time wondering with a hint of envy as how Chris and Erica were getting on in Paris…. she promised to tell all when they got back over coffee on Tuesday morning.

Mike and Sarah arrived clutching a few bottles of wine, and just to prove that they were "paying attention", a bottle of Jack Daniels. We'd just finished the first course when the phone rang and I heard Paul saying things like "yes great…that would be good…yes no problems…. hotel…Heathrow…look forward to it!". My ears had pricked up, I was like a Meerkat on speed. Paul came back to the table grinning…saying it was Olivier from Paris and he was coming to London the following Thursday on business and was bringing Claudia, he'd extended his stay, so they wouldn't be leaving Heathrow until the Saturday afternoon and would love to meet up again. They were booked into the Sheraton Heathrow for both nights and had reserved a suite.

The dinner went down well and we retired to the lounge, all four of us a bit frisky and flirty by this stage. Mike had brought a very artistic porn DVD that Paul put on and within minutes we'd paired off, Sarah was all over Paul and he seemed to be enjoying all the attention. So Mike and I decided we'd have our own bit of inappropriate behavior. He was a very slow sensual kind of lover; with a wonderful electric touch, in no time at all, he had me at his mercy. I glanced across at Paul and admired the way Sarah was administering a very enthusiastic and verbal blow job…I considered it only polite to show Mike my own variety of skills…. he certainly had a lot for me to work on…. this was now turning into a very decadent and debauched evening, and I was loving it. Mike suggested that we leave Paul and Sarah to it, and we went to the kitchen, where he soon had me in all kinds of trouble.... taking me authoritatively over the work surfaces, across the table and against the wall...we stopped every now and then for a little tipple, but he continued to pound me hard, and didn't even break his stride when Sarah wandered in to refresh her and Paul's drinks, she just slapped his bottom and called him a pervert!... much to my amusement. After a good two hours of pure sexual athletics Paul and Sarah crashed and burned. Paul put her into the spare room to sleep, and shouted down that he was also retiring and needed to get some sleep. This left me and Mike together, back in the lounge, both wired by the excitement of it all, earlier he'd popped out to their car and brought in a small overnight bag...presumptuous but wise in hindsight!

    We continued to play enthusiastically, intimately exploring each others bodies, with both fingers and tongues. By now I'd completely surrendered all my inhibitions, and was pretty much game for anything. After a while he subtly produced a small vial of "amyl nitrate", which I'd vaguely heard of and told me to lie back and relax as I was about to have my "G-Spot "tap" turned on. He instructed me, that when I felt an orgasm approaching that I should take the top of the vial and sniff the powerful vapours with both nostrils.... I was very apprehensive, but trusted him. I lay back across the sofa, whilst he probed and manipulated my vagina, with one hand expertly working my clitoris, whilst the other was stimulating deep inside me, searching for my G-Spot....it was heaven....I followed his instructions, and as I felt orgasm approaching I took a large sniff from the small bottle.....then all hell broke loose...my body felt unimaginable pleasure exploding as wave after wave of orgasm hit me; simultaneously my G Spot had been switched on; my pussy started to squirt fluids uncontrollably and powerfully ...I didn't know what was happening, and quite frankly didn't care, as this was a mind blowing out of body experience, indescribable pleasure...intense...insane...but wonderful! I continued to gush for what felt like an eternity as his deft fingers expertly probed deep inside my body.

    After a few minutes things calmed down a bit as we took a breather, and he explained what had just happened and announced proudly "welcome to the club". He assured me that my G-Spot was now switched on, and I would experience this level of orgasm forever more (he was not wrong), and that I'd be able to gush at will. As a thank you we finished the evening with me sucking his extraordinary cock enthusiastically, until he himself had a big sniff of this magic fluid and proceeded to ejaculate like an erupting fountain, it was everywhere, I was drenched but in a very good way, insatiably drinking in his cum. Satisfied and exhausted we fell into a deep sleep, to be awoken by Paul a good few hours later with a strong cup of tea each. He looked at us both and called me a "slut" and went off to the kitchen chuckling to himself.

Once everyone was showered and changed we went off for a spot of lunch at a local pub, where we all decided it might be nice to all meet up again the following Friday, and introduce them to Olivier and Claudia, Paul said he'd call them and arrange it and let Mike know the details by Wednesday evening.

Paul had also arranged with Mike to go shopping together, as they both were in the market for a home computer. Mike had done a lot of research and was going to buy an Apple Mackintosh and suggested we do the same.

We'd only met the previous evening, but we parted firm friends (an what has turned out to be, long time lovers), we just seemed to have clicked and bonded...we had so much in common, apart from just awesome sex!

I met Erica as arranged, she was still on a high from Paris, she said that it was all that we'd said it would be.... but much, much more, and she so wanted to sell up and go and live there, so she could send Chris out to work, whilst she fucked her way through the men of Paris! They had been treated like visiting dignitaries at ChrisetManu2, and she said they'd both let themselves get swept up in the atmosphere, and it had simply reenergized them both sexually... they were well and truly hooked.

She gladly agreed to have the kids to stay over with them on Friday evening, so we could party without worry of interruption.

Paul had rung and arranged with Olivier that we'd pick them up at their hotel at seven thirty, and that we'd be meeting Mike and Sarah at a lovely restaurant in nearby Chiswick at nine, giving us time to have a quick drink at the hotel bar and re-acquaint ourselves, and also briefly describe who and how we'd met Mike and Sarah.

We had a pleasant meal and were seated at a nice secluded table, where it very quickly became apparent there was a great amount of sexual chemistry between the six of us! After the meal it was agreed we should all make our way to their hotel and see what the rest of the evening had in store!

Once back at their hotel and having a drink at the bar the boys arranged for some drinks to be sent up to the room, so we wouldn't have to keep ring down for room service, as Olivier said we'd probably empty the mini bar very rapidly.

Over dinner we'd discussed the wonders of Mikes little vial, which he referred to as his "poppers" and Claudia was very eager for a personal demonstration…. ah ha, I thought ", at least there's something we can teach our newfound French cousins!"

The suite was enormous, and the bathroom had a large Jacuzzi, which, everyone agreed should be filled and utilized to the full. It wasn't long before everyone's inhibitions went flying out of the window, and there were six very horny people, relaxing in the sensual hot bubbling water, each with a glass of champagne in one hand, whilst the other was making and renewing acquaintances under the water. It was amusing to see three very enticing erections breaking the surface at regular intervals. I made it my personal ambition to have all three of them before the evening was over… strangely, as it turned out Sarah and Claudia must have read my mind, and each claimed a "full house" before the night was over!

Mike treated Claudia to his G-Spot extravaganza, complimented by his vial of poppers, which literally blew her mind…Olivier was intrigued and couldn't get enough, while Sarah and myself gave him lots of attention with our tongues…Paul lay back on the sofa taking in the debauchery happening in front of him, simultaneously sipping a large Jack Daniels on the rocks…. I could tell he thoroughly approved of the scenario. At one stage, I was being pleasured by both Olivier and Mike, whilst the girls set about Paul…they were insatiable and he was loving every single minute and he decided it was time he tried, the now much in demand vial of poppers …… I could tell by the look on his face that he approved of their heightening effect on ones overall sexual feelings.

During a break in the proceedings Olivier arranged with Mike to get him a supply of poppers, and deliver them personally to Paris! ...Which is what actually occurred a month or so later.

Chapter Thirteen: Internet...Early Days

Mike and Paul had met up for lunch, and armed with computer magazines discussed and debated the route to go in this new approaching era. After much deliberating they both pumped for an Apple Mac each, apparently the salesman in the Tottenham Court Road Computer shop was impressed with their new found knowledge and was more than helpful, the shop even agreed that they would deliver and install the machines for both of them.

Once installed and set up we spent hours searching the web, albeit very slowly in those days, but we did stumble upon a "swingers site" run by a guy called Phillipe and his partner Christine, he coincidentally worked in the Music Industry in Paris, and ran the site in his spare time...in the early days his site was much visited and a lot of valuable information gained and contacts made.

Paul contacted Phillipe, and they immediately hit it off - he invited us out for dinner and to be their guests during our next visit, at a new very private club, that had recently opened ......a club, that a while later unintentionally led me down a different path and opened up a whole new level of hedonistic pleasures.

We made one more visit in this year to Paris (however, a little bit of Paris came to me for Xmas!), this time we were accompanied by Mike and Sarah, as Mike had a nice little gift of a dozen vials of his magic poppers for Olivier, which he'd had specially delivered from a contact in Amsterdam, as poppers were very popular on the large Gay Scene there and freely available.

We'd arranged to join Olivier and Claudia for dinner, we'd also arranged to meet Phillipe and Christine, who were going to take us to the new club, it was tucked away in the 20th Arrondissement with a simple brass plaque on the door inscribed with the words "Privé Association S.A.S" confusing but absolutely nothing whatsoever to do with the British Army!

The club had a traditional reception coatroom area, then you descended into a space, which had once been a large wine cellar, and had been converted into a beautiful bar area, which was surrounded on three sides by tunnels, which led to various rooms and a dimly lit maze. There was also a grope box, which was a small box room, where a lady could go and shut themselves inside; there were strategically placed holes on all sides, where gentlemen could put their hands through and also holes to insert their penises, as an offering, in the hope that the lady would anonymously suck on them. There was room around the box for up to six men (a few years later a club opened where the grope box was the centre piece and could accommodate up to twenty men). The absolute "Pièce de résistance" of this club was the hidden stairway, up to a level that had very comfy sofas and an amazing and unique floor, which had strategically placed glass tiles, so you could look down, and view the activity in the various nooks and crannies below. This was a very popular spot for the avid voyeur, and Mike and Paul could be found cradling a Jack Daniels, whilst Sarah and myself were having fun below with Olivier and one or two of the select gentlemen that were allowed entry, purely due to their prowess and sexual skills. This club attracted many and varied people from the French "show bizz" circle, they were certainly what you'd call "a diverse and glamorous crowd".

It was here that I experienced my first real taste of full on all female fun! It all happened so naturally. We were all at the bar chatting and drinking, when I became aware that Christine was giving me a certain look, that as well as made me nervous, also intrigued me, she was a very elegant women who was born and bread in Paris and was one of their top eye surgeons, she just had that certain " je ne sais quoi" that a lot of French women seem to have….. an assured confidence. After a short while she took my hand and said she wanted to show me the "Maze", once inside it was all lit by ultra violet tubes, which made her skin look gorgeous and bronzed, coupled with her long blond hair, she oozed sex from every pore. There were a few couples in various stages of lovemaking as we wandered through, when suddenly she put her fingers to my lips and whispered "shhh" and opened a secret door, which led to a very small room, which inside was, all I can describe as a Y shaped padded massage table, which had padded Velrco fastenings for the ankles, and wrists restraints attached to the wall at the head end. There was only just enough room for the two of us standing….so with no words spoken she slid my dress over my head, and then expertly removed my panties, leaving me completely naked apart from my heels.

      She'd obviously done this on more than one occasion, and motioned for me to climb up on to the table, where she nimbly fastened my ankles to the ends of the Y shape with the restraints, and then swiftly moved around to the head end and similarly restrained my wrists. From her clutch bag she retrieved a black velvet blindfold, similar to what you get on a long haul flight. She had me totally at her mercy and I simply loved it! She began by gently running her fingers all over my exposed body, whist kissing me with vigour and passion, then gently licking and sucking on each of my nipples in turn, which were rock hard and very sensitive to her expert touch and warm, wet tongue. She let her mouth and tongue roam all over my body, which I knew must be glowing, as I felt so hot, with my body going into big, long lasting spasms of pure pleasure, the blindfold heightened the sensation in a way I thought not possible ….she teased my thighs with her tongue and finally went to work on my pussy, licking and nibbling my lips and deftly squeezing and teasing my pulsating clitoris, building me to a crescendo, until I simply couldn't hold back any longer, I tensed and gushed my juices all over her mouth and tongue, in great powerful jets. She let out a moan and softly cried "oui..oui, plus, plus" as she continued to probe me with both tongue and fingers and drink my secretions, I could feel myself building again towards another climax, and as she inserted a finger into my anus I submitted to the pleasure, and again exploded with an intense liquid orgasm, I could feel myself squirting and gushing uncontrollably, she swallowed torrent after torrent of my juices, it was immense and so satisfying! Eventually, she undid the Velcro restraints, removed the blindfold and gave me a peck on the lips, and said in whisper "Incroyable"…. I lay there for a few moments trying to compose myself and get some energy into my system before returning to my much needed drink.

      Once we were back at the bar, she questioned me regarding my orgasms, particularly on how intense they were. I told her the story of the evening when Mike had taught me how to attain this level of body pleasure and control, she was intrigued and more than a little excited by what she'd heard. A short while later I saw her leading Mike by the hand into the maze…I had a distinct feeling that she'd be the one on the Y shaped table this time round! I wasn't wrong!

At one stage during the evening I was casually watching Sarah on all fours in one of the rooms being ridden by a young guy, whom she'd spotted earlier and had immediately put on her "to do" list, whilst his friend was simultaneously using her willing mouth for his pleasure! I glanced up and saw Mike and Paul, drinks in hand grinning, watching in admiration the activity below through the glass tiles. As soon as Sarah realized this, she really played up to her audience. Giving them a master class in pure filth.

Shortly afterwards we ordered three taxis, one to take Phillipe and Christine home, as they had work the next day, whilst we all jumped in the remaining taxis and headed for our little jazz bar for a night cap. Mike snuck back to the hotel to get Olivier's special present and with a grand gesture handed the gift wrapped vials of "magic" to him…Olivier immediately got itchy feet and whisked Claudia back to their apartment…to sample the gift, we assumed! Correctly, as it turned out.

We were all still wired from such a great evening of food, drink and lots of outrageous sex in each others equally outrageous company, so another round of drinks was ordered before we all retired for a well deserved sleep.

We met up in reception at midday, refreshed and ready for the day ahead, which we decided would be spent shopping and generally doing the sight seeing tourist thing, which actually turned out to be great fun. I also took Sarah to The Galeries Lafayette where we both spent an eternity in the lingerie department and bought some exciting items to wear during the forthcoming evening.

We'd booked a table for the four of us at "ChrisetManu2", we were excited, as this was going to be Mike and Sarah's first time there, so we wanted it to all go as we'd explained to them previously, on many occasions. We had nothing to worry about, as Jesse greeted us as enthusiastically as ever. She also told us that our friends Chris and Erica really had a ball and they were among the last to leave every evening!

Both Mike and Sarah were totally blown away by the quality of the food, and even more so by the elegance and stunning good looks of many of our fellow dinners…. Mike was on tenterhooks, as he was full of anticipation at what was awaiting downstairs, Sarah had to tell him to slow down and chew his food.... we all laughed as she admonished his impatience, as if he were a naughty schoolboy!

The club area was in full swing and Sylvia embraced us like long lost friends, and gratefully accepted the selection of C.D's that Paul had brought. After the introductions we took our drinks, as per normal to our favourite little alcove (creatures of habit), and let Mike and Sarah get accustomed to the surroundings, after a while I gave Sarah a guided tour of the fun areas, she was very excited by all the action, which was by now in full swing and couldn't wait to get back to Mike and get amongst the fun!

They very quickly disappeared into the rooms, whilst Paul and I relaxed with our drinks, as by now we felt like regulars and didn't need to rush anything. On this particular night there seemed to be a more than normal amount of "beautiful" people present...after a bit of investigating we found out that there was a major fashion show and exhibition going on, therefore the club was teaming with "fashionistas".

We took a wander to see how Mike and Sarah were getting on, eventually finding them participating in a bit of group fun and games, they looked to be thoroughly engrossed in the situation, so we left them to their own devices. As we entered one of the smaller rooms to engage in our own bit of sexual shenanigans, I became aware of a gorgeous looking man of about thirty approaching us with his blonde partner, no words were spoken as he started to caress me, whilst simultaneously the "blonde" took Paul to a secluded cushioned area in the corner, where she immediately started to administer some enthusiastic oral pleasure on him, my admirer very soon had me in all sorts of trouble, I quickly removed my panties and was soon coming over his expert fingers. I couldn't get over how stunning looking this guy was, with shoulder length swept back black hair, and to top it all off, he had the most enormous penis I'd ever had the pleasure to have in my hand...and then rather rapidly in my willing mouth, I moaned with pure lust which he took as a signal to rhythmically start to fuck it....I could feel him stretching the sides of my mouth and I was taking as much as possible, but still there was a good amount to hold on to, it was such a thrilling feeling as he fed my his manhood...this was the start of my infatuation and quest for "big cock" and I rapidly became a connoisseur of size! I was on my knees and climaxing without any physical stimulation at all

... simply this beautiful man using my mouth for his pleasure gave me immense gratification. It wasn't long before he was filling my throat with his hot semen; I swallowed all I could, endeavoring not to waste a single drop! It was a wonderful but brief interlude. As we were making ourselves presentable, I noticed Paul gesticulating that he'd meet me at the bar shortly. I kissed my nameless lover on the cheek and whispered in my best French "Merci" and made my way to the bar area.

A short while later Paul joined me, looking absolutely shell shocked, and took a large gulp of his Jack Daniels and said "do you know who that was?"…..I said that I had no idea, but they were a very sexy couple….when he told me that the blonde was a very famous female tennis player…the most well known at the time in fact, I simply thought he must be mistaken, until they reappeared and joined us at the bar (where he subtly handed me my panties, which I had left on the floor). They were a very pleasant pair, and spoke excellent English, and it was who Paul thought it was! Her partner at the time was a very well known French socialite/racing driver. Shortly Mike appeared and said he'd left Sarah in the very capable hands of a young couple, his jaw dropped and he was rendered speechless when he realized who we were drinking with….to this day, one of his greetings to Paul is "Game, Set and Match to Zee Eengleesh". A short while later there was a bit of a commotion as a world famous supermodel arrived with a small entourage, immediately she started to strut her stuff provocatively on the small dance floor, much to the appreciation of many of the men (and ladies) watching in admiration…she was later to be spotted (by Mike) being pleasured in a back room by at least five men. This had certainly turned out to be a very memorable evening indeed!! One that Mike didn't want to end…we eventually left at dawn and all strolled contentedly back to the hotel to rest and recharge our very depleted batteries.

Saturday morning was missed completely, as we all slept in. We didn't meet up in the lobby until gone one o'clock; we went and found a small bistro across the Seine in St Germain, where we all tucked into a feast of Beef bourguignon and crusty bread and a nice bottle of Cabernet Sauvignon. We all agreed, as Mike and Sarah wanted to experience as much as possible and this was the last night, that we'd take them to "Au10Bis" after dinner, unfortunately Olivier and Claudia had a family commitment, so could only meet us for a brief drink.

Paul and Mike wanted to go wandering around the Rue Saint Denis to buy a few new DVD's and to check out a few computer shops (bars!). Sarah wanted to have her hair done at a small hairdressers near the hotel, called Chez Stephan, which left me at a loose end with a few hours to kill…On the spur of the moment I decided to take the bull by the horns and try and fulfill a fantasy that I'd been running over in my mind for a few weeks. No time like the present!

I rushed back to the room and freshened up, whilst having a large brandy from the mini bar for Dutch courage. I put on a new pair of sheer hold-ups with a lovely crimson and cream lace design at the top and my black court shoes, then slipped on my long black leather coat. I grabbed a carrier bag and put my jeans and a t-shirt in it and stood in front of the mirror for a moment…I was ready to take the leap and go for it…the anticipation was driving me wild, and making me very wet…wondering if it would all come together as I'd fantasized! I casually left the hotel (being completely naked under my coat was so erotic and exhilarating) and headed towards the Rue Quimcampoix to my favourite shop "Phylea". I casually walked by at first, and took a sneaky look through the window, to my immense pleasure I noted that the shop was empty and Michel was sitting at his desk. Composing myself, I took a huge breath; I knew that I was now at the point of no return, and strode purposefully to the shop door and walked in, smiled at him and said with a lustful look "we have unfinished business…yes?" and opened my coat to show him my naked body…he smiled and walked to greet me, bolted the door and led me through the velvet drapes to the back room….I felt hot, horny and at home as I stood proudly in my nakedness. He seductively removed my coat and hung it up. He plucked, what looked like a feather duster from the shelf of toys and proceeded to tease me with it, flicking it over my nipples and stroking it down my back, the feeling was amazing - I could feel my juices starting to run down my inner thighs. He then surprised me and took a beautiful penis shaped clear glass dildo from the selection of toys, and made me lick it whilst he disrobed. As soon as he was naked, he lay me on the chaise longue and gently inserted the dildo into my soaking vagina, whilst offering me his penis to suck, like a greedy child in a sweet shop I enveloped him in my mouth. I started to cum with huge spasms as he plunged the glass penis into me, all the time talking dirty to me in broken English, calling me a "Salope" over and over again. I was in a completely different world of unbridled passion and pure wanton lust. This was both physical and mental fucking on such a grand scale, he realized I was wound up, ready to explode and he turned me over and expertly replaced the glass penis with a human one. He penetrated me hard and very deeply, which had me screaming with complete joy, I felt my orgasm building - it was fast approaching and with an intense rush my vaginal muscles started to rapidly pulsate and contract around his cock, milking him viciously, I whimpered as my pussy exploded and drenched him in my love juices, my legs gave way and I collapsed on the floor, exhausted but wanting and needing more, and out of the corner of my eye I caught a joyful sight…amongst the sex toys I spotted several small bottles, of what I was sure was poppers, I just pointed and he quickly grabbed a vial and opened it , offering me the first inhalation, which I accepted with relish, in an instant a second tidal wave of orgasm washed up through me, shaking me to the core. Then he athletically straddled my chest, taking a big sniff himself and started to slowly stroke his throbbing cock, as my tongue was wrapping itself around its bulbous head, it looked so angry and hard, his free hand reached behind and started to expertly work my clitoris into a frenzy again, gently fingering my anus simultaneously…I was in a constant state of climax, my body shaking and quivering, as he salaciously rubbed his cock all over my lips, occasionally slapping it against my cheeks, we both had another large sniff, as I built towards another gushing climax he started to breathe heavily and I could feel his thighs begin to tremble and quake - my mouth automatically opened as wide as possible, ready to take his orgasm, and just as I began to cum again he unleashed a huge torrent of hot semen into my willing, eager mouth, I was struggling to drink it all, there was rivers of it, he just didn't stop ejaculating for a good two minutes, my face was literally covered in it and my hair was a mess, his cum was everywhere…but did I care….categorically NO! We stayed in this position for ages, until he threw his jeans and shirt on and ran upstairs; reappearing with a well deserved and needed bottle of chilled white wine. I cleaned myself up as best I could and put on my jeans and t-shirt, and we chatted and drank like old friends, all very civilized. Before I left he presented me with a carrier bag, which had the glass dildo, poppers, and a beautiful new pair of hold ups inside and with a wink he said "a gift to show your husband where you went shopping". Before leaving, I gave him my new personal Email address, so I could let him know when we were visiting again, and also so he could let me know of any new designs they had that might interest me! Any excuse for a repeat performance.

I got back to the hotel before anyone else, so nobody was any the wiser as to where I'd been, and even more, what I'd been up to, which gave me the chance to hide my presents in my luggage...this had been an encounter so brazen I wanted to save it for Paul to savour at a later date. I would tease him with all the details when we were making love alone, together at home, as I knew it would turn him on massively.

The Saturday night was very chilled, with great food and we had a brief farewell drink with Olivier and Claudia. The club was very busy and Mike and Sarah indulged themselves. Paul and myself played together and briefly joined in with a Swedish couple in one of the rooms, it was fun but not that memorable. I think purely because I was still trying to come down from my spontaneous afternoon of debauched lustful pleasure, and simply couldn't concentrate on any new sexual encounters. I felt exhausted, but in a good way. We, as per normal rounded off the evening in our little Jazz bar with a few drinks, and toasted to what had been a wonderful weekend of fun and debauchery. When we eventually got to bed I still had a slight taste of Michel's cum in my mouth...yummy. I was still amused that in a few hours time I'd revert to being a housewife and mother again, and be pushing a trolley up and down the supermarket aisles, with nobody any the wiser as to what I'd been doing over the weekend...it was still a very surreal experience! My big guilty pleasure!

The coming weeks were taken up with organizing Christmas; also we were in the process of deciding to move to a bigger house as Paul had been given a big promotion at work, which included a substantial salary increase and a much larger bonus potential. Also, I was rapidly learning to master the computer and explore the exploding Internet. I would spend a couple of hours each day playing and searching the web, it was all so new and very exciting, but still very slow due to dial up connections and abysmal speeds.... ADSL was a little way off still.

During this time I had told Paul snippets of what went on that "memorable" afternoon in Paris, he was enthralled at my new found confidence and sexual awareness, he said it was a real turn on for him and he got massively aroused every time he thought about it. He positively encouraged me to explore these kinds of scenarios and liaisons further. I was sure I could, and would in Paris, but had my doubts that it would have the same kind of thrill in the U.K...only time and the right opportunity would tell!! I certainly wasn't the remotest bit attracted to private house parties in suburbia, it just seemed it would be a massive let down compared to the thrills Paris offered.

Chapter Fourteen: An Unexpected Xmas Present

A fortnight before Xmas, I received an Email from Michel, saying he was coming to London with his head designer and business partner for two days, as there were a few shops that were interested in stocking a large range of their "fetish wear" and they were bringing samples and had a few meetings arranged. He said that they had the Thursday night free before they flew back to Paris on the Friday lunchtime, and he wondered if I would like to go for dinner, as he had a little Xmas present for me, in the shape of a dress, along the lines of the initial one I'd purchased. He said that he'd be staying at "The Royal Garden Hotel" in Kensington and it would be no problem to arrange for a taxi to take me home after dinner.

I was excited and hugely turned on by this unexpected turn of events. I showed Paul the Email after dinner that evening when the children were tucked up in bed. He said there was absolutely no way that I could refuse the invitation, he said it would be rude, and would severely put back Anglo/French relations, plus finally, he reminded me that when he'd first met me I'd go anywhere for food and a new dress thrown into the deal! To say I was excited at the prospect of an evening out alone with Michel was the understatement of the decade. So with Paul's complete blessing I replied, saying it would be my pleasure to meet up and join him for dinner and would look forward to details of times etc. All the next day I checked the Email every hour, growing ever more impatient, eventually late afternoon, ping and there sitting in my inbox was his reply, saying that he'd be finished with his meetings by six and suggested we meet in the hotel at Berties bar at Eight, and dine in the Park Terrace restaurant at nine. Perfect I thought, and was pleased that Paul said that he'd work from home that day so he could drop me off at the hotel, to save me getting trains and tubes and that he'd take the children for pizza on the way home…even more perfect!

The days flew by, with Xmas planning and the various festive work functions that we were obliged to attend, especially with Paul's new promotion, he had to put in some serious networking.

D. Day arrived, and in the morning I had hair, manicure and pedicure booked and had bought a very sexy and chic black business suit for the occasion, and of course some very expensive and stylish black hold-ups, that were incredibly sheer and silky to the touch. I started my Paris pamper routine late in the afternoon, and eventually after perfecting my make up I was ready to go…. but not before I slipped a little vial of poppers into my clutch bag. I was highly aroused, my pussy was tingling already, and I was not even there yet, I just felt this was going to be a wonderful and erotic dinner…it turned out to be completely off the scale!

Paul dropped me off fashionably late (at least one minute)! And told me to have fun and enjoy myself. I nearly leapt out of the car, but I kept my composure, and kissed the children goodnight, saying that I'd see them in the morning. I confidently made my way through the revolving doors at the entrance. I quickly got my bearings and made my way up a small flight of stairs to Berties bar, where an immaculately dressed and smiling Michel was stood, casually leaning on the the bar. After a flourishing, yet typically French embrace he ordered a bottle of Champagne and three glasses ….. three glasses!? I was now very intrigued! We found a free table overlooking the foyer, and in no time the waiter was elegantly opening the Champagne and pouring two glasses, leaving the third empty. Michel could see my confusion, and explained he'd asked his partner Frederic to join us for dinner, especially as he'd designed and had made my gift with so much care and attention! I wholeheartedly agreed, and was more than a little excited by the prospect of dinning with two Frenchmen, but was a bit apprehensive as to what his partner looked like, my trepidation was very short lived, when a very elegant and handsome man of about forty arrived and proceeded to greet me with considerable flamboyance and affection…. wow I thought to myself! … this one's a real charmer, a true ladies man. I noticed he had the most beautiful flawless skin and very piercing blue eyes; he was also immaculately well mannered. The conversation flowed easily, and they were interested to hear about my recent experiences of the Parisian nightlife, it was the first real conversation I'd had with Michel since "that" afternoon… and I was sure he'd told his partner, Frederic!

We finished the Champagne and made our way up to the restaurant, and were shown to a table with a spectacular view over

Kensington Gardens and the London skyline. The food was wonderful, as was the very flirtatious company. The drinks flowed, and we all agreed, that after coffees we'd retire to Michel's suite, so I could give them my opinion on some of the samples they'd brought over ,and also try my present on! I was already wet with anticipation, but showed great willpower by sipping my brandy and prolonging the inevitable!

    Eventually we took the lift to the top floor, where Michel had reserved the "Royal Suite" at a very good price, as the Manager was a very old friend of his, and used to work at the George V in Paris. It was stunning suite of rooms. Michel immediately got us all some drinks from the mini bar, and we relaxed in the comfortable deep sofas. Frederic went and fetched a large case full of sample outfits, and another with several pairs of wild and very high heeled clubbing shoes. There were some very beautiful styles of dresses, many in very exotic silks, along with a number of very detailed and intricate leather designs. Also they had brought a wonderful pair of soft ivory suede chaps, the feel of them was stunning, so subtle, and they had two matching suede braces to cover the nipples. It was stunning, but you would have to be a real exhibitionist to wear it in public, they could see that I was enamored with it and suggested that I try it on, as they felt I'd compliment the design, and as it was just a sales sample I could keep it if it fitted. I jumped at the chance, Michel said I could try it on in there, pointing to a bedroom, but on one condition, "that I would let them see how I looked with it on", I agreed readily and took it to the room and undressed. I swiftly removed my suit, bra and panties and hold-ups, as it was designed to be worn simply as it was, it was such delicate soft suede… I was extra careful not to get any marks on it. I eventually got it on, buckled up and strategically covered my already erect nipples with the braces. My shoes didn't do it justice, so I slipped on a pair of outrageous high Perspex ones that were in one of the cases, luckily they were almost a perfect fit, just a tad tight. I looked in the wardrobe mirror, and was amazed at how incredible the ensemble looked, even with my pussy and bottom fully visible, and prominently on show.

    My confidence, along with my sexual appetite was riding high as I walked through into to the lounge area…. to an immediate and very positive reaction, from Michel, along with a very vocal "Mon Dieu, Magnifique" from Frederic. I retrieved my drink whilst they admired and commented on how my body enhanced the outfit. I strutted around posing and showing off the ensemble as provocatively as I could! I could tell that they both recognized how turned on I was, as my pussy was so wet now, its lips gleaming prominently due to the rooms subtle mood lighting. It was Michel who took the lead and stood, he came over and gave me a long slow, deep passionate kiss whilst I stood there with my legs slightly apart, showing Frederic my engorged pussy, in all its glistening glory! He looked on approvingly, lewdly licking his lips...I didn't want to ruin the suede with my now abundant juices, so I whispered to Michel to take it off for me, which he did in a slow seductive ritual, soon I was stood fully naked, apart from the massive heels, in front of two very attractive, horny and experienced Frenchmen. I could sense, I was going to be used expertly by them, and they in turn sensed that I was very eager to please them, in any way they desired! Michel reached into his pocket, and produced his own bottle of amyl nitrate, I took a huge sniff from it. As always it had an instant and gratifying effect, enhancing all my nerve endings. Michel took the outfit into the bedroom for safety, leaving me on the verge of climax, alone with Frederic, who was staring intently at my body...I just sucked my fingers and rubbed my exposed, swollen clitoris forcefully, instantly climaxing with a huge spurt of my juices, cascading onto the floor and pouring down my thighs. Frederic had a look of pure lust in his eyes as my vagina visibly flexed and opened for him to see. Michel was soon back, this time naked, with a very proud and angry looking erection. I immediately fell to my knees and started to lick his balls, spending time licking and sucking each one in turn, running my tongue up and down the entire length of his beautiful cock, whilst staring across into Frederic's piercing blue eyes as saliva ran down my chin. I shamelessly slurped on Michel's pulsating erection. Shortly, Frederic got up, took a large mouthful of scotch and disappeared into a different bedroom, returning a few moments later, naked and with an erection so large, and intimidating, the sight of it made me gasp and immediately another orgasm came flooding through me, powerfully squirting from me in great streams. He came straight over to me, picking up the bottle of poppers and taking a huge hit himself, then offering them to me for a hit, the effect was stunning, his enormous cock twitched and seemed to grow even larger. Michel withdrew his cock from my mouth, which was immediately replaced by Frederic's. It was a real challenge getting it into my mouth, but I worked on it in this position for a good fifteen minutes, whilst Michel was avidly watching and instructing me what to do, all the time in that sexy French voice. I was putty in their hands and they were using me as their personal sex toy...I was loving every moment.... eventually, I couldn't wait any longer and I begged them both to fuck me...Michel lay back on the sofa, and Frederic picked me up and lowered me onto me on Michel's waiting cock, I proceeded to ride up and down on it rhythmically, whilst continuing to work on Frederic's oversized member with my eager tongue. I sensed they had done this before, and that I was in highly accomplished hands. Eventually positions were swapped, and I climbed on top of Frederic's massive member and felt my vaginal walls stretch to accommodate his enormous girth.... god it felt good and once he was fully inside me, I started a steady agile grinding of my hips, whilst Michel was now steadily fucking my mouth. We were passing the poppers around between us, which was giving the situation a whole different dynamic...my internal organs felt like they were exploding as Frederic's monster was pounding me relentlessly...I was in a state of permanent orgasm, squirting uncontrollably. After a while they carried me through to Frederic's bedroom, where they placed me on all fours, and Frederic produced a small chrome dildo, which he inserted slowly into my anus, they then took it in turns to fuck me hard and very deeply from behind, in rotation, all my three holes were being stretched and filled, being put to some serious use. I was just moaning and crying out with pleasure...I was experiencing yet another level of intense pleasure that I never thought possible. I could feel the muscles in my anus gripping this divine chrome plug, whilst my vagina was gripping two different hard French cocks in turn. After considerably more intense and heavy fucking, they knelt me on the floor and we all sniffed some poppers, then they started to stroke and rub their cocks over my face, gently slapping my cheeks with them. Two gorgeous cocks engulfed my face; my tongue was darting over each one eagerly awaiting their semen. Michel was first to unleash a massive stream of hot cum down my throat, and over my lips, the sight of this had an instant effect on Frederic, who then let loose with his own very powerful orgasm, spurting torrents of hot sticky cum into my mouth, I was swallowing as much as I possibly could, but this was a total semen outpouring, I was thoroughly drenched, it was everywhere, dripping off my chin and running all over my breasts and down on to my thighs.... what a glorious feeling! What a wonderful end to a perfect evening! I just had time for a quick shower, before my cab was due to arrive and whisk me the thirty or so minutes home…. taking with me a bag containing my wonderful suede chaps and new black number that I'd never got round to trying on…. also sneaking my new little chrome friend in to my bag as a memento to a fine tripling!

    As true gents, they escorted me to my cab and slipped the driver his fare, we said our fond farewells and wished each other a merry Xmas. I sat quietly in a warm satisfied glow on the journey home content with the knowledge that I had so much to tell Paul, and felt sure he'd fully approve of my antics and the retelling of the session would run and run over time!

Chapter Fifteen: New Horizons

Paul's parents joined us and the children once again for Xmas and the New Year festivities. Over drinks on Boxing Day they dropped a small bombshell. They told us that they were seriously contemplating selling up and moving to South West France. They'd already been and visited some old friends, who'd taken the plunge five years earlier, and had never looked back. Their plan was to buy something that was suitable to run as a small, but upmarket Bed and Breakfast business. They were going to go over by car in late February to have a good look at what was available.

Also, Paul and I decided, that as the children were now growing up quickly and his new position was bringing in substantially more money, it was time for us to move to a larger property.

We spent a number of Sundays just driving to various areas, and eventually decided that we'd like to find a suitable property in or around Kew, which would make Paul's commute into the West End, that much easier. After much searching we found an ideal property, close to Kew Green, the previous owner had passed away and the family wanted a quick sale. It was a lovely five bedroomed detached house, with a nice manageable garden, it was well under market value, but needed lots of work to bring it up to how we wanted it. After many late into the night discussions, it was decided that we'd take the plunge and fortunately our house sold quickly. We took out a much larger, but manageable mortgage, which would give us the funds to restore the house and remodel it to our tastes.

We'd have a few fun evenings with Mike and Sarah, and had remained in touch via Email with all our French friends, but with all that was going on we'd sadly had no free time for a naughty excursion to Paris for a while.

Eventually things leveled out, and we had a firm completion date on the Kew house. Paul decided, that as the year was flying by and it was now late April, we should have a big blow out in Paris just prior to exchanging contracts, as we'd be fully committed for a while after the move, with builders and everything that we had planned for the house.

Paul, once again booked our itinerary as before....same flights...same hotel. We were both fatigued by everything that had been going on during the previous four months, but we were excited and couldn't wait for our first jaunt of the year.

We didn't tell any of our French friends we were going, as we just wanted to do our own thing, we'd maybe ring them if we had time. We arrived on a beautiful warm and sunny spring day. It wasn't long before we found a lovely old bar by the Seine and sat outside and relaxed with a well-deserved bottle of chilled Chablis.

A very nice looking Thai restaurant had opened opposite the hotel with a very romantic looking outdoor eating area complete with large patio heaters, so we decided we'd have dinner there that evening, then go back to the room and get ready for our first night of fun in a long while. We were both feeling incredibly horny and full of anticipation for the night ahead. We'd decided we'd go back to the S.A.S Association club, as we'd so enjoyed the whole ambiance of the place previously, especially the glass paneled floor, plus I also wanted to give the grope box a try. Paul had picked up their card on our last visit, so we would have no problem explaining to a taxi driver where we wanted to go.

After a lovely meal, we showered and I prepared myself for some naughtiness French style. I had brought a lovely black Armani jacket that resembled a gentleman's tailcoat that could be just worn by itself, underneath I just wore a skimpy black g string, I decided to go bare legged, as I'd recently had a few sunbeds, so my legs had a nice healthy glow to them. I wore a pair of elegant black heels to finish off the outfit.

Around eleven thirty we jumped in a taxi and handed the driver the card and off we went, after about ten minutes we were dropped of at the corner of the road where the club was located, as arriving from this direction it was no entry, as it was a one way street. We got out, paid and started to make our way the hundred metres or so to the club...we were completely surprised to find it closed and with no signs of it opening anytime soon…. we were flummoxed…. until Paul suddenly announced "Plan B" and we swiftly made our way back to the main street and waited for an empty cab. Eventually after waiting a good ten minutes, one pulled over and we jumped in. Paul said to the driver "Rue le Regrattier, Ile Saint Louis S'il vous plait". He told me it was a new club that Phillipe had recently recommended on his website, and that was "Plan B". He knew no more! We were in the lap of the Gods, so to speak.

Ile Saint Louis is a small island in the middle of the Seine, and is a very upmarket area; we walked along the street not knowing the actual full address of the club. We soon found it - a discreet canopy which had the club name on it and an inconspicuous "video entry camera" by the buzzer. The club was very aptly called "L'Escapade" (recently renamed "Au Lys en L'Isle"). With trepidation we rang the buzzer, and were soon ushered into a large and very opulent reception area by a lady called Amanda, who informed us in perfect English, that she and her husband Costas were the owners and we were very welcome. She offered to take my jacket, but after a brief explanation that there was not a lot under the coat, she laughed and winked approvingly. She explained that the club had been only open for a few months, and it had a policy of allowing very select single men entrance, only after being strictly vetted by her and her husband. They already had over seventy of the most eligible "Cocksmen" in Paris as members. They were aiming the club at couples and single ladies that enjoyed being in an environment of more than "just couples". She told us, they were also open from two until seven in the afternoons, as they had a clientele of French ladies who attended, whilst their partners were at work and whom enjoyed the extra attention they received in a safe and opulent environment…I was getting very excited already…. She went on to say, that the club was fairly quiet, as they had been expecting a couple from the South of France to be visiting, but they'd been delayed until the following day, however, we were more than welcome to go down into the club and have a drink and a look around! It was all very relaxed and hospitable.

She led us down a very elegant marble stairway, where halfway down a large oak bar came into view, and at the sound of a pair of female heels about dozen very elegantly dressed men looked up…my legs went to jelly…. praying that they didn't let me down, I gripped Paul's arm and the balustrade firmly, smiled and descended, to an enthusiastic greetings of "Bonsoir Mademoiselle, Monsieur" from the men. I made it to the bar without stumbling, and Amanda introduced us to Costas, who immediately poured us a welcome glass of champagne. Amanda presented us to a few of the men, some of whom were in full evening dress. The club was an converted ancient wine warehouse, and from the bar area it led, through a pair of heavy drapes to a small intimate dance area, with a small room with two bedded/sofa areas with a lockable iron gate off to one side... It was just like a small prison cell! Further on into the club there was a large room, with relaxing sofas where you could relax, flirt, drink, or simply watch whatever was happening at the time. Leading off from that area was a larger room, beautifully lit with a large circular bed as its centre piece, there were also smoked mirrors strategically placed, both on the walls and ceiling. There was also a very nicely appointed bathroom/dressing area, complete with a large wet room to shower and fresh towels and perfumes close by.

Whilst Paul was chatting, in his now almost passable French to Costas, several of the men who spoke English started chatting to me and wanted to know all about what brought us to Paris, and were we having a good time.... I kept the details to a minimum, but revealed enough information, so that they understood that we'd been to Parisian Clubs previously and knew the etiquette. I also told them we'd come here due to the S.A.S club being closed...one of the men explained that it had been shut-down, as it didn't have all its papers in order and the authorities had closed them a few weeks ago.

After a while a very suave guy asked me if I'd like to dance, Costas controlled the music from behind the bar and was playing some slow French mood music, I caught Paul's eye to let him know that I was going for a dance. I was led to the dance floor and was immediately in the arms of my elegant partner, who danced very sensually and was running his hands over my lower back, he enquired as to what I was wearing under the jacket, and my response of "not much" had an immediate effect on him. He became more adventurous and soon started kissing my neck and stroking my bottom through the material of my jacket. As soon as the music ended, we made our way back to the bar, I only had time for a brief gulp of Jack Daniels, when another man whisked me off to the dance floor.... this happened several more times and I was getting more and more turned on by the minute. Any reservations that I may have had went rapidly up the stairs and out the door... it was however; very reassuring that Amanda kept popping her head through the drapes to make sure everything was, as I wanted! I simply adored being the centre of attention amongst all these charming men.

During one of the dances a good looking man, who it later turned out worked for Chanel and became a good friend and lover, (I was never short of their No.5 range of products) decided that I should remove my panties.... I declined with a wink, saying maybe later....we'll see...all said with a teasing and seductive look in my eyes as, I suggestively squeezed the front of his trousers as we left the dance floor...he pinched my bottom and said "naughty girl".

I declined any further dances for the next twenty minutes or so, as I wanted to soak up the atmosphere, and revel in all the attention being heaped on me, and savour my JD with a nice menthol St Moritz cigarette.... I was teasing myself, making myself wet with anticipation. Paul enquired if all was good and did I feel comfortable with the situation? I told him, I loved all the attention and was game for whatever occurred...he grinned and whispered "Salope". Shortly, I went to freshen up and lustfully removed my panties and hid them discreetly in one of the cupboards in the bathroom. I returned smiling inwardly to myself thinking, "OK Emma your biggest challenge to date, lets see what you're made of?"

I returned to the bar and had another tumbler of JD with ice and a slow cigarette.... my insides were churning with desire, huge waves of expectation and desire were sweeping over me....I really did love being the object of lust amongst all these elegant and sophisticated men....it was like my own personal porn film.... one, that had me firmly in the starring role! And one that was going to need a whole lot of improvisational skills, as never before had I entertained more than two leading men!

It didn't take long for me to catch Mr Chanel's eye, and once more he escorted me through the drapes and onto the dance floor. One of my all time favourite slow grooves was playing, "Float on", I hoped this was the long ten-minute version! It didn't take long before he was softly kissing my neck again and enquired in a sexy French accent "had I misplaced anything from under my jacket", to which I replied a simple "maybe" and gave him a mischievous wink ...he took this as an invitation to find out and slipped his hand under the tail of my jacket and gently started to explore, caressing my buttocks and slowly running his fingers up between my cheeks, when satisfied that I had discarded my panties he whispered "tres bon", and swiftly moved his hand around to the front and began to gently rub in between the lips of my vagina, commenting on how deliciously wet I was. Soon we were joined by another man from the bar, who I'd not danced with, he looked on in appreciation at my semi exposed body being stimulated in front of him. Amanda was obviously keeping a close eye on me and soon popped her head around and gave me a look that said "everything fine?" to which I simply gave her the universal thumbs up and she disappeared. At this juncture the other guy said something to Mr. Chanel which I didn't understand…but soon became obvious…as he proceeded to lift the tail of my jacket, fully exposing my bottom and slowly pulling my cheeks apart, giving him a great view and an open invitation to play…without hesitation, he stepped forward and caressed my cheeks from behind, deftly and expertly teasing my anus with a flicking motion of his fingers….I soon started to cum at the hands of the two skilled men, legs splayed, giving them easy access, and a sure sign to continue playing with me.

     As Monsieur "Chanel" was undoing the three buttons on my jacket to expose my breasts, I sensed out of the corner of my eye another man enter and admire the scene. Soon, the guy behind me took his cue and slipped my jacket off over my shoulders and handed it to the new gentleman, who went and hung it on a peg near the drapes…Yummy….I was now naked, in heels, on a dance floor, in the presence of three elegant men…I was in heaven. They soon led me through to the large room with the circular bed, and to my relief, on a little side table I spotted a bowl of condoms and some lube…not that I needed any. Whilst the new gent sucked on my erect nipples and stroked my pussy, the other two were undressing and carefully hanging up their clothes, shortly a forth guy appeared with a drink for me, which I gratefully took a large gulp of, whilst sizing up the erections now at my disposal! Soon there were four naked Frenchmen…then five…then six…then I stopped counting! I began concentrating on the task in front of me. A plethora of naked men, all proudly showing and offering their erections to me…. which, joyously ranged from large to bloody enormous! At first I knelt down and started to suck and lick any and every cock that was put to my lips, sometimes as many as four at a time, trying to force their way into my mouth. I was climaxing almost continuously, as hands and fingers deftly explored and probed my pussy and anus from behind, eventually several pairs of hands lifted me up me and bent me over the bed, spreading me open, and one swiftly penetrating me from behind, whilst several of the other men knelt on the bed in front of me as I greedily slurped and guzzled on their throbbing cocks…. I had rapidly transformed into a complete slut, playing the role with total commitment! The men were all vocal in their encouragement of each other, which spurred the gentleman behind me to pound into me even harder. I kept glancing in the various mirrors, I watched intently, as a guy held me open for the other to penetrate me deeply. I was experiencing even more explosive orgasms by the sight reflected back at me. At one stage, I caught a glimpse of Paul watching in complete admiration, before disappearing back to the bar; also Amanda kept a watchful eye over the proceedings. Over the next few hours I got well and truly used, in a great variety of positions, never at any stage without at least two cocks at my mouth, with another pounding into me. I had cock after cock pleasuring me, and at times felt I was drowning in a sea of hot sperm, it was everywhere…it was pure debauched ecstasy… I lost count of how many times I gushed, but I knew I'd lost a lot of fluid during the evening. Eventually Paul appeared and told me there was a present for me at the bar…he asked me if I was coming…and to great amusement the chap who was currently fucking me said "she hasn't stopped monsieur!" It had been a fantasy for quite a while and it was definitely well worth the wait. My confidence was sky-high, knowing all these men desired my body, and the satisfaction of pleasing them all was beyond belief!

After a quick shower, I retrieved my panties and headed back to the bar, and as soon as I stepped through the drapes all the gentlemen gave me a spontaneous round of applause, each and everyone of the men presented me with a bottle of Champagne and commended me on my stamina, enthusiasm and all round energetic performance!

Costas and Amanda offered to ship the back Champagne back to the U.K - after we explained that we'd never be able to carry all fourteen bottles back on the plane. However, we eventually agreed the best solution would be that we took two bottles and that they would keep the rest on reserve for us behind the bar, ready for our next visit… On top of that, they gave us a lift back to the hotel and wouldn't take a penny off us…saying that I'd had been the star of the evening and they'd sold a lot of Champagne! By now I was absolutely wiped out, physically drained and had the munchies, so Paul and I ended up in a late night bar with a nightcap and a large plate of cheese and bread, accompanied by some knowing nods and smiles from the other late night revelers.

From a false start nearly six hours earlier this "Plan B" had turned into the most wonderful night of complete decadent fun. Paul said he'd come and checked on me at least half a dozen times, but said I had a look of pure lust in my eyes and didn't want to interrupt my fun. He laughed and told me he had my back covered at all times, but let the guys "cover" my front. I told him with a roll of my eyes that his sense of humour was extraordinary!

We surfaced around lunchtime on the Friday, remarkably refreshed, but were both in desperate need of a caffeine fix, so after throwing on some jeans and sweatshirt, we made our way to the nearest café/bar where we replenished ourselves with coffee and a large "croque monsieur" each. We talked endlessly about the previous evening and both decided this was one gem of a club, and we'd return again that night, I'd have preferred the Saturday, but that wasn't possible as we'd already booked our table at "ChrisetManu 2" for the the final evening.

We had decided to have a relaxing afternoon and after perusing the latest edition of "Pariscope", we decided to have a few hours at a "Sauna Hammam" close by, on the Rue Rivoli, very close to Le Louvre. We spent a wonderful few hours alternating between the sauna, steam room and large Jacuzzi. The place was fairly quiet, with only about another twenty people, all focused on relaxing. It was an oasis of tranquility and we lounged on the confortable bed/chairs and detoxed with some exotic juices, all the time extolling "L'Escapade" and what a great find it had been. This really had a calming effect on both of us and we left totally revitalized, ready for another wild night!

Upon returning to the hotel later that afternoon I had a wonderful surprise when I opened the door, as there on the bed was a large burgundy leather hold-all full of Chanel No.5 products, it looked like the entire range, topped off with a large 30ml bottle of "Parfum Grand Extrait" "Incroyable!"…but well deserved!". There was also a compliments slip, signed by - Thierry, and a phone number!! It transpired that Paul had mentioned to him in conversation where we were staying, and also gave him one of his business cards, as they were going to meet up in London the next time he was there on business (I expect both Paul and he had something extra on the agenda that would include me)…well I hoped so!"

We decided it would be rude not to telephone and express my thanks and deepest gratitude for the totally unexpected gift. So, with my first glass of wine of the day in hand, I phoned and said what a lovely and overwhelming gesture it was, he said "it was his pleasure and that I deserved to be showered with Chanel for eternity"… charming swine!

He enquired as what our plans were for that evening, and would we like to go out for dinner - as his guests? I remember blurting "yes please" and handing the phone to Paul to arrange, as I was getting in a tizz about what I'd wear and how long to get ready etc.

After much deliberation, I decided on wearing a nice respectable trouser suit with a white silk shirt underneath, as Thierry had told Paul it was a very chic old Parisian restaurant and that I could pop back to the hotel to change before going to the club.

We arranged to be outside the hotel at nine, and on the dot a taxi pulled up with Thierry inside, we got in and were very quickly (about three minutes) driven to a wonderful old traditional Parisian brasserie called "Bofinger", situated on the rue de la Bastille. It was in a wonderful old building in a very "belle époque" setting. Thierry told us that it had been founded in 1864 and was considered to be "most beautiful brasserie in Paris". It was a truly magnificent restaurant and was very busy, but all the staff seemed to know Thierry, and ushered us to a beautifully set table in a booth with quilted black leather benches. It was a stunning setting, and the large selection of seafood's on display outside, arranged on a big cart of ice really got the taste buds tingling. We asked Thierry to order for us, as he knew the menu inside out, so to start with he ordered "The Royal Bofinger", which consisted of a whole lobster, half a dozen large langoustines, a whole crab, prawns, eighteen assorted oysters, brown shrimps and shellfish, all on ice, arranged spectacularly on a huge three tiered platter, complemented by a nice chilled bottle of white wine, and for the main course we all had pan-fried beef fillet with a green pepper sauce and gratin dauphinois potatoes. I stayed on white, while Paul and Thierry got stuck into a bottle of Beaujolais. He insisted that we all had a dessert of Profiteroles with warm Valrhona chocolate…they were awesomely good. We all indulged in a brandy and coffee, soaking up the atmosphere, whilst our food settled…we were all well stuffed!

It turned out that Thierry was forty-three, and had a seventeen year old son who lived with him, he'd been divorced for three years and was simply living life to the full. He was a creative marketing director for "Chanel", and his position saw him travelling frequently to all the major European Capitols. He had an apartment in Paris and a house near Versailles. Evidently not short of cash!

We decided to stroll slowly back to the hotel, so as I could change into my more revealing "club" wear. I chose to go all out for the "Wow" factor and wore my new black crepe de chine halter necked evening gown, which around the cinched waist hung a dozen ribbons of silk, which parted as I walked, to reveal my body from ankle to hipbone (zero underwear needed), and the huge black and red heels, both courtesy of Michel…. this was sure to be a head turner…. I wasn't wrong…I slipped my coat over this highly revealing and provocative outfit and rejoined the men in reception. Whilst waiting for the cab they were both trying to get me to show what I had on under the coat…. I played the teasing game and told them to wait and see! Their patience would soon be rewarded.

Amanda welcomed us with great affection, and when I removed my coat there was an audible gasp from Amanda, both Thierry and Paul just stood starring, completely open mouthed… exactly the kind of reaction that makes a girl horny! I prepared myself for the long walk down the stairs, where I would be completely exposed for the final eighteen or so steps to anyone at the bar below, as the strips of the dress parted easily as I walked…once again, gripping the balustrade for all I was worth, I began my slow descent. Costas immediately popped a bottle of "our" champagne, and Paul signaled to him that third glass was required.

It was much busier, as I noted a few people already on the dance floor and several couples floating around, and the obligatory suave single guys in attendance. Soon Amanda drew me to one side and introduced me to a very sexy looking Swiss lady, named Severine, who was there by herself, she spoke perfect English. She was around late forties and had been living in Paris for a couple of years and she came to the club when she wanted and needed some male attention, without any of the preamble of a "date". I admired her honesty and attitude…she was a real bubbly outgoing person and I immediately invited her to join us, which she readily accepted!

After a few drinks Severine and I went for a little wander, to see what was happening in the back rooms, by now she'd discarded her jacket to reveal a stunning sheer black dress, which showed her body off well, un-spoilt by either bra or panties, her large nipples prominently visible through the clinging material. There were several couples and singles that were already making good use of the circular bed. We were stood casually watching the action, when I felt a warm hand deftly slip between one of the strips of silk that barely covered my bottom and gently start to stroke in between my buttocks, caressing my pussy from behind. I simply parted my legs slightly, to give the anonymous hand full access, which he took full advantage of, bringing me very swiftly to a very wet orgasm. I noticed Severine was also on the verge of climax, I glanced down to see that whoever was behind us, was also skillfully playing with Severine…. He definitely had his hands full! We stayed a while, watching a scene akin to a Roman orgy taking place in front of us, whilst letting "Mr. Anonymous" continue to pleasure us both with complete dexterity. After a short while, we both decided to return to the bar…. but not before saying a big "Merci" to a very distinguished man in his sixties, but undeniably very elegant.

When we got to the bar, Paul was busy in conversation with a couple I recognized, but couldn't place immediately. As soon as introductions were made, it came to me instantly…it was the couple from our very first night in Paris; Monique and Anton, whom we'd had a drink with in Harry's Bar.

Paul immediately asked Costas to pour them a flute of champagne, we all clicked instantaneously and as the drinks flowed a very hedonistic and sensual feeling became very apparent between our little group.

After some very inappropriate dancing between various combinations of the now six of us, and some very open and exhibitionistic flirting, especially from Thierry, who couldn't keep his hands off me, which in truth I pretty much encouraged and returned his advances with fervor. Paul appeared to be getting into Monique, whilst her husband Anton had disappeared into some small nook or cranny with Severine for a brief dalliance…. the entire atmosphere was electric. A while later, Thierry suggested we all get taxis and reconvene at his apartment to continue the nights activities…his son was visiting his mother for the weekend, so there'd be no interruptions. Everyone was in complete agreement. Whilst waiting for the taxis Amanda asked me if we could come back the following afternoon around three, as there was a private and very intimate afternoon get together, that she said we may enjoy! I agreed and said we'd definitely attend.

    Thierry gave each of the taxi drivers his address and we jumped in, myself, Thierry and Severine in one…Paul, Monique and Anton in the other. After a short drive we arrived at his apartment, which was on one of Paris's most desirable streets…Rue du Faubourg Saint-Honoré…very close to one of the Chanel Boutiques.

    We all followed Thierry, and from nowhere a fully uniformed doorman appeared, doffed his cap and let us in with a small bow, then escorted us to the lift and bade us all a "bonne soirée". The lift deposited us on the top floor of the building - the doors opened on to large pink marbled lobby area, with several lounge chairs and a collection large exotic plants in elegantly decorated porcelain pots. To one side was a huge pair of mahogany doors, which Thierry unlocked, and led us in to what can only be described as the most magnificent and sumptuous room I'd ever stepped foot in, it was like a ballroom, filled with antique sofas and elegant lounging areas, two huge crystal chandeliers and tucked in the corner a very well stocked bar. The room led out on to huge terrace with uninterrupted 360 degree views of Paris. Under a large awning there were four sofas, arranged around a large marble drinks table - in each corner there was an outdoor patio heater. The lighting was like something you'd see in a Vogue photo shoot, all moody and discreet…this was style on an titanic level…. everyone was stunned by the pure scale and sheer opulence of it all! "Magnifique" didn't even come close to describing these surroundings. Thierry left to prepare the drinks, whilst we settled into the sofas, which if you weren't careful could and would swallow you whole.

    Monique was really making her moves on Paul and he was really relaxed, and seemed to be fully enjoying all her overt flirting, whilst

Severine and Anton were slowly and erotically playing with each other, they seemed oblivious to everybody else. Thierry arrived with the refreshments, which were on top of a substantial drinks trolley.

    Thierry poured and served the drinks with elegant panache, and soon settled in beside me on the sofa, he proposed a toast "amour et plus amour", which made us all giggle, as he tried his best effort at a translation…"fuck and more fucky!"

    Shortly, Thierry suggested he gave me a tour of his apartment, and I couldn't wait to follow him. As we walked through the huge salon he told me it had been in his family since 1929, and that he'd been living here since 1985. There were several large elegant rooms at one end, whilst his son had his own private area at the other. Off to one side of the salon there was a very long dinning room, which led through to a very large and spectacularly equipped kitchen. From the kitchen there was a stunning spiral stairway, which led up to a breakfast room with inspirational views over the Paris skyline.

    He certainly saved the best for last, as we returned to his suite of rooms…. he opened a large door that was partially disguised as a large mahogany panel, what I encountered was quite magnificent, a master suite with a large panoramic curved glass window with similar views as the terrace, but even more awe inspiring when seen through tinted glass from a king size hand crafted mahogany four poster bed! To the right, a door led through to a dressing room and walk in wardrobe, to the left there was a very modern, chrome, slate and glass wet room and grooming area.

    Instinctively we embraced, very deeply, it was incredibly sensual, his hands were roaming all over my body, soon my breasts were exposed as he gently pulled the material to either side of them and started to gently suck and nibble on my now very erect and sensitive nipples, whilst his fingers were playing a mesmerizing game in between my legs. He sensed my legs tremble as my arms gripped his shoulders for support, as he began to rhythmically fuck me with his exquisite fingers…soon the tremble became a shuddering, intense and very wet gushing orgasm. I held on to him for a while to regain my balance and strength, as nowadays these orgasms were increasing in power and were very energy sapping for a few minutes, until a second wind took over. Once a level of normality returned to my body, I stepped out of my dress, whilst he swiftly undressed and for brief second we stood and smiled at each other, until I dropped to my knees and opened my mouth invitingly for his gorgeous pulsating erection to use. It was as hard as a rock and was a feeling of pure joy taking it in between my lips, encircling him with my eager mouth, as I locked eyes with him, my tongue darted all around its large glistening head. He tasted, and felt monumentally good! After a good while he lifted me to my feet and carried me to the huge bed where he gently placed me on all fours with my bottom pushed up skywards, open and inviting him to do with it as he pleased…I soon felt his warm breath and tongue on my pussy, slowly licking up and down, probing…sucking…. gently nibbling my lips and frequently exploring my anus with both fingers and tongue…it was wonderful. I was begging him to take me, but he made me wait until I'd had another huge climax on his tongue before he entered me. The feeling was incredible; all my senses were on fire. He was a wonderful and skilled lover, soon we rolled over and he instructed me to ride him, taking his entire length deep inside me, whilst he tweaked and teased my nipples with one hand and inviting me to suck the fingers on his other, like a substitute penis. This was "total" sex in its most basic and animalistic form…two people experiencing and pleasuring each other's bodies with absolutely no limits whatsoever. I felt we were welded together as I rode him for what seemed an eternity until he himself started to shudder, then utter a volley of guttural noises as he exploded forcefully deep inside me…it was an intense, hot wet climax, as I joined his pleasure and simultaneously gushed as he came, soaking his thighs in my warm juices. We lay together exhausted. Eventually, we decided to rejoin the others, he threw me one of his Polo shirts to put on, whilst he slipped on a long silk printed robe.

    We wandered through to the salon and found the others locked in a limb-tangled foursome, with lots of moaning and groaning. I was pleased to see Paul abandoning his inhibitions and really letting his basic sexual instincts take over, we left them to it and went and relaxed outside with a drink, absorbing the wonderful ambiance of the glowing Paris skyline.

    We eventually made it back to our hotel in the early hours and gratefully collapsed into a long overdue sleep.

The following day we surfaced around midday and went out for our ritualistic Coffee-Brandy-Ciggy, and discussed the evening, from one another's perspective. Happily, we were both of the opinion that we should "make the most of every situation that arose". Even though, we were both running low on energy, we were very excited as to what the afternoon would bring…I felt that being in a club like "L'Escapade", during the daytime hours would only increase the excitement and the debauchedness of it all!

Sufficiently rejuvenated by the typical French "Steak Frites" and more coffee, we returned to the hotel to prepare for the afternoon. Not really knowing the etiquette as to dress code, Paul put on a pair of trousers and casual Polo top and I wore a simple short black dress and hold-ups…. nothing overtly revealing. Simple, elegant, but with an air of hidden "naughtiness".

We decided to stroll to the Ile Saint Louis, and stopped off around the corner from the club at a small watering hole, and had a nice specialty of the bar, which was raspberry vodka and tonic with crushed ice, which after five minutes hit the spot, giving us both an instant energy boost and a devilish attitude.

Amanda gave us her customary warm welcome, and took my coat, whilst explaining that this was a private party, for a particularly attractive and well known female French television presenter…it was her fortieth birthday and her current beau had arranged it, as a little afternoon treat for her. He had instructed Amanda that he would like the crème de la crème of her male members, and a few select couples to attend. I must admit I felt honored to have been invited; it was like being accepted into an inner circle of French Society. Costas poured us both very large Jackie D's (as he now referred to our drink of choice) and introduced us to a few of the stunning looking men at the bar, everyone seemed to have stepped straight out of a designer clothes store, all very elegantly attired and oozing with sensuality.

The guest of honour was a very elegant woman, she certainly didn't look forty, and she had that typical Parisian look of sexuality and confidence about her.

Apparently the "birthday girl" was a complete and utter exhibitionist and loved being the centre of attention in a group of men.

She was a very typical French temptress, who just loved all the admiring men, and of course her celebrity status. I asked Amanda wasn't the "lady" worried she'd be exposed in the papers, to which she laughed and explained that the French had very strict privacy laws, and anyway the French people would just smile and probably even applaud her courage...."Pas de problem!" She exclaimed.

Her current man eventually proposed a toast, we all raised our glasses as Costas brought down a gorgeous birthday cake, and everyone was given a slice. Suddenly, with much flamboyance, he announced that proceedings should begin. He led her to the dance floor area, on which a very large circular bed had been erected, her boyfriend instructed two of the men to undress and prepare her... I was intrigued...once she was naked, apart from her heels, she was quickly surrounded, by various men, who were taking turns to massage oil into her body, quickly she was glistening with a shiny-oily sheen. Then, once she was ready the drapes were parted and her special "presents" appeared....two very well oiled muscular black men, both proudly stroking two of the most enormous penises I had ever seen. The other men respectfully stepped aside, as she knelt down on a small pillow, that had been placed strategically in front of the bed, and waited impatiently as her "presents" moved enticingly towards her, offering their pulsating cocks for her pleasure...it was an amazingly erotic spectacle...everyone was silent, quietly watching with admiration, as she endeavored to suck these huge men.... she was moaning loudly, and her eyes had rolled back into her head, it appeared as if she was in a trance! Her boyfriend was like a circus master, issuing instructions to the two guys and they were both more than eager to please, both him, and the lady in question. After a long period of her administering her oral skills, the two guys picked her up, placing her on her hands and knees on the bed as they positioned themselves at either end! They simultaneously entered both her pussy and mouth; she let out a piercing scream, only to be silenced as the huge black cock filled her mouth. Her boyfriend was enjoying every minute as she was being monumentally fucked by the two guys.... occasionally they swapped ends, continuing to pound her vigorously until she climaxed, after a while her legs just simply gave way. Her boyfriend quickly gave her a glass of champagne, before she was subjected to "round two", again, they proceeded to fuck her mercilessly...she was absolutely loving it.... the harder they worked her mouth and pussy, the more she seemed to want, until eventually she begged them for "la crème". This appeared to be the agreed word, as the guys immediately knelt her back on the floor and proceeded to stroke themselves in turn, into her eager mouth, often slapping her face with their cocks, until they both in unison…like a well practiced routine…started to flood her mouth with copious torrents of their semen…she was in a complete orgasmic world of her own, whimpering lustfully, as they continued to ejaculate into, and all over her. I along with everyone else was speechless, and when they had finished we all burst into a polite spontaneous applause. It was such a depraved, but wondrous sight, seeing her exhausted, with her perspiration mixing with their semen as it dripped down her body!

Once everyone had refreshed their drinks it was open season for all the other guys to join in, and several of the other women took it as a signal to participate and help out. Sadly, time was against us, as we needed to get back to the hotel and freshen up, as our table at ChrisetManu 2 was booked for 9.30p.m.

We thanked Amanda and Costas for a lovely and somewhat educational afternoon, and left saying that we would visit again as soon as time would allow…. basically, we felt we wouldn't be able to keep away!

As per usual we had a wonderful meal at ChrisetManu2, but we were both drained from the previous few days, and mentally overloaded with what we'd witnessed that afternoon, so we simply relaxed with a few drinks and watched a selection of debauched couplings, not having the energy to get involved ourselves. We left relatively early for us, and had a well earned six hours sleep, until it was time to get a cab to the airport, boy did we have plenty to talk about on the fight, and I certainly had lots to tell both Erica and Sarah, as I knew both would want to hear every detail. I felt sure Erica would be pestering Chris for another Paris trip and certainly a visit to L'Escapade!

Chapter Sixteen: The Move and More

The next few weeks were a bit of a blur, with lots of packing and general things to sort out regarding our impending house move, whilst also having Paul's parents announce that they'd actually found somewhere and would be definitely "upping sticks" and moving to a small town in South West France called Blanquefort, which was close to Bordeaux. They had bought a lovely old farmhouse, which had the potential to accommodate four "Gites" in the grounds, the actual farmhouse was ready to live in, but they estimated it would be at least nine months work to get the "Gites" built to a high standard; as getting the various licenses and paperwork required was a slow process in France, with lots of red tape to get through. They were fully committed and had great plans for the place. It did look amazing.

It felt like the entire family was in a state of upheaval, and that we were all entering a new phase in our lives.

Paul was extremely busy at work, and his new position came with a lot more responsibility, and as we expected demanded a lot more of his time…. he would be away at least one night a week, sometimes two and there was a few of overseas trips as well. Therefore, it was basically my domain to manage the children and arrange all the finer details regarding the move, including all the hassles that came with it. Also, as the house required a lot of work it was down to me to arrange all the necessary meetings with interior designers/builders, the list went on!

On top of all this, there was also the weekly visits to check on my Aunt in the Cotswolds, that needed to be shoehorned in to my already packed schedule. I used the drive there and back to drift off, into what I now saw, as my alternate life, one that was increasingly based around sex and the encounters and adventures I'd had over the last few years. However, I wanted more, much more and the more exhibitionistic and furtive the better. I used to lay awake at night, replaying some of the highlights of my erotic journey so far, over and over again in my mind!

It was during a visit to my Aunt, a few weeks after we'd finally moved into the Kew house, that she dropped the "bombshell".

We were having our customary glass of wine and a sandwich in her garden, when she broached the subject. She said she'd thought long and hard about her situation and said she wasn't getting any younger, even with Celia there, she now found the house a bit of a dinosaur and that she wanted to sell and move closer to Paul and I. She explained to me that I was the "Main" beneficiary of her will and she didn't want me to be burdened with it when she was gone. She roughly explained her finances; the house was fully freehold with no mortgage. She said that she just wanted to simplify everything, so there would be no complicated taxes and any stress for me when she passed on.

I tried to reassure her that she had a good few years left, she agreed, but explained that she felt burdened by the house and grounds, she was simply fed up - as she put it, "rattling around in a big box waiting to die".

Her idea was to cash everything in and rent a small flat near to us in Kew, I said I'd have a word with Paul, and see what his thoughts were when I got back home that evening.

The following Sunday, we all went to visit and take her out for lunch, to see if she was still in the same frame of mind.

Paul and I had come up with an idea, that there was the option that we could convert the basement of the Kew house into a nice self contained apartment for her, so as she could enjoy a much slower pace of life, with no worries of bills, or the complications of running and maintaining her house.

She loved the idea (I think it was in the back of her mind all along). We explained the situation with the house, she agreed, that once a lot of the basic work that we were having done was completed, that she would come to Kew and stay for a few days, to make her final decision. She couldn't wait and was on the phone a couple of times a week for progress reports!

Chapter Eighteen: The Request

Having kept in frequent contact with all our Parisian friends by Email since our return, it was a lovely surprise when out of the blue, one afternoon Thierry rang and told me that he'd be in London for two days the following week, and would we both like to meet up, as he had a small favour to ask us, or more to the point me!

We met him on the following Thursday lunchtime, at a restaurant near his hotel, as both his evenings were taken up with business dinners and meetings.

Paul had taken some time off, so we all met at the restaurant, we chatted about Paris, he was enthralled by our latest discovery, telling him about our experience at L'Escapade on that first infamous Saturday afternoon. From our description, he felt sure that he knew the "Celebrity" in question. He said he was definitely going to make further enquiries as he put it!

Over coffee he told us that his son, Laurent, was coming to the U.K for the last two weeks in August and the first week in September, to stay with an English family, a few miles from us in Chiswick, as he was going to be attending an intensive English Language course at a specialist college.

Thierry was hoping that we could keep an eye on him during his stay, and use us as a point of contact. We told him that there would be no problem whatsoever, and that we'd help in any way we could. He explained that Laurent, was spending July with his Mother in the South of France and would be back in Paris to celebrate his eighteenth birthday before coming to London.

This was coincidental timing, as our children were going to be in France with their grand parents, during a similar period, as the builders were due to be doing the planned reconstruction of their bedrooms during that time.

Paul said his good-byes, and went back to his office, leaving Thierry and I to have a Brandy. It was then that he winked at me and told me the true nature of his "favour". I was both shocked, yet excited when he asked me if I would "teach his son the art of lovemaking". He said it was fairly typical for a Father to arrange for his son to be shown the ropes, as it were, by an experienced older Lady. He said he'd be honoured if I would accept, and be the "One" to educate his son and refine his technique in the "Boudoir". I was, to say the least stunned by this request, but also hugely enthusiastic at the thought of it…. I told him that I'd need to time to think about it…Thirty seconds later I agreed! Thierry settled the bill and told me he had a few gifts for me back at his hotel and that we should get them now, as he had an important meeting very soon.

    I was also on a tight time schedule, as I needed to be back for the children by five, to collect them from the after school club. We hurried back to his hotel. Once in his room, he gave me another identical leather "Chanel" hold all, once again it was brimming with their products, but this time a classic vintage "Chanel" white silk tuxedo blouse was the "piece de resistance", it was absolutely gorgeous.

    I seized the moment and took it into the bathroom, returning moments later, wearing, just the blouse, open and tempting; I smiled seductively, as I offered myself to him. He made no hesitation in bending me over one of the chairs and knelt down behind me, and he started to probe my pussy with his tongue, it was a matter of seconds before I was flooding his mouth with my powerful orgasm, he firmly held my thighs, as they trembled uncontrollably. He stood up and opened his trouser fly and in one swift movement penetrated me with his gorgeous thick cock, he simply fucked me like a rabid animal, hard and rough, all the while slapping my bottom, it was intense, lustful and oh so good. He eventually climaxed inside me with a huge powerful, final thrust, engulfing my insides with his hot semen…. and whispered in my ear "my son is in good hands" and winked.

    We had a quick drink at the hotel bar, until it was time for him to go off to his meeting and me…. back to "normality".

    I told Paul of Thierry's proposal, he thought it was a fantastic and very erotic idea, and one which he said I should plan with great care. He assured me that he'd find it a massive turn on to be at work, whilst knowing that I was seducing our friends' eighteen-year-old son!

Chapter Nineteen: The Instructress

Work on the house was progressing well, and was ahead of schedule, the only delay being the new kitchen, which wouldn't be completed until sometime in October, due to the late delivery schedule of the Italian work surfaces.

By this time, Paul's parents were living in France, but returning frequently to finalise all the various paperwork and legalities. They also took this opportunity to transport all their delicate, personal effects to their new home, by car.

August came, and soon the children were packed, ready and waiting for their grand father to pick them up, in his newly acquired French registered "Range Rover", he said it made him feel like a "land owner", to which there was much mirth, and general Gallic piss taking.

The children were highly excited, and couldn't wait to start their holiday adventure! We loaded them into the car for the beginning of the two-day drive, via Calais to Bordeaux. Both Paul and myself waved them off, with a degree of trepidation and a tear in my eye…, which, I shrugged off as a mild attack of hay fever!

Paul returned to work… suddenly, everything seemed calm and quiet, so I took the opportunity of having lunch with Erica, on Kew Green at the "Coach and Horses", which along with "The Greyhound" had become our local pubs of choice, they both served wonderful English Pub Grub and had a really relaxed atmosphere about them.

Erica came and inspected the work in progress on the house, as was her norm she enthused lewdly about what she'd do with one of the builders in particular, given half a chance! I was a tad concerned as "half a chance" would be all she'd need! I swiftly marched her to the pub to have a good catch up…. And keep her out of harms way.

I told her all about Thierry, the gifts and all the fun we'd had at "L'Escapade". She was doubly excited, as she said they'd booked a weekend early September and could I ring ahead, as before and make an introduction for them.

I saved the best till last, finally telling her about Thierrys request regarding the educating of his son in the finer details of lovemaking...the dirty bitch offered to help and assist in any way she could. It turned out that she had a major weak spot for the younger man. She said she loved to be in control and shock them, and that the previous year she'd had a short fling with a Dutch art student, who was staying near them. We laughed about it, but she did give me a few tips that would later prove very useful!

Thierry rang to give us Laurent's itinerary, as well as emailing all the relevant contact details. He told me "he was sending a boy to London and wanted him to return to Paris a man! With a mischievous giggle, I said, I'd do my best and that I'd give the task my fullest attention.

A few days before Laurent was due to arrive in Chiswick, I went to visit my Aunt, to give her a verbal progress report and arrange a date for her visit. We eventually settled on mid-September. She told me she'd been busy and had started to get things in order, and that she'd had the house valued; and already had an interested buyer get in touch, so she was very positive, that once things were finalized, that it wouldn't be a long drawn out process.

The children rang us every other evening and were having a great time helping their grand parents settle in to their new way of life, and they were enjoying the glorious sunny weather they were having. They'd had a few days at the beach, which was a twenty-minute drive away and according to Paul's mother, they'd quickly adapted to the French way of life and had even picked up a smattering of French words. They were amazed that both the children loved Mussels and ate them at every opportunity, and also adored the "croissant au chocolat" for breakfast. Apparently, they slept like angels and awoke refreshed and excited early every morning, and there'd not a been single tantrum. It was a relief to both of us that they were having such a good time, we felt it was broadening their outlook on life and experiencing a different culture first hand could be only a good thing, and serve them well in later life.

We'd been out for dinner several times since they'd been away and both of us were at it like rabbits, with the house to ourselves and with Paul loving it, when I told him details of things I'd gotten up to in Paris, he positively encouraged me to be even wilder, and live out each and every fantasy that I may have (it didn't take much persuading). He said he'd hate it if we both got to our old age with regrets, and the attitude of "I wish we'd done this and that....!" He'd instilled in me a very positive "Carpe Diem" attitude to life.

The following week Thierry called to say his son had arrived in London and was getting well settled in with the family, and that he'd be calling sometime over the next few days...I was apprehensive but excited, as to how this little scenario would play out.

The wife of the family rang to introduce herself and told me that Laurent had settled in well and it would be nice if I could pop round the following morning, before he went to his lessons and have a coffee and say hi! Which, I readily agreed to.

They had a comfortable, if not compact home and made me very welcome. We took coffee in their new conservatory, she said Laurent would be back shortly, as he'd gone to buy a few cakes; we made small talk until he returned.

I was slightly taken a back, as the boy in the photographs in Paris had grown somewhat and resembled a younger Thierry, but with his mothers olive complexion. He immediately came across as a very confident young man and had a cheeky grin, one that would melt many a girl's heart in future years.

We arranged to meet for lunch on the following Monday, as he had an afternoon free from lessons, and wanted to practice his English in a real environment. We arranged to meet at the "Coach and Horses" at one o'clock. I wrote the directions down for him and he said he'd take a taxi, as it was only a short distance.

As it was a gloriously hot sunny day, I decided to wear a nice summer dress, which showed off my figure well, accentuating my tanned legs, especially when worn with a pair of high wedge strappy sandals.

He was already sat outside with a drink and was enthusiastically waving at me as I walked across the Green to the pub. I felt a tad self conscious as I got closer, as I could feel his eyes mentally undressing me!...Just like his father! He immediately jumped up and greeted me with a kiss on both cheeks and offered to get me a drink. He reappeared a few minutes later happy that he'd been able to order in his limited English and a few moments later a nice bottle of chilled white wine arrived...I was impressed and definitely felt more than a little horny, especially as three women sat near by were obviously ogling Laurent and trying to work out what the relationship was, I could tell they were more than envious! Here I was a married woman in my thirties lunching with a very tanned and fit looking eighteen-year-old French boy. His body appeared well toned in his cargo shorts and typical French "Lacoste" polo shirt. We each had a nice summer salad and he told me in broken English the things he'd learnt so far. It was embarrassing as already his English was miles ahead of any French I'd picked up! He explained he'd met a couple of nice English girls who lived near where he was staying, but said they were nice but he much preferred girls who were older than him as they had a much more mature outlook on life, to which I inwardly smiled to myself.

I asked him if he'd like to come back and see the house where I'd make him a proper cup of coffee. The garden was still a jungle but we'd put a few loungers on the large decking area that was situated across the entire rear of the house.

After giving him a tour of the house and showing him the work in progress, we decided to take coffee outside in the sun.

I was getting very tingly and excited at the prospect of how and when I was going to seduce him. The fear of the unknown was really making me horny. I soon decided that there was no time like the present and told him it was fine if he wanted to take his top off to sunbathe, as in England we needed to grab and make the most of the rare sunny days when we could....he casually slipped his shirt off, to reveal a very ripped and bronzed chest and smiled at me when he caught me peeking at him. He playfully asked, if I was going to join him, this was the catalyst that I was hoping for, so I said, I would, but I would first go and fetch some suntan lotion. I went and quickly stripped off and put on the tiniest bikini bottoms I had, and grabbed the lotion and returned to the garden.... the look on his face said it all as he appraised my breasts and my already hard and erect nipples. I could sense that he liked what he saw, as it was obvious that he now had an erection!! He kept discreetly looking at my body, but I could also sense his hesitation as to the next move, so I took the bull by the horns and asked him if he'd like me to put some sun cream on his shoulders for him. In a flash, he said, yes please…that's all the encouragement I needed…it was now "game on". He sat up as I gently massaged his shoulders with the cream, letting my hands stray down to his chest, stroking his nipples, he made it very clear that he was enjoying this, by letting out a small moan. I continued my way down his chest, which meant I had to lean even further over him, and he shuddered as my breasts brushed against his shoulders, I could feel him tense, as he felt my hard nipples pressing into his back. I reached down even further and helped him undo his shorts, typically French he wasn't wearing any underwear. I gazed down shamelessly, as a beautiful thick, hard cock sprang from its confinement. He was every bit as endowed as his Father, if not more so. I encouraged him to remove his shorts completely and I came and knelt in front of him, between his powerful young thighs, I gazed with lust at him for a few moments before I went to work on him with my mouth and over eager tongue, I told him to keep eye contact with me whilst I ran my tongue up and down the length of his manhood, also licking and sucking on his balls…after a few moments of this, his youth and inexperience took over and he shuddered and unleashed an enormous torrent of hot semen over my tongue and lips…..I greedily accepted, and lapped it up, swallowing every last drop!

    He was embarrassed by the speed at which he came, it was then I knew that I was going to make the most of teaching him, and enjoy every single moment of my task.

    Hesitantly he leant forward to kiss me, I returned his kiss with fervor, and it wasn't long before he was playing enthusiastically with my nipples. After a short time his penis sprung back to life with the same intensity as before. I stood and invited him to remove my bikini bottoms, which he did with the deftness of someone twice his age. I spread my legs slightly as he stared briefly at my vagina which was only inches from his face…he looked at me for approval and gently started to run his fingers over my lips and tenderly parted them, as he did so I moaned encouragingly, whilst guiding his fingers to my swollen clitoris…. as he played with me, I could see his penis flexing and throbbing angrily. I took control of the situation and pushed him back down, so as he was laying full length on the lounger and I slowly mounted him, easing his penis into my soaking pussy, my muscles gripping him and pulling him deep inside me. He groaned as I slid down on him, taking his entire length inside me. I just stayed still for a while, smiling at him, whilst he played with my nipples, tweaking, pulling and sucking each in turn. I knew that it would be actions not words that would teach him self-control, and all the techniques he'd need in the coming years. I rode him nice and slowly, enjoying the warm sun on my back and a young hard cock inside me...I was having mini climaxes of my own every few minutes.

I could see a look of total concentration on his face, trying everything in his power to prolong our pleasure. I wanted to change position, so as he could take me from behind, but I knew that if we tried, he'd loose control quickly. So I just gripped his length with my vagina and encouraged him to increase the tempo and not to worry if he came, as we had plenty of time! Encouraged by my pleasure, and the gasps I made each time his entire length filled me, he started to match my rhythm until, with a cry I climaxed comprehensively, as he pumped me full of his hot young sperm, my vaginal muscles milking him dry …..it was a magical and memorable feeling!

We collapsed totally spent for a while, I was smitten by his boyish good looks and his enthusiasm to please. I was already planning ahead for our next lesson!!

After a quick shower, we dressed and I said I'd drop him back in Chiswick, as I had to go to the supermarket to get some groceries. I felt like a naughty teenager when he asked me if we could meet again. I readily agreed…I had so much more to teach him…. And we set a date for two days time, when he had his next free afternoon. I wrote the address down for him, and told him to come straight to the house! I'd be ready and waiting for him.

Paul and I enjoyed a long relaxed session, during which I told him a few of the high points of my afternoon, as we had the house to ourselves we indulged in a few glorious hits of a new brand of poppers Mike had given us, it was even stronger and more potent than previously, and had me gushing continuously. Before we retired, exhausted to bed, as promised I sent Thierry a progress report, my Email simply stating "Lesson One Successfully Completed".

The warm sunny weather the following day saw me relaxing and sunbathing in the garden, whilst plotting scenarios for Laurent's next lesson. I had to be a bit careful, as the builders were back putting the finishing touches to the new downstairs cloakroom, as finally the taps we'd ordered had arrived. Also the main builders were returning the following week to start on the new driveway and the re-roofing of the detached double garage. Also laying the foundations at the rear of it, as Paul was having a large home office/den built. Luckily, the previous owner already had similar plans already approved from a few years prior, so the local planning licenses were very straightforward.

    I spent the following morning preening and pampering myself, whilst preparing a few little nibbles for when Laurent arrived.

    Bang on the stroke of One the door bell chimed, and there, stood grinning at me, was my young, confident and simply gorgeous French boy…. who, was now, in my eyes well on his way to becoming a man! Over a few drinks outside we flirted and practiced his improving English. Trying to discuss in depth anything sexual was difficult, with the languages getting mixed up, it seemed much easier to simply let the actions do the talking. I took his hand and promptly led him upstairs to the bedroom, where, we slowly undressed each other, taking time, kissing and stroking each other. I had decided that for this second lesson I was going to be a little selfish….I was going to teach him how to take a woman to heaven and back, by solely using his tongue! We lay together, kissing and touching on the bed, his body as hard and responsive as before. I took the lead and gently offered him my nipples to suck and nibble on, also encouraging him to work his way down towards my vagina, slowly and teasingly. Instructing him verbally as best I could, that he must take it slowly and not to rush to the target area. I showed him where on my inner thighs to concentrate his efforts (I had my own agenda by now!). I made him spend a good twenty minutes licking and nibbling my labia with his tongue, before opening myself up fully to give his tongue the freedom and encouragement to suck and probe everywhere, slowly at first but building to gentle nips on my lips and clitoris with his teeth…he was certainly learning fast, he did everything I asked and more, bringing me to a powerful shuddering wet orgasm. I could sense he was proud and elated by what he'd achieved, and when I told him to straddle my chest he moved into position like lightning. I propped a pillow under my head and started to slowly lick his testicles, taking my time and paying full attention to each of them in turn. Looking up into his eyes and seeing a young man in total ecstasy spurred me on to lustfully run my tongue up and around his cock and over his fingers as he masturbated into my face. It was a sight I will always remember and it still makes me wet to this day! Soon, I could sense he was approaching orgasm, at which point, I encouraged him to relax and let his pleasure erupt…as I continued to whisper verbal encouragement to him I felt his entire body tense as his climax took over and he ejaculated a gigantic torrent of cum, drenching my face with his hot young semen…I was willing him on until the last drop oozed out of him. He collapsed forward and I took his still erect but spent penis in my mouth and cleaned him with my tongue!

We both lay exhausted on the bed for a while. Once we'd got our breath back we took a shower together, we kissed and soaped each other for ages, simply enjoying playing with each other, until without any instruction, he bent me over and proceeded to take me from behind…. my legs were shaking uncontrollably as he rhythmically fucked me with long powerful strokes until I came…. gushing over his thighs…then he fucked me some more, making me climax again ferociously as he continued to pummel my pussy mercilessly. As he was approaching his own climax, he unexpectedly slapped the cheeks of my bottom, and as he exploded deep inside me, filling me with his young seed, he uttered my favourite French word "Salope". I knew there and then, that I could Email his Father that evening, and simply say, "mission accomplished!"

Over the following couple of weeks, he'd come round to continue his "training", when his schooling allowed. Each visit he became more and more confident and certainly much more adventurous. We worked on his oral techniques, and perfected his own self-control. I felt elated that he was returning to Paris, having enjoyed his time, both at school and in my bed. He is now in his mid thirties and we still meet up a occasionally, so as I can give him a few refresher lessons, which in honesty are not needed but intensely erotic! He even once embarrassingly introduced me to one of his young girlfriends as "the woman who taught me how to fuck!".

Chapter Twenty: Order Established

The children were back from their Grand Parents and were excited that Aunt Helen was coming to stay the following week. I had spent a good few days, ensuring that her room and bathroom were ready for her and that she'd be comfortable and feel at home.

In the meantime, Erica and Chris had been on a visit to Paris and were given the full welcome treatment by Amanda and Costas. They had also spent a night at ChrisetManu2, where they'd met a French couple and had struck up an intimate friendship. They had also got themselves a computer, which was giving Erica hours of immense pleasure. But was driving me mad with her constant phone calls on how to work it!

I drove down to the Cotswolds to pick my Aunt up and bring her back to Kew, for her much-anticipated visit. On the drive back, she told me that, simply by word of mouth and local gossip she had several people wanting to buy the house, and that she realized it would be a big upheaval, and an emotional decision, as she'd be leaving a huge part of her life behind, not least many happy memories.

That first evening we all went out for dinner at the pub and introduced Helen to a few of the regulars that we'd got to know already, she was welcomed warmly. It was wonderful to see a little twinkle in her eye again. The following day we took a walk around the area, so as she could get a feel for Kew and what it had to offer. She loved the house and was already planning what needed to be done with the garden. We didn't pressure her, just letting her come to her own decision and agreed we'd all sit down and see what her thoughts were when she felt the time was right and she had a more positive idea of what would suit her.

On her final night she had an outline of a plan in her head. Basically, she wished to come and live with us, and asked Paul if he was in agreement, she'd like us to get an architect in and draw up some plans for the basement conversion, and that she'd meet all costs involved.

Over the next month we had several sets of plans drawn up and eventually, after a few visits Helen had settled on the one that would most suit all her requirements, whilst at the same time enabling us (and her) to maintain a level of privacy and independence, but also giving her a feeling of security. She arranged with Paul that she'd deposit a sum of money in an account, which would be available to pay builders and suppliers.

The schedule had been provisionally set, that the conversion would be completed by the following March, and that we'd start to move her valued possessions into storage at our house during my visits. She officially put her property on the market and passed all negotiations over to her long time solicitor, who was a valued and trusted family friend. There was so much to do, and between us we called in a local auction house, which listed all the items that she was prepared to part with. It was an emotional time for her, but she handled it stoically and the sale raised a substantial amount of money, far more than she had anticipated.

Once again the house was in a state of turmoil, as our kitchen had now arrived and was being installed, whilst work was in full swing on the basement and Paul's office/den. It

During this period the only bit of amusement was another sexually decadent evening in London with Michel and Frederic during one of their sales trips. True to form they had me modeling some of their designs for their pleasure…. and mine. It was during this brief trip that they offered me a part time job, of sorts!…. one, which I immediately knew I wanted, but, also one which I didn't feel I had the time or confidence to accept! The job entailed me going to Paris for a week every few moths to model their new creations in a "Private" apartment for selected buyers from around the world, who were retailing their every increasing and much in demand creations. My fee for the week would be the equivalent of two thousand pounds (a huge sum back then) plus all living expenses and any of the outfits I desired…it certainly was tempting and after talking it over at length with Paul, we agreed, that I should give it a go, if only on a trial basis. They were delighted when I Emailed and accepted their offer, they said the first showing would be early in the New Year and would send me dates well beforehand, once all agreed they'd set up the client viewing times.

The following couple of months flew by, with the house being a hive of activity, with builders coming and going and Paul's work taking up most of his time during the very busy Xmas period, as it was historically, the music industry's busiest time.

On top of everything else, we had to squeeze in a flying visit to Paul's parents and also get the children kitted, out as they were off to boarding school in Sussex, in January…so time was very tight…every minute was filled with dramas and stress.

It was a huge relief when everything started to come together early into the New Year and a very faint light was becoming visible at the end of the very long tunnel.

My Aunts house was finally sold and contracts completed, an exchange date had been finalized for early April. She was remarkably calm about it all, and was busy planning the finer details of her move and the start of her new life in Kew.

Life at first, with the children away at school was strange, as once the builders had finished for the day, the few hours before Paul came home were bizarrely peaceful and quiet, allowing me a relaxing bit of "me time" over a nice glass of wine, also enabling me to catch up on Emails etc.

The much anticipated day arrived, when an Email from Michel in Paris dropped into my inbox, outlining some proposed dates for the first private showings…excitement immediately started to bubble up inside me, especially as he'd attached some sketches of the new range of outfits I'd be wearing. After a bit of Email Ping-Pong, we arranged for five days late February, and I left it to Michel to organize the itinerary.

I had taken advantage of the forthcoming trip to arrange to see both, Olivier and Claudia, and of course Thierry

Thierry invited me to stay at his apartment, but on this occasion it was out of the question, as Frederic had an apartment leased for the week in "Le Marias" district, which was a large loft conversion, which he said, would also be perfect to use for the "buyer" showings. I decided I'd try and squeeze a few sunbeds in before the trip to loose some of the dreaded English winter pallor.

It coincided nicely with the children's school half term break, so it all worked out fine with timings. Paul had arranged to work from home, so as he could be on hand for the builders, as the work was nearing completion on the basement conversion and his study/chill out area.

Everything was running smoothly, a sense of calm and a definite end of all the madness and upheaval was in sight. So I could go and enjoy my five days of business and pleasure in Paris with an easy conscious. I could finally unwind and enjoy all that came my way, whatever or whoever it maybe…. It was a wonderful feeling of independence.

Chapter Twenty-One: Spreading My Wings

Finally, the day arrived and Paul drove me the few miles to Heathrow, he grinned and wished me a "fun" few days, and reminded me to charge my new mobile phone, called the "banana", which we'd both acquired the previous week courtesy of Paul's company.

The flight was all on time and a customary half bottle of Champagne was consumed, courtesy of Air France. I had an increasing tingling sensation building throughout the flight, and I'm sure in hindsight I had a mini-climax as we touched down at CDG airport; such was my excitement and anticipation.

Frederic was waiting to pick me up and ferry me into the centre and soon we were negotiating the narrow streets of "Le Marais", until he pulled into a small courtyard and parked in one of the half a dozen reserved residents spaces.

Grabbing my bag, we got into a tiny old lift and ascended the five flights to the apartment. On entering, I was immediately taken by the sheer size of the open plan area, with gorgeous wooden flooring and large floor to ceiling windows, all along one wall, overlooking the courtyard and part of the street. It had a large kitchen and dining area at one end, and two en-suite bedrooms at the other, with a guest cloakroom and a further lounge area on a raised level. An American, who fashioned it on the latest Manhattan loft designs had renovated it, but was letting it, whilst he was abroad on a six month work contract.

Frederic had arranged to meet Michel at a small café a few minutes away, as since they'd expanded and were doing well they'd taken on two people to run the actual shop end of things, whilst they got on with the design, manufacture and sales part of the escalating business. Over a typical leisurely Parisian lunch, they explained that they had also leased a small warehouse where they worked, and the actual seamstresses etc were all spread throughout a large area on the second level, full of individual workspaces, fabrics and constantly buzzing sewing machines. They now had nine full and part time workers and orders were coming in steadily, but they wanted to take the business to the next level and had several backers, who'd injected "funds" into the enterprise. They were both very motivated and enthusiastic about the future development of the enterprise.

The first evening was spent, with me in a permanent state of undress, being fitted into the range of new outfits that they wanted to promote, and making sure all were finished to a high standard. They'd decided on ten various outfits, and a wide range of accessories, from shoes and boots, through to a fabulous range of exotic masks…. which I found amazingly stimulating and sensual.

The following morning they'd booked me a hair an make-up job at a salon near to the apartment, and the first showing was scheduled for six o'clock, with a German buyer, who had fourteen fetish/club-wear shops across their major cites.

Canapés and a wide range of drinks were organized, and the spare bedroom was used as store/dressing room. He arrived at six sharp, with three assistants and it was all very clinical and businesslike with Frederic introducing and describing each item in depth, whilst Michel helped dress me…It was a very uplifting and liberating experience, nearing the end, I was completely exhausted with the concentration required to show the outfits of to the best of my ability.

Finally, at around nine o'clock they left to go to their hotels and freshen up and returned within an hour with their order. Then we all headed out for dinner at a nearby Indonesian restaurant.

I could see Frederic was on tenterhooks, but said that he felt it all went very well and he was confident that they'd been impressed. It was a lovely meal, but I was nervous for Michel and Frederic that their expectations may not be fulfilled, but fortunately over coffee and brandies the "Boss man", passed across his order to them, duly signed.

The anticipation of that first order was intense, and we couldn't wait to get back to the apartment and do some sums! To say they were ecstatic, was an understatement…they'd ordered a wide cross section of outfits and accessories for each of their shops (Frederic was hoping for only five or six) and they calculated the approximate order value would end up around four hundred thousand French Franc (about forty thousand pounds), we were all exhausted but buzzing with excitement, so the three of us retired to celebrate the initial success at a late night drinking club they frequented.

The following day was almost a replica of the previous, however, this time with a selected assortment of smaller buyers from London/Italy and Spain, again the reception was fantastic, with a similar level of orders. The showing had finished slightly earlier, so I took the opportunity to call Thierry, and we arranged to meet for a drink after I'd freshened up. He asked if he could also meet with Frederic and Michel and take us all to dinner, which they both agreed to enthusiastically, once I'd explained to them who he was.

In his honour, I decided to wear the Chanel blouse, with a high side split black pencil skirt and hold ups and of course an obligatory pair of leg extending heels. Thierry picked me up by cab and we returned to the scene of the crime "Le Bofinger". Michel and Frederic were waiting at the bar and I made the introductions, they seemed to have a lot in common and started chatting away in French and broken English…. Along with much talk regarding both their businesses, they also seemed to have a very similar outlook on the Paris club/party scene. During dinner, Thierry complimented me on my handling of his son, which led to me having to describe the entire encounter, in detail, to "tuts" and much to the delight of Michel and Frederic…who both found my behavior exemplary, but proudly proclaimed that it was all well and good corrupting a young boy, but I'd be well out of my depth with three experienced men! A dare, if ever I'd heard one! With a nice glow from the afternoon showing, coupled with my now sky-high ego, enhanced further with a few flutes of Champagne I scoffed at him, announcing firmly "they'd be no contest for me!"… A challenge had been firmly thrown down and we made a toast to the 'last man or lady standing" at the end of the evening. I was high on the sheer prospect of what may occur later, and we were only half way through the meal. The conversation kept coming back to what they were going to do to me later, to which I simply gave them a "Gallic" shrug of the shoulders saying "give it your best shot boys!". I could sense that the three of them were aroused by my sheer arrogance and bravado.

I decided to tease them for a while after dinner, by insisting we paid a visit to L'Escapade, so I could say hello to Amanda and Costas, and check on my "Champagne Reserves". We duly arrived around midnight, and Amanda was intrigued at what I was currently up to, and was interested in everything that was going on with Paul, the house etc. I introduced Michel and Frederic, who fell in love with the club, its layout and atmosphere, they thought it would be a perfect location to unveil their designs to Parisian movers and shakers. Thierry was well known to Amanda and Costas, and we all spent a pleasant while catching up. Amanda told me what our friends Erica and Chris had gotten up to... She told me Erica was a big hit with the men and wouldn't leave until dawn. She would also return alone for a few hours in the afternoons as Chris catnapped at the hotel... She certainly made hay, apparently she simply couldn't get enough! I made a mental note to meet up with Erica and get the finer details of her exploits.

We decided that we'd all grab a cab back to Thierry's apartment, as Laurent was staying with friends in a small town south of Paris.

Let the games commence, I thought as we arrived at Thierry's. Both Michel and Frederic were as equally impressed as Paul and myself had been at the "Grandeur" of the apartment, he took pleasure in giving them an extensive guided tour, whilst I made my way to the bar area to fix the drinks. It was way too cold, even with the outdoor heaters to sit on the terrace, so I set the drinks on the large occasional table in between the large sofas. The three of them seemed very comfortable with each other and there was no hint at any competition or reticence, in fact it seemed to be the most natural thing in the world for them (I'm convinced this is a very French thing, must be in their genes).

After a while, Thierry refreshed the drinks, I slipped off to the cloakroom, where I took a sneaky hit from my ever-present vial of poppers that I carried in my handbag in anticipation of a situation such as this. I immediately came up to a level approaching orgasm, intensified by the fact that I'd undressed and was stood naked in my hold ups and heels with three hot French men waiting a few feet away on the other side of the door. I took another large sniff, and took the bull by the horns and entered the salon, to a look of pure lust from three pairs of male eyes! I returned the look, with interest and invited them to do their "worst", the next few hours were simply a madly intense and experimental session of sex that I'd ever experienced.... periods of long and slow erotic licking and sucking through to heavy and hard moments of deep penetration.... I was stretched and pushed to my limits, every possible position was achieved, every orifice used. I was amazed at my own flexibility and knew I'd be sore and aching everywhere a few hours later…. did I care? Nope, I just wanted more, in fact they threw everything they had at me, and eventually, true to my earlier boast they waved the white flag and declared me the outright winner…. not before each of them stood in front of me and in turn stroked themselves into my willing mouth, giving me profuse amounts of their hot, sticky sperm to drink! Thankfully, Thierry suggested that, we all just crash and get some well-deserved sleep.

Thankfully, I had a free day with nothing planned, where as Michel and Frederic had to return to their offices slightly worse for wear. I took the opportunity to have a long and luxurious soak in Thierry's Jacuzzi bath and ease my aches and pleasant pains, before I met him for brunch in a nearby café. I was a bit overdressed, but nobody seemed to notice.

I spent the afternoon wandering around the elegant boulevards of Paris without a care in the world! I kept in touch every day with Paul, thanks to the mobile phone, which was proving to be a godsend. He was pleased that I was having fun and said he couldn't wait to hear all the "lurid" details at the weekend.

Around four, I decided I'd go and have a sauna and massage at a new place that Michel told me had recently opened in "Le Marais". It turned out to be very close to the apartment, so I popped back first and threw on some jeans and sweatshirt. The next few hours were blissful just lounging in the steam rooms and was topped off by a ninety minute massage at the hands wonderfully skilled Moroccan lady. I drifted in and out of consciousness as her hands soothed and manipulated my muscles, with dreamy atmospheric music in the background and beautiful scented candles adding to the ambience.

Thankfully a quiet meal was planned that evening with Frederic and Michel, to discuss the final showings, which were to a few domestic buyers, along with the head honcho from a chain of shops across the Netherlands, Amsterdam in particular.

During dinner, I tentatively made a suggestion, which over the forthcoming years would take the business global. My proposal was, that now that the Internet was growing at a very fast rate and was starting to become a mainstream marketing tool, that they should have their own website! I explained to them all that I knew from using our Mac daily back at home in the U.K. They both admitted that they knew very little about how to go about it, and in short immediately offered me the opportunity to research the idea further, and if there was any mileage to be gained, they would finance it! My brain clicked into gear and I told them to give me a few weeks and I'd come back to them with a solid proposition…. to which they readily agreed.

The final days showings went well, with the "Dutch" connection placing a substantial order, even buying a thousand masks of varying designs.

All told the few days of showing had generated a full to bursting order book for them, and I picked a couple of my favourite designs along with two pairs of shoes and a selection of masks as my bonus present. I had earmarked the money I'd earned to be spent towards a family holiday.

Both Michel and Frederic had a business trip to Belgium, to see a fabric supplier planned, and they wouldn't be back till late, therefore I had the following day all to myself. I decided I'd just have a leisurely lunch, followed by a sneaky solo trip to L'Escapade in the afternoon, on the pretext of saying my good byes to Amanda and Costas and I would play the final evening by ear.

I nipped in to the Lacoste boutique on the way back from lunch and bought Paul a couple of Polo shirts, I also picked up a couple of things for the children, in the very chic kids department.

I decided to go to the club in a slightly daring, short clingy dress and heels, hidden during the stroll there under my long coat. I felt I was becoming a bit of a regular when Amanda greeted me like a long lost sister. Immediately, she demanded to know the "ins and outs" of how my time had been since we'd last spoken. Eventually, she took my coat and I followed her down the stairs, still gripping the balustrade as I went. Costas was already pouring me a glass of "champers", which was ready as soon as I got to the bar. The club was fairly busy, with several couples drinking and relaxing at the bar and a few people obviously already enjoying themselves in the playrooms. I was very much the centre of attention, being a single lady, and English to boot! There was one charming, but much older gentleman, who enquired to Amanda "as to who I was", and she translated for me, as he offered me a drink, but it was unnecessary, as it turned out he spoke perfect English. Very swiftly I was caressing a beautiful crystal tumbler complete with a large measure of Jack Daniels on two rocks of ice. Even though, as he later told me, there was nearly thirty-year age gap, we had an immediate rapport, and a definite sexual attraction was apparent. He exuded charm and sophistication. He was a very flirtatious person by nature and sparks flew when we talked further. Amanda subtly gave him her seal of approval with a knowing look and nod, so I relaxed, as we discussed our various lives. It turned out he was a widower and had just celebrated his sixtieth birthday, at his house near Cannes and he was back in Paris at his apartment for the spring, as he said spring in Paris was the best time for "amour". He was definitely from a breed of Frenchmen, who could at any given moment charm the pants of a lady…. fortunately I wasn't wearing any, as not to spoil the clingy effect of the dress and it also made me feel very horny!

    He was very interested in me as a person, and paid full attention whilst we were talking and there was never any mention of anything overtly sexual, I must admit I found this both refreshing and arousing. He gave me a potted history of his life and that he'd held a post in the French Diplomatic Corps most of his working life and was still employed by the French government, in an advisory role, he was incredibly interesting and very well travelled. I found him most attractive, even though, as he put it, he was old enough to be my father! This made us both laugh. The ease at which he discussed all kinds of subjects was highly entertaining, and the conversation flowed, as did a couple more drinks.

    After subtly finding out that I had no firm plans for the evening he insisted I join him for dinner later, after I'd agreed (without a moments hesitation) he told me to be ready for eight. I agreed that I'd be waiting outside the apartment at eight sharp to save him parking. He told me he was taking me to his special club, twenty minutes outside of Paris, where the food was exceptional and it had a very strict and selective membership…. I was intrigued! Oh and he told me to dress elegantly, but "les culottes" were strictly banned…. I was even more intrigued and excited!

Amanda had, at the request of Yves ordered a taxi to take me the ten minutes back to the apartment to get ready. I had decided to wear the elegant but very revealing evening dress of long ribbons of silk material that I'd worn to L'Escapade previously (also Amanda recommended it, once she knew where I was being taken). I wore it, with an outrageously high pair of shoes I'd acquired from the "showings". I spent ages moisturizing my body with my Chanel No.5 velvet body lotion. I was ready with exactly five minutes to spare and took one last look in the full-length mirror, put on my coat and made my way to the entrance.

Outside, was a very large black Mercedes Limousine, with a man in a chauffeurs uniform, holding the back door open for me, there sat all elegantly in an evening suit was Yves, holding a rose and a glass of Champagne for me. He explained, that as part of his work with the government, one of the perks was having a car and driver on call 24/7.

He told me we were going to a small town called Ville d'Avray, which was close to the Palace of Versailles. The club was called "le Roi René" and was the oldest club of its kind in France. It had been open since the early 1940's, and had since become a favourite and discreet haunt of the rich and famous. It was popular with high ranking government officials and their wives and mistresses. Legend has it that the wife of a very famous Prime Minister used to go on a Thursday afternoon, to be entertained by selected endowed young men… Yves mentioned no names, but assured me it was true and it was not at all unusual to see well known faces there …a bit of "what goes on inside the club, stays inside".

We pulled up outside a very discreet building, on a quiet leafy suburban street, where upon stopping, a uniformed doorman was quickly by the car door to greet us, holding it open for me, whilst Yves's driver did the same for him. Yves said something to him and he nodded, saluted and drove off.

Upon entering a beautifully decorated reception/cloakroom area a young man stepped forward and took my coat, as people greeted and fussed around Yves, when suddenly the young man enquired, whether I'd respected the "Non Culotte" rule, I told him yes, but hilariously he still produced a long elegant cane, with a small mirror on the end and checked for himself saying "tres bon entrer Mademoiselle". It took vast effort on my part not to giggle, but with a flourish, we were escorted to our table for the evening.

There was a pianist playing at a grand piano in the corner, and everything seemed to be conducted in very hushed tones. Already seated at the nine or so other tables, was a mix of elegant ladies my age with much older distinguished men, and older ladies with much younger consorts!

An aperitif was brought to the table, whilst we looked over the menu, again I passed the buck, asking Yves to surprise me and order on my behalf...basically I didn't have a clue what most of it was!

We started by sharing a dozen fresh oysters with Tabasco, cracked black and pink peppercorns and a fiery herb salad, this was followed with a sorbet to freshen the palate .The main course was a beautiful sea bass in a citrus sauce, it was light and perfectly presented. Throughout dinner he regaled me with stories of his life, whilst seeming fascinated with my own situation. After a dessert of fresh raspberries and cream we adjourned to the smoking lounge and settled in a sumptuous leather sofa, whilst he took a cigar with a cognac and I opted for a Jack Daniels and a welcome St Moritz cigarette. There was definitely an under current of sex permeating from the surroundings and after a while he suggested that we move through to the bar area, as he felt it was time to see the club in its entirety and the bar was the starting point.... I soon discovered why!

At the bar were about a dozen stools, however, some were stools with a difference...a big, big difference! They had a heart shaped hole cut out in the padding and were reserved for the more "adventurous" ladies! We were served a fresh round of drinks, and he suggested that whilst he paid a visit to the bathroom, I should choose a bar stool and see the reaction it had. I chose one reserved for the " adventurous ladies" and instantly an elderly, but distinguished gentleman approached, said "bonsoir" and as he was ordering his drinks, I felt his fingers nimbly reach under the stool and start to stroke my vagina, very subtly I adjusted my posture and parted my thighs, this encouraged him to gently insert two fingers into me, whilst continuing talking to the bar man, I could barely contain myself, my pussy was soaking already, when suddenly, I felt another hand reach under from behind and a warm finger slowly entered my anus, both gentlemen seemed to work in unison, as they brought me to my first explosive silent orgasm of the evening. I glanced into the mirror behind the bar and saw Yves watching the situation unfold, with obvious pleasure on his face. After what seemed like ages, but was only a few minutes Yves rejoined me and with a curt nod, the men instantly disappeared back to whence they came. He was pleased that I'd enjoyed the brief encounter and suggested we took our drinks to a quieter lounge area, on the way we passed a few interesting alcoves, with a variety of sexual shenanigans taking place. He gestured for me to sit on the sofa whilst he sat opposite in a large easy chair. He took a sip of his cognac and asked me if I was enjoying myself, I told him it that I was having a wonderful evening and that the atmosphere was very stimulating and hugely erotic. He asked me if I was turned on by it, I told him I definitely was, he said that he'd be honoured if I would show him just how much! This didn't take much encouragement or effort, as I simply shifted a few ribbons of the silk to one side, and seductively parted my legs, to show him my glistening wet pussy, that was open and inviting attention. He looked on in admiration, and encouraged me to pleasure myself; I slipped one of my breasts from the dress to allow him to see one of my very erect nipples. I started to stroke myself slowly at first, increasing in intensity, until I gushed heavily over my fingers. I quickly sensed somebody had joined us and glanced sideways, to see one of the younger guys from the restaurant, watching admiringly, whilst gently stroking a rather impressive erection. Yves smiled at me and enquired whether I'd like to have him, to which I simply licked my lips and he nodded and beckoned him over. Without any hesitation my fingers were replaced by this young mans tongue, as Yves issued verbal encouragement to both of us. I lay back and let this anonymous young man bring me to a number of very wet orgasms, before I suggested he should take my place on the sofa. I climbed on top of him and made sure Yves had a perfect unobstructed view, as I slid myself down on to this large mysterious penis, I thrust my bottom out, so everything was exposed, as I rode up and down on my new best friend.... Yves was very vocal in encouraging us, which made it all that more pleasurable, I knew he was enjoying seeing this big cock penetrating and filling me up. Finally, I was placed on all fours and taken expertly from behind with smooth powerful thrusts, until he couldn't hold back any longer, and with a final flurry of hard pounding strokes he began to fill me with his hot semen, at the same time I exploded with my own brutal orgasm. I stayed on top of him for a while using my vaginal muscles to milk the final drops of his semen from him. To which Yves quietly applauded saying "bravo, bravo, magnifique". I excused myself and went and found the ladies bathroom area and cleaned myself up. I quickly made myself respectable again, and returned, to find a very welcome fresh Jack Daniels waiting for me. Yves explained to me, that nowadays he took his own pleasure, simply by seeing ladies such as myself letting go of their inhibitions and expressing their sexual desires fully. He paid me a huge compliment, and told me I was the most sexually aware and enthusiastic woman he'd met in many years, and he'd like this to be the start of a long friendship. I readily agreed, saying that I was very interested in exploring all areas of my sexuality, and that my husband had given me a free reign to accomplish my goals. I gave Yves my full permission to arrange some interesting future situations for me; I promised him he'd receive my full co-operation. He smiled knowingly!

I was flying high and had abandoned all inhibitions. I finished off the night on the dance floor, with a few of the younger French ladies, as we danced provocatively to a selection of seductive dance tracks, there was much appreciation from the gentlemen who were avidly watching. It was certainly a night to remember and it was clear to me that a lasting bond had formed between and myself Yves.

Right on cue, his driver was waiting outside to take us back into Paris, however, we stopped off at a small bar, over looking the Seine for a final coffee and a nightcap. We exchanged contact details and I savored my final moments of the last night, of what was a very memorable few days flying solo, in the most romantic and sexually charged city on earth. It wasn't the end, but the beginning of a beautiful voyage! One, which had many years, and adventures ahead. After a gentle peck on each cheek, we said our goodnights, and I watched in awe, as the large black Mercedes disappeared into the Parisian night.

After a few hours of sleep, it was soon time to have a last meeting with Michel and Frederic, before being dropped off at the Airport. We had a quick run through of how successful the "showings" had turned out, and I agreed to definitely do it again in a few months time, when they anticipated they'd have several new designs ready. I also reiterated that I felt that the rapidly growing Internet market should be targeted and I'd keep them updated on my research and ideas via Email.

Whilst sitting in departures at CDG, Yves rang me on my mobile to wish me "bon voyage" and said that we'd keep in touch and definitely meet again very soon, he also surprised me by saying that he would also like to meet Paul!

Paul was at Heathrow to meet me, and couldn't wait to hear about the previous evening; also, he said there was a surprise awaiting back at home!

Chapter Twenty-Two: A Manic Few Months

My surprise was evident immediately, as we pulled up to the house, firstly the drive way had been finally completed and amazingly Paul's pride and joy had been finished, he had his own office/den. He'd obviously been very busy, getting all the final touches in place whilst I was away. He'd done wonders and had transformed it into a real comfortable work/play area with all the toys installed and working…I felt a tiny bit guilty that I'd been having my fun and games, while he'd been a busy beaver.

We also decided that we'd move our computer into his den and we'd invest in the latest Apple Mac for me, so as I could put heart and soul into exploring the increasing business opportunities that the Internet was throwing up.

The following week was taken up with ensuring that Aunt Helens new home was completed in time for her impending move.

The children had really settled well into their new school and had made many new friends and were growing up at a rapid pace.

Finally, the day arrived and the last of Aunt Helens personal items arrived, delivered by the removal company, they were put into the garage, until the following day, when I'd arranged to go and pick her up and bring her back to her new home. It was a very emotional time, but she coped stoically as she said her goodbyes to a community that had been a major part of her life for nearly half a century. She'd made a pact with Celia that they'd remain in touch, and she would come and visit once she'd got settled. With a small tear in her eye she handed over the keys to the new owners and touchingly told them to "look after the house" as if they did, they'd have many happy years ahead. We didn't drag it out more than necessary, and started the journey back to Kew.

We spent the next few days sorting out various personal things, such as signing with the local G.P and Dental practice. She was frail but really got stuck into the task of transforming her basement rooms into a cozy self-contained home of her own. One concession she made, regarding her independence, was to have an intercom system fitted, so if she had any problems one of us would be on hand to help.

To keep her active and her mind focused, we gave her the task of redesigning the garden area and together we'd arrange to get some quotes and input from some of the local Landscape Garden companies in the area. She insisted on funding this, as a little "thank you" present, for ensuring, as she put it, "her twilight days would be happy and stress free".

Over the following few days I'd got to grips with my new computer, and was more than pleased with our new faster Internet connection…I could now settle down and put together a preliminary design for Michel and Frederic.

I found a vast array of product related web sites, that were already trading on the internet, I basically took what I felt were the best bits of each and mocked up on paper how I thought the various pages should look and what would link to what, it was before any easy web design software was available, so it had to be built from the ground up as it were.

I sent my ideas via Email to Paris, thankfully they loved it and gave me the green light to go further and gave me an initial budget to work with.

After much digging around some of the "geeky" chat rooms, I made contact with a young IT Student, called Jon, who was studying at the LSE and happened to live in nearby Barnes. We agreed to meet up for lunch to discuss my project. He was everything I pictured from our phone chats, anorak, long hair, jeans, T-shirt and trainers. He had a lot of ideas of his own and was excited about researching the project further. He asked me to give him a few days and he'd put together a simple web site for me to see, before we took it any further. I agreed and we arranged to meet the following Monday at the house, so as he could give me a demo on the Mac, which fortuitously was also his system of choice.

During this period I kept in touch with Yves, it was a pleasant and much needed interlude when he rang. It was during one of these calls that he invited both Paul and myself for dinner, as he was shortly going to be in London on business at the French Embassy. He said he'd be staying the night at his rooms at the Consulate in Knightsbridge, and suggested, that we ate at "San Lorenzo" in Beauchamp Place, it turned out the owners were friends of his and he'd been a regular patron since they opened in 1963. I readily accepted and told him, we'd be delighted and would meet him there at Eight-thirty on the day in question.

The following Monday Jon arrived at the house with a bag of cables and boxes, and after a cup of tea we went to my computer room and hooked up one of his external hard drives. After some techie stuff, he proceeded to show me some pages and ideas he'd put together...I was very impressed and enthused by what I saw, so much so that I agreed there and then to have him come on board. We agreed in principle that he'd get paid a percentage upfront, and the balance of his fee in a lump sum upon completion of the design and its initial implementation. It turned out to be a good deal for him (as he quickly made a name for himself within web design circles and still today runs a very successful company, with many high profile clients) and an even better investment for Michel and Frederic.

I kept Paris updated and we agreed that once we had a fully functioning site ready to go, they'd come to London for a demonstration and discuss any input they may have.

With, a high degree of planning we arranged to have a week at Paul's parents new, and almost operational business in France. We, also arranged for Celia to come and stay, to keep an eye on my aunt, and to be on hand for any unforeseen problems, which thankfully wasn't needed, as they had a fine old time. Especially overseeing the team of landscape gardeners, that was busy transforming the current "jungle" into an area of calm. Thankfully it was designed for minimal maintenance on our/my part, simply a bit of pottering about for Helen and tending to a small manageable herb garden.

Jon rang everyday with updates and progress reports, and gleefully told me, that we'd have enough to present an almost finished working site to Frederic and Michel within a few weeks.

This enabled me to relax and enjoying the family all being together and make the most of the laid back way of life in this wonderful region of France. Doing very little but eating, drinking and sleeping

Chapter Twenty-Three: A Memorable Dinner

On the evening, we were ushered into "San Lorenzo" like visiting "Royalty" and shown to a discreet table, and were informed that the "Général" would be arriving shortly and they took our order for drinks. "Général"!, we both looked baffled at one another, I told Paul that I was equally as confused as he was. I simply knew him as Yves! All became a bit clearer over a beautiful dinner. At first Paul was a bit in awe of Yves and his effortless charm and the commanding, authoritative aura he exuded, but soon relaxed and they genuinely seemed to enjoy each others company. Yves was as interested in Paul's work, as much as Paul was captivated with some of Yves stories! Especially, when they veered towards the more salacious accounts of some of the French "high society" summer orgies in the South of France. Where Yves had a wonderful home, situated nr Cannes, in a small town called Valbonne.

Paul was enjoying hearing about the night Yves took me for Dinner at "Le Roi Rene", and I could tell he was enjoying hearing it from Yves point of view. I found it amusing that they were both discussing my behavior, as if I'd suddenly evaporated into obscurity.

Yves skated around his title, but said it was bestowed on him during his military career and subsequent "Diplomatic" work for his government. With a smile and a nod we left it there!

Over coffee and brandies, Yves told us about an interesting "Masked Ball" that was held on the first weekend in December, at a chateau south of Paris, near to Orleans, he said it was an annual event going back to the mid seventies. He explained, that it was arranged by a very wealthy Count and Countess, who were very well known in Parisian Society and it was a very select and sought after "invitation" only affair. He said he'd been attending for many years, and this year he said he'd be honoured, if Paul had no objections, that I would be his companion for the event!! I could sense Paul was excited by this request and I subtly signaled my interest and willingness to attend. Immediately, Paul gave the go-ahead. Yves was delighted, saying he would arrange everything, and forward all the details, complete with itinerary, within a week.

Chapter Twenty-Four: Going Global

Since the success of the initial showings, Frederic and Michel had taken the decision to put all the various areas of their business under one identity. They rebranded and changed the company name and logo, giving it a striking new look. After much discussion, we all agreed that this branding should be carried through to the impending Web Site.

Jon and I were now in a position to show them all the work that we'd done, and how the site would eventually look and operate. So, they arranged to come over to London for a flying visit. Arriving early morning, I'd arranged that I'd pick them up at Heathrow and we'd spend the day with Jon, at my house going through it all, then they'd catch the last flight back to Paris.

I duly picked them up and we went straight to my house, as Jon arranged to be there for ten thirty with all his techie bits and pieces, ready to do his presentation.

They were knocked out with what he'd achieved so far. They could envisage how impressive it would look, when proper photographs of the products were placed into the relevant pages, and when the whole site was linked to a "shopping trolley" software sales system, which would be running through a merchant account billing system, that between Jon and Frederic would be simple to set in motion.

We all had lunch at my local on the Green, which the French contingent enjoyed hugely, sampling some of the more traditional English pub grub, such as steak and kidney pie!!! They found it bizarre, but loved it.

After a few more hours' discussion, with copious notes being taken by Jon, it was agreed to go ahead full steam. Jon would continue to finesse the site, and await the first set of product photographs, along with prices, item codes etc. It was also decided, that the customers would be given the option of being billed in either Pounds Sterling, Dollars or French Francs, this would prove a little complicated, but between them Frederic and Jon had it covered.

Once Jon had left we sat down and discussed my involvement and payment structures etc. We made it simple. I'd be paid, as before to do the next "show" in three weeks, and also receive an extra bonus payment on top, as they wanted to get a professional photographer to shoot me in the outfits and that we'd use these on the Site. Also, as it was my initial idea, I'd run the Internet business autonomously and would be paid a percentage of sales. Plus, they agreed that Jon should host and look after all the technical areas. Everyone was happy. I was a good feeling eventually getting the "green light" from Frederic and Michel.

Paul arrived home and I introduced him to two Frenchmen that he felt he knew, but had never met!! Only heard about (in bed)!

As they had a few hours before needing to be at the airport for their return flight, we all went to a local Bistro in Kew and ran Paul through where we were in the venture. He was very positive and expressed his complete approval. He offered to help in any way he could…. which, mainly was allowing me the time needed, both in Paris and at home to drive the project forward.

The subsequent showings were much more hectic As well as presenting the new range of outfits, shoes and accessories to the clients, we also had to squeeze in two days with the entire range of products for photographs to be taken to use on the website.

This was fun, as they'd arranged a friend of theirs, who had one of the latest digital cameras, to arrange and do the shoot; also he came with hairdresser and makeup girl. It was such a busy few days, plus the photo shoots lasted well into the night, which meant that there was no time for any, real fun and games "Paris" style until the final day. During which, both Frederic and Michel were busy going through all the pictures, matching product codes and prices to them. They wanted me to return to the U.K, with everything Jon required to complete the web site.

I was feeling a bit guilty, that I'd not contacted Yves, or for that matter Thierry whilst I was in Paris, but the work schedule was just so chaotic, it wasn't possible. I decided that I needed some "me" time during my final afternoon/evening. I decided that a relaxing morning wandering the Marais and doing a bit of shopping was in order, followed by a mid- afternoon sauna and massage, before a solo visit to L'Escapade during the evening.

Feeling refreshed and very horny after the massage, I ate alone at a wonderful little café I'd passed by on several occasions, traditional simple French cooking with no frills, it was perfect, just sitting alone reflecting on events, with a carafe of wine and a lovely salad with bread. I was feeling daring, so I decided I'd wear one of the new outfits we'd promoted, a transparent lace, body hugging, full-length dress, that had a split right up to one hip. I felt it showed off my body to great effect; also it made me feel elegantly slutty, whilst modeling it earlier.

I rang Paul whilst I was getting ready and filled him in on my plans for the rest of the evening.... He fully approved and said enjoy, and that he'd look forward to hearing all about it the following evening!

I took a cab to the club and spent a good half hour in the reception area having a good catch up with Amanda; we both loved having a good old gossip! She wanted to know all about my evening with Yves during my last trip, she informed me that, he was a bit of a high profile-well respected and admired Government official, and was often mentioned in Society Magazines such as Paris Match and Hello!

Eventually, I made my way down the now very familiar stairs and experienced a lovely warm tingling feeling as several pairs of eyes watched me descend with lustful approval. I knew immediately, I was going to have "fun" tonight. I felt I'd definitely checked any inhibitions in with my coat!

As usual, a glass of Champagne was waiting courtesy of Costas, and as ever a welcoming smile. It wasn't long before I was being engaged in conversation with several gentlemen, each trying to out do the other in the English speaking prowess department, which was proving very amusing, but a real turn on at the same time. It was massively arousing having a throng of elegant males vying for my individual attention There were a few other couples already having fun and flitting and flirting around the club, however, as a young solo female, I was very much the main focus of many of the men. I simply adored the attention.

Once I'd had a few sips of my first Jackie D, I sneaked off to the bathroom, where I took a nice, big relaxing hit of my poppers, just to get all my juices flowing. This always empowered me and rapidly took me to a level, where, just a simple touch would ensure a gripping orgasm would soon be forthcoming.

I felt outrageously horny and decided to take my drink and have a cigarette in the room, which had the lockable ornate metal grill. No sooner had I settled into the sofa several men approached, looking through expectantly, it gave me a feeling of control and allowed my exhibitionistic side to fully show itself.

I swiftly allowed my hands to provocatively run themselves seductively over my body, sensuously licking my lips, much to the obvious vocal enjoyment of the guys, who were watching safely locked on the other side of the grill. Soon, after much erotic eye contact with each of the men, I seductively removed my dress until I was reclined on the sofa fully naked apart from my heels. With much vocal encouragement from the various men, I started to play with my nipples and showing them to my audience how hard and erect they were, and how turned on I was by this scenario. I stroked, tweaked and pulled them, never loosing eye contact with the engrossed spectators. It didn't take long until my legs parted, exposing my soaking wetness, my lips already open and swollen, my clitoris exposed and throbbing in anticipation. My fingers began to rhythmically stroke my self to a huge, squirting orgasm, with much verbal appreciation from my captive audience. I surveyed the men, who by now, all had their erect cocks out and offering them to me through the grill…. it was all wildly erotic. I soon found myself slowly crawling towards them on all fours, reaching out to touch the nearest ones briefly. Once I was in position I began to lewdly and lasciviously lick and suck each and every one from the safety of my cage, running my playful tongue over all the numerous shapes and sizes, savouring each and every one. Also taking moments to stand, with my back to them, whilst they reached in through the bars and played with me, I was climaxing regularly as many pairs of anonymous hands played with my breasts, receptive pussy and anus, soaking many of them in the process…it was pure animal sex at its rawest form. Eventually, I could take it no longer and needed some hard fucking, so I simply unlocked the gate and chose two of the best looking guys, inviting them in to use me, much to their delight! I grabbed the poppers from my bag and we all had a good long sniff as they began to ferociously fuck me from both ends.... I was whimpering with pleasure, both at what they were doing to me, as well as the effect it was having on the very aroused audience gathered at the door, all hoping that I'd pick them next. After the two guys had become a spent force, showering me with their cum, I regrouped and after a quick refresh in the powder room I returned to the bar to have a much-needed breather and a welcome pick-me-up JD and St Moritz!

It wasn't yet midnight, which gave me a feeling of contentment, knowing that there'd be a good few hour of debauched playtime left. It was an exuberant and exhilarating feeling having a selection of men of vastly varying ages vying for my attentions. I'm sure some of their chat up lines would have been hilarious, if only I understood them; still they all sounded sexy to me!

After a few bouts of inappropriate dancing with a few of the men, I got a second wind and another rampant urge of sexual need raging through my veins, I felt it was time for a bit more "playtime".

I weighed up my options and returned to my "cage", with a line of men casually following.... I felt a bit like the "pied piper". However, this time I didn't hang around, I whipped my dress off as soon as I was in and had my protective door locked. I immediately pressed my naked body against the grills and offered it to the eager groping hands. I managed to get one leg up on the edge of a door hinge, which enabled my pussy to be opened wide by the abundance of probing hands and fingers, my lips were fully stretched and held apart...there was much gasping, as I ejaculated powerfully and profusely over them, it was like the floodgates had opened. I was urging them on in the most lewd and vulgar language possible (even though they didn't understand, I'm sure they got the gist of it!). Eventually I gave in to temptation and unlocked and opened the door to what can only be described, as a complete free for all. I was naked and engulfed on all sides by men, most of whom were offering me their throbbing cocks to play with, a few of the really adventurous one were knelt in front and behind me, simultaneously working on my anus and pussy with their eager tongues...Occasionally, Amanda would come and check on my well being and with a nod from me would disappear back to the bar. At times, I had multiple erections eagerly offered to my willing mouth...all shapes and sizes.... I was spoilt for choice.... at times I was gushing, as the men were cumming, there were huge jets of semen flying everywhere. I'd never seen, or experienced anything quite like it.... but boy it felt good! Towards the end I was lifted up and held aloft by four men, whilst several took turns working their cocks into my wet, willing and insatiable pussy.... They weren't just fucking me, they were positively pounding me into submission! At the finale of this mad session, I had semen dripping from every inch of my body. It ended equally erotically, as I was joined in the large shower and was washed and soaped clean by three very attentive and appreciative men! Thoroughly cleansed, dried and freshened up I returned to the bar with a look of total innocence on my face, along with a smile a mile wide and gratefully took a much needed slug of my Jackie D. After another cigarette and nightcap, I said my farewells and thanks to everyone and headed back in a taxi, to get a few hours sleep before my final meeting with Frederic.

Over a leisurely brunch, we went through all the various bits information they'd put on disc for Jon, everything he'd asked for and more. So, just my flight to catch and back to home life, a bit of normality and much work to be done.... Until the next time!!

After a relaxing weekend with Paul, coupled with a visit to the children at their school it was back to the grindstone.

Monday morning was soon upon me, Jon was due, to go through everything I'd brought back from Paris for the site. During an intense few hours fuelled with copious amounts of coffee, accompanied by a fair amount of "Geek Speak" from Jon, we'd decided on the final layout of the website.... So over to him, for what he said would be about a week of solid graft, then a week of testing everything to make sure it all functioned as it should...Then the big launch. We agreed to meet up again the following Monday all being well and between us work out a strategy for splitting the testing procedures equally, to save time.

Frederic had paid me as per usual, plus an extra amount for the photo shoot. He'd also given me the agreed amount owed to Jon. So all was moving along nice and smoothly.

Between discussions with Paul and Frederic, it was decided that in order to keep everything legal and above board that I'd open a French Bank Account in my name on my next visit, which all being well would be around the first week in December, to accompany Yves to the "Masked Ball".

During that week, I met up with Sarah for lunch and a girly update, I must admit she was very envious and told me she'd loved to have been the French T.V Presenter and she'd love such a debauched birthday present. She also told me the Michael had booked a Xmas trip to a Swingers Resort in Jamaica, so she'd hopefully be treated to some "black meat" as she lewdly put it.

Also Yves rang one evening and gentlemanly rechecked with Paul that it was still fine to "borrow" me for the weekend, once Paul had fully agreed with Yves proposed plans and given his full blessing, he said he'd Email all the details within a day or so… I was frequently checking my Inbox! Finally, my itinerary arrived, with, I was sure a louder more pronounced "ping" than usual. I was booked Air France First Class to CDG, where his driver "Bruno" would be waiting to collect me and take me to my accommodation. My ticket would be waiting for me at the 'Air France" desk at Heathrow. I was flying out on the Friday morning and returning on the Sunday evening. I was so anticipating the Email that I must have read it a good half dozen times! However, I was still confused by the last line of the message that simply stated " Revelry Clothes Provided".

Between us, Jon and myself finally were almost good to go with the Website; all that was needed was the "green light" from Paris. Once they'd had a good look and did some basic trials themselves they gave the definitive go-ahead…. To say they were impressed with it was an understatement. We agreed to make it publically available on line immediately. Jon had cleverly hidden a hit counter on the webpages, so we'd know on a daily basis how many people had visited the site and where the main interest lay. Also he had submitted it to all the available search engines. Frederic and Michel had now included the Web Address on all their paperwork, flyers etc, and had put a few select teaser adverts in various French fetish magazines. All that was left to do was wait and see…The first few days were a bit slow with only a handful of visits each day, but then suddenly, around the second week the site had a deluge of hits, producing a good healthy level of orders across the entire range, strangely a high proportion were from Japan of all places. It was a telling time, hoping and praying that everything worked as planned, especially the "billing" system. Thankfully there were no major problems, just a few little hiccups that you'd expect on any new venture such as this. Between us we decided that we'd update the site with any new products on a monthly basis, and we positively encouraged customer feedback, which in most instances was taken care of by myself. Jon had really earned his money in putting together, this all-encompassing easy to use site. The various products generated a very encouraging eighteen thousand pounds in its first month trading, which when all costs had been deducted left a very encouraging profit. One, which just grew out of all expectation over the subsequent months, and years. The company expanded at a rapid rate.

On the home front, thankfully everything, including the garden was finally finished, enabling Paul to now work from home a couple of days a week, which was a blessing, as we felt it prudent to have someone on hand if Helen had any sudden health problems.

One big relief was that her accountants advised her, that she should make arrangements to start "gifting" the children and myself; in order to minimize any tax and death duties - as I was the major beneficiary of her will. Between them they worked out a legal and very beneficial structure of payments etc. Firstly, she paid off a big percentage of our mortgage, also buying the children some stocks and shares, in their name, with Paul and I as the overall administrators of the portfolio, until they reached adulthood.

Chapter Twenty-Five: You May Go To The Ball!

Finally, my much anticipated weekend trip had arrived, and after a lot of careful preparation and packing (still confused by the "Party Clothes statement in the Email), Paul dropped me at the Air France Terminal, where I duly collected my ticket and was escorted to their First Class Departure Lounge. I was welcomed with a glass of Bucks Fizz and offered a selection of mouth watering canapés! You certainly got a massively different level of service in First Class, for a start back then, the Captain came and had a chat before "take off" and enquired if all was to your satisfaction…. I politely replied, "yes thank you" even though I felt like grabbing him and whisking him of somewhere quiet for some pre-flight fun!!

At CDG a member of Air France collected my luggage and escorted me to the First Class pick up area, where Bruno was waiting beside the car, after greeting me once again by doffing his cap and showing me into the rear of waiting of the Mercedes, he took my luggage from the member of staff and subtly tipped him, before stowing it in the boot and driving off towards Central Paris.

After helping myself to a glass of wine from the mini bar things started to become clearer when Bruno informed me, that we were first going shopping for my outfit for Saturday night, and that The "Général" had given him detailed instructions and I should just sit back and relax. A glass and a half later, we pulled up out side the "Dior" Flagship Boutique on Avenue Montaigne. Immediately, I was helped from the car by the uniformed doorman, and once inside, was handed over to a charming lady, whom it turned out, was a director of their couture division. I was shown swiftly to a private dressing room, with an elegant seating area, where she explained that she was tasked with recommending and presenting me with a variety of gowns and accessories, and to pick which ever one I liked the best, and then after any final adjustments, she would help me accessorize, with shoes, lingerie and anything else that took my fancy… I was speechless, as I imagined the dress alone would cost a small fortune. After a good two hours I was done, and after a small glass of Kir Royale, was informed all the purchases would be delivered the following morning at ten thirty, to the given address...At least she had an address, I was still clueless!

Back in the car Bruno informed me that I'd be staying at an apartment that Yves owned, and had just finished having it refurbished. It was a few minutes away, on fashionable Rue Marbeuf and that the "Général" would telephone me shortly once he was out of his meeting. I was to relax and unwind until then and to help myself to anything I wanted.

It was a beautiful apartment, very elegantly furnished in traditional French style, not a large as Thierry's, but equally elegant and impressive...not too shabby for a spare apartment in the Centre of Paris!

Across the street from the apartment I could see a traditional Café/Bar, so I decided to relax with a coffee and a snifter of brandy whilst I waited for Yves call with "further instructions!". It was very busy inside, and was a lovely warm retreat from the late afternoon Paris chill. Eventually my mobile buzzed and vibrated on the table, it was Yves, and after a brief conversation he told me to be ready at eight-thirty, as we were going out for dinner, he said casual/chic, nothing too outrageous.

He took me to a lovely little restaurant, discreetly tucked away in a small street near the "Bastille". Over dinner we chatted away like we'd known each other forever, he divulged very little about his past, but, however, told me he'd married in his mid twenties but his wife had died suddenly six years previously, due to his work they'd never had children. He had lived and travelled to many places on behalf of his government and was now just keeping busy in an advisory capacity.

He explained the following evenings agenda, which comprised of arriving between seven-thirty to eight for pre dinner drinks and generally meeting old and making new acquaintances. Dinner would be served at eight-thirty and the entertainment would follow, which had for the last few years been a "Slave Auction", which he said had proved very popular amongst, as he put it "the good and the great and the often bad" of French Society. He wouldn't tell me anymore, except that he was sure I'd enjoy it! He also had arranged for me to be visited at the apartment by a hair and makeup lady at five the following day in preparation of Bruno collecting me at six forty-five sharp. He also said he'd bring his mask of choice, for me to wear for the evening.

After a very enjoyable meal he dropped me back at the apartment and told me to get a good rest, as "tomorrow" would be a long night! I rang Paul, who was as intrigued as I; he said he wished he could be a fly on the wall!

As promised, my outfit was delivered promptly, I marveled at these exquisite items for what felt like an eternity, before going out for a wander around the local area.

The excitement and anticipation of the forthcoming evening was making me very horny, and continued to throughout the day. Whilst I was out casually perusing the shops, I stopped off for a drink and in my state of arousal I discreetly exposed my pussy to a guy sitting at a table directly opposite me in the busy bar, I could tell it was driving him to distraction but as he was with his partner, he was powerless to respond…naughty I know! But having a quick climax in front of a helpless stranger was a huge turn on…a game that over the years I have played many times to some fantastic responses! More of these later.

After my makeover and help getting dressed it was soon time to leave, precisely on time Bruno buzzed me down to the waiting car, where Yves was waiting, with once more a red rose and glass of Champagne plus my mask for the evening. It was a beautiful genuine Venetian black & cream Harlequin shaped half Mask, just the feel of it made me warm and tingly.

We settled back and relaxed as the Chateau was about a thirty minute drive, I told him I'd been horny all day and this pleased him a great deal and I could sense he was really looking forward to my reaction to what lay ahead.

The driveway up to this massive old French house was at least a mile long, which eventually led to a semi circular dropping off point and a line of elegant limousines, all patiently waiting to deliver their high profile occupants. Yves explained this event was for the wives only, and that the mistresses would be compensated later, by way of extra Xmas gifts or an increase in their allowance! Only the French! I thought grinning to myself.

Eventually, after having my coat taken and Yves standing back and clasping his hands in admiration at the stunning Dior gown, whispering "you are simply divine my dear", we were escorted through to a beautiful library room that was full of gorgeous antique furniture and stunning large works of art, it was like standing on a movies set, there were male and female waiters gliding discreetly everywhere, with ornate trays of Champagne and Canapé's at the ready. There were some stunning evening gowns on show, and all the men were all dressed in tuxedos and many medals were being proudly worn.

It seemed everyone knew Yves and were waiting their turn to greet him. I played along perfectly each time, as he introduced me as the "Daughter!" of an old British friend, whom he'd worked with in Hong Kong in the Seventies. Each time, he would subtly wink at me…. how I kept this elegant façade going, I'll never know. Even with their Masks on, I could tell that many of the ladies were fifties upwards and were discreetly giving this "thirty" something the once over…. I could certainly feel a degree of envy from behind the masks.

Once all the guests had arrived I did a rough headcount and estimated there were around fifty or sixty couples present. After a while the large double wooden doors opened and a footman announced that, dinner would be served. Then with a commanding voice he commenced announcing couples by name, whom, when walked forward were escorted to their table. We were the last to be announced as Yves was on the "top table" with our host and hostess and two other distinguished couples (I thought I recognized one couples name…but basically I didn't have a clue, as to how high up the social ladder they were…. but very near the top I suspected).

It was all very highbrow and elegant, with a classical string quartet playing in the corner of the large ballroom, but with a distinct under current of sexual tension.

Discreetly placed with each of the ladies place setting, was a small booklet, which was highlighting the male and female "slaves", that were to be auctioned later during the evening! During dinner, apparently the ladies would make their choice and their husbands would do the bidding. Yves informed me that, as last year, there were five male and two female "lots", so expected he the bidding to be fierce. If successful you would have forty-five minutes alone with your purchase in one of the prescribed private fun rooms on the first floor, after that they would be joining the guests in the large Arabian Nights themed room, decorated for the occasion. All very civilized! He told me that the males were hired for the oral skills, as well as their very impressive endowments and the ladies for their beauty and enthusiasm (and acting ability he told me with a smile!).

Thankfully, when the food was served everyone followed the hostess's lead and removed their masks; it gave everyone a chance to have a good look at their fellow guests; smiles and little regal waves passed between the tables. It was all very surreal.

The food was out of this world, the main course being a whole baby roast suckling pig per table, with a selection of local grown vegetables, for dessert crepes were flambéed to spectacular effect. The fine wines and Champagnes had been flowing abundantly and things were starting to "buzz" in anticipation of the auction.

Yves asked me if we should make a bid on any of the "lots", I said I'd leave that up to him, but I wouldn't be adverse to it if he did.

After dinner wines and or spirits were served, and as the chandeliers dimmed the stage was lit, to rumblings of anticipation from this normally, I suspected, reserved congregation.

The first "slave" up for bidding, was a very tall and slim girl with jet black hair who was led on to the stage with a chain attached to her "slut collar", she wore a long sheer gown with heels so high she towered over the auctioneer.... as Yves predicted bidding was rapid and she was eventually secured by a couple seated near to our table, accompanied by much merriment and polite applause. The winning bid was thirty thousand Francs!! I was bemused by the decadence of it!

The first male "slave" was finally sold to another couple for twenty five thousand Francs. He was led on, to much "oohing" and "aaahing" from the ladies, he was wearing a very skimpy loincloth, which left nothing to the imagination. All the "lots" were sold for between twenty and thirty five thousand Francs.

The final "slave" was led on to gasps from everyone, he was a very muscular, mixed race man with a beautiful smile and quite simply the largest penis I'd ever seen anywhere.... and I'd seen a few by now!.... His body was glistening with oil, Yves gave me a playful squeeze on my knee under the table and whispered " I will buy him for you …. yes?", I picked my jaw up off the floor and just discreetly nodded my interest.

We followed the bidding with interest, as many of the gentlemen had been firmly instructed by their wives to bid, astonishingly the bidding soon reached fifty thousand Francs, when it looked like he'd been sold, Yves, with a subtle tipping of his glass trumped the room, with a massive and mindboggling "one hundred thousand Francs", the room was on its feet, clapping, whistling and shouting "Bravo Général Bravo". All eyes were now focused on me…I was flushed with embarrassment and a large degree of apprehension at the unfolding events. People now started to mingle and some went off to the "smoking rooms". Also all the ladies were in the powder rooms freshening up and reapplying their "Masks", as was the etiquette that was strictly adhered to! Many of the ladies congratulated me on my prize and wished me a wonderful liaison! It all made a bit more sense, when Yves explained that all the money raised during the auction, plus the large contributions from all the other guests was donated to the Parisian equivalent of "The Army Widows Fund".

After a short while, Yves told me my "slave" had been prepared and was waiting for me and that I should go and enjoy myself. He explained that he'd be watching, along with the host and hostess in an adjoining room, which had the viewing side of the two-way mirror that was in the boudoir… My emotions were already in turmoil, but now heightened with the added pressure of a small, but distinguished audience to play up to!

I unlocked the door to the room with the large brass key Yves had given me, and entered apprehensively, and there, spread-eagled and restrained to the large four poster bed was my prize. Lying there at my mercy was this gorgeous man, with the beginnings of the most enormous, gargantuan erection. I quickly realized that no words would be spoken, no small talk, just simple animal passion. I smiled and slowly and provocatively started to remove my gown, all the time fully aware of unseen eyes watching my every movement. By the time I'd carefully placed my gown over the large wingback chair in the corner. I saw with glee, that my undressing had given him the most colossal and pulsating erection, his body was completely hairless and very well toned. I wanted to prolong this moment of sheer expectation, we both so obviously felt. So, I started to gently stroke and play with my breasts, showing him my hard erect nipples, swiftly, my vaginal muscles started to rapidly flex and contract as I reached my first small orgasm. He moaned appreciatively as I discarded my small-embroidered silk panties and stood before him solely in a pair of silk hold-ups and my black patent heels, his beast of a penis flexed and twitched with appreciation of my body. I approached the foot of the bed, stood and stared at his body for a good minute, whilst suggestively licking my lips. I slowly crawled forward onto the bed running, slowly my tongue over each of his legs, making my way to his wondrous, muscular brown thighs, gently biting and licking them in turn, all the time with my eyes watching his huge abnormal penis throbbing angrily. I eventually couldn't tease him any longer and began to slowly run my tongue up and over his swollen testicles, taking each one in turn into my mouth, he was quietly moaning, as I pleasured his engorged sac, I then paid rapt attention to his shaft, teasingly running my tongue up its entire length, whilst staring intently into his smoldering black eyes, until I reached its bulbous head, flicking at it like a lizard. Then with my eager, willing mouth took him in, slowly at first, allowing my mouth and lips to adjust to its size. Then inch by inch I took him to the back of my throat, as his hips started to buck rhythmically, he began to powerfully fuck my mouth, his sheer size was restricting my breathing…that coupled, with an explosive orgasm on my part, squirting my juices everywhere, I needed a breather. I knelt up and straddled his chest whilst gulping a few lung fulls of much needed oxygen. I opened my pussy wide with my fingers for him to see and started to play with my swollen clitoris as he watched intently. I brought myself to another series of powerful spurting climaxes, soaking his chest; the aroma of my juices and his body oil was completely intoxicating. He gestured with his eyes that he wanted to taste me, I moved forward and lowered my wet pussy onto his face, where his tongue immediately went to work skillfully on my lips, nibbling and sucking on my clitoris, occasionally probing my anus, much to my delight… his technique was both skilled and enthusiastic, I could sense he was fully enjoying my taste, and with my body starting to go into spasm, I powerfully gushed another orgasm into his very receptive mouth, he drank my juices keenly, we were both groaning with the intense pleasure that we were giving each other. It was now time to fuck this man, I slowly moved down his body until my vagina has hovering over his gargantuan, pumped erect cock...all the time hoping, Yves and his guests were enjoying the spectacle as much as I. With one hand I guided the huge head of his penis into my wet and open vagina, hesitantly at first whilst my opening gradually stretched to accommodate his monstrous girth, slowly I continued lowering myself, until I could take no more of him...god he was enormous. I settled for a moment to regain my composure, and then began slowly and rhythmically riding up and down his length, my vaginal muscles gripping him with such intensity, I felt as if my orgasms would go on and on. I increased the rigorousness of my movements over time, until he started to breathe heavily, groaning as my internal muscles worked his cock to the point of no return.... with a huge shudder I could feel his semen explode into the depths of vagina, filling me, as my muscles milked him ferociously until he was spent!! I collapsed exhausted and overflowing onto his chest. I lay there savouring the moment, until it was time to release him from his restraints (Velcro is wonderful thing!). I went into the en-suite to tidy myself up, cleansing myself on the wonderful cushioned bidet. My drained lover, with a smile helped me into my dress to resume the evening!

Yves was waiting for me when I exited the room, he was grinning from ear to ear, complimenting me on such a wondrously decadent exhibition, he informed me that the hostess was playing with herself throughout, and that her husband had given her permission to go and play with him herself, now that he'd been released from his "Slave status", he was now free to party and entertain the various needy ladies! Before he did he thanked me and complimented me on my dexterity!

I gratefully accepted a large crystal tumbler of Jack Daniels on the rocks that Yves had commandeered for me, and took it to one of the elegant smoking rooms, for a much needed and well-deserved cigarette. The host joined us; he was very complimentary on my unreserved exhibitionistic behavior, as he said, that any English people he'd met were very reserved and cold... I explained to him that there was a small select group of us that had firmly cast off the old "British Reserve", but you had to know where to look to find them!! This amused him greatly and he asked if I'd allow him to give me a tour around his private wine collection in the cellar, as he'd like to choose me bottle of something special, as a memento of the evening. Yves nodded his approval (I felt sure they'd discussed it already). After finishing my drink and another cigarette, he led me through the immense kitchen to a vaulted doorway, he tapped in a code and the door unlocked; we entered down a marble stairway into a vast cavernous cellar with floor to ceiling racks full of wine, as far as I could see...row after row! He gave me a brief tour and potted history of some of the vintages, when we reached the Champagne he selected a stunningly beautiful bottle of Perrier Jouet Belle Epoque Magnum 1990 Vintage Champagne as my gift. At the far end of the cellar was an elegant air-conditioned "tasting" lounge, where he suggested that we had a brandy and a cigarette, which I readily agreed to. We both removed our masks and I settled back into a sumptuous armchair, whilst he selected and poured a fine smooth Cognac, it was divine and I was savoured its rich oaky taste. He asked me, where I'd learned to achieve the intense orgasms he'd witnessed earlier, so I proceeded to recount in great detail the story of how Michael had turned my "tap" on several years ago, and that I could now control and achieve them at will in almost any situation. His face lit up, I could sense, he was enjoying my openness, as there was a very mischievous little sparkle in this elderly French aristocrats eyes! In his near perfect English he expressed his interest, that as we were alone and nobody could interrupt us, that it would be a great pleasure for him, if I would give him an intimate, personal demonstration of this rare skill. He said that he would be highly honoured, if I'd allow him to drink my juices as I climaxed. He quickly informed me that he'd got Yves blessing, however, the ultimate decision was mine. I admit I was massively aroused by the thought of this scenario and eagerly nodded in agreement. I asked him to help me out of my dress, which he carefully hung on a coat stand in the corner. I then instructed him to kneel in front of me and remove my rapidly dampening panties. I was once again naked, except for my heels and hold-ups. I lifted and placed one leg up on the arm of the chair and invited him to open me and closely inspect my pussy. I was rapidly juicing up with the whole scenario. I sensuously placed myself back in the armchair and lewdly opened my legs as wide as possible, letting them drape over its soft cushioned arms. He was transfixed, as I went to work with my fingers, opening my labia ever wider whilst tweaking my clitoris, I told him to lean in closer and see how my vaginal muscles flexed and gripped under my control. I invited him to lick my anus whilst I held myself open for him, he accepted his task with great relish and started to gently run his tongue around my precious bud in deft circles and probing it deeply inside, making my sphincter spasm and pucker uncontrollably. It was a very erotic scene looking down at this beautifully dressed gentleman feasting on my most private of places, it wasn't long before I could feel myself building up to an intense climax, I verbally signaled my intentions, and as he knelt before me like a hungry child with his mouth wide open, I let go a powerful orgasm and squirted jet after jet of my hot sweet juices into his waiting mouth and over his ecstatic face. I just continued pulsing and squirting, drowning him in my juices. Eventually I was a spent force and decadently told him, to lick me clean, whilst I enjoyed the rest of my Cognac…, which he did with boundless enthusiasm!

I rejoined Yves in the Library for a final drink, before Bruno was scheduled to pick us up, he told me many of the guests were enjoying themselves in the Arabian nights room, where the young, and now free slaves were entertaining various guests and generally ensuring the eroticism of the evening continued. Shortly, our ride arrived and we bade our farewells to our hosts, and with "my gift" in hand, slid into the rear of the waiting limousine.

After thanking Yves for such a wonderful and very eye opening evening, and giving him a gracious peck goodnight, I made my way up to the apartment, where after undressing, I collapsed into the large comfortable bed and drifted off into a long restful sleep.

As arranged, the following day Yves picked me up and we went for a long leisurely lunch before my evening flight back to Heathrow, to an excited Paul, who'd want to hear all about my exploits in minute detail. To be honest, I was really looking forward to the comforts of my own environment and just enjoy a few hours of "slobbing out" in sweat pants and t-shirt, after all the exertions of the previous couple of days had exhausted me. Followed by a long, slow soak in the bath and even slower lovemaking session with Paul…complete with commentary by myself for his delectation!

Chapter Twenty-Six: The Ideal Mix

Over the coming months, I worked hard at ensuring family life blended well with my more and more demanding business commitments.

The website was generating ever increasing orders, and between us we decided that I'd concentrate more on the creative marketing aspect of the business. Meaning I could take more of a back seat at the "showings", since we'd hire professional models for the forthcoming photo shoot. This was a big relief, as the range of clothing and accessories was growing rapidly. At the same time, the range of high-end exclusive "toys" had started to sell in quantity.

Paul's Parents business was going well and they now had four fully operational "Gites". Their reservations book was looking very healthy, even during the low season, which was a relief to all of us.

The children were happily, doing well at school and were frequently going on school trips and visiting various school friends' families during the holidays.

The only major worry was that Aunt Helen was becoming frailer and needed an increasing amount of help with things on a daily basis. We contemplated getting in some home care, but she was very adamant that she didn't want to be beholden to a stranger, especially at this stage in her life. After many discussions and a few scares along the way she relented, eventually agreeing she'd be happy with a live in carer, but only if it was Celia! So after much to-ing and fro-ing and a little bit of pleading Celia agreed that she'd move into Helens spare bedroom and once again resume her previous role of paid carer and general companion.

Paul's job was still very demanding, as his company was in the middle of a very successful period, with many of their "artists" performing well in all the relevant music charts globally. We had to juggle schedules a lot, as Paul now was at a level, where he was attending monthly planning meetings in New York and a quarterly three day round of meetings in Los Angeles.

We, however, ensured our social life didn't suffer too much and frequently held or attended small dinner parties with our well-established close circle of friends.

I always made time to have a girlie lunch, at least once a fortnight with, either Erica or Sarah, so we could swap stories and notes as to what we'd all been up to. They were both hugely envious of my night with Yves at the ball, and were always making little quips and calling me "The Generals Toy" or "plaything"… I didn't know whether to be offended or amused by the title…they meant it in good heart, and Sarah was always threatening/begging to join me on my next visit to Paris!

Over the following months I had a few flying visits to the company for planning meetings and also an all too brief coffee with Claudia.

At one stage, Thierry came to London on business, for a new important product launch at the Chanel Flagship store in Old Bond Street. Needless to say a few goodies were forthcoming along with a lovely watch, as a late birthday present. Both Paul and I joined him for dinner, but sadly there was no fun and games, as a very prudish older lady accompanied him on the visit, she was on the board at the "House of Chanel", therefore everyone was on their best behavior. Shame!

Yves telephoned or emailed once a week, usually on a Thursday evening, an event I always looked forward to with joy.

Paul had also bought a new toy, a state of the art, and top of the range digital stills camera. He loved having me dress up in some of the outfits and have me model them purely for him, as a prelude to a night of heavy sex. Now, he could put them instantly onto his computer, safe in the knowledge of not having to worry about having them developed and going astray in the post, or worse, being opened accidently by Aunt Helen…heaven forbid!

The big talking point at this point in time, was the recent introduction of Eurostar and how it would take the stress out of travelling to Paris. The boast being, how it would whisk you in comfort directly to the heart of the City. I was due to attend a new collection launch shortly, and was going to see if it lived up to all the "hype".

I was in the process of working some dates with Frederic for the proposed new showing and web site photo shoot, when Yves telephoned and said he'd like me to come to visit, as he was shortly hosting a small evening get together, for six influential high ranking officials, who had all served in some senior level before their retirements. I told him that I was due to come on business very soon and if the dates coincided, then it would be my pleasure. I was intrigued as he briefly explained that it was an all male get together, but he'd like me to attend during the "brandy and cigars". He said he'd explain more, when I was in Paris. I was fascinated and more than a little excited by the intrigue. I was also relieved, that Yves had had the courtesy to telephone Paul and get his blessing prior to inviting me. Always the gentleman!

With a degree of planning and a bit of juggling here and there, I booked my "Eurostar" first class ticket on line, and was due to travel on a Tuesday mid-morning returning Saturday mid-afternoon. I cleared everything with Celia and Aunt Helen, whilst reassuring them that Paul would be either at his office, or working from home during that week.

I email Yves and told him that I'd reserved my tickets and my arrival time at the Gare Du Nord, his reply was brief and succinct, Bruno would be waiting to collect me and I would again be staying at his empty apartment for the duration. I asked him should I pack anything special, to which he replied "travel light, think minimal"!

It was a simple tube ride from Kew to Waterloo, with only one change at Westminster to the then Eurostar terminal, where the first class ticket area was a simple show up show ticket and board system. As soon as I boarded, I was directed to a very spacious and comfortable seat, in my allotted smoking carriage, and was immediately served with a glass of Champagne and a small menu card, with the day's food choices. It was, as they boasted, all so easy and so very relaxing. The only downside, was on the leg from London to the Channel Tunnel the high speed super train could only trundle along, due to there being no high speed track at that time, however, after about fifteen minutes under the English Channel the train emerged into French daylight and stopped at Calais to drop of and pick up passengers. Then, once underway it rapidly accelerated up to its speed of nearly 190 mile per hour, only stopping once, at Lille. It was fantastic feeling flying through the French countryside at this speed, whilst being served a delicious light lunch and drinks of choice, all included in the ticket price, which was a lot cheaper than flying, as they were now in a cut throat price competition with the airlines. In less than two hours we were pulling in to Le Gare du Nord, in the heart of my favourite city! I immediately began to get that feeling of "Joie de vivre".

Bruno was there to meet me as expected and whisked me straight to the apartment to dump my luggage, and as I was meeting Yves for drinks and supper at Eight that evening, I got him to wait and next drop me in Le Marais, so as I could get some work done and plan the next few days schedule with Frederic and Michel. Enabling me to be in a position where I could instantly available, for whatever Yves had planned. They had some great new designs and some wonderful leather based accessories, which we were going to show the buyers and have photos done for the web- site. Also, we had a very positive financial update and there was a surplus of profit in the main company account, for which the website accounted for a good percentage of this. So, between the three of us we agreed to paying ourselves a nice "bonus" for all the hard work, this was paid electronically into my healthy and fully operational account at the BNP Parisbas. Frederic also gave me a nice envelope, with a bonus in pounds sterling for Jon, I knew he'd be over the moon, so I gave him a quick call and told him. He was very pleased and begged me to let him meet me at Waterloo on Saturday, after winding him up a little, I readily agreed.... I'd suddenly become his favourite person on the planet!!

Yves arrived, surprisingly unaccompanied at eight and we strolled to a nearby restaurant, La Fermette Marbeuf, it had a sumptuous art nouveau interior, with a stunning stained-glass ceiling, ornately mirrored walls, the "belle époque" rooms are an amazing experience for locals and tourists alike. As per usual, Yves was greeted and fussed over like a returning war hero! We were shown to a discreet and private table in the main dinning room, where with great theatrics, the menus were presented. I decided to go with the Blue lobster ravioli and mushrooms to start and followed with a mouthwatering Scottish Salmon fillet with braised leeks and chestnuts, on Yves insistence I finished with Crème brûlée with vanilla ice cream from Tahiti, it was historic! Over the meal I updated him on my life in general and he was genuinely interested to hear about Paul's current successes at work. It was at this precise moment, that he suggested that I should use the apartment on a permanent basis, which would make my business life a lot simpler, and obviously would also enable me to be available to him, as and when his time permitted! I must admit he made a very strong argument that this would be in my best interest, it really was a no-brainer to accept, which I did, but with one stipulation...that I'd do it on a six month trial basis and only with Paul's full support (which I knew would be forthcoming). During the obligatory coffee and brandies he explained that he was hosting this small dinner for a small group of retired "grandiose" officials, in fact, one of them being the host from the masked ball. He explained to me that my body, my exhibitionistic flair and most importantly my tremendous G-spot orgasms, overwhelmed both himself and the host, and the apparent control I had to achieve them at will, and he would be most gratified if I would demonstrate this highly erotic and personal "art" to this small distinguished gathering after they'd dinned. I didn't have to think too for long! I told him with a cheeky grin, that it would be my pleasure to attend! We made a toast to a long lasting friendship and many more fun filled erotic adventures in the future! With all that was happening, I felt I was well on course to achieving the perfect mix of business/family and fun.

Chapter Twenty-Seven: Playing To The Room!

After a full day at the offices with Frederic and Michel, pricing and organizing what we'd be getting Jon to launch on the site during the forthcoming round of updates, I called it a day and headed off for a long soak in the large tub at the apartment, with a deserved chilled glass of vino.

Yves had called during the day and told me that Bruno had been to the apartment and dropped off the outfit that he'd like me to wear that evening. He told me Bruno would be picking me up at 10.30 prompt.

When I entered the apartment, I immediately noticed that a wonderful flower arrangement had been placed on the large dinning table along, with an envelope. Inside the envelope was a note informing me that Bruno had hung my outfit in the bedroom and that he had also filled the fridge with a selection of food and wine to enjoy at my leisure.

Feeling horny and excited I rushed to the bedroom, to find a full-length silvery black mink fur coat hung up inside a Perspex protector, a very erotic looking pair of black heels with built in ankle cuffs and a beautiful pair of Antonia Silk Noir Lace Top hold-ups. The only other item present was a matching black "Bella Morte Choker".

I had a nice couple of hours to relax, so I raided the fridge and made myself a lovely mixed salad, with some cold slices of roast beef and a large glass of chilled white wine, I took the opportunity to check in at home and update Paul and hear about his day. He told me he'd met a very interesting woman, who was working in management for one of the artists signed to his company, he said she'd very openly flirted with him and in the line of business had invited him out for lunch later in the week…I told him to investigate further and I'd expect a full report on Saturday evening…. we both chuckled!

I poured a lovely hot bath, with some nicely scented bath oils and took my glass of wine in with me and layback and daydreamed about my naughty solo performance, that was fast looming. The sheer calmness of the wine and the distant background sound of the Parisian traffic was intoxicating and heating me up very nicely…. I resisted the temptation of giving into any self-stimulation, as I was determined the gathered gentlemen would experience me in full "flow". Quite literally!!

It was a magnificent feeling putting on the gorgeous hold-ups that slid on with ease over my lightly oiled legs. I massaged a nice palm full of my Chanel Body Velvet moisturizer into my breasts; I instantly gained a good few inches as I slipped into the cuffed shoes, finally adding the finishing touch by putting the choker on. I stepped back and admired myself in the full-length mirror. I looked the part and boy did I feel lecherous. My final luxury, was applying a liberal amount of the "Body Velvet" over my recently waxed and already wet pussy. At exactly ten twenty-nine I slid on the fur coat, which fell level to my ankles, the effect with the shoes was electric!

At precisely ten thirty the intercom buzzed and Bruno told me he was waiting by the car, I had one final look in the mirror and went down to the entrance, where Bruno tipped his cap and told me that "Le Général" would be pleased at how I looked in his "late wife's" favourite coat. He explained that it was a great honour and privilege to be invited to wear it and that I was the first…an honour indeed He mentioned that he'd not seen the coat since she passed away; I admit I felt both touched and slightly nervous, as to Yves's reaction…I needn't have worried in the slightest!

Bruno explained that we were going to an old French Military Institution, where highly decorated officials and special guests met for unique occasions, and was used as a focal point for them when in Paris. He told me that we were going to a special area of the The École Militaire in the 7th arrondissement. It was a very esteemed building and it was founded by Louis XV in1750. We would be entering through a very private and little known access point. We drove into a small courtyard, through a set of electronically operated, solid metal gates, where several identical Mercedes cars were parked. We pulled in to a reserved bay, close to the only visible entrance, which was lit solely by an ornate carriage lamp, with a discreet CCTV camera set back in the corner. Bruno escorted me to the door, where he pressed the buzzer and looked up at the camera, then he wished me a pleasant evening and left. Shortly the locks clicked and the door opened, I was greeted by a young uniformed man, who swiftly beckoned me inside to a small oak paneled lobby area. He said that I was expected and asked me to follow him; we took the marbled stairway to the second floor and entered a small ante chamber, where conveniently waiting on a small table was a large Brandy balloon, with a large measure of the warming amber liquid inside. He handed it to me and explained, that when I felt that I was ready, I was to knock on the door of the "inner sanctum", he then bizarrely, stiffened to attention, saluted me and said "Bon courage Madame", winked and left.

    I took a good mouthful of Brandy, delved quickly into my bag and for added pleasure, and to settle my nerves indulged in a large sniff from a brand new vial of amyl nitrate. Within seconds the combination of the alcohol and amyl had my blood warming and rushing to all the relevant pleasure receptors in my body, my nipples grew rock hard and erect and my clitoris started to throb intensely…. It was time to go!!

    As I knocked twice on the solid oak door I could hear the faint murmur of male voices, upon opening, Yves was standing there and took a moment to take in the sight of me in the coat, he leant forward and kissed me on both cheeks and whispered that his wife would be looking down and smiling approvingly!

    As Yves led me into the room, I was met by a small group of very distinguished gentlemen, all regaled in full Military uniform, with a vast array of medals on show. I was a bit intimidated at first, but was soon put at my ease, as they were all smiling admiringly as they stepped forward for Yves to make the introductions. Several of them expressing their approval, exclaiming, "magnifique, tres belle". There were also a wide variety of many other flattering comments. After a little small talk, a tall gentleman, who was addressed as "Le Compte" and appeared to be the most senior, in both age and Military Rank took my hand gently and said "Young lady you have been invited here to our gathering on the highest of recommendations of certain gentlemen present, and I personally am looking forward with great interest to witnessing your special talents".

    Yves stepped forward and released the two clasps that held the coat closed, there was a noticeable rise in anticipation from the group as the first glimpse of my flesh became apparent, as the coat was gently slipped from my shoulders the tension increased massively. As I was now stood in front of them fully naked, nipples erect and my moist and glistening pubis now effusively on show. I felt, both in control and vulnerable at the same time, it was a strange but highly sensual feeling.

A beautiful large antique Chaise Longue, covered in dark crimson velvet, was discreetly placed in a position close to the array of armchairs, which ensured they all had an unrestricted view. I took one last sip of my Brandy and handed it to Yves and discreetly winked. I elegantly moved across to my little "stage", making sure they all had a good view of my bottom as I walked, even getting a few gentle slaps on the way. I was starting to really get aroused and could feel my much anticipated orgasms start to bubble under the surface, as a warm flush spread rapidly through me. I lay back on the Chaise seductively and slowly spread my legs, until I could feel myself opening up. My entire vagina started to tingle and throb profusely; I simply lay there watching their reactions, as they all focused intently on my open and very wet sex. I remained in this position for a number of minutes, relaxing and contracting my vaginal muscles, while quietly whimpering. I could feel their eyes burning into me as my climax started to build; I slowly reached down and pinched my nipples, on my way to fully exposing my engorged and pulsing clitoris to the captivated audience. I pushed down in to my vagina, as my orgasm was fast approaching, and as if on cue, as the senior gent exclaimed loudly "C'est Incroyable", I climaxed and powerfully let forth a huge arcing stream of my ejaculation, followed by more and more fluids. I started to feverishly slap my pussy as I built to a crescendo of pure animal pleasure and lust. There was enthusiastic applause and much verbal appreciation, and I saw a look of pure pride on Yves face!

Yves brought my drink across to me, so as I took take a breather and compose myself, he enquired if everything was fine and if I was comfortable, I grinned and told him it was perfect and I was incredibly horny and was ready to "go" again. Once the gents had settled back down, I indicated, I had more to give and proceeded to reposition myself, this time kneeling on the Chaise with my back to them and one heeled leg cocked up exposing my parted buttocks, after reaching under and opening myself up and slowly inserting two fingers, I started to pleasure myself furiously and brought myself to another powerful, squirting orgasm, which after a moment, I controlled with my internal muscles. By now my confidence was so high, that I stood and approached each of one of them, displaying my vagina for them, encouraging them personally to feel me. I firmly encouraged them to slap my clitoris and tweak my labia, until I was ready to gush again. I targeted Hugo the "Host" from the masked soiree, to be the recipient of my climax, which, as previously he enthusiastically accepted, gulping it down greedily.... I tried my best to ensure my abundant squirts avoided his pristine uniform, alas; he did get a little wet! However, he was delighted and thanked me profusely and showered me with compliments, whilst kissing the back of my hand.

Yves returned the coat to me, to reestablish a degree of dignity, whilst I finished my Brandy, and shortly before I left I was presented with a memento of the evening and token of their appreciation, which Yves instructed me to open once back at the apartment. Shortly the young uniformed officer was there to escort me back to Bruno, with an appreciative round of applause, I took a small bow, said goodnight and left...smiling from ear to ear, but desperately needing a large drink in a very quiet room!

The young escort handed me over to Bruno, and saluted as I climbed into the rear of the car. Bruno smiled, as if he could read my mind and as he pulled up outside the apartment, he said he'd taken the opportunity to buy me a bottle of Jack Daniels as instructed by Yves. I took it off him most gratefully and looked forward to pouring myself a large measure on ice. It was almost one in the morning, so I sat in the salon of the apartment, lit dimly by a small sidelight, content with my Jackie D and long overdue St Moritz cigarette and contemplated my evening of sheer exhibitionistic indulgence! I suddenly remembered my leaving gift and retrieved it from my handbag, after unwrapping it carefully, it revealed a deep red "Cartier" Moroccan leather box with gold lace borders, with rising excitement I opened it to reveal the most elegant ladies Gold Cartier "Tank Francaise "watch set into a black velvet plinth.... My only reaction was a huge gasp, followed in an instant by phone call home, from one very spoilt lady.

The new ranges went down well with the buyers, and the photographer had done a very professional job, especially with the new accessories and toys. It was a relief not to have to model the outfits, as this enabled me to fully concentrate on the Internet and focus fully on what Jon and myself needed to achieve over the coming few months. Plus the fact that the new model was a very erotic looking young French girl with long jet black hair and olive skin, she was of Algerian background, but had lived in Paris for most of her life. She settled in immediately and I could tell Frederic and Michel were going to work their charms on her soon, if they'd not already done so!

Yves rang during the day on my mobile, and complimented me on my little performance, saying he'd had many messages of thanks and praise for his erotic interlude from all his colleagues, all expressing a very strong interest in meeting me again, laughing, he told me he said he'd pay it due consideration! We both laughed when I told him I was exclusively his, unless he authorized it, he seemed very pleased by this, saying he may consider letting one or two "play with me" at some stage, all things are possible he said with a definite teasing tone in his voice. I was intrigued as to where this may lead, and what little scene he'd want me to play out for him in the future! I didn't have to wait that long to find out, as he dropped by the apartment that evening for a brief drink whilst on his way to an official function. Before leaving, he arranged to meet me for "dinner and games" the following evening, and that he'd pick me up at eight-thirty.

After a long call home, I called Thierry to see if he was available for a drink, sadly he answered his phone, but was in Germany. I eventually decided a visit to L'Escapade was in order, as I was in Paris, alone, and everything was readily available to a young woman about town on a Thursday night. There was no way I was going to have an early night with a book and a mug of cocoa!

It was still early by Parisian nightlife standards, so I slipped on a clingy LBD, heels and obligatory hold-ups, I popped a short blazer on top and with smile wandered across the road to the small bar. I went all-French and ordered a "Pastis" with a small carafe of water, and sat in a window seat, watching the night time unfold. I had put my hair into a simple pony tale, and glancing at my reflection in the window decided it looked damn sexy! I was also feeling a need for a little hands-on male attention, after my exploits the previous evening had left me drained but a little frustrated!

After another "Pastis" which certainly hit the spot, I stepped out and grabbed a taxi to the club. As usual Amanda greeted me and we sat in reception having a good old catch up, she was completely in awe as to what had transpired with Yves and his comrades! Thankfully, she went down into the club and returned with a nice plate full of nibbles, as I'd completely forgotten to have any dinner. During our catch up several couples and a variety of single men arrived. It was fun vetting them as they checked their coats in. Amanda said that word of mouth had been a major factor in their now virtually closed membership book; they were only accepting the cream of the crop or member recommendations when it came to single males. I was surprised, when she told me that amongst their members eighty-two were single females and this demographic was growing steadily.

I went down to the club area to the ever-present predatory eyes. I surprised Costas by ordering a "Pastis", and was quickly approached by a few nice looking men, all acting courteously and making polite conversation, by this time my knowledge and command of the French language was pretty good and I was able to converse on a reasonable level. Which got me into and out of a few situations!

After some general flirting and a couple of dances I wandered off through to the back room play areas and had some fun watching various groups of people engaging in a variety of interesting encounters. I watched a very vocal lady being taken from behind mercilessly, by a well-defined black man, whilst her partner looked on in awe. It was always fun anticipating as to whom the discreetly caressing hands belonged to, that were having a quick anonymous fondle! After a short period of watching, I knew I needed a good, hard uncomplicated "fuck". So, when a handsome young chap I'd locked eyes with on several occasions earlier sidled up behind me and slipped his hand under my dress and started to play with my bottom, I swiftly parted my legs slightly making it very obvious to him that I was up for more. He gently slipped my panties to one side, sliding a finger inside me as I firmly pushed myself backwards towards him. I could distinctly feel his erection throbbing against my bottom. I was groaning and very wet by now, I quickly reached around and took hold of his hard cock and guided it to the entrance of my very wet and receptive pussy. I gasped loudly as he drove himself into me powerfully. He pulled my dress up over my hips and started to pound me, whilst a couple of people beside me stepped aside a little and watched as I was taken to heaven and back by this sexy stranger. His strong hands were firmly holding me by my hips, he intensified his thrusts until, with a load groan we climaxed together. We both laughed at the sheer spontaneity of what had happed.

I went of to freshen up and joined him for a drink at the bar.... It was the first time we'd actually spoken! He turned out to be a really lovely guy, called Gerrard, and had only become a member a few months previously when he was brought to the club by a couple he knew, and they regularly went out as a threesome. Just by chance in the conversation he mentioned that he'd met the other couple by chance and the wife "Claudia" was.... I stopped him mid-sentence and laughed as I said "is her husband called Olivier?" he was completely taken aback and nodded, as I said "small world"!

He gallantly gave me a lift back to the apartment and wanted to come in and as he put it "fuck me properly", I was sorely tempted, but didn't want to do anything that might offend Yves, so I just took his number and gave him a lingering kiss goodnight in his car.

I rang Claudia and we arranged to meet for a coffee late morning in Les Halles. My opening line was "Gerrard sends his regards", she looked shocked, until I told her all about my recent encounter at the club, she grinned and called me "Grande Salope!". She was excited to hear all about what I'd been up to and insisted we have a "girls" night out on my next visit, I agreed wholeheartedly. I, however, made no mention of Yves, I felt that with his high profile status amongst the French people it was best kept as quiet as possible.... not that the average French person would give a hoot, but I certainly didn't want or need any of the predatory U.K tabloid press getting wind of anything, as back then, as now, they tended to sensationalize everything and quite frankly could ruin peoples lives. She told me about a wonderful new club they'd been going to twenty minutes from Paris and strongly suggested we visit at some stage. She also told me about a wonderful new man she'd met the previous year, his name was Nikolas and he was a "Tantric Masseur" and was a "Yoni Master", she giggled and told me to look at his web site...She he gave me his business card. She said he was in high demand with a certain breed of Parisian women. She insisted I contact him, as she knew I'd enjoy the experience!!. When I called I was to say that she'd recommended him and that would be a major "ice breaker". We had a big parting hug, and I promised we'd meet up again in a few weeks, on my next trip.

The following few hours were all business, getting all the bits and pieces ready that Jon and myself would need for the updates and any final bits of paperwork finished. Both Frederic and Michel were very pleased when I told them that I'd arranged an apartment that I could use as and when I needed…. they saw this as a further commitment to the business on my part.

I returned to the apartment and had a good few hours to relax and get ready for the evening, Yves told me just look elegant!! I rang Paul and had a good old chat, he was pleased that Jon was going to pick me up at the station and drop me home. I was excited when he told me he had lots to tell me regarding his lunch date. I begged him to tell me more…but he teased me and told me, I'd have to wait till I was home!! He simply said, I'd be proud of him…. whatever that meant. I poured myself a drink, ran myself a bath, and as it was filling I had a good clean around the apartment, as I wanted to leave it as immaculate as I'd found it.

Yves telephoned, saying that Bruno was on his way and would be dropping off a little present, one that I should wear that evening, and not to rush as he was running a bit late. Minutes later the entry phone buzzed, Bruno was stood with a large carrier bag, I asked him if he could come up as I was only in a robe, which he did and as he handed me the bag, he said he'd be back at a rescheduled nine-thirty prompt.

I immediately took the bag into the bedroom and took out the protective carrier and hanger to find a gorgeous figure hugging full length black Valentino dress, with accompanying crimson velvet "Bolero" jacket. It was exquisite and very tasteful; I was intrigued as to where he was taking me…. I would just wait and see! I got ready nice and slowly until it was almost time to go… I finished my wine and had a quick cigarette on the small terrace. I had earlier bought some really good powerful spray breath freshener that masked the smell of tobacco. It was quite expensive but I'd never seen it for sale in London, so I bought three.

In the car Yves said that we'd be spending the evening at a very well known, but invitation/reservation only club, where the food was renowned, as were the play areas. It was called Le Cleopatre (Le Cleo) and it was situated on the Avenue d'Italie in the 13th arrondisment of Paris. He said it was the haunt of the rich and famous, many politicians, actors/actresses and a variety of well-known Parisian socialites and "nightflies".

It was a good twenty minute drive to the club, which was set back off a very busy main road in a fairly modern building. It's entrance was a very discreet, heavy black door, with the customary CCTV cameras, within moments of pressing the buzzer we were welcomed in to a small foyer, where our names were ticked off in the reservations book. A waiter appeared and with great formality escorted us upstairs to the main bar, where he presented us with that evenings menu as we ordered an aperitif with the very dignified looking barman.

Shortly, a very elderly gentleman walked towards us with the aid of a cane and flamboyantly embraced Yves, who introduced us, he was the owner and apparently Yves had known him and his lady wife for many years. With a cheeky wink he tapped my bottom with his cane and with great glee told Yves that he had a beautiful and exceptional "Daughter", Yves smiled nonchalantly and said "many a tune was played on an old fiddle", which had us, especially me in stitches! The elderly owner then said as he started to leave…" I should go and find him, if ever I needed a real man". Yves chuckled and told him it was way past his bedtime and his mug of cocoa was waiting!

There were some very elegant couples already there and the dinning area was over half full. After having a good look at the very extensive menu, we decided we'd share a seafood platter on ice, followed by Chateaubriand, accompanied by a very nice bottle of house red wine, which Yves said was a personal favourite of his, as he knew its maker…enough said!

Yves discreetly pointed out a few people who were celebrities in France, I thought I recognized one or two, but I was more intrigued by the way people were wandering ofF with their own or other peoples partners in between courses. He said it was a tradition at this club for people to have an intimate sexual encounter whilst awaiting their food. The thing that had me biting my lip to stop me laughing uncontrollably was the sight of a man in full evening suit and a top hat, playing a Grand Piano with a pair of white gloves on…. I felt like I was in a scene from "the mad hatters tea party" for adults! Yves was highly amused by my interpretation and said "just wait, it gets much madder!!"

After the wonderful meal, we took our brandies and coffee into a large subtly lit lounge area with sumptuous sofas and grand armchairs, soon I realized why…there was a little boutique selling very erotic outfits, very reminiscent of what we were marketing, the one big difference was, that from the lounge area there were several large one way mirrors, so you could see right into the changing rooms. Yves told me that many men sent their exhibitionistic wives and girlfriends in to try on the items…as sensually and provocatively as possible!! He said maybe "I'd like to try and buy later". He guaranteed, I'd draw the biggest crowd of the evening! Boom! Out came my exhibitionistic streak. I smiled a definitely maybe smile and sipped my brandy.

The club was really starting to get busy, with couples in various degrees of undress appearing and disappearing into alcoves and along corridors to the fun rooms. Yves beckoned a waiter over and ordered a Jack D on ice for me and a vintage cognac for himself, he suggested whilst waiting for them to arrive I should take a look in the large room to the left of the bar, and he'd explain all when I returned… my curiosity got the better of me, so off I wandered with one or two admiring glances along the way. I was simply blown away when I peaked in the room, the heavy drapes were shut with a little sign beside saying "open midnight", through the gap in the drapes, I saw a room with bean bags all around the walls and taking pride of place in the centre, was a large mechanical "Bucking Bronco", and protruding from the saddle was a very large black replica penis! Now I was more than curious and made my way quickly back to Yves, who was happily chatting to a man, whose wife was exposing herself in one of the changing rooms to the delight of a few avid voyeurs. He was highly amused by the look on my face and patted the sofa for me to sit and have a drink and he'd reveal all. I took a sip of my drink and listened intently, as he explained that they ran a competition every Friday and Saturday evening, where the more exhibitionistic and agile females would straddle the machine and would impale themselves on the large black "dildo", the pre-programmed "Bronco" would buck and twist at increasing speeds, until the participant was flung off in a very undignified manor, naked and onto the padded landing zone! The Bronco did start at a slow speed for a brief period, so the women would receive a nice initial pleasuring! The winner was the lady who set the best time of the evening. As her prize she was given a nice bottle of Champagne, and her and her partners evening paid for. He laughed, when I said that it would remain solely a spectator sport for me!

I did however, wander off into the shop and picked a few items to try on, I made sure I put on a little bit of a performance in doing this, much to Yves's delight and the crowd of on lecherous lookers. One of the ensembles I had tried on was a very skimpy "French Maids" outfit, which I thought to be a bit predictable, but Yves loved me in it and had it bagged up for me.

We sat and discussed my next visit and what sexual adventure would I like arranged…. I simply said "your choice, surprise me". This gave him great pleasure and I could sense his mind already working overtime.

We went and watched a few brave ladies take on the "Bronco", one very petite oriental girl being tossed into the arms of a group of encouraging men, then to be carried off to a private room, to receive her just rewards! Then a very well built middle-aged woman proceeded to ride it like a true equestrian, until she let out a climactic scream as she was flung unceremoniously on to the mats, still squirming with pleasure.

The debauched behavior, of these supposedly respectable and model citizens was truly an eye-opener; it was all very decadent and reminiscent of a "Roman Orgy". We took one more drink in the lounge, accompanied by a plate of cheese, and then we left, apparently long before the real debauchery took place. It was a very interesting evening, with fantastic food, but all a bit "pretentious" with a "don't you know who I am?" feel about it all.

Yves was leaving early in the morning for his house in the South for a few days, so we said our goodbyes, giving me a good few hours sleep before catching my "Eurostar" back to London.

Chapter Twenty-Eight: Moving Forward

After an uneventful, but very soothing train ride back to Waterloo, it was nice to see Jon's smiling and expectant face. We went and found his little Ford Fiesta, in a nearby car park and had a very easy journey back to Kew, where Paul was waiting with a nice welcome home hug.

As Paul was making us all a very welcome cup of tea, I gave Jon his cash bonus, which made his day…if not his year! We agreed that he'd come a little later than normal on Monday to go through the debrief, as he wanted to go and pay some outstanding suppliers and pick up a new piece of computer kit.

After popping down to see Celia and Aunt Helen to catch up on their week, Paul and I decided to go and have dinner at the Pub and give each other edited highlights of our respective week! I usually kept the really naughty bits for our lovemaking; also I was desperate to hear Paul's news… I was not disappointed!

I was all ears, as he told me he'd gone for lunch with the woman who'd openly flirted with him at a business meeting, it turned out she was heading up the European management team, for one of the new up and coming bands signed to his company world wide. She was called Antonia, but liked to be called "Toni", she was thirty-six and separated from her husband, who still lived in America. She'd just moved back and was starting to build a new circle of friends. Paul said she was very open, and was definitely the kind of woman that I'd get on with and she definitely would be no "shrinking violet". He said he'd mentioned a few of the things we'd experienced in Paris, she said she was very intrigued envious and that she'd love to see for herself sometime. He'd only given her a very brief outline, so I suggested, that he should invite her around for drinks or meet up at a bar. I could tell he was more than interested in having a little liaison with her…. Which, I positively encouraged! So I left it to him to make the arrangements.

Jon was buzzing over the coming weeks and months as the web site grew at a much faster rate than we'd ever anticipated. Also a major factor was that he'd put a "customer feedback" page online that seemed to verify the quality of both the products and the high level of service that we provided. It basically gave potential customers confidence in ordering. We also had a no quibble returns policy, which also was a big factor on establishing a high level of customer confidence. Jon was also very happy, as with the salary and good bonuses he'd earned from our venture, his fledgling company had really expanded and his client base was growing monthly. He was in the process of moving to larger premises and employing staff, but he never lost focus and has always given me priority.

The children also benefited from this, as Jon had streamlined his new company. He'd invested in new hardware, so he kitted them out with a nice Mac set-up each, put together from all his surplus custom equipment. He also sorted them out a printer. He even put in a new bigger hard drive for each of them, keeping his old ones securely under lock and key.

It was shortly after, that Mike and Sarah invited us to a private house party at some old friends of theirs, who had recently moved back to the U.K and were celebrating the completion of work on their large private country house, it was situated at a small village near East Grinstead called of all things "Horney Common" (yes its true).

Paul had arranged an evening drink with Antonia, and with the blessing of Mike we invited her to attend the party, which she very readily agreed to. She was everything that Paul had described and was a really open and approachable person, most of all she had a wicked sense of humour. It was soon agreed, that as it was a good ninety minute drive from us, that we'd pack an over night bag, as the hosts had two large marquees erected in the grounds and everyone was welcome to stay.

Antonia and I met for lunch the week prior to the event, and I gave her a few ideas as what I may wear, but we all agreed it would be easier to get ready at the "party" house, which was not a problem, as there was plenty of room, and the hosts had set aside a few of them, solely for this purpose. There was a going to be a wide variety of guests, with one couple flying in from South Africa for the event. Toni was very easy to talk to and we bonded immediately, she asked my advice as to how to play it as a single "female" and the etiquette. I told her to stick to Paul and/or Mike and they'd see she was "looked" after (in more ways than one, as it turned out!). This relaxed her and she seemed really excited by the prospect of meeting some new people. One's that were sexually liberated and just out for a "fun time" with people with similar lifestyles and sexual interests.

Chapter Twenty-Nine: Horney Common

Antonia arrived at our house on the Saturday lunchtime, as we thought it would be pleasant to have a nice lunch on the river somewhere and generally relax before we set off at six-thirty-ish, as we were hoping to get there around eight, giving us plenty of time to get ready.

After lunch I showed Toni around the house. I had spoken to Mike and Sarah earlier in the week to confirm the dress code for the party and they said it was "elegant but erotically revealing" for the females. As Toni had nothing really too wild to wear, I gave her tour of my "samples" wardrobe, which contained all the outfits I'd collected over time from the business. She, however, really loved the "French Maids" outfit that Yves had bought me at Cleopatre, and as she was a very similar size to me, apart from having larger breasts, we decided she'd borrow it for the occasion. Her larger boobs would only enhance the effect of the outfit.

After a few wrong turns, we arrived at the lane that led us through the woods, to a magnificent large old farmhouse with stables and various outbuildings. We were met by Louisa, the hostess and told to dump our bags in the hall and follow her through to the massive kitchen to say hello to a few early birds, who had the same idea as us. Introductions made, we had a glass of wine and made polite small talk until Mike and Sarah appeared and we introduced Antonia to them. Immediately, I saw that unforgettable filthy look in Mike's eyes. They took us, and showed us the two marquees that had been erected in the garden, one was full of soft comfy cushions…. it was like a Bedouin tent in the desert, the other had a dozen or so tables and chairs, a small dance floor and along one side, a huge buffet and a BBQ area that was going to be run by the caterers they'd hired in…. all very impressive. Situated to one side of the large terrace was a large twelve-person hot tub and behind, there was an outbuilding that had been transformed into large massage area, with two large massage tables and some scented candles to be lit as darkness fell.

Mike introduced us to the host, his old friend of many years Patrick, who turned out to be a real "tech" freak and had the interior and exterior of the house fitted with CCTV cameras, all linked up to a very nice powerful Mac with two large split screen monitors attached, in due course this would be a major source of entertainment.

He showed us his pride and joy, which was a very large drawing room that was completely dark and devoid of any furniture, apart from taking pride of place in the centre of the room, there was a very large old style black leather dentist's chair. There were a multitude of cushions placed around the walls, all softly lit from above by a dim spotlight! Very kinky.... Toni's interest was really peaked now, and I sensed her excitement levels were intensifying!

Antonia and I followed Sarah to a room she'd commandeered for us to use and get in to our party outfits. It was a large room, with two double beds, a sofa and large dressing table...Sarah said, we could all use this room, as and when we needed to "crash" and she had a key, so we'd lock it after we'd got ready, and to, just come find her as and when required!

Sarah had brought an outrageously revealing black and red satin and leather Basque with an eight strap, suspender belt, sheer silk seamed stockings and a black lace thong, all topped of with amazing patent black platform heels.... She looked fantastic. I'd eventually settled on a translucent black halter long dress with thigh high split and an incredibly low back line, matched with lace top hold ups and a pair of my killer Parisian shoes. Antonia, decided to stick with the "Maids" outfit, with hold ups and lilac platform heels, she looked a million dollars, especially as her breasts looked tantalizing and certainly seemed to have a mind of their own...I was sure they'd be make many appearances, whether intentional or not during the hours ahead.

Mike and Paul appeared wanting to get ready themselves, as people were now starting to arrive in numbers. So we left them to it and went downstairs. Sarah went and helped Louisa and Patrick welcome people, as a good proportion of them she'd met at parties they'd attended, before we got to know them. There were a couple of open-minded girls from the catering company serving drinks, and generally running that side of things. Initially, drinks were taken in the large lounge area and out on the terrace. As per usual groups started to cluster in the kitchen as well. Antonia and I chatted with some of the couples we'd met earlier whilst waiting for Paul and Michael to appear. Antonia was definitely starting to warm to the situation, as she realized there were several single females present, as well as a few select male friends of the hosts.

As soon as it was dark the subtle garden lighting came on, as did the hanging lanterns in the "Bedouin" styled marquee. It was all very conducive to some very adult fun and games.

Amongst the guests there were some very outrageous and daring ensembles…. I thought I was back in Paris!! The atmosphere was starting to build from hot to volcanic very swiftly. Many guests had brought drinks with them to compliment the vast range that the hosts had provided.

Paul and Mike were chatting with Patrick and a very attractive woman, so Toni and I made our way to get a bite to eat and check out what was developing out in the marquees. We got a steak each from the BBQ and some lovely exotic salads and grabbed a table. Most were occupied, and it wasn't long before a couple came and joined us and we had a good natter, they were very interested in the Paris scene and I gave them all the information, they told us they'd been to club in Germany, but were very disappointed as it was full of aggressive people in leather, with no finesse whatsoever. So they were grateful for any help and advice that I could give them. With my business head on, I gave them my business card, which also had an email address they could contact me on. I'd also brought a handful of flyers advertising the web site, which Patrick happily let me leave on the kitchen table for people to take.

By now the party was starting to get into full swing. Patrick had gone and locked the entrance gates, so no unexpected visitors could crash the party.

There were people chilling out in the hot tub, and it was obvious by some of the girls squeals that there was a lot of under the bubbles antics occurring.

Louisa came and dragged me off to meet their South African friends, as they were also off to Paris during their visit, so wanted pointing in the right direction. I told Toni to find Paul or Mike and enjoy herself, and that I'd catch up with her later… Eventually, after chatting to the South Africans and giving them my card, I went for a mingle myself, when a rather handsome young man approached and said hi. Before I knew it, we were deep in a very flirtatious conversation. We soon gravitated towards the "Dentists Chair" chamber, and began to watch a very vocal middle aged lady, getting an absolutely vicious pounding by a man, that was quite obviously not whom she arrived with! My new best friend asked me "if I'd like some of what she's getting", whilst he glided his hand seductively down my spine, which made me shudder heavily with sheer anticipation! I remember smiling my naughtiest smile and saying, "indeed, I most certainly would!" We were immediately kissing and exploring each other expectantly; he took my hand and guided me swiftly over to the far corner of the room and gradually lifted my dress up over my hips, he gasped in delight to discover a very wet and willing pussy that was completely unhindered by any panties, he was on his knees in no time, with his eager young tongue working its way feverishly all over my wetness… my kind of guy! He worked me into a complete frenzy, his tongue working every inch of my engorged pussy… he adored it when on several occasions I climaxed, flooding his mouth with my juices, there was no stopping him, he was a true connoisseur in the art - totally dedicated and fully tuned in to my pleasure! Through the ambient lighting, I could vaguely make out several more people, across the far side watching the frantic activity taking place in the chair, whilst engaging in their own personal pleasure…. I wondered if Paul was amongst them, possibly with Antonia!

    The lady who was getting some very personal attention in the "chair" was by now quite obviously on a continuous level of orgasm and was eccentrically, alternating between screaming instructions to her lover and singing snippets of popular "Opera" songs! It was most bizarre, but speaking to her at length the next day, she explained that she was a semi-professional "Show" singer and once she was approaching and achieving her orgasm she uncontrollably burst into song, she couldn't explain it, but said it had made for some very interesting scenarios and a lot of curious looks.

    My young "oral" specialist wasn't distracted one bit by her "warblings", and continued dispensing pleasure with his untiring tongue and fingers, eventually I felt it my duty to repay his endeavors and administer some of my own oral skills. As he rose to his feet, I sank to my knees and released his very hard, straining erection from his trousers and began working eagerly on him with my tongue. I could sense by his breathing and body movements that it was going to be short and sweet, so I gripped his hips and verbally encouraged him to "fuck" my mouth. Driven on by this he gently placed his hands on top of mine and started to rhythmically thrust his length into my mouth, occasionally slowing, so as I could take him fully to the back of my throat…. his face was contorted in pleasure as he watched me completely devour his cock. Something I'd mastered over the years, with much practice on Paul. After a few minutes of this he indicated he could take no more and with a flourish began to urgently rock his hips back and forth, powerfully thrusting himself into my mouth, until with a huge roar of ecstasy he unleashed his own orgasm powerfully into my willing mouth, I didn't spill a drop, he tasted so good, plus I didn't want any tell tale marks on me when I returned to the general drinking and chatting areas. We thanked each other, and giggled as we left the room, noticing that the "singing" lady was being taken by her second or maybe third man…. she was having a serious "check up". I noticed a few ladies encouraging her to finish and to let them have a turn, in the by now very popular room!

    I went and grabbed myself a drink and a cigarette and decided to go check in with Paul. As I wandered out on to the terrace I saw Sarah enjoying the attention of a couple of men in the hot tub, she immediately noticed me and grinned motioning that I should sneak a look in the "massage room". As I approached I could hear the unmistakable sounds of some sexual shenanigans drifting from inside. A very pleasant sight greeted me as I entered, there lying prostrate on one of the massage tables with a look of complete contentment was Paul, and sat astride him moaning and skillfully riding his manhood was Antonia, they looked like they'd been locked together in this position for quite a while. They were both shimmering in the candle light, with a film of perspiration on their bodies. Mike suddenly appeared from nowhere, naked and proudly erect as ever and said "lets leave them to it, they've been at each other like rabbits for ages". As I was being dragged out by Mike, I caught her eye and gave her the approving thumbs up gesture, to which she looked relieved and reciprocated… I cheerfully left them to enjoy each other uninterrupted be me "the wife". Mike and I went and retrieved the key from Sarah, who was too engrossed in her own fun to even acknowledge us. We must have made an amusing sight, as Mike led me through the lounge, with his impressive erection nearly knocking some poor ladies wine glass out of her hand and me trying to keep up, whilst giggling uncontrollably!

Once in the room, there was no stopping us, in quick time he had me naked and squirming wetly on his expert fingers. It had been a while since we'd had fun together, which made it all the more intense. It wasn't long before he produced a little bottle of poppers and we both took a huge hit- as always the effect was almost immediate and he had me gushing powerfully over his fingers…. I always came in a slightly more intense and personal way with Mike, as it was him who'd turned my G Spot on, all that time ago, so I considered it was like a teacher/pupil thing. He had a technique that made me climax more forcefully than anyone I'd ever met…. many have come close, but he is definitely the unrivalled Master! He also had mastered total control over his own orgasm and could last indefinitely, whilst deeply penetrating me everywhere, in a vast array of positions. We seemed to be completely in harmony with each other's sexual pleasures and desires when in a situation like this and we instinctively knew what each other wanted next. However, after a few more popper induced climaxes, coupled with some hard and powerful fucking, we freshened up, as we didn't want to appear rude and lock ourselves away for the duration!

We returned to the main congregating area and got a long refreshing high sugar drink to quench our thirsts and replenish our energy levels. We wandered off together and found Paul with a very "pleased with himself" look and Toni, sat having a drink, we all gave each other knowing looks and I was pleased that Paul had let himself go and that Antonia had relaxed into the whole situation. By the look on her face she had only just started and wanted to have a lot more fun! I nudged Mike under the table; he soon took the hint and whisked her off into the "Bedouin" tent area. I grinned at Paul and told him that I'd witnessed a little bit of his fun, and teased him a bit about his look of total concentration, he agreed that he'd really had fun, but it would have been even better if I'd joined in with them!!! Mmmmmm, I thought and agreed that we should make it happen, whether here, or on another occasion. This really got him excited again at this prospect. I must admit the idea of this turned me on as well and my mind drifted back to Paris and the S.A.S encounter with Christine and the Velcro restraints.

We finished our drinks and went and mingled, eventually catching up with Sarah, who looked suitably contented. Paul went and fetched us all some drinks. I collapsed laughing when she told me, that whilst she was having fun in the hot tub, a woman got in and as the was getting pleasured burst into a selection of popular show tunes…I recounted my "musical "encounter in her presence…we were both uncontrollable!!

The BBQ was still going strong, so the three of us went and got a plate of barbecued chicken wings and some dips and joined Patrick the host, who was grinning from ear to ear at the success of the party and vowed to hold at least two every summer and also an annual Halloween Party which were destined to be a huge success. There is always something unsettling, but erotic being made love to by a man dressed up as a corpse with a knife in his back!

I went to find Antonia to see if she was okay and in need of food or drink, only to find her impaled on top of Mike, whilst hungrily sucking on the male part of the South African contingent.. I didn't feel it good form to interrupt a girl who was so obviously engrossed in enjoying what she was doing!

Eventually, everybody crashed and burned, and when I awoke, several hours later to bright sunlight, I went to see if there was any coffee or juice on offer; it was like walking through a war zone, pure carnage…. I grabbed a coffee and helped Louisa and one of the girls from the catering company, who'd joined in the activities and ended up staying, to regain some semblance of order. Luckily it was mainly superficial, and with a concerted effort we filled at least a dozen large black bin sacs with empty bottles, cans and general detritus from the festivities. There was about half a dozen people groggily waking up in the marquee, some with the look of "good morning…who are you?" on their faces, always an interesting moment during a weekend party.

As the morning progressed and the sun started to warm up, a dozen or so people happily sipped coffee, with the more hardened taking a "hair of the dog" brandy with it…myself included. I felt remarkably fresh, but, thankfully, I'd not really over indulged on the alcohol front.

After a few hours, and by now the sun was overhead and warm several people began to get a bit frisky and started playing again, after things had heated up and several sexual exhibitions were evident. Paul and Mike came and got me, they took me into Patrick's study, where he was sat engrossed in front of his computer screens. He was like the ultimate peeping Tom, as he had his monitors split with each screen showing four CCTV cameras feeds. In six of these there were various people in various stages of sexual encounter. Mike was chuckling as he was glued to camera feed 2, where Sarah was fervently giving the young guy who'd entertained me the previous evening a vigorous blowjob, oblivious to their audience, suddenly, we all were really riveted when Toni appeared on the screen and started to share the guys cock with Sarah, both obviously enjoying using the guy for their own fun… he was just a lucky victim of two very horny ladies. I couldn't resist the temptation and quickly stripped off and went to join them and help "abuse" the guy. The look on his face when I suddenly appeared was a joy to behold. He just knew he was now in big trouble and just muttered "oh fuck!". Give him his due; he did do a good job in satisfying three very wanton older women…. I couldn't resist at intervals looking directly into the discreet camera and gesturing and pulling faces to the assembled three peeping toms'!

After a few hours Paul, a very happy-smiley Antonia and myself, thanked our hosts profusely and also said our goodbyes to Mike and Sarah…both independently giving their full approval of Toni.

We stopped off on the way back at a superb pub in Epsom, called "The Rising Sun" and had a late afternoon Sunday roast, whilst listening to Toni barely stopping to breathe, while telling us what a spectacular time she had had, and generally, re-living the entire evening again. We quietly ate and listened intently…. remembering how we were, after our first night in Paris, all those years ago and how our minds raced with all the new adventures, discoveries and sexual enlightenment! We dropped Antonia off and went home to some much-needed peace and quiet.

Chapter Thirty: A Devastating Blow

Things were running smoothly, in both Paul's and my work and we'd just taken advantage of having a long weekend at Paul's parents in France with the children. We'd all had a relaxing few days, however, on the evening before we were due to fly back from Bordeaux, we had a call from a very distraught Celia. She informed us, that without any warning, whilst pottering in the garden Aunt Helen had had a stroke, a much more severe one than she'd experienced several years previously, and that she'd been rushed to Charing Cross Hospital, where she was in intensive care. Luckily our flight was early the next morning and with the time difference, it meant we'd be able to get to the hospital by midday at the latest. We agreed with Celia that we'd stop off at the house first and drop our bags off, and collect her, so she could come to the hospital with us.

It was a very subdued final evening and flight, which only got worse upon arrival at the hospital, where we were told, that unfortunately Helen had deteriorated overnight and now had several complications. Basically, the prognosis was not positive and it was only a matter of time. In fact it turned out to be only 48 hours, during which time she never regained consciousness and peacefully slipped away.

As per her wishes she was cremated, and we held a small memorial service back in the Cotswolds, which was attended by many of her old friends. Celia was deeply saddened and wanted to move back and try and take up where she had left off, before she came to Kew to look after Helen. We wished her well and helped in every way we could over the following months. It would take time, but we were sure that she'd be able to rebuild her life, especially as she had so many good friends in the village.

Shortly afterwards, we were contacted by her Solicitors, for the reading of her "Will". It was a very somber occasion with Paul and myself, the children and Celia present. She'd left the children a lump sum each, once again to be administrated by Paul and myself - to help pay for their University education, she'd also left a rather nice lump sum of fifty thousand pounds to Celia, at the point this was read out, I thought she was going to pass out, instead she simply went white and speechless, the remainder and bulk of her estate was, as we already knew was left to me. We went to a nearby pub afterwards, as poor Celia needed a stiff drink. We then dropped her off at Paddington for her return train journey to the Cotswolds.

Bless her; Helen had left things totally in order down to the last detail. Paul and I agreed to continue with the services of her trusted accountant to help and guide us through the transfer of monies, payment of duties etc.

Over the coming few months everything carried on as before, however, the house seemed eerily quiet without Helen, but that eased off gradually, once things calmed down and all the paperwork and legal issues had been taken care of.

Paul's workload had remained at a manic level as the company was going through another successful period, with several new U.K artists breaking through in America, which meant longer periods in New York. But the rewards were good.

Yves rang as always every Thursday evening without fail, this as ever was a welcome diversion, and he always had some little tale to tell, which raised my spirits. Eventually, I couldn't put a business trip to Paris off any longer, as I'd already missed one and had sent Jon over on a flying visit to keep the web site updated as normal. However, the fact that Internet connection speeds had increased massively, it meant a lot of images could be sent in Emails.

Paul and I decided that we'd reincorporate the basement back in to the main body of the house, and seek the help of an interior designer and planner to oversee the project. We agreed to make it into one large entertaining area with access from the main house hallway. We also planned to incorporate a small kitchen area and a large wet room with shower and sauna at the rear, with a small pair of French windows, opening up to the small courtyard with steps up to the garden. With everything approved and plans in place, work was started.

I scheduled in a Tuesday to Sunday trip to Paris and booked my Eurostar ticket online. I must say, it was well overdue and I was really looking forward to this trip and even more so. When I told Yves my dates, he simply said the time was right, and that I needed to start "living and loving again" and that he'd arrange a special evening on the Wednesday. As always I didn't ask any questions, just left it in his capable and trustworthy hands to organise.

The web site was now scoring well on all the new search engines and was generating a steady increase in traffic weekly, mostly due to Jon's endeavors. Also out of the blue we received an online order for well over three thousand pounds worth of goods; from some certain South Africans that I'd met!!

The only difference about this trip, was that I'd relented, (doesn't take much) and agreed that Sarah could join me for a few days and I'd show her Paris "my way". She'd booked a little solo trip, as she'd also been having her share of dramas with Mikes elderly mother. So in her words, she needed to "get rude" and unwind for a few days. Mike rang me, and gave me his blessing to make sure she had a good time and let her hair down, as she'd had to put up with a lot recently.

Yves had no problem with her staying at the apartment with me and looked forward to meeting her, as he'd heard so many "good!" things about her.

Chapter Thirty-One: "My Return To Form"

The Eurostar continued to live up to all its "hype" and it certainly did take a huge amount of stress out of getting to Paris, no waiting around airport departures, no journeys to and from airports… just city centre to city centre in style, comfort and most of all swiftly.

I told Yves that there was no need to have me picked up, as I would be going straight to the offices in Le Marais.

It was great to see Frederic and Michel again and we went to a local bistro as soon as I arrived and I caught up on all the news and gossip. They also had an idea regarding the web site and wanted my feedback.

They had been talking to the photographer, who suggested, that they should stage their own "Catwalk Show" for their forthcoming designs and film it. He said the exposure would be a great boost to the business. Also having it on the web site would send out a clear message that this was a professional and trustworthy company and that people could place orders with 100% confidence.

I agreed in theory, and between us we put an outline proposal together. We planned to hire three models for the occasion and find a suitable venue and invite a range of people, from fetish club patrons to press, basically anyone who had any influence in this area of fashion. Eventually, I gave my full backing to the event, leaving it to them to work out the finer details. After we'd been back to the office and sorted a few outstanding issues, I took a cab to the apartment and relaxed and waited for Yves to call. Yet again waiting for me in the bedroom was a selection of presents from him, this time included, was an exquisite Azzedine Alaia cream and burgundy silk fitted cocktail dress and a pair of matching evening court shoes. Hung on a hanger next to the dress was a beautiful three quarter length single breasted black Yves Saint Laurent cashmere coat, he'd really spoiled me this time, I couldn't help but wonder, with a degree of trepidation and excitement what was planned for Wednesday evening.

He called early evening and told me he had a dinner to attend at nine o'clock at the Ritz Hotel, and he'd like me to meet him there for a quick drink at eight in the Hemingway Bar. He told me he'd send a taxi for seven forty-five, as Bruno would be driving him there.

As I was going to be free from around nine, I did a little preplanning of my own, as it had been lurking in the back of my mind for a long time. I fished out of my purse the card and details of Nikolas the masseur that Claudia had given me when we'd last met. With a tumbler of Jack Daniels in my hand for "Dutch Courage", I called and explained who I was and pleasingly, he said that he remembered Claudia mentioning me quite a while ago. I explained my situation and told him I was in need of some relaxing therapy and would be free later if it was convenient.

He explained that his Tantric studio was in a building adjacent to his apartment, which was situated in Saint Germain, only a ten to fifteen minute cab ride from the Ritz. He told me he'd be expecting me between nine to nine-thirty. Anticipation and excitement of which I'd not felt for a while grew, as I lay back in the bath tub for a soak prior to getting my new outfit on…. hoping that Yves had meant for me to wear it for our brief drink-date!

Even though I say it myself the dress fitted a treat and really accentuated my long lightly tanned legs. I felt more relaxed and in the mood, than I had for quite a while. I'd also had a flash of inspiration as to what little treat I'd try and get arranged for when Sarah got here on Thursday afternoon. I knew she'd want to cram in as much fun as she possibly could and I wanted it to start with a "bang".

Yves was waiting in the Bar as I arrived and looked his usual elegant distinguished self, after a four peck Parisian greeting he ordered me a "Bellini" from the discreetly hovering waiter. We had lots to discuss, but little time on this evening. He told me that the following evening was going to be an evening I'd never forget. He asked if I knew about the tourist boats that did romantic night time cruises up and down the Seine, when I nodded, he said grinning "its like that but a whole lot different". It turned out that the only remote similarity was the River!

I also explained my idea regarding a surprise for Sarah, which immediately got his thought processes going into overdrive, he said he'd look into the possibility and let me know, but absolutely adored the scenario! He escorted me back through the elegant and busy lobby and saw me into a taxi, wishing me a pleasant massage and to enjoy the rest of the evening and that we'd talk in the morning.

Fifteen minutes later the cab was pulling up outside a graceful old building, in an elegant side street just off the famous Boulevard Saint Germain.

As per Nikolas's instructions, I pressed the buzzer on the assigned door, shortly a very handsome man, with dark olive skin and the most smoldering pair of eyes answered and ushered me inside, whilst simultaneously kissing both my cheeks and introducing himself. He showed me to what was his studio, which, was a beautifully decorated area. I immediately noticed it was comfortably warm and had an infectious aroma of mixed spices. In the centre of the room was, as he explained in great depth, a custom-made massage table. It was built like an inverted Y shape, with a small area near the top cut away for the face to rest, and on the Y shaped section two padded openings for the feet and toes to slot into. The leg area was on lockable castors that could be maneuvered to suit the person and give Nikolas unhindered access to whichever area he was focusing on. He swiftly took my coat and complimented me on the dress. He went and fetched a padded hanger to place it on. In the corner was a hydro shower, which he explained was should to be taken as hot as possible, so the resultant open pores on the skin would absorb the mixture of oils he used. He said, that when I was showered and dry to ring the buzzer, and he'd return and begin my treatment, which would last around ninety minutes.

With huge excitement and growing anticipation, I showered and pressed the buzzer, he quickly returned wearing a pair of white sweat pants and a V-necked white t shirt, he was carrying several small bottles of warm oils. He took my towel from me and helped me up on to the table, he delicately pinned my hair up, and as he slipped on a black velvet blindfold explained, that with my senses confused the effect of the massage would be far more enhanced and pleasurable.

He put on some very relaxing and soothing music, and as I was face down he placed my feet securely into the slots. I had a definite impression that the legs of the table were being slowly moved apart, until he was satisfied with the positioning. I could definitely feel my thighs and buttocks spreading open voluntarily as the adjustments were made. He then instructed me to relax, enjoy and place my entire body into his hands.

    He commenced by slowly covering my entire back and legs with warm oils, softly applying them over my skin. He then spent a good amount of time massaging each foot in turn, finding and putting small amounts of pressure on various tingly nerve endings, it was an amazing, indescribable feeling and the erotic sensation when he massaged each individual toe was mind-blowing, but incredibly relaxing at the same time. He then proceeded to powerfully, but sensually concentrate on each of my calves in turn, steadily working up to the backs of my thighs, focusing on each leg individually, on several occasions straying tantalizingly close to my most erogenous area. I sensed him move to the head of the table and continued by working my shoulders and each arm in turn, also erotically working on each individual finger. He firmly massaged his way down my spine, spending a good while on my coccyx, which I surprisingly found was an awfully sensitive area. I could feel my self beginning to tingle all over and a powerful feeling of arousal flowing through my veins, this was massively heightened when I felt him trickle the warm oils on to each of my buttocks. I shuddered as I felt some of it trickling down between my cheeks and over my anus…it was sheer delight. His hands firmly worked each cheek in turn, at times firmly, then switching to gentle strokes and soft pinches, occasionally one of his fingers would flick over my anus, making my lower body arch and quiver involuntarily in response to these brief tempting, teasing touches. Soon I could feel the legs of the table being moved further and further apart, until my already swollen wet labia parted, exposing my vagina in all its glory. I could sense him looking and admiring it for several prolonged moments, before massaging the very innermost tops of my inner thighs, and gently brushing his fingers over my lips as he worked on one thigh, then the other… I was screaming inside, I knew I wouldn't be able to take much more before I succumbed to my climax. I felt he sensed my urgency, as he immediately started to gently massage my anus with his fingers. Delicately stroking, tweaking and probing until a delicious and powerful orgasm erupted from within me as I felt his long slender finger slide, smoothly into and up my anus, the feeling was explosive, my vagina spasmed furiously as I gushed a profuse jet of my juices, my internal muscled were on fire as I responded to his skillfully probing fingers. He worked me for what seemed an eternity bringing me to several more shattering orgasms. After a few moments of no contact, he asked me to sit up and remove the blindfold, and to my eternal gratitude said that we should have a five-minute break to let my body relax before he worked on my front. He suggested a nice glass of wine was in order, which was music to my ears! He asked me if I was fully enjoying the experience, to which I simply nodded and said that I was fully looking forward to the second part.

After this pleasant and relaxing interlude, it was time for part two. He replaced the blindfold and once more skillfully positioned me back on the table, this time face up! It was a wonderful feeling lying there naked and exposed, with no sense of sight, and my vagina fully open and on show, knowing it was going to get some masterful manipulation very shortly. At first he was stood behind me, working on my shoulders in turn, tantalizingly working his way slowly to my breasts, my nipples were excited and very erect, desperately wanting and needing some attention! He poured some freshly warmed oil over my chest area, I could feel it slowly running down and pooling in my navel. He worked each of my breasts in turn, tweaking, pinching and flicking my nipples, until I was groaning in ecstasy, verbally encouraging him to squeeze and pinch them harder. He soon started manipulating them both together, he then held each individual breast one at a time and gently slapped and flicked the nipple, until with a huge groan I began to climax…my entire body core was erupting, every nerve was ablaze as I let my orgasm totally take over me.

After a brief period of silent, gentle, feather like strokes over my legs, he began circling my navel with his fingers, scooping up the pooled oil in to his hands and letting them slowly and enticingly drip onto my vagina, which was on fire! He continued by administering long slow strokes up and down the length of my labia, then repeated the process he'd used on my nipples on my swollen and protruding clitoris…it felt like small electric shocks hitting my most precious and sensitive of areas. Subsequently, I felt two fingers slip inside me and curl themselves around to the front wall of my vagina, they immediately found and started massaging my G spot, until I screamed uncontrollably as a massive orgasm ripped through me, he continued working my G-spot with one hand, while the other was rhythmically slapping and pinching my engorged clitoris... this sensation took me forward to a whole new plateau of sexual gratification, I was squirting profusely - I begged him not to stop. After the crescendo began to subside a little and I started to get some feeling back into my pleasantly aching body, I heard him open and close what sounded like a door and shortly another sensory overload began to develop, as what can only be described as feeling like a flame had started to dance across my nipples and on to my aching clitoris, it was both soothing and intense at the same time, it was like no other sensation I'd ever experienced, it was only when he suddenly put it up to my mouth and teasingly ran it across my lips did I comprehend what it was! As I tasted the raspberry spiced droplets melting in to my mouth. I gently started to flick my tongue over the end of it and began to suck it into my mouth, as the cold ice melted he moved my hand up to hold the stick as I continued my lewd licking of this raspberry flavoured popsicle. As the last of the ice melted it was immediately replaced by a wholly different sensation, one that I was very familiar with, a very warm and hard penis was being rubbed gently over my lips and across my face, my tongued shot out and by feel alone circled the head of his cock as it lay twitching across my open mouth. I turned my head to one side to enable me to get more of him into my mouth, I sucked and slurped on it just as I had on the popsicle for a few minutes, until he took my hands and helped me down off the table, so as I could kneel and continue to please him with my mouth in a more manageable position. Simply imagining the sight of what I must look like, knelt naked and blindfolded, shamelessly sucking on this mans large cock brought on another series of orgasms. I worked my tongue all over his energetic erection and took each testicle in turn into my mouth and softly sucked on them. Soon he reached around and cupped the back of my head in his powerful hands and began to slowly fuck my mouth, deeper and deeper, with each thrust getting more and more ferocious, until I could sense and feel his cock start to throb and twitch violently as I worked my mouth and tongue in harmony on him. I was in a state of orgasmic euphoria as he pumped my mouth faster and faster, until he unleashed torrent after torrent of hot semen into my throat, there was so much, I was swallowing as much as I could but could feel the excess running down my chin and splashing onto my breasts. It was incredible; he just continued to cum and cum, I'd never experienced anything quite like it, when it eventually subsided I heard myself muttering in French

"Incroyable, impressionnant, superbe" amongst many other expletives. He removed my blindfold, and as my eyes became accustomed to the light again, the sight was truly mind blowing, I was covered in semen and a handsome Frenchman was leaning back against the wall looking exhausted, with one very large and contented penis staring back at me. I simply had to crawl forward and gently lick the last remains of his orgasm off him. We shared a final glass of wine whilst waiting for my taxi and I promised to give his card to a few of my contacts. I discreetly handed him his one thousand Franc fee and departed, one very happy and satisfied lady. Thankfully Bruno had re-stocked the fridge at my apartment enabling me to chill out with a nightcap and a light salad before collapsing into bed.

Chapter Thirty-Two: "La Nuit Des Sapeurs-Pompiers"

The following morning I indulged in a breakfast of hot chocolate and sweet lemon and honey crepes, before heading off to Le Marais to continue finessing the forthcoming Internet marketing campaign.

A friend of Frederic was exhibiting his successful range of Erotic furniture at a forthcoming Adult Erotica Show in Berlin and had agreed to distribute our flyer for us from his stand, however, it was decided that as it was a few weeks off we'd put together something more substantial and professional. It became my job along with Jon to design the catalogue as we had all the relevant high quality images and once done an acquaintance of Frederic's would have them printed locally. It was one more piece of the jigsaw, which grew over the years into a simple but very effective marketing tool, always generating a high degree of interest and more importantly firm orders, both wholesale and retail. Plus it also sent a lot of traffic to the web site.

Yves called and we arranged to meet for a simple dinner early evening before revealing the surprise he'd arranged for me. He told me that he'd talked to a few people and had a provisional plan in place to welcome Sarah to Paris the following day.

I had a catch up call with Paul, but it was only brief as he was in New York for meetings and was up to his eyes in work, but he told me he'd spoken to Michael before he'd left and arranged that on Friday evening they were going out for dinner in Kew, and he'd invited Antonia along who was more than happy to accept. I laughingly told him to tell Mike from me to "turn her tap on". He chuckled and said they'd already discussed it!

Yves arrived at precisely eight, as arranged, looking very distinguished in a smart charcoal grey pinstripe suite and crisp white shirt and tie. I, as instructed wore a simple but chic black cocktail dress and heels and my gorgeous YSL coat. We strolled to a nearby restaurant called "Le Bistro Marbeuf ". It was a very typical Parisian bistro that specialized in "Lyonnaise Cuisine". To start we both had the Foie Gras with a prune chutney and warm crusty bread, it was delicious, to follow I had a simple roasted chicken with a salad. Yves decided on one of the daily specials - Sea Bass cooked in a fruity sauce, it looked divine. Over the food and a nice bottle of Beaujolais he piqued my anticipation when he explained my "little present". I was going on a trip up the Seine, on the high-speed boat that was used by the Parisian Fire Department to help patrol the River. I would appreciate Paris in all its glory, seeing all the landmark buildings whilst illuminated and from a different perspective. I was then to be entertained for a while afterwards in the Brigades barracks. Sounded fun, even more so when Yves told me what I'd be wearing for the trip! I had wondered what was in the box he'd left in the apartment! He told me it was a very special favour arranged by a friend of his who worked at the fire department and ran the "station. He explained that all Parisian firefighters were Army trained and seconded to firefighting duties on rotation.

    He also told me what was tentatively arranged for Sarah and if I approved (which I did very enthusiastically) he would confirm it in the morning.

    We went back to the apartment so I could get ready, as Bruno was collecting us in a short while.

    Yves had very naughtily bought me a pair of patent leather thigh high boots with a nice high heel and a string of pearls. I said, "Is that it?"...To which he replied, "no, the Fur coat as well". Obviously it took very little time to get dressed!

    Bruno drove us to the mooring on the river, adjacent to the Brigades head quarters. The Station chief, who bowed, and saluted to Yves, as he led us aboard the fire launch, was there to greet us. There were three, very swarthy firefighters on board who also saluted Yves and then went and prepared a glass of Champagne for us as we took our seats inside. Shortly we were underway and were slowly cruising along the Seine; The Musée d'Orsay, Notre Dame, Assemblée Nationale and the Eiffel Tower, were amongst the many famous landmarks, pointed out proudly by Yves as we sipped our drinks. This was certainly a unique and unforgettable way to see Paris, all lit up and looking magnificent... I couldn't help but wonder what was in store for me back on dry land...the very thought was turning me on massively.

    The return journey to the station house was exhilarating to say the least as the Captain put the power down and we raced along at high speed with siren blaring and lights flashing, all for my benefit. It was a very privileged position to be in and I was loving ever moment. Also, the second glass of champagne had made my exhilaration levels hit the roof. The feeling of sitting there, just wearing a Fur coat, the boots and absolutely nothing else was sublimely erotic and enhanced my already high state of arousal.

We were soon back safely at the mooring area, where, we were met and escorted off by the Chief and ushered the few yards to the entrance to the Brigades HQ. Once inside, we went into a small anteroom, where both Yves and myself were offered a brandy. The Chief informed us that all was arranged and the men were in readiness and looking forward to the encounter. We were told that a strict sixty-minute period was allotted, before the men needed to be back on their shift duties. Once that was all made clear, Yves smiled and asked if I was ready for my treat, I nodded my full agreement and asked if would he be in attendance. He very quickly said "no, as he was too well known, and couldn't be seen in this environment", however, he'd be watching from a special vantage point with his brandy, accompanied by the chief.

They guided me along a corridor, which had several doors leading off it, which, I could only assume was offices, until we passed a stone staircase leading upwards and then two steps later, a similar staircase leading down. I was instructed to go down the steps, and in front of me along a corridor there was a large door, I was to remove my coat and place it on the hanger provided, then I was to simply knock and wait to be let in.

Yves pecked me on the cheek and told me to enjoy and make the most of my hour, as he turned I watched him, brandy in hand follow the station chief up the stairs.

With a big breath and a little trepidation, I descended the curving stone stairway until I reached the bottom, and as instructed walked slowly but purposefully along the corridor towards the large wooden door. With another huge breath I took my final opportunity and reached into my coat pocket and took a big sniff in each nostril of my poppers, which I'd secretly put there earlier. Immediately I felt the rush and the rapid feeling of euphoria sweep through me as I slipped the coat off and hung it carefully on the quilted hanger. I stood for a good thirty seconds, naked apart from the boots and a string of pearls, absorbing a few pre climax tremors that had started hitting me in between my thighs. My whole groin started to throb and my pussy was already drenched in anticipation. I knew the time had come to knock and reveal my entertainment.

There was an antique knocker on the door, which with an unsteady hand I grasped and gave two quick raps and waited. Seconds later the door was opened by a very dark muscular man wearing only a pair of firefighters bottoms and a very seductive smile, he took my hand and kissed it and said "Bonsoir Madame". He led me through an archway, into a large communal changing area, where I was confronted by a group of handsome muscular firefighters, all smiling at me, and all only wearing towels. I noticed very quickly that off to one side was a large group shower area, and I glimpsed a couple of rather well endowed men closest to the entrance showering and lathering themselves. I found this a massive turn on and felt my vagina start to ache greedily. I was immediately made to feel at ease, as I was introduced to them by the man who was still holding my hand, who then grinned and in French said "we are your present" as he tweaked my hard brown nipples. As one the group of men exclaimed "tres belle, magnifique" I felt myself rapidly relax into this wholly debauched scenario. Any trepidation I had swiftly disappeared, as they all removed their towels. Many already were aroused and were proudly exhibiting their endowments for me to appraise. They swiftly surrounded me, all stroking and playing with me from all sides, hands were everywhere, with fingers skillfully entering me. I could hear my wetness as many different men played with me, opening me up and pinching my clitoris and fingering my anus. The sight and feeling of having fingers from three different men inside my stretching my sex was astounding. I was quickly offered two different sets of fingers to suck on whilst I began to orgasm, I quickly started to squirt profusely as a shuddering climax hit and my juices splashed loudly on to the tiled floor, mixing with the wetness already there from the showers. It was like all my wildest fantasies rolled into one. A few of the guys climbed and stood on the bench beside me and offered me their large erect members to suck, I slurped and sucked on them ravenously, one, two, three at a time! Occasionally gagging, as the sheer amount of man-meat was overwhelming, and I wanted to devour as much as I physically could! It was mind-blowing; my climaxes were coming in rapid succession as my pussy and anus were being skillfully manipulated by several of the men. I noticed the two men from the shower and another I hadn't seen were now stood nearby watching and obviously enjoying the scene, as they slowly stroked their very impressive erections. Also the gentleman, who'd led me in, was now naked and had begun flexing one extremely large and beautifully sculptured penis. After I quick assessment, I realized I was at the mercy of nine of Paris's finest firefighters. I pledged to myself that they'd all be well and truly satisfied before the sixty minutes were up! I made it abundantly clear to them that I was theirs to use as they saw fit!

After seemingly gorging on all these exquisite cocks, which were continually being thrust into my mouth, I was picked up and unceremoniously carried to another bench, where I was gently lowered on to the man who had originally greeted me. I could feel his huge penis begin to stretch me, as I was slowly impaled on him inch by inch…. I can remember letting out a scream of joyous ecstasy as my vagina yielded to his immense length. I immediately had my screams stifled by another large penis being placed into my willing mouth. I continually had a wide choice of cocks to suck on and didn't waste anytime pleasing them all…there'd be time to breathe later! I was soon lifted and placed on all fours and ferociously fucked from behind, whilst having my bottom slapped and various fingers playing simultaneously with both my clitoris and anus. It was a testosterone overload. They were all taking turns to penetrate me, showing off to each other as to how hard they could pound me, it was sublime…. I just kept gushing as they all took turns in fucking me. I lost all sense of time and was away on a different planet, as various cocks would shower my face with sperm while others would ejaculate deep into my throat. I remember at one stage lying back on the bench playing with my clitoris and squirting over a mans waiting tongue, whilst four guys masturbated over my face and breasts, all covering me in their hot semen. I even saw cum dripping off the tops of my new boots. Then before I knew it, I was lifted and lowered onto yet another waiting cock and someone held my cheeks apart, whilst his colleague slowly entered my anus…. pain, pleasure, pleasure, pain…all became one amazingly lustful sensation as I was simultaneously taken in both orifices by two very skilled men. The others watched admiringly and stroked themselves in appreciation.

After a period of intense, deep penetration, I felt the two men ejaculate inside me, and I was overcome with this new sensation of hot semen being delivered deep into both vagina and anus at the same time. I screamed as my orgasm mixed with theirs. I felt used, abused and wonderfully fulfilled. After a short break my boots were removed and I was forced to kneel whilst three final men used my mouth for their pleasure, until one after the other they unloaded their cum into my willing mouth, saturating my face with copious amounts of their sticky sperm... filthy I know, but oh such fun! To a round of applause and whistles I was carried into the shower area, where I was soaped up and literally hosed down until I was eventually restored to a clean and pristine condition. It was a perfect finish, when several of them towelled me dry before leading me back to the door to retrieve my coat. I needed just a few moments to compose myself, before climbing the stone stairway to be met and quietly applauded by Yves, who said "You have earned a large drink my dear"..... He wasn't wrong there!

Bruno was waiting outside to whisk us away, but with one final act of debauchery, we stopped off at the Ritz and went in, where I had a rather large and welcome Jack Daniels on ice, I took a sip and sucked a cube of ice into my mouth, and after replacing the drink on the table, I discreetly moved the coat to one side and opened my legs, so Yves could see my well used pussy. I retrieved the ice cube from my mouth and rubbed it over my hot aching labia and clitoris before inserting it. I grinned innocently at Yves and said "it just needs cooling down"! We casually finished our drinks and left smiling.

I was very glad to eventually climb into bed and drift of into a heavenly deep sleep.

These brave firefighters have entertained me on many separate occasions over the years, and I also shared them with a few special select female friends. In fact on one evening both Sarah and I were their guests of honour, after several of them had received medals for bravery at an awards ceremony, and they wanted to celebrate afterwards in their own special way! There were at least half a dozen more at this little soiree, much to both Sarah and my pleasure.

Chapter Thirty-Three: Sarah's Initiation (Paris Style)

A had very little to do until I had to meet Sarah at the Eurostar arrivals area at La Gare du Nord later that afternoon. So I had a leisurely breakfast in the bar opposite and went and did a little bit of present shopping for the children. I popped in briefly to see Frederic and picked up the couple of items that Yves had asked me if I could get for the evening.

Yves rang and told me everything had been confirmed regarding Sarah's first night surprise, and that it was all scheduled for ten o'clock. He suggested that I took Sarah to dinner near the apartment, as Bruno would be picking us up at nine forty-five. Precisely, as always! You could set your watch by him, which is funny as he is half Swiss.

Sarah's train was spot on time, and we were soon on the way back to the apartment, both speaking ten to the dozen trying to catch up. We just dropped her bags and my shopping at the apartment, which when I gave her a quick tour around she gasped in awe and said "what does a girl have to do to get this?!, I laughed and said, "I'll tell all over a drink".

As we'd just sat down in my now customary outside pavement table and ordered our drinks my mobile chimed, it was Yves with a suggestion that he would meet us for dinner at seven-thirty, as he'd finished all his business earlier than expected and if it was okay by us he'd book a table somewhere pleasant. All agreed I said Sarah was looking forward to meeting him and we'd see him later.

Sarah was really excited, as she said that Mike had given her "carte blanche" to enjoy herself as she saw fit. Once I'd told her about my week so far she was squirming in her seat with envy. I put my fingers to my lips and said "sshh" and got out my mobile phone and found Nikolas's number in my contacts list and called. The look on Sarah's face was a joy when she heard me say "Hello it's your Tuesday evening client, my friend Sarah is in town and she'd would like a very similar massage as myself, in fact identical!. She nearly came on the spot when I ended the call by saying "fine I'll bring her along at three-tomorrow afternoon". She got even more aroused and frustrated when she asked what was planned for later and I just tapped the side of my nose and said surprise, you'll have to wait and see! It was lovely just sitting, relaxing and having a good long girlie chat over a few drinks and watching the world go by, whilst every five minutes Sarah, upon seeing a good looking guy walk past, would comment " I would oh I so would".

We both had fun getting ready and Sarah was in a flap as what to she was going to wear, and after much deliberation decided to wear a very understated, black silk cocktail dress, which certainly showed her figure off. I gave her a pair of sexy hold-ups to compliment the dress. I wore my new Azzedine Alaia outfit…. we were "ebony and ivory" and most definitely in the mood for the night ahead. I was going to take a bit of a back seat and let Sarah enjoy all the fun and attention, that I knew she was craving, also my limbs still ached pleasantly from all the sexual gymnastic exertions with the "firefighters" less than twenty-four hours earlier.

Bruno collected us and informed me that Yves was already at the restaurant, as he'd met an old colleague for an early evening drink.

We arrived only a few minutes later, at a wonderful old traditional Parisian eatery called "Au Pied de Cochon" on Rue Coquillière. It is hugely popular with both locals and tourists alike, who all get drawn in by the vast array of seafood/shellfish on display outside, all looking mouthwatering piled up on large beds of ice.

Yves saw us and made great overtures as I entered with Sarah just behind, trying to keep up, whilst at the same time trying to take it all in. Yves greeted Sarah like an old friend and I could see by the twinkle in his eyes that he was loving the admiring glances of the other diners and casual drinkers, especially when our coats were taken and Yves took a step back and approvingly clasped his hands together and exclaimed "Ah my two favourite Mistresses", and winked as he got some envious looks from many of the men. There was much good hearted laughter, when one man nearby said "Bravo and good luck, shall we keep a doctor on stand-by for later when these beautiful creatures put too much pressure on your old ticker". Yves loved the attention and it was obvious many people recognized him. Sarah was looking slightly bemused by it all, and very unsubtly knocked her glass of champagne back in one.

We were shown to our table and a complimentary bottle of Moet was brought, much to the delight of Sarah, whom I sensed was in a complete state of mental overload, her mind was racing. We all shared the magnificent "Royal Seafood Platter", followed by one of the house specialties, Sea Bream grilled with sliced fennel and orange. Delicate, mouth wateringly tasty, and at Yves's insistence, Crêpes flambéed with Grand Manier at the table as the finale.

Throughout the next few hours we both teased Sarah regarding her forthcoming surprise.. She was so excited, but we didn't give her any clues! During the meal, when Yves had popped to the bathroom, she sneakily showed me a fresh vial of poppers Mike had given her for the trip and asked would she be needing it tonight, she gave me a huge lecherous grin when I said, "you definitely will".

Bruno was waiting for us as usual outside, and once the staff had all bowed and scrapped, saying their farewells, more to Yves than us, we departed to begin Sarah's surprise. Bruno wound his way along the Rue Rivoli, onto the Champs Elysee, which added to Sarah's excitement. Her head was spinning taking in the sights from the comfort of the limousine. Also the shot of cognac Yves had poured from the mini-bar accentuated the occasion. Shortly after passing L'Arc de Triumphe we took a turning into a very grand residential street and abruptly entered our final destination through a set of security gates, onto a short gravel drive and parking area. Bruno was out quickly to see us from the car and with a discreet wink wished us both a pleasant soiree!

There on the porch to welcome us, were my old "friends", the decadent French aristocratic couple, Hugo and Reine, who had hosted the masked ball, the owner of the house Jean Paul with a very attractive woman in tow, who was around my age called Flavie. We were greeted in usual Paris fashion with over the top kisses and hugs and general "bon homie". We went through to a very elegant drawing room, where a young oriental housemaid served drinks. Yves took me to one side and asked had I brought the items and explained what I was required to do. I was getting aroused just listening to what was about to unfold. But was fully confident that Sarah would handle it all with aplomb.

After a few drinks and a lot of good-natured flirting with many double entendres, all aimed at Sarah, who was loving being the centre of attraction, the host Jean Paul announced Sarah's surprise was ready and waiting. This was my cue; I took Sarah by the hand and we followed him out of the room and went down a stairway to the basement. We passed a couple of closed doorways, until we reached one, which was open, and he showed us in and indicated to another door, which was padded and said to Sarah "that her entertainment was through that door when she was ready". He gave me a wicked little smile as he left.

    I helped Sarah out of her dress and panties, until she stood in front of me naked, except for her heels and hold-ups. I admired her flawless body and completely smooth pubic area for a moment. Then, I produced from my handbag, the leather studded "Slut collar and chain-link leash", she gasped with pleasure as I put it around her neck and fastened it, and she trembled with expectation as I attached the leash. I told her now would be a good time to have a little sniff of her amyl, it turned into one big inhalation, which I could tell had an instant effect, hugely enhanced as I slipped on the black velvet blindfold. She was now ready and prepared for her "Parisian" initiation!

    I took her by the leash, and walked her to the large padded door and opened it, the room was lit perfectly for the occasion, it had a full-length mirror running along one entire wall, much like a dance studio. Then, as instructed by Yves, I led her to the large velvet cushion that was in the middle of the room, immediately in front of the large raised circular bed. I knelt her down and whispered in her ear "enjoy, but I'm here if you need me". When the door at the far end opened and in walked my "slave" from the masked party, I was surprised, as Yves had kept his attendance a secret from me. Following him, were three more equally stunning black men, all four of their bodies glistening with oil. They were all in a semi erect state and all wearing leather and chrome "cock rings" which, only enhanced their massive organs even more. It was an awesome sight; one I knew Sarah would take full advantage of, as her love of all things "black" knew no bounds.

    I grinned at them, and they grinned at me as they silently lined up in front of her. I stood her up with a gentle tug on her leash, and watched as the men silently admired her body, gently stroking her breasts and bottom, whilst they appraised her, occasionally giving her nipples a firm pinch and her bottom a gentle slap…. I could sense her first climax building as they quietly discussed between themselves, what they were going to do with her. I translated for her as best I could and she shuddered as an intense orgasm ripped through her. I then knelt her back down and crouched beside her and whispered in her ear, "this is my gift to you" as I removed the blindfold. The effect was shattering and immediate, as four over-sized erect black cocks confronted her, only inches from her grasp...she whimpered a "thank you" as I turned and left. Leaving her at the mercy of these truly magnificent male specimens.

As I left the ante room Yves was waiting for me in the hallway, and guided me through another door way, along a short corridor, which led through to a long and narrow room with sofas and armchairs. I should have guessed, we were on the other side of the mirror with a full panoramic view of the events unfolding. Our drinks had been refreshed and brought down to us, as we got comfortable and decadently prepared to watch and comment on Sarah's performance...... Which was truly magnificent, the more they gave her the more she wanted. They had more than met their match, they had her in trouble on a few occasions as they penetrated her savagely in both her holes, but her body quickly adapted and accommodated their huge members. It was a strange sensation watching, but not hearing anything apart from a few very muffled screams. At one time, she was trying to get two of them into her mouth at once, whilst straddling number three with number four ruthlessly pounding into her anus. I found it erotic to watch, but was worried she'd get lockjaw, as she was going at them with such vigour and determination!

Yves was very impressed by the power and wetness of Sarah's orgasms, and I explained, that her husband Michael, was in fact the man who turned on my G spot and my ability to ejaculate almost on command. He was very interested in Michael's technique and we laughed when Yves said he could make a fortune in Paris if he set up a "G spot clinic", catering to Parisian society ladies of a certain standing!

I could sense that Reine and Flavie were itching to join in the action, and get their hands on those black bodies, so after about an hour of Sarah having all the pleasure, it was decided, that if the ladies wished they should go and help her.... not that she needed any, she was coping admirably. Trying not to show their eagerness, both the ladies sipped their drinks, waiting to see who would give in and go first. Eventually it got too much for Reine, and she scooted off in the direction of the room, followed microseconds later by Flavie. I discreetly shook my head, when Yves looked to see if I was going to follow and raised my glass for a top up. He understood that my previous evenings activities had taken their toll, and I just needed to chill out and be a voyeur for a while.

In double time the door to the room opened, and Flavie and Reine entered, both naked, except for their heels. Flavie had an extraordinary body with small pert breasts and large hard chocolate brown nipples, Reine on the other hand, whilst in very good shape was showing her age, which I put at mid to late fifties, but when it came to sexual enthusiasm, she behaved like a woman twenty years younger, encouraging the men to fuck her in a great variety of gymnastic like positions. Sarah took a well-earned break. I handed her a much needed large and refreshing Vodka and Tonic that I'd asked the waitress to make. She fully understood, when I told her I was taking a rain check on the fun, due to my antics the previous evening. Cheeky bitch called me a "Light weight". I'd make her suffer at a later date for that remark!

I rejoined the men, who were intently watching their ladies getting pleasured by these strapping, black fucking machines. I thanked them all for arranging such a lovely evening for my friend. They said it was a pleasure and it made it all worthwhile seeing the look of sheer joy on Sarah's face. They saw it as their duty to ensure their ladies had pleasure, in any way they desired. I thought that was such a civilized attitude, one that I wholeheartedly agreed with. As the sexual shenanigans were winding down our host had cheese and fruit served with a large balloon of a fine smooth reserve cognac.

Sarah couldn't thank everybody enough; she was high on life and sex in particular as we said our farewells. Bruno was waiting with the doors open, ready to whisk us back to the apartment. I whispered my appreciation and thanks to Yves as we were pulling up; he put his hand on my knee and told me I deserved everything and more, a really sweet sentiment.

We watched as they drove off into the distance, and we decided to have a nightcap in the bar opposite. Sarah was beaming, she ordered us two brandies and we indulged in a few St Moritz cigarettes. She proceeded to tell me what happened when I'd left her in the room with the black men, I suddenly realized, she had no idea we'd been watching her performance from behind the two way mirror. She gasped with delight, as I explained that we'd seen it all, she giggled, as I told her she represented us "English ladies with style and panache". Her performance was nothing short of exemplary.

After a good sleep I took her for a lovely lazy brunch and generally showed her around the local designer shops for a few hours, before taking her to Le Marais to see the operation and to meet Frederic and Michel. All throughout the morning she couldn't stop talking about her evening and how it was all her secret desires becoming a reality, and that she was now looking forward to her encounter with Nikolas.

I introduced her around the office, showing her the design and manufacture area, that had by now expanded even further and we'd leased more space to cater for the continued rise in demand, for both the outfits and the incredibly popular range of accessories/toys. I could see both the boys' eyes light up when I introduced her to them. They both sat silent and open mouthed, in both admiration and astonishment, while she happily recounted her evening to them, no blushing or shyness with Sarah! I could see they both would love the opportunity to give her the same "treatment" that they'd given me when they'd first come to London. Before we left I told them we'd be going to L'escapade later that evening after dinner, and it would be great if they could join us. They immediately accepted the invitation, and told Sarah to have a look in the stockroom and pick herself an outfit to wear to the club, which was a lovely gesture. Between us we picked an (in)appropriate "crowd pleasing" number.

I'd arranged with Claudia and Olivier that we'd meet up for dinner, as they wanted to meet up with Sarah again, as it had been a good few years since they'd last met. I'd also invited Thierry, as I'd not seen him in nearly a year.

We popped into a little bar for a coffee and a cognac, before I took her to St Germain for her massage. I introduced her to the delights of Pastis with ice and water.

The cab dropped us outside Nikolas's studio. Sarah was flushed with excitement as he welcomed us in, winking at me very obviously. I made the introductions, and before I left I discreetly slipped him the fee for the massage. I arranged for him to put her in a taxi after the session was over, and to have her dropped off at L'escapade, where I was headed for a few hours, to have a girlie gossip with Amanda and enjoy a relaxing drink.

I left her smiling, and headed off. I window-shopped during the pleasant fifteen-minute stroll to the Ile Saint Louis and the club.

I sat for a while on a bench overlooking the Seine and managed to get hold of Paul and give him a brief outline of the week so far, he said he was looking forward to his evening with Mike and Antonia. I told him that I was looking forward to hearing all about it when we were alone on Sunday evening. A huge smile crossed my face as I noticed a "River Seine" Firefighter boat cruising along, patrolling the river.

Amanda was on top form and full of some outrageous stories of a few of the choicer moments and outrageous happenings at the club since my last visit. She looked forward to seeing Sarah when she arrived, as she thought she remembered her from before, when she and Mike had been on a previous visit. My original stock of champagne long since gone, I arranged with Amanda to run me a tab, as the evening was my treat and I told her that my partners Frederic and Michel may arrive before me, so make sure they were looked after!

She told me, that the club had gone from strength to strength, and they'd now taken on a young barman to help Costas and a hostess called Pascale to oversee the general proceedings. They worked on Thursday, Friday and Saturday nights, so I'd get to meet them later. After a chatting for a good few hours the buzzer went, and there on the CCTV monitor was Sarah, looking flushed if not a little disheveled!

It transpired that Amanda did recognize Sarah and embraced her warmly and ran of down to the bar to get her a requested and much needed Vodka and Tonic. Sarah spent the next eternity extolling Nikolas's skills and how she was in love with his hands! And another important part of his anatomy! I was astounded, when she coyly told me she'd booked yet another massage for two o'clock the following day. I admired her stamina, but recalled what I was like in the early years. Simply cramming in as much fun as possible in the time available! I'd since found myself in such a position, that I could pace myself, safe in the knowledge that everything would still be there the next day/week or month.

Eventually Sarah stopped talking, drew breath and took a large gulp of her drink, when a stunning looking guy turned up.... I looked at her and shook my head and firmly said "No, Sarah no time", she put on her sad face, but then grinned, as I told her we'd be returning later after dinner and she could run riot then, but now we needed to get back to the apartment and get ready to meet Thierry, Claudia and Olivier. Amanda called us a taxi; we finished our drinks just as it arrived.

Thierry rang to confirm and arranged to meet at the apartment as he had a few gifts for me, and a small present for Sarah. Also Claudia was bringing her club outfit with her, so us ladies could come back to the apartment after dinner to dress more (in)appropriately for our soiree at L'Escapade.

Upon our arrival back at the apartment, I immediately saw that Bruno had been, as there, on the table was a card and a small gift for Sarah from Yves, and a little note telling me to look on the bedroom bureau. Sarah opened her gift excitedly, and to her astonishment inside was a very exquisite pair of pearl earrings from Cartier. The card simply said "In memory of a very entertaining evening, Yves". We were both stunned at the unexpected show of generosity. She rang him and left a message on his answerphone, thanking him profusely, and saying she'd thoroughly enjoyed being of service. Filthy little minx!

I went into the bedroom to find another Cartier gift box, nestling inside was a most wonderful 18ct gold " Cartier Love Bracelet with matching screwdriver". I immediately put it on and with the screwdriver locked it in place; it has rarely been off my wrist since that day! I knew I'd be thanking him at some stage soon, in the only way I knew he liked. This relationship has never ceased to thrill me, and we have never stopped pushing the boundaries of both our imaginations. His vision and ability to be so in tune with my needs and desires, and always fulfilling them, is a true gift. Also, his amazing capacity to turn even the most outrageous fantasy into reality at the "flick of a switch" is outstanding, a most enviable skill.

Both Sarah and I dressed casually chic for dinner, in simple cocktail dresses, with Sarah proudly wearing her earrings.

Thierry arrived bearing gifts as promised, which once again piqued Sarah's excitement levels as he presented her with a very nice

Chanel sampler gift box. She thanked him by draping herself around his neck and giving him an over-enthusiastic kiss…not that he was complaining!

As for me, he'd brought me a few essential top ups that he expected I'd be needing, but the pièce de résistance was a magnificent black Chanel Vintage Quilted CC-clasp handbag. It is still to this day my personal favourite. It possesses enduring quality and style.

Claudia and Olivier rang from the bar opposite announcing their arrival. We joined them minutes later for a pre-dinner drink. They were pleased to see Sarah and wanted to hear what she'd been up to in Paris….where to start?! We decided to return to "Au Pied de Cochon" as the food was so good, and the atmosphere is always very loud and fun. It's an ideal location for a group get-together.

Thierry was in his element, sat in between Sarah and Claudia and they were both fully playing up to him, with Sarah flirting wildly. Olivier and I were reminiscing about "Au Dix Bis". They'd been recently, and Olivier said he'd often thought fondly about our liaison there, all those years ago! It was a great fun start to the evening, very raucous good-natured banter, with Sarah getting frustrated, when we all spoke French whilst giving her knowing looks! Claudia was pleased that I'd taken her advice and visited Nikolas, and thought it most amusing that Sarah had experienced it earlier, and had re-booked already. As usual I remained very tight-lipped regarding my relationship with Yves, and thankfully everyone respected my discretion. Sarah would occasionally make in inappropriate comment and would look suitably chastised by just a stern look from me!

Olivier and Thierry decided they'd take a walk to the club, leaving us girls to return to the apartment to get our clubbing outfits on and we'd meet them there. This was the easiest solution regarding the taxi situation.

Claudia's outfit was very minimalistic, a sheer lace body stocking, with a very short ra-ra skirt to wear on top, just to initially cover the strategically cut away area and keep her modesty intact.

Sarah looked amazing in her new outfit - courtesy of my boys; it was a tight fitting black satin dress, which had many strategically placed zips, so it could become very revealing in an instant. It was very effective and a real head-turner.

I wore a white "showgirl" tailcoat, to show off my tan, with a tiny white and pearl string thong. I matched this with a pair of turquoise platform heels. We were now ready for some fun!

When we entered Amanda told me everyone had arrived and that the club was already fairly busy. As usual there was lots of heads turning, and appreciative eyes following us down as we descended the stairway. I flashed my thong at Thierry, much to his delight!

Amanda introduced us to Pascale, and the gorgeous new barman François. Drinks were already flowing and Frederic and Michel were in high spirits and made a beeline for Sarah, and complimented her on how wildly tempting she looked in her outfit. Everyone was introduced and re-introduced to each other; we all raised our glasses and toasted to "a night to remember".

Sarah absolutely loved all the flirtatious attention from the guys, not just the ones in our group, but also many of the handsome younger men drinking at the bar...she was like a kid in a sweet shop! Pascale was turning out to be a great addition to proceedings, ensuring everything ran smoothly, she made sure the dance floor was always busy, she'd often drag us all for a "boogie". This always guaranteed a number of men watching and encouraging the ladies to be more and more daring and outrageous. There was lots of comings and goings through the drapes to the rear fun rooms. It was a great crowd, and the men were very respectful and made sure that it was all about the "ladies" pleasure.

As I thought, the first one into the action was Sarah, whom I saw busily engaged, and by the sound of it thoroughly enjoying the attentions of both Frederic and Michel in my favoured gated room. They were dispensing some of their well-practiced tag-team moves on her. When Michel returned to the bar for a breather, Olivier went to join them. I knew there'd be no holding her back, she was simply rampant! At one stage when I took her a drink she was skillfully riding Olivier, whilst working Frederic's cock with her mouth, she took a long sip of her drink and handed it back to me without breaking her stride...I was impressed by her dexterity, and full commitment to the rather large task in hand.

Thierry and Claudia had disappeared into one of the back rooms to reacquaint themselves, as only the French know how, this left me chatting at the bar with the new barman François, as Michel was deep in conversation with Pascale. He was twenty-six and came from a town in the South West of France and had been in Paris for two years. He was by day a self-employed interior designer, who was slowly building a reputation in Paris for his creative work. I told him a brief synopsis of my situation, which he was enthralled by and wanted to hear more. Further into the conversation he expressed to me of his interests in the BDSM scene and told me of an intriguing sounding club called "Chateau de Lys" in the 18th arrondissement. The club fully catered for people who were into the more adventurous fetish side of life. He invited me to his apartment the following afternoon for a drink and to see his latest design project, saying that he'd explain more about the club then, as he could tell I was intrigued. I tentatively said yes, but would ring to confirm at midday. I thought it could be fun, and it coincided with Sarah's return match with Nikolas the masseur!

They say a club is only as good as its clientele, and this particular night went a long way to confirming this general assumption. The mix of couples and singles was dynamic, with everyone in tune with each other. At one stage whilst seeking out Sarah, to check on her current status, I found myself in a brief but very sensuous encounter with a very attractive woman, who with no words spoken took my face in her hands and started to lick my lips and probe my mouth with her very lively tongue. I automatically responded and soon found myself in a very passionate and sensual clinch. We maneuvered each other into a secluded corner of the dance floor, partially obscured by a stone pillar, which she had pushed me up against. With much fervent kissing she slid a hand between my thighs, and without any hesitation I moved my legs apart to signal my willingness for her to continue. I was already very aroused and as she stroked the pearls on my thong I could feel myself starting to tremble. As she eased my thong down, I jiggled a bit and it fell completely to the floor enabling me to step out of it. In no time her deft stroking and probing had me in the throes orgasm, she increased the urgency and intensity of her probing as I came powerfully and wetly over her slender fingers. I stepped back slightly, so I could repay the pleasure, she let out a moan, as between us we removed her panties, and as my fingers found her exposed clitoris she started to gyrate her hips and ferociously thrust herself on my hand as she began her own potent climax. The whole encounter was made even more carnal, as now, just a step away was a young guy watching intently, whilst slowly masturbating his rather impressive erection. We all were at a high level of arousal, intensifying our gratification by watching each other's sexual play. It didn't take long for him to join in with our games, he was definitely ambidextrous, as he played and pleasured us simultaneously, whilst we both stroked his granite like penis. It was a frantic few minutes of pure sexual abandon between three total strangers, whose sole intention was giving each other enjoyment and sexual fulfillment. The whole dynamic between the three of us was electric, with each person egging on the other, to more and more extreme levels of indulgent delight

 Eventually, between us we brought our male cohort to the point of no return, and as I continued to stroke him my mysterious lady knelt down in a flash to accept his fast approaching climax into her open mouth, culminating in her looking up at us both and lewdly licking her lips, waiting in anticipation for her reward. I always was and still today am in wonderment and have total respect when people adjourn to the bar as if nothing had happened, with that look of complete innocence…. Remarkable, as I'm sure I always look as guilty as sin!

 Eventually, with most of the groups desires taken care of, we all decided to have a farewell drink whilst waiting for the taxis and agreed to meet at a traditional Parisian late night watering hole, to round of the evenings entertainment, Michel knew just the spot, called the "Café Charbon", situated on the ever-bustling Rue Oberkampf, the Café/Bar is according to Michel an institution that has been attracting nocturnal Parisians for more than a century. First opened in 1900 in what was then an artisan's quarter, this café dates from the Second Empire of Napoleon III and has all the style of the brasseries of another era, with its shiny bar, red banquettes, tarnished mirrors and high ceilings. It catered to a very mixed clientele. Michel ordered everyone a large balloon of cognac and a large plate of cheeses and warm crusty bread. Sarah's face was a delight, what with the cognac and all four men still playing up to her, whilst Claudia and I looked on. A perfect end to a wonderful evening with good friends! And I couldn't help but wonder if Paul and Mike had entertained Antonia with such aplomb…I was sure they'd made sure she was more than satisfied.

Once back at the apartment, Sarah kept us both awake, verbally reliving her day and evening…yet again. Eventually, we both managed to sneak in a good six hours sleep, only to be woken up at half past ten by Yves apologizing that he would not be able to see us that day as he had to attend to some family business in the South of France and his helicopter was waiting. He asked to say "au revoir" to Sarah and he hoped he'd see her soon, along with as he had christened him "Mike-Le Legende de Le Digit". He gave me Bruno's number if we needed anything, or to be driven anywhere. I said a huge thank you for my bracelet and told him that I was always at his disposal and to say a massive thank you to the fire chief, and I'd be back for more!

Chapter Thirty-Four: The Aspiring Bitch

    I put some coffee on, and whilst waiting for it to filter through I took the bull by the horns and called François to confirm I'd visit at two o'clock, whilst Sarah was at her massage. He seemed very pleased and gave me the address, which turned out to be only a short cab ride away, in an area near Montmartre, called Place de Clichy.

    Once coffee's and showers were completed, we ambled across the road to the bar and upped the sugar levels with two large plates of crepes, one with sugar and lemon, the other with a divine rich chocolate sauce…. an absolute winner every time, especially if accompanied by a strong black coffee and a cognac. It is the ultimate way to rejuvenate, after a grueling Parisian night out. I'd thoroughly recommend it to anyone. The effect is immediate… a sugar rush extraordinaire!

    We went back to change for our varying liaisons and I gave Sarah the full addresses to give to the taxi driver, both the apartment and Nikolas's business card. With instructions to meet me in the bar opposite if I wasn't back…. and no wandering off!

    I decided to look casual, but slightly alluring, so I decided to wear a pair of new Ralph Lauren skintight black jodhpurs, with a soft cream cashmere, loose, off the shoulder jumper, finished with the black patent thigh boots Yves had bought me. I saw Sarah off in her taxi, then quickly put on my coat, locked up and hailed my own and was quickly on my way to see young François.

    He lived in an attic apartment, decorated in a very modern minimalist style. He welcomed me eagerly, and took my coat; my attire instantly impressed him. Heaping praise upon the boots, saying I must wear them when I accompany him to "Chateau de Lys". He poured us both a large Pastis, with ice and water. He proceeded to show me some of the latest designs he had been commissioned to work on, by a company who were reforming an old building into six apartments. It was all very modern and tasteful with fine use of space. However, it wasn't long until he started telling me about the club, he said it was close by, behind Montmartre, in a beautiful thirteenth century building with a tower and many themed fetish rooms with lots of relevant BDSM equipment. It attracted a mixed crowd, where people went to explore their submissive or dominant side. He wanted, in fact, insisted we went together on my next visit. I was fascinated and to his delight I tentatively agreed. He explained that he was a submissive and his fetish and obsession was being dominated by older women.... well, that's me I thought! He told me about one lady in particular, who he visited occasionally, who insisted on him being naked, on all fours, whilst she sat on his back and masturbated herself with a large black dildo, stopping to spank him every so often with a leather paddle. I told him I'd never acted in this role before, as usually I was the one being dominated. He asked if I'd like to try, and I decided it would be fun and agreed, thinking he meant at the club! I was wrong on that assumption, when he disappeared briefly to an adjoining room, returning a few minutes later with a large travel chest on wheels.... he called it his "box of many moods". I realized he was working under the assumption of "no time like the present". I was now very inquisitive and my interest was piqued, as he explained to me what some of the things were, and in what situation they'd be used...it was all new to me and definitely an exciting diversion from my normal kind of sensual amusement.

    I agreed to have a trial run dominating him, starting softly with handcuffs and leg dividers. At his suggestion, I went to the bathroom and undressed, leaving only my boots on. Standing there naked, instantly made me very wet and aroused. I returned to the lounge area to find him stood naked, with a very large erection, adorned with a leather cock and ball harness, which accentuated his arousal even more so. He told me to handcuff him and fit him with the leg spreaders, which once accomplished, he instructed me to paddle his bottom and generally use him as I wished. He encouraged me to be vocal and forceful, which at first was difficult, but after another large Pastis it all became a bit more fluid, and I actually found myself incredibly turned on, having this strapping twenty-six year old at my mercy. I soon started to enjoy myself, making him kneel, albeit awkwardly in front of me. I forcefully ordered him lick my boots, each one in turn. He relished this and was soon licking and sucking on both the heel and toe of each boot, and running his tongue up and down my legs. I went to the box and retrieved the collar and chain that I'd noticed; very similar to the one Sarah had worn. I gently secured it around his neck. I made him continue licking my boots and, as a treat every so often I'd pull the leash, so his face was opposite my groin and I'd make him to beg to lick my vagina, lewdly calling it "my wet cunt", I didn't let him immediately…I wanted him to really grovel in front of me. I would let him get just close enough to allow him to sniff at me and breathe in my scent for a moment, then gently slap him back down. He adored it and was saying that I was a natural and encouraging me to continue. The Pastis was making me feel much more adventurous and I kept him prostrate and powerless on the floor, with his erection throbbing intensely, due to the tightly fitted cock ring. He groaned with joy each time I slapped it. His cock was standing proud, glistening as a huge amounts of his pre-cum ran down it's shaft. I dominantly walked around him, then stood above him, legs apart, so he could look up at me exposing and casually stroking my vagina, whilst he was restrained - totally helpless! It was a feeling of pure unbridled power over another human being, albeit a handsome and hugely aroused Frenchman. Our eyes were locked together as I opened myself up to him, showing him my wetness, exposing my clitoris fully, slipping a finger in teasingly, bending down occasionally and making him taste the juices on my fingers. I made great play in deciding out loud how I was going to punish him next, and what I was going to make him do to me. I was bringing myself to the crest of orgasm time after time, letting it subside, building myself slowly to one long powerful ejaculation. I instantly knew that in my handbag I had a little something that I could bring to the party. I promptly retrieved my little vial and saw a look of both joy and terror on his face as I waved it above him, with a shameless look of pure lust in my eyes. I brazenly flicked his erection, with the toe of my boot and firmly ran my heel over his testicles, he moaned with a mixture of fear, passion and pain.

    I left him for a few moments staring at my body, whilst I sat in an armchair and lit a long cool St Moritz whilst sipping my Pastis, continually opening and closing by legs, lewdly fingering my pussy and anus in turn, playfully slapping my lips. The longer it went on, the more confident I became. Playing, teasing and generally frustrating him until I decided it was time for my pleasure.

    I stubbed my cigarette out, and went and stood above him again, all the time asking him if he was thirsty and if he wanted to drink my woman's "holy water". He just gasped in ecstasy and pleaded for me to quench his thirst! I lowered myself slowly into a squat, with my vagina open and inches above his face, I unscrewed the bottle and took a huge sniff, then lifted his head, enabling him to do the same, instantaneously we both ascended into an amyl induced trance like state, both cresting on a climactic sexual wave. I lowered myself further and instructed him to eat me. He was working his tongue over me like a man possessed, sucking and nibbling my swollen labia as I gyrated my hips back and forth, instructing him on which area I wanted him to focus his attentions on next. I turned around, so I was looking down towards his straining wet penis, twitching in desire and need, whilst at the same time demanding that he worked my anus with his unrelenting tongue. It was heavenly feeling his tongue deeply probing and penetrating my rectum. I could soon feel myself bubbling up to a gargantuan orgasm as I took another sneaky snort of my poppers. I swiftly pivoted back around and repositioned my gaping pussy directly above his mouth; I tweaked and rubbed my clitoris, then rapidly released a colossal bone-shaking climax, with squirt after squirt of my juices flooding in to his willing and eager mouth. I was nearly drowning the poor boy; he was swallowing as much as physically possible, but still it was overflowing everywhere. As my orgasm reached its crescendo, I felt a lovely warm sensation hitting my lower back, as he spontaneously ejaculated with me! Jet after jet of his hot, sweet semen exploded from his restrained penis. He came with such ferocity I though he may pass out, his eyes momentarily rolled back into his head; thankfully it was just the sheer gratification of the moment. He continued to lick and nibble me, long after his climax, until my legs simply gave way!

I unleashed him from his restraints and we collapsed together exhausted on the sofa. We both lit a cigarette as he paid tribute to my debut performance in a Dominant role! I felt like taking a bow, but my legs were unable to summon enough energy, so I just kissed his cheek. I made him a promise before I left, that I would attend the club with him on a future visit, as long as he supplied me with a fetish outfit of his choosing...he hastily agreed to this, saying it would be an honour and a privilege.

I had a quick shower before departing and left fully satisfied. I was back just in time to catch Sarah sat outside the bar waiting to order a drink. We both had stories to swap, so a nice long drink was required and promptly ordered.

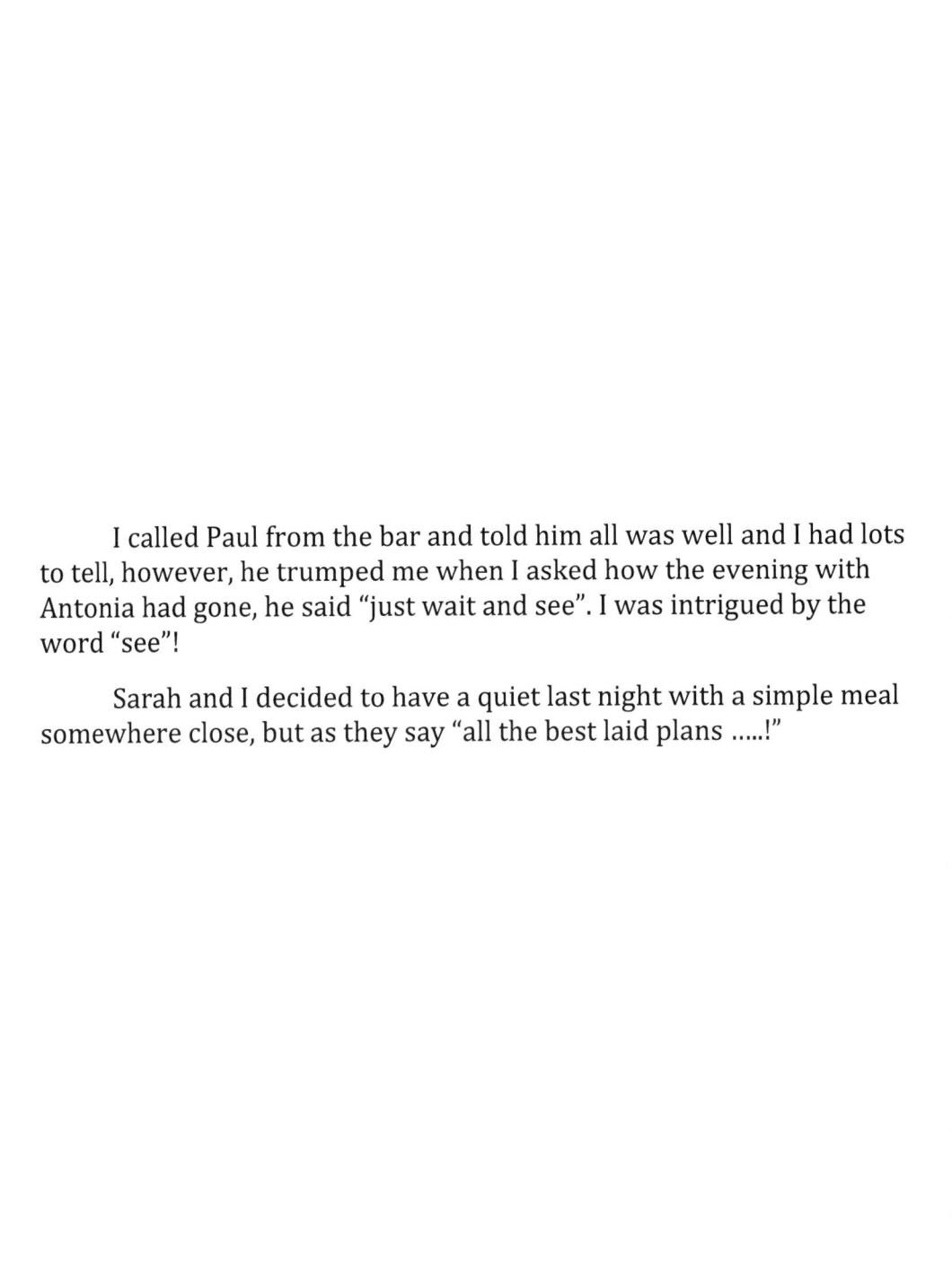

I called Paul from the bar and told him all was well and I had lots to tell, however, he trumped me when I asked how the evening with Antonia had gone, he said "just wait and see". I was intrigued by the word "see"!

Sarah and I decided to have a quiet last night with a simple meal somewhere close, but as they say "all the best laid plans …..!"

Chapter Thirty-Five: Sarah's Grand Finale!

After a few hours power napping back at the apartment we were feeling fully refreshed with any ideas of an early night starting to quickly evaporate over a glass of chilled white wine, as Sarah said, she was getting a second wind and it would be a great shame and such an anti-climax, if her final night in Paris ended in a whimper…she said she'd much prefer a "bang"! Plus she was still in a highly stimulated state after her latest visit to Nikolas!

In a moment of inspiration I telephoned Claudia and mentioned our predicament, she said to give her fifteen minutes and she'd call back, in fact, she called within five minutes with a plan. She'd got the okay from Olivier to have a spontaneous "girlie" night with us. She suggested a new club they'd heard about, but had not visited yet, but was getting many very favourable reviews. I suggested that we all had dinner together and then take a cab to the club, which was a twenty-minute journey. It was called "The Quai17" and was in the 19th arrondissement in the northeast section of Paris. All was agreed that Olivier would drop Claudia off at the apartment at eight-thirty, so we had a nice relaxing hour to get ready, I poured us a glass of wine, whilst we decided on our attire for the evening.

After showering, I couldn't help admire my wrists, Cartier watch on one and the "love band" on the other. Most elegant, and made me feel very special. I'd freshly applied some of my new Chanel Le Vernis nail colour to both toes and fingernails, it was a beautiful vivid shade called "Rose Exubérant ", which came with a matching lip gloss…. now I was definitely feeling my sensuous cravings creeping up on me… again!

Sarah wore a very vibrant patterned body hugging dress, with stylish pair of emerald green suede heels, whilst I went for a more subtle stretchy black, backless mini dress and high black platform heels with the ever present sheer hold-up stockings.

At Claudia's recommendation we went to eat at a fabulous and rammed to the rafters Thai restaurant in the 11th arrondissement, called the "Blue Elephant", for sheer ease we ordered the "degustation menu" for three. Still to this day the most fragrant and tasty Thai food I've had outside of Thailand. The black pepper prawns with lime were to die for! The atmosphere was very lively and the aromas wafting through the restaurant were delicately fresh and aromatic. The two bottles of light fruity wine that was recommended were exceptional. The overall ambience was vibrant and very relaxing. After the superb food we strolled to a small back street bar to take our coffee and brandy, as we didn't want to get to the club too early, we aimed for midnight as this seemed to be the "witching hour". We lost count of the number of suggestive but good natured comments we received from various groups of men out for a wild Saturday night in Paris....We giggled amongst ourselves and all clearly thought "boys, if you only knew!".

    When we did arrive at the club we were given the V.I.P treatment, being three single women, who certainly looked the part. The very attentive and complimentary doorman ushered us in. The place was already quite busy and the manager gave us a guided tour of this large purpose built "adult" theme park. Everything was classy and stylish; there were playrooms of every size and description at every turn. And much to the delight of Sarah there was a large "grope box/glory hole", she squealed with glee when it was pointed out to us. Our host explained that on a Saturday evening there would be about 70% couples and females and 30% single selected males, so we wouldn't be overwhelmed by groups of predatory males. They definitely had it all well organized and beautifully laid out. Also the DJ was excellent and the dance floor was always rocking.

    The three of us started with a large house cocktail, which was gorgeous, but tasted very potent. We were all very quickly in tune with the club and the three of us hit the dance floor and let loose! The DJ kept us dancing as he played a great selection of 80's funk.... Everyone was in a full on party mood. It was a intoxicating mixture of hedonistic eroticism and scantily clad people, all looking to have fun. However, between Claudia and myself we made a pact that we'd keep an eye on Sarah, as she was definitely in the mood for some more fun and games and I didn't want to loose her in Paris on our last night. That would have taken some explaining to Mike.

    There was certainly a wide selection of good-looking men "on offer", and we had a constant stream of admirers chatting to us and refreshing our drinks, generally trying to seduce us into one of the variety of rooms. Then suddenly Claudia and I looked at one another, as two very attractive tall black men appeared at the bar.... We knew it was game over, as Sarah's eyes nearly popped out of her head.... talk about over-eager glances, the manager saw our concern and quietly told Claudia that there was absolutely no problem, as they were members and very nice respectful men, so we could relax...which is exactly what we did!

The club management had a very similar agenda to L'Escapade, in that they were aiming to attract only people with a high degree of social standing and personal hygiene, people who followed the expected behavior and adhered to the club etiquette at all times. They certainly didn't allow entry to just anyone, especially where single men were concerned. This policy seemed to work extremely well.

The club was in full swing by one-thirty, and many of the play areas were being put to good use, and it was good to see there were discreet bowls of "preservatives" strategically placed around all the rooms.

Claudia and I kept a watchful, but unobtrusive eye on Sara, who by this time was in the "harness room" with her two black admirers. She was naked and suspended on a sling like support, which was secured to the ceiling on hooks. She was being rocked rhythmically back and forth, as the men took turns in pleasuring her both with their tongues, hands and their more than impressive black "wife pleasers". There was another couple enjoying the spectacle and were busy making love themselves, as they watched Sarah, lustfully demonstrating one of her loud and powerful climaxes. Luckily, the music and the general level of people experiencing similar scenarios drowned her screams of ecstasy out. A while later, whilst having a little bit of a voyeuristic wander around the rooms, I noticed that the "grope box/glory hole" was a hive of activity, upon closer inspection, I saw Sarah and another attractive blonde girl happily knelt sucking on a variety of penises that were being frantically presented to them through the strategically placed holes. She'd obviously used and discarded her two black admirers and on to pastures new.

I remained a very chaste lady that evening, apart from allowing a very cute younger guy to feast insatiably on my pussy for a short while, as I was still recovering from my time with the firemen! Also I wanted to be on top form for Paul the following evening. Eventually Claudia and I managed to rescue Sarah from one of the group rooms, for one final drink at the bar before our taxi came. We bade the club and its staff farewell and said we'd return.... which, I did on a number of occasions, both with Paul and several times with Claudia.

After dropping Claudia off on the way, we both flopped into our respective beds exhausted and happy. With the prospect of a nice lie-in, followed by a leisurely brunch I drifted of into a deep and much needed sleep.

Over brunch Sarah excitedly told me that the two black guys hosted their own parties in a luxury apartment once or twice a month, where a group of select black men attended to and fulfilled the fantasies of elegant married Parisian ladies. They had swopped contact details and told me they were going to arrange a party in her honour.... This I'd have to see! Her love of black is as strong today as it ever was.

After a relaxing and speedy Eurostar journey back to London it was great to eventually be back home, alone with Paul, where over a glass of wine he told me of his and Mikes evening with Antonia, and much to my entertainment, he accompanied the account with pictures on the computer monitor, which they'd taken with his digital camera... his pride and joy.

Apparently they'd all met up in Chiswick, and gone for a meal at a local Bistro/Wine bar, there was lots of flirting and covert touching going on, Antonia had made a point of telling the boys she'd come prepared and, in her words "had gone commando". Paul told me she took ages to eat her food, as she had to keep stopping to compose herself, as Michael and Paul took it in turns stroking her pussy under the table, bringing her close to climax again and again, stopping just to let her take another mouthful of food. Paul said she was being totally outrageous and both he and Mike were fully encouraging this new exhibitionistic streak she was displaying.

She, according to Paul, insisted, that as Sarah and myself were probably having fun and games in Paris, it would be remiss of her not to deputize for us, and let the boys use her body for a few hours of debauchery. Apparently, once back at our house she was naked before

Paul had opened the wine. He said one thing very rapidly led to another and before long all three were stark naked. Paul was egged on by Mike to get the camera, which resulted in a memory card full of high quality photographs of Mike administering his legendary G Spot massage and the resultant "tap opening" was vividly captured in glorious Technicolor. Once Mike had her at fever pitch, he introduced her to the delights of poppers. Which she took to like a seasoned player, judging by the photos? She was gushing everywhere, and was, judging by all accounts extremely vocal. There were dozens of photos of the boys taking her in every conceivable position, and many great facial close-ups of her ecstasy. The final photo was a comical one, with her lying back covered in the boys semen, holding a piece of A4 paper up with "Didn't I do well?", written on it, and a huge lecherous grin.

Paul and I had a wonderful and prolonged love making session after this visual depiction of their evening, and it got better and better as I was re-living my evening with the firefighters…I just wished I could also have had it also captured on camera (I indeed did, at a later meeting, and put the memory card inside Pauls' forty-third birthday card, as a surprise treat). He thoroughly enjoyed the explicit visual souvenir, and spent many hours looking at and playing with on his Mac. This was the real start of our love affair with all things digital, whether it was photo or video!

Chapter Thirty-Six: Unexpected Turn Of Events

During this period Jon and I had completely re-designed the web site, taking it on a progressive journey, from the initial early format, to a now slick, professional and very user friendly site, a template of which was copied and used by hundreds of other on-line web marketers and designers over the proceeding years. The site was now truly global and orders were being received daily from some of the most unexpected of countries. However, it was a very long time before we got a single order from China, we tried, but rarely even got a reply to our Emails. They simply didn't trust westerners, especially when it came to doing business on the Internet. Still to this day it's a negligible market for our kind of products. The reverse however, was true regarding the Americas, with demand continually outstripping supply. This was starting to become a problem, one that we seriously needed to address.

To cut a very long story short, in early January of 1999, an approach was made to acquire the business, by a large American group, who were expanding exponentially, and obviously had very deep pockets and wealthy investors. They were primarily interested in buying the Internet side of the operation, as the web site had gained a very high presence on all search engines and was receiving a level of daily visitors that they could only dream about.

Frederic, Michel, Jon and I had a meeting with them in London, and over the coming few months a deal was put in place, where everything in Paris would continue as it was, both creatively and from the manufacturing side and distribution. It would however concentrate on the more expensive "couture" and individual bespoke outfits. A separate personalized identity and sales area would be created for the Paris products. The Americans would take care of the manufacture and distribution of the mass-market product lines.

The offer was more than fair, and it was agreed that as the web site had been my idea/project from day one, that the financial split would that I would receive forty percent, Jon happily accepted ten percent as he was going to be continuing to work with the new owners, albeit in a more advisory role. Michel and Frederic were each delighted with their twenty-five percent.

The deal was signed and sealed in New York in early May of 1999! It suddenly hit me that the new Millennium was just around the corner and I was, in the not to distant future going to be a lady of leisure.

Paul and I went away for a week with the children to his Mother and Fathers place Nr Bordeaux, to regroup and generally throw some ideas around as to what direction we wanted our lives to go next. Aunt Helens money was very much untouched, and the proceeds from my share of the sale sat nicely in an account in the Channel Islands, our options were very much wide open!

What we both discovered during this trip, was that Paul was really burning himself out physically as well as mentally with his job, as the expectations from the board of directors grew ever higher and unrealistic; the more success the company achieved, especially the U.K division, the higher the targets, and in all honesty, I could tell he wasn't getting the same "buzz" out of it now as in the early days. He said it was now too corporate, and more and more the industry was being run by accountants and lawyers, rather than by "music people". It was now all about the bottom line!

We left Bordeaux with an understanding that for us as a family the new Millennium would also be a good starting point for a whole new challenge. I could see the relief on Paul's face when I suggested that the first thing he should do when he went back into work was hand in his notice and work out his six month contract. That would give him peace of mind and a good few months to come up with a tentative plan for the future. It would only be a few years until the children would be away at University and thanks to Helen the bulk of the costs would be taken care of by the trust fund she'd set up for them.

I had two more business trips to Paris to plan to fulfill the terms of the buy out contract. These were basically needed to tie up a few loose ends and guide the new owners through various updates that were in place but not uploaded yet. In reality, trying to help engineer a seamless a transition as possible.

Yves was also a very good listener and guided both Paul and myself during this important time in our lives. He insisted that to celebrate we visit him in August and spend a week with him and his various friends at his house in the South of France. He said it would be good for both of us to relax, and at the same time he'd arrange one of his legendary summer parties and we would really celebrate my successful business deal in style. He said the children would be welcome, however, Paul and I decided they would prefer to be with their grand parents, as during their many visits to Bordeaux they'd built up a close circle of friends their own age. We accepted that they were not children anymore, but fully fledged teenagers, with their own agendas and needed their own bit of independence.

It was a rough couple of weeks for Paul, as the company tried everything to get him to reconsider, but thankfully, as it turned out he stuck to his guns, and they eventually accepted his decision.

To announce all our "news" to our closest friends, Paul and I thought it would be ideal to put on a themed dinner party in our house. I decided to recreate the "Masked Ball" London style.

Chapter Thirty-Seven: A Celebration In Kew

The event was to be small and intimate, but with a twist that took some major planning. We invited Erica and Chris from the old days, along with Mike and Sarah, Oliver and Claudia, Frederic and Michel (unfortunately, Michel couldn't make it as his Mother was very ill), Antonia who was single again after a brief fling with a chap she'd met at work, Julia and James who were new friends of Mike and Sarah and came highly recommended! Thierry promised to come if he could arrange to be in London with his work, and finally, after much deliberation I invited Jon and his new girlfriend. I explained to him that it may not be for the "faint hearted", but he promised he'd scrub up well, and Jill his new love interest would jump at the chance.

I designed all the invitations, and arranged with Frederic to send me a selection of masks over from Paris, so I could have them delivered with the invites.

Paul and I planned that the dinner would take place outside, under the awnings, and the party itself would be in the basement, which would be ideal. We decorated to emulate L'Escapade, and we even had a small grope box built for the occasion, by a friend of Mikes.

We hired in a local catering company to come and take care of the food, which we'd decided would be a medieval Hog Roast with all the trimmings, with large flagons of cider on ice. I found, through a local papers free ad's section, three students, whom I employed to dress up as medieval serving wenches for the evening. I also hired a young trained barman to be in charge of drinks, this turned out to be a masterstroke.

The French connection came on the late afternoon Eurostar, and I'd arranged a local cab firm to collect them. Thierry was already in London and had a room booked at his regular Hotel, and would be making his own way to the party.

I'd spruced up the spare bedrooms, and Olivier and Claudia would be in the unused larger one, with an en-suite. I'd allotted one of the other en-suite rooms for Frederic. Chris and Erica would have one of the children's rooms. Mike and Sarah said they'd just sleep anywhere. However, in the end, we'd organized a second sofa bed in Paul's office area, so there was plenty of room for any eventuality. Jon and his partner said they'd just go with the flow.

The day of the party was a frantic whirl of activity, with drink deliveries, and the huge rented eighteen-seater garden table, along with chairs and a few smaller tables scattered around the garden arriving as arranged. The caterers arrived mid afternoon with a very large mechanical contraption in tow, which was used to slowly roast the suckling pig. They'd made a wide variety of salads and other complimentary dishes. There was also a large outdoor gas cooker, where they were going to make a large dish of potato/green peppers and onions in olive oil.

By late afternoon everything was organized and prepared, and the suckling pig was merrily beginning its slow roast.

When the French contingent arrived a while later, we welcomed them with a jug of the quintessential English Pimms.

I'd shown everyone to their relevant changing/bedrooms to prepare for the main event, which we'd scheduled for eight.

My little twist and surprise for the "ladies", telephoned to confirm, that as requested he'd arrive at ten-thirty and text me when he was outside our house. Also, Julia rang and apologized, as they'd unable to get to us until around ten o'clock, as James's flight back from Edinburgh was delayed by three hours, and was it still fine to come, of course I said it wouldn't be a problem, and to turn up as and when they could.

As arranged the three "serving wenches" arrived at seven and slipped into the outfits I'd rented for them. They certainly looked the part, with their breasts pushed up and spilling out of the lace tops, also exposing an inch or two of flesh above the top of their hold-ups. The young barman also arrived on time and I gave him a quick tour of where all the relevant glasses and accessories were kept. He immediately got busy organizing things, I'd explained to all four of them that things would probably get a little out of hand later…. they all giggled and said that it wouldn't be a problem. I was surprised when two of the girls said they'd been to a well-known fetish club of the time called "Submission". So they were pretty broadminded and not easily shocked!

We'd instructed everyone to gather in the garden around seven forty-five for drinks.

After slipping into a new elegant Dior cocktail dress that Yves had surprised me with on my last trip, Paul and I went and put the finishing touches to the table. I'd bought three, large five-arm Candelabras in a local junk shop, which would look stunning all lit up when darkness descended.

Paul had got a young product manager from his companies "dance music department" to burn him a few CD's of music for the evening. Everything was set and the hog roast smelling fantastic and the caterers' two chefs were cooking up a storm. Once completed they were off to another event, so it was down to my "wenches" to take over from them.

We started the evening in Parisian style, with everyone being served a flute of "Kir Royale" as they arrived, either from upstairs or via the front door. Everyone arrived on time, all looking elegant in their various slinky outfits, the look complemented by the masks of varying designs being worn to great effect. Thierry, as always looked ravishing, draped head to toe in Chanel, and came armed with little gifts for the ladies. Erica's face was a treat; in fact I'm sure she drooled as he embraced her. Antonia made a spectacular entrance in a sheer, see through stretch lace evening dress and killer heels... There was an audible intake of breath from the men!

The complete shocker for me, was when Jon arrived with Jill his new lady friend, a simply gorgeous redhead, who came dressed to party hard, and Jon who'd ditched the geeky tech-skater look, and was in a very expensive Hugo Boss black suit and a white silk Tom Ford shirt. This was a massive transformation and both Paul and I stood open-mouthed appraising his new look. He grinned at us and said "I thought I'd make an effort!"

It was wonderful to have some of my closest friends and sexual confidantes in one place, only Yves was missing, but our relationship was of a very different kind and on a much deeper level. I knew that if he was present, he'd be charming and act the part, but it wouldn't really be his thing. We'd celebrate in our own way at a future date!

Everyone got into party mode very quickly, with old friendships being rekindled and new ones just beginning. Sarah and Claudia had really bonded again and were in boisterous mood. Frederic and Thierry were flirting with everything that had a pulse, and Antonia was being Antonia, just oozing sex from every pore. Jon's girlfriend Jill was deep in conversation with Olivier, whilst Erica was outrageously coming onto Mike, and jokingly kept inspecting his fingers while winking at me!

As we toasted everybody prior to eating, Paul told them our news and our tentative future plans, everybody applauded and wished us well and Frederic gave a lovely little speech as well. It was all very emotional, but in a positive and uplifting way.

The young ladies served the food provocatively, and the brilliant, extrovert barman was in his element, and kept calling me "Madame", with a very inviting glint in his penetrating blue eyes. Paul was being the perfect host, making sure all the guests' needs were being catered for and busy taking photographs of the occasion. I was keeping a watchful eye on Jon, but he really showed me a whole new, relaxed and attractive side to him, one I'd never seen before, in fact I would have sworn it was a doppelganger he'd sent in his place!

At one point I was chatting with Antonia, telling her how much I enjoyed seeing the evidence of her filthy, debauched evening with Paul and Mike, when Erica joined the tale end of the conversation, she made it plain, that she too wanted to become a fully paid up member of the "Mikes Magic Fingers" appreciation society. I chuckled and said I'd put in a good word for her.

Just as people were finishing their "Roast", James and Julia arrived complete with masks and a thousand apologies for the shortcomings of Easy Jet, they were immediately introduced, watered and fed in that order. Julia was a very sultry looking brunette, with incredibly long legs and a smoldering "come hither" look, whilst James could have passed as Michael's younger brother. Mike wasn't at all happy, when I ribbed him about this, especially when the word "younger" entered the equation. He simply said "but only I have the Midas touch darling" winked and flounced off.

After much frivolity my mobile vibrated, and there was a text from the evenings surprise entertainment! I discreetly made my way to the front door and quickly led Daniel down into the basement. Daniel was a well-known black exotic dancer on the London scene; he was famous for his physique and his legendary endowment. I'd got his contact details from a well known adult entertainment web site and had telephoned him, and when I explained what I envisaged he went into overdrive telling me he thought it was a fabulous and wickedly erotic idea, and he'd be more than flattered to do it.

Nobody had been allowed into the main basement room, as I didn't want anyone guessing what the twist was. I had acquired a full size massage table, which I had strategically positioned in the centre of the room for the occasion. I'd placed a tall floor standing spotlight to illuminate it when the allotted time arrived. I showed Daniel to the large wet room, and told him I'd see him in a few minutes, once I'd fetched the goods!

I went upstairs to the kitchen and luckily one of the serving wenches was bringing some used plates in for the dishwasher. I explained what I was up to and she positively jumped at the chance to help me in my time of need.

We collected everything that was needed and returned to the basement, to be met by a freshly showered Daniel standing by the massage table wearing just a towel. Nikki the serving wench gasped at this six foot two black, man mountain and muttered "Wow", and when he removed his towel, we both muttered "Oh my God" in unison. Both salivating slightly!

He nimbly leapt up on to the table, and Nikki and myself set about decorating his body with an array of fresh fruit and meringue's; I could sense Nikki was getting quite aroused as we sprayed little peaks of cream on his chest, stomach and thighs. The "piece de resistance" was when I opened the large tin of pineapple rings; we took turns in positioning six of them on his gargantuan black, thickly veined penis, one for each lady! Nikki winked at me and requested that we put an extra one on for her! All the time we were placing the rings on his cock it kept growing, it would have taken the whole tin, with room to spare. I gave him the cable with the switch for the spotlight and told him that when I said the word "dessert", he should turn it on. I turned off all the lights. Nikki went back up stairs, and I went out the French windows up to the garden.

I summoned the ladies, telling then to follow me - as dessert was now being served in the basement. I led them down the steps, crocodile fashion, all holding hands in the dark, like a train, until we were in position. This was going to be fun, who would participate, who would be shy and only watch coyly…. I was fascinated to see what their various reactions would be.

I simply said "Ladies your dessert is served", instantly the spotlight came on, revealing Daniel in all his glory, covered in fruit and cream with seven pineapple rings around his huge rigid penis. As one, they all shrieked, with what can only be described as a "lustful animalistic howl" of pure delight, with Sarah typically saying, "Back off ladies, he's all mine".

I explained to them that there would be no cutlery available, and it was purely a mouth and fingers style self-service buffet, and the pineapple rings were available by mouth only! Everyone stood mouths open and gawping for a moment, until Sarah led the charge, and started on the raspberries and cream on his chest, after a mouthful, she looked up and said "ladies, please dive in and help me". Soon there was five horny ladies, erotically eating the fruit and licking up the cream, until it was just the pineapple rings left. I quickly went in search of Nikki, and when I returned with her, four of the rings had been eaten and Jill was lustily eating the fifth. Nikki suggested that her and I eat the final two together, which was greatly appreciated by both Daniel and the other girls. Between us we made a great show of eating them and him, as slowly and erotically as possible. I looked up and noticed Antonia and Jill were already naked and furiously kissing each other, whilst Daniels hand had found Claudia's pussy and she was contentedly grinding away on his fingers. Moments after Nikki and I had finished the pineapple our mouths were immediately replaced by Sarah and Julia's who both proceeded to suck and lick his cock together, both of them literally drooling. Erica was looking on in total awe. It was a thoroughly wonderful and debauched scene… It was the perfect plan, with an even more perfect execution! Unexpectedly Nikki started to kiss me, and we were soon locked in a passionate embrace, with our hands briskly exploring each other's bodies. I decided it was time to involve the men and Nikki and I broke off our kiss. I then turned all the proper mood lighting on and the spotlight off. Then we went upstairs and got our barman Jamie to pour all the men brandies. The chefs had packed away, and had told Paul they'd return the following day for the equipment.

Once the brandies were served, I asked Nikki to invite the men to follow her into the basement, which she did without hesitation. I took the opportunity to tell the other two girls and Jamie the barman, that their work was done and paid them what they were due, plus a nice bonus, as a thank you for a job well done. I told them that I'd arrange a cab for them, or alternatively they were more than welcome to stay, and join the party, to which they grinned, as cheeky Jamie replied "we thought you'd never ask", and one of the girls asked cheekily "any spare pineapple rings left?"

They eagerly followed me down into the basement area, to be greeted by a scene Caligula himself would have been proud of. Daniel was having his massive member test driven by Claudia, whilst Sarah was squatting over his face, encouraging him enthusiastically to make her climax with his tongue, various couplings and intermingling's were happening everywhere. Jamie and the two girls took it all in, and whilst Jamie stayed close to me, the two girls went in search of their own entertainment, in short order they were being taken care of by a very rampant looking Frederic, who was now completely engrossed in the situation. I noticed Jon sitting back with a contented look on his face, watching all the action unfold, whilst Olivier was paying avid attention to Jill's body with his over-active French tongue, she was moaning loudly with intense pleasure. Antonia was being well and truly put through her paces as James and Paul were operating as a well-practiced tag team, working her hard from both ends, much to her intense pleasure. Chris and Nikki were rampantly enjoying each other. At various stages the grope box was put to good use, one of the younger girls was in and out several times, always exiting licking her lips with a smile on her face, especially as on one occasion Daniel put his deadly weapon through one of the holes for her to play with as she saw fit.

Jamie was helping me refresh everyone's drinks, he took great pleasure in interrupting peoples pleasure to enquire whether they would like a top-up. On one trip up to the makeshift bar in the kitchen he told me he thought my cocktail dress was stunning, but he was sure

I'd be more far comfortable now if I discarded it and partied myself! I agreed wholeheartedly, excused myself and went up to our bedroom and wiggled out of it, freshened up and returned to the kitchen naked, apart from a different pair of extra high bright red "Fuck me Shoes". As I re-entered the kitchen, I enquired, "Is this better?" as I stood with my hands on my hips with my legs slightly spread, accentuating my glistening pussy, whose lips were already parting in anticipation. He promptly approached me, and immediately I was enthusiastically kissing and being caressed by this very confident and desirable twenty year old. He was soon sucking and nibbling on my very erect nipples as his tongue was making its slow journey down my body. Eventually his mouth found my pussy and his eager tongue started to eat me with passion, he found my pulsating clitoris very promptly, especially for one so young and proceeded to gently bite and suck on it very skillfully. I was rapidly approaching orgasm, but was very apprehensive that I'd scare him to death if I unleashed a huge torrent of my love juice, so I held back, controlling myself, just enjoying measured multi-mini climaxes.

During this wonderful oral attentiveness from Jamie, a very lustful looking Erica appeared dragging Mike behind her. He explained that he was going to give Erica his legendary "G-spot Treatment", however, he though it would be easier and a much more relaxed experience for her if they were in a quieter place, where she could let herself go fully. Jamie looked bemused and was intrigued as to what this treatment was!

I suggested we all went up to our bedroom, where we wouldn't be disturbed. Once in the bedroom, I motioned to Erica to get comfortable on the chaise longue, whilst I went and got some fresh towels in anticipation of the outcome of Mike's treatment. When I returned from the bathroom, Mike was already starting to dispense his unrivalled finger ministrations, whilst Jamie observed in bewilderment. I went to my bedside table and retrieved a fresh bottle of poppers and very subtly slipped them to Mike with a wink!

Jamie and myself watched intently the unfolding scenario, and soon I was relieving him of his clothes, to reveal a very taut and athletic torso with a most desirable and granite hard manhood. After a sustained period of Mike's fingers probing and stimulating the insides of Erica's very wet vagina he unscrewed the poppers and encouraged her to take a sniff up each nostril. She did so, hesitatingly, until she looked at me and I nodded reassuringly. I told Jamie to watch and learn, as with Mike's technique, coupled with the amyl, I knew she was imminently about to achieve her first intense G-spot orgasm. With much encouragement, from both Mike and myself, she slowly started to tremble and her legs started to shudder as her hips bucked wildly, it hit her like a huge tidal wave, and she let go, as Mike withdrew his fingers and worked her clitoris, she bit her lip and squealed loudly, as she squirted her first and simply colossal jet of her juices, followed by several more, to Mikes delight, he proclaimed "the tap is now on, let it flow". Poor young Jamie, this was certainly a baptism by fire, as I knelt, and slowly took him deep into my mouth, whilst he was still processing what he'd just witnessed. I took full control and after a period of teasing his cock and balls with my tongue I gently pushed him back onto the bed and straddled his face, presenting my open vagina to his eager young mouth. I positively encouraged him to make me cum with his tongue, now confident that he'd not freak out, after just having witnessed it first hand. Also, Erica was in the throws of another bout of gushing climaxes as Mike was massaging her G-spot, whilst she sucked hungrily on his mighty erection. I ground my pussy hard into Jamie's face as I manually stimulated myself and shortly came with a massive deluge in to his young expectant mouth. He was both, pleased and grateful, as this was a major first for him. I slowly slid my body down over his body and guided his throbbing penis into my wetness, gripping his length with my vaginal muscles as he penetrated me. I rode him slowly to begin with, as I didn't want it to be over quickly, but with his full encouragement, I started to gradually increase my rhythm, as he was busy squeezing and sucking on my responsive hard, erect nipples.

    It was building nicely, and for one so young he had an extraordinary level of self control, always putting my pleasure first as I attained a high level of fulfillment, his constant thrusts giving me wave after wave of pure sexual bliss. I was determined that his orgasm would be monumental and one he'd never ever forget, so I lewdly asked Mike to toss me the poppers. I ceased all movement for a moment, and just sat on him with his erection buried deeply inside me, clamping my muscles around his shaft, gripping him like a vice. I slowly unscrewed the cap on the little bottle of joy and with a look of pure sex, I took a big hit, and immediately held it under Jamie's nose, urging him to follow my lead, he did so eagerly. I replaced the cap and felt my inner glow rapidly arrive, whilst simultaneously his face began to flush and he let out a loud groan of delight at this new sublime sensation. As I again began to work my hips into a pounding tempo, working my pussy on his pulsating cock, I sensed his urgency, as he matched my thrusts equally, until we were both riding on a pure wave of pleasure, with a ferocious bout of powerful thrusts I watched as his eyes as they rolled back into their sockets as he began to flood me with his hot and powerfully squirting semen. The feeling of this young man filling me with his seed was truly sublime. We were both lost in the moment, as I had simultaneously gushed my own juices all over his balls and abdomen, soaking both him and my freshly laundered duvet. I eventually rolled off him and casually watched as Mike was impressively fucking Erica viciously from behind, she was pleading with him to stop, in a "don't you dare" tone of voice, as she matched his thrusting by slamming her bottom back onto his cock. I excused myself and went to the bathroom to freshen up, and was staggered upon my return, to be greeted by the sight of Jamie now pounding Erica brutally from behind, whilst Mike was feeding his cock into her ever agreeable and very greedy mouth. I helped them along by passing Mike the poppers to enhance all their senses. I left to return down to the basement with Erica's screams of animal passion ringing in my ears.

    I caught up with Paul, who was now busy again with his camera, as Daniel had Antonia, Jill and Julia bent over gripping the massage table as he took turns in penetrating each of them with large powerful strokes with his awesome, immense black cock. Jon was reclined on one of the sofas watching and enjoying the spectacle…. even more so, when I knelt in between his legs and looked him in the eyes and gestured with my two fingers "ssshhh" and commenced to blow his mind, as well as his erection. Paul edged over and rattled off a sequence of shots of me with Jon in my mouth! Thierry was alternating with James in keeping the young serving wenches well and truly satisfied. Chris was oblivious as to where Erica had got to, as Sarah was keeping him fully occupied. Frederic being Frederic couldn't resist sneaking up behind me whilst I was sucking Jon, and slipping himself inside me before I knew what was happening, after about ten minutes or so I glanced over my shoulder, only to see Thierry had replaced him, I was on such a sexual high, I never noticed them swap over. A true slut!

Eventually, I realized nobody was leaving, so I locked up and went in search of a nightcap. I was dead beat and looked forward to crawling into bed and starting the recovery process.

Around mid-morning people started to surface, and the consensus of opinion was that we should all go to the "Coach and Horses" for a full on English fry-up, to replace some much needed energy and soak up the excesses of the previous evening, before everyone headed off, to return to whence they came! All totally fed, watered and fucked!

Much thanks and big hugs and kisses later Mike and Sarah helped Paul, myself and Antonia clear up the final remnants of any evidence from the party, also the caterer dropped by to pick up his equipment and final balance of payment. It was late afternoon before all was in order and we could relax on the patio with a nice chilled "Sancerre", we all fell about when Paul looked up and said with a smile "same again next week?" Many complimentary Emails only substantiated what a success it had been on every level. Also on a positive note Antonia had more than widened her circle of "friends" and had invites to Paris and a dinner date with Daniel planned "filthy lucky bitch!" She'd really become a valued friend and we definitely had a very similar taste in men, and what we enjoyed doing with and to them!

Chapter Thirty-Eight: French Riviera Revelry

We were due to visit Yves for five days in late August. Having driven to Paul's parents and spent a relaxed week there, with the whole family together, doing plenty of nothing but eating, drinking and sleeping in the South Western France's magnificent hot summer weather.

Paul's parents had, with our blessing, bought the children a couple of 50cc motor scooters that they could get around on whilst there. They were over the moon and couldn't wait to enjoy their newfound freedom. The relevant paperwork and insurance was a nightmare, however, Paul's father "Mr. Organised" sorted it all out efficiently as usual.

We had a few wonderful days on the stunningly beautiful and vast beaches of the Atlantic coast, Paul even taught me the basics of surfing, as he used to surf a great deal himself in his youth. He explained it was a bit like riding a bike, once you'd got it, you'd never forget it! I never really got it, so had little or nothing to forget.

We'd arranged with Yves to meet up on the second Saturday at the Noga Hilton hotel in Cannes, as it was the simplest and most convenient place to park the car, whilst he took us for a welcome lunch at one of his favourite eateries in the area.

We'd left Paul's parents on the Friday, as it was a much too long a drive to do in one go. We left after breakfast and took a leisurely drive on the very good French road system, and we were arriving in our planned stopover, a small town called Marseillan at around lunchtime. It was ideally situated, a short drive off the main motorway (E80). We were very fortunate, as whilst stopping to fill the car with petrol I got chatting in French to a lady, who like me was waiting to pay, she told us about a wonderful boutique hotel nearby, that she thought would suit our needs, and as she was driving back home that way we followed her until she indicated and pulled over and told us it was two minutes further on. We thanked her, and two minutes later we were parking up outside a wonderful looking old French building, which had been given a full refurbishment a few years previously. It's called "Les Chambres d'Andrea". It was ideally situated, just one minute's walk from the town centre and two minutes from the very pretty harbour with restaurants, bars, cafés and shops. After a brief freshen up, and a quick drink in the garden by the sparkling swimming pool, we took a walk to the little harbor and slowly feasted on a huge bowl of mussels, salad and a jug of iced larger. It was heavenly.

We were very close (semi-purposefully) to a place that we'd heard about from many of the friends we'd made in Paris. It was legendary among Parisian hedonists and the "libéré", namely Cap d'Agde, a haven for nudist's, swingers and every imaginable kind of hedonistic pleasure seeker.

We had decided to go and check it out for ourselves and maybe stay for a day or two on our return journey from Yves's.

We grabbed the car and headed off the two or three kilometers to the beach resort itself, although not venturing into the "Naturist Village", where it is frowned upon to even wear a pair of shorts…. even in the supermarket, not really my kind of thing. However, we parked up and scouted out there area and had a few refreshing drinks in the many and varied bars, picking up leaflets and flyers along the way. Unknown to us at the time, we would enjoy many an erotic adventure on the beaches and in the clubs over the coming years.

After a good amble around we made it to the beach, which was a very long stretch of golden sand, which late afternoon was packed with naked people of all shapes and sizes. We'd been informed that it was a definite no-no to try and wander around fully clothed. So as good respectful Brits abroad we stripped of and replaced the towels in our sports bag with our shorts and t-shirts and went to explore further.

It seemed the further along the beach you walked, the more exhibitionistic people became, with many couples openly having sex, either together or in groups. We were very amused to pass a gentleman, obviously talking to a family member on his mobile phone, whilst a nubile young lady was giving him a blowjob! There was also an intense amount of activity in the sand dunes and bushes all along the back of the beach. There were distinct areas for all different sexual persuasions.

After finding a spot to park ourselves and enjoy a bit of people watching near a small beach hut/bar, we went and got a drink and surveyed the endless parade of naked flesh on view. It was a bit overwhelming at first, but we soon became oblivious to all but the most beautiful or bizarre!

Occasionally there'd be a few beach police patrolling on horseback and dune-buggies, making sure things weren't getting too raucous, it was amusing to see people, who seconds earlier were indulging in all kinds of exhibitionistic play, suddenly pretending to be innocently engrossed in reading books and magazines.

The beach suddenly got very busy around the time most beaches would be emptying, we soon discovered why! We've since realized that as the sun goes down the real exhibitionists came out to play, and the various areas at the back of the beach became packed with people watching others putting on "shows" and groups of people generally engaging in all forms of debauched behavior. We joined a throng of people watching two rather spectacular looking women enjoying each other and playing up wildly to the circle of men who were all masturbating around them. For any females like myself watching, it was a bit like walking into the proverbial lions den, as hands and fingers reached out to grope and fondle in the hope that you'd respond in kind, which on this occasion I declined to do, simply wanting to get the full lay of the land, before indulging myself! We wandered off and passed a middle-aged lady taking on a large cross section of men, to the great delight of her partner, who was issuing explicate instructions to the various participants, as to what he wanted them to do to her (all with her full consent), she was enjoying her own little fantasy. It was a real eye opener. Being fully accustomed to the strict etiquette in the Parisian clubs, it was an initial shock to the system to see it in broad daylight. It was obvious that everyone was very at ease with his or her own bodies and any hang-ups were left in the car park.

We got talking to a young couple, called Elodie and Louis, who had an apartment there and had been visiting for the previous five years. We went with them to a small bar for a drink where they gave us the full run down of everything "Cap D'Adge". Particularly of interest were the various clubs, of which there are now many, however, then the top club in the area was L'Extasia, it was about a ten-minute drive from Cap

D'Adge, in between Marseillan and Mèze. They gave us their phone number and said they'd be happy to take us as their guests, if we returned, as planned the following weekend.

We returned to the hotel and showered, made love rampantly and went in search of a suitable restaurant for dinner. We found a complete gem, called "La Taverne du Port", it was located right on the port, and had been family run for nearly eight generations. It was incredibly authentic, with a wonderful atmosphere and the smells were simply exquisite. I started with a sensational hot Camembert salad, Paul had a traditional fish soup with bread, and we swiftly followed with a massive platter of "fruits de la mer" between us. All accompanied by a wonderful bottle of a local white wine "Picpoul Domain Creyssels", absolutely gorgeous and slipped down a treat.

We ended the evening with a brandy and coffee, whilst soaking up the outstanding ambience, and watching the boats gently bobbing up and down on the calm waters of the harbor.

The following morning after a lovely rustic breakfast beside the swimming pool we set off towards Cannes, not before rebooking for the following Saturday evening!

We got back onto the AutoRoute, and began our journey to Cannes. Yves rang on the mobile mid morning to check on our progress and we arranged that we'd meet him at the terrace bar/café at the Noga Hilton as soon as we arrived.

Driving into Cannes in August is a slow business, it seemed like the whole of Paris was there, every other car registration was suffixed by the number 75 (Paris registered), plus the fact that many were just cruising, and showing off their flash sports cars to anyone who cared to look... It was a definite poseurs paradise!

The "Croisette", the main boulevard along the sea front I Cannes was nose to tail in traffic, however, we eventually made it in time and found a spot in the hotel's underground car park and excitedly took the lift to the main hotel reception area.

We found Yves resplendent in the traditional wealthy French man "on holiday" attire and looking very Riviera chic! He said he'd arranged with the hotel to leave our car there for the week, as it would be easier if we just used Bruno, who always was on call. By this stage Bruno and I had developed a good friendship and always shared a joke or two when we were alone in the car. He had a tremendous sense of humour and was completely loyal to "Le Général". As if by magic the man himself appeared to whisk us all off for lunch.

We headed out of Cannes, passing through a small town called Mougins, which Yves informed us had one of the best clubs in the area and, we should visit while we were here if the chance arose!

Eventually, we arrived at a very exclusive looking establishment called "Le Bois Doré". It was Yves's favourite eatery in the South of France, and only minutes from his home.

Translated the name means "Golden Wood" and we sat on a beautiful terrace, shaded by tall trees and surrounded by gorgeous flowers of all varieties. There was a wonderful scent of mimosa all around. After all these years Bruno was invited to join us for lunch (it turned out he dined with Yves frequently during the month of August, when, he was more a companion, than a employee).

We ordered from the "Menu Bois Doré", where, I had lobster salad to begin followed by Sea bass in a salt crust with fennel seeds, it was sublime, I avidly remember Paul indulging with Yves, in a dozen Fines de Claires oysters, due to the look of complete orgiastic pleasure on both their faces. They both had grilled Lobster for their main course, and as always, Yves ordered a selection of outrageous desserts, including hot Chocolate dip with fresh fruit on skewers! Bruno, however, was a man of simple tastes where food was concerned, and simply had a selection of cheeses and meats with bread, it was a standing joke between them, with Yves always trying to get Bruno to broaden his horizons and try new things… sadly, to no avail.

Yves's house has to seen to be appreciated, it is a gem of a pink stone palace, enormous with ten en-suite bedrooms, with three guest cottages built around a large swimming pool and decking area. The views are outstanding, looking down over Cannes and across the shimmering Mediterranean Sea. It was such a tranquil setting, with large grounds, where you could get lost. He employed six staff during Augusts to cater for him and his select circle of friends.

We were shown to a very large bedroom in the main house, with his and hers en-suite bathrooms and a very large terrace, where you could simply sit for hours taking in the spectacular vistas.

We took a late afternoon drink with Yves, who explained, that he had guests staying, all good friends from various hedonistic circles and they were all down on the beaches along the Riviera and would probably return around six to relax and prepare for the evening's festivities.

Bruno was available to drive us wherever and whenever, also there was a little jeep we could use if we just wanted to pop down to the coast for the day.

Yves had drawn up a "suggestions" list of things we should or may possibly want to do and see whilst we were there. He said to keep Wednesday free, as we were invited to lunch on a close friend of his boat, which was at present in Saint Tropez for the summer. Both Paul and I were excited at this prospect, as many years before had been invited to a party on a large boat in Marbella, but we couldn't make it, as we'd both gone down with a touch of food poisoning. We always regretted missing that opportunity, and were thrilled that the chance had come around again.

Yves had arranged a "small" party for later in the evening as a welcome to us, and as a celebration of our recent decision to initiate a fresh challenge for the new millennium!

The party was centered around the pool area. We were staggered at the transformation that had taken place whilst we were having a little "siesta" time. The staff had been very busy! There were numerous tables and chairs set out, and a large DJ console was in place.

The theme of the evening was Moroccan, with caterers generating some wonderful aromas. There were open spits roasting large legs of lamb, and huge tagines being attended to over an open clay pit fire. It was a hive of activity, with people buzzing around like flies getting everything prepared.

The invited guests started to arrive around ten, as the searing heat of the day was replaced with a cooling breeze coming off the sea. When we made our way to the large bar area Bruno appeared, and explained there'd be upwards of fifty people attending, and it was a mixture of couples and wealthy single acquaintances of Yves. There were five lithe topless girls, along with a similar number of well-defined young men who were simply there to serve drinks, entertain and add an air of decadence to the proceedings. He told us they were also hired for their open and free attitude to sex. This piqued my curiosity, as I'd already noticed one or two very erotic male specimens circulating.

After being introduced to many of the guests, Yves appeared resplendent in loose white trousers and white silk shirt, this appeared to be the uniform amongst the men, while the females were all dressed very provocatively, many wearing very little, apart from the obligatory "fuck me shoes", as Paul loved to call them. We, for our part blended in with the crowd, as I'd decided to wear a very micro and clingy white dress, which showed off my tan to good effect and generated many admiring glances from both the men and various ladies.

Once everyone had arrived Yves began proceedings with a charming little speech in French, introducing us formally, Paul just smiled, as he had no idea what was being said! Everyone raised their glasses and toasted our good health and then Yves declared the party officially open and food was served.

We joined Yves at the large pink marble table beside the pool, with a very sexy mid forties lady with her considerably older partner, they were very old friends of Yves and always attended his frequent parties. She was called Eloise and she kept flirting madly with Paul, telling him in broken English, how she was going to take him into the woods later and seduce him. He took it all in his stride, telling her it would be his pleasure. Yves was on top form and was really in full flow. He had Eloise squirming with pleasure, as he recounted the story of Sarah's all black experience in Paris. She was almost begging him to arrange a similar evening for her!

After the delicious food was consumed things really started to heat up, with lots of people shedding their clothes and frolicking in the swimming pool. Set back from the pool was a large changing area, which had been transformed with beanbags and cushions into a group fun room, and there was lots of "toing and froing" going on. It wasn't long until I saw Paul being dragged off by Eloise, whilst her partner was enjoying his drink and the rapt attention of one of the young waitresses.

Yves gesticulated to me to circulate and enjoy myself. I didn't have to be told twice and went in search of my own entertainment.

I spotted, and made a bee-line towards one of the fittest looking of the male waiters at the bar and asked him for a drink. We instantly struck up a natural, but overtly sexual conversation. He made some very suggestive, but flattering remarks regarding my dress and how it was a big shame that it was hiding my best assets. It was all very flirtatious, and he definitely was an experienced player. He seductively and humorously told me, that he'd been bringing his "penis" on holiday to the Riviera for a number of years and "its" reputation now preceded him and "it" was in constant demand at the many "high society" soirees along the coast at this time of year. He grinned, when I told him I'd be honoured to be introduced to "it" sometime. He said, there was no time like the present as it was about time for his break. He took my hand, I was compelled to follow him as he led me down some nearby steps into a wine cellar and general drinks storage area. Immediately, without a moment's hesitation, he slipped my dress up and off my body. He stood back for a few moments appraising what he saw, he deftly removed his shorts and revealed the most colossal erection I had ever seen on a white guy, it was huge, he held it proudly in both hands, grinned and said, "meet Enrique". I stood frozen to the spot for a few moments, drooling and staring achingly at it. We kissed lustfully and I could feel his monstrous manhood throbbing against my thigh. I was so turned on, that as his fingers reached my clitoris I exploded in a massive bone shaking orgasm, my juices making the noise of a heavy rainstorm, as they cascaded onto the tiled floor. I just couldn't stop gushing, it was truly amazing and he gasped "formidable, tres formidable". We stumbled over to a large wooden worktable, where he bent me over and continued to explore both my soaking vagina and anus with his fingers, stopping occasionally to powerfully slap his heavy cock across the cheeks of my bottom. It was magical the way his slim fingers probed and teased deep into my rectum; he was enamored by the way my sphincter muscles gripped them so tightly and willingly. After his anal treatment induced several more wet and substantial orgasms, he laid me back across the table; I held my legs in the air, as wide as I could possibly get them, as he guided his oversized penis into me. I could feel it slowly stretching me, as he forced its massive girth into my throbbing vagina. Its length was overwhelming, and I could only accommodate about three quarters of it. He remained completely still, as my vaginal muscles adjusted, to compensate for the immense pounding, it was inevitably going to take. He complimented me on my prowess, saying many women were usually alarmed when they saw it, and only played with it with their hands. He said it took a true aficionado to accept his exceptional size, especially so eagerly. I simply groaned "its all yours, fuck it", which spurred him on into giving me one of the most ferocious and merciless hammerings I'd ever experienced from one man!! Let alone a tanned and physically immaculate one. I was in seventh heaven, urging him not to hold back, I was cresting from one orgasm to another, each time the intensity rising to deliver more and more forceful bodily releases. He continued his thrusting like a well-drilled machine, asserting his complete authority and supremacy over my willing body, until he demanded that I knelt in front of him. I immediately began to lick and taste his precum, which was oozing copiously from him. I had lost all self control and my mouth went at him like a wild animal, slurping and gagging on his gargantuan organ. I was totally lost in the moment, worshiping his mighty cock as he began to pump stream after stream of hot stick sperm into my animated mouth and over my animated face. We had both been swept away by the intensity of the situation and his body started to relax as I greedily drank the last remnants of cum from him. It took several minutes until I had any semblance of feeling return to my battered body. It was like I was drowning in a big bowl of "euphoria". Once we'd got ourselves back together and freshened up, we made our way back to the bar area, where I retrieved my much needed drink. Yves caught my eye and gave me a knowing wink; I raised my glass in return.

 A few years later, whilst on a trip to London I reacquainted myself with "Enrique" and had an intense afternoon of anal fun. He was overjoyed, as he explained it was incredibly rare that he could indulge in his passion for anal sex, simply due to his size. I must admit I was at first a bit apprehensive, but I never shirk from a challenge…even one of such magnitude.

 Shortly afterwards Paul appeared, with a naked giggling Eloise from the wooded area behind the guest houses, looking very much like how I felt, shortly followed by a nearly naked smiling waitress. Paul gestured to me to get him a drink ready, and he'd be back in two minutes. I knew, that he just had to go freshen himself up and catch his breath!

We briefly swapped experiences at the bar, until Yves called us over to introduce us to a few more of his "inner circle". One of whom was the owner of the club in Mougins called Le 606 (now le club Absolu), he said, that he'd be delighted, if we'd be his guests at the club on following Thursday, and he'd ensure a table was reserved for us. He was a very flamboyant character, who said he'd snuck off for a few hours and had left his wife Alexandra in charge of the club. He told us it was a pity that we weren't still here on the Sunday, as the last Sunday of every month was "Firefighters Delight Night", Yves smirked at me, as I knew exactly where that idea had emanated from!

By around three in the morning there was sexual shenanigans taking place all over the place, with a very athletic lady enjoying the attention of several men on a sun lounger, whilst her husband was giving her "unnecessary" words of encouragement.

Paul and Yves were deep in conversation; so I went for my own little wander in the woods, and casually watched, as one of the waitresses was being expertly taken from behind, by a lady wearing a large glowing purple strap-on dildo. It was a mind-boggling scenario; several of the people watching were murmuring their delight at this mini exhibition. Two of the waiters came and played with me for a short period, until I excused myself and returned to the bar. "Enrique le Cock" had thoroughly exhausted me, and I was ready for bed. I said my goodnights and thanks to Yves, telling Paul that I'd see him later and to enjoy himself, if he had anything left in the tank!

When we awoke the following morning and stepped out on to the bedroom terrace, we were both staggered to see that there was absolutely no evidence that there'd been a wild party only a few hours previously. Bruno later explained, that there was a house rule, that the parties must end at five a.m. prompt, as Yves paid the local garbage collectors to stop off on their rounds and clear away any devastation and party detritus. Typical, well organized Yves.

We spent the Sunday just relaxing by the pool and socializing with a few of Yves other guests, the ones who'd not gone off to the coast for the day. The staff took care of our every need. The evening was a nice relaxed affair; a group of us strolled down the hill into the centre of Valbonne, to a small and very authentic French eatery called "Le Cadran Solaire". Guy the owner is a local celebrity for his legendary nourishing fish soup/stew, which everybody indulged in, with freshly baked warm crusty breads, and jugs of red and white house wine. It was very tranquil and everyone was in high spirits. Yves was not present, as he had one of his many social functions to attend.

    We took a few trips into Cannes, and ventured onto the famous beaches. Bruno took us on a little guided tour to some unbelievably beautiful locations, such as Antibes, where we had a wonderful few hours, ambling through its maze of streets, all of which were brimming with designer shops. You needed serious money to have a property there. But window-shopping is free; well almost, as we'd inevitably end up in a bar or two! Out of uniform and not standing on ceremony, I saw a completely different side to Bruno, and he and Paul really became bosom buddies during the few days here. Paul even invited him to visit us in London, so as Paul could repay the compliment (he did just that a year or so later). He was a great source of information regarding the inner workings of French High Society, but was however, a soul of discretion, never mentioning names! He would just wink and tap the side of his nose and give the Gallic shrug. Paul actually got this off to a fine art over this holiday. He even "out shrugs" the French sometimes. Which, always reduces me to fits of laughter. In August it seems like the most beautiful people in France flock to the area, to see and be seen! It has to be seen, to be believed.

    The Wednesday morning was a typical gorgeous Riviera's summer day Yves, Paul and myself set off with Bruno, whilst two other couples followed in their car, as we made our way towards Saint Tropez and our scheduled lunch on the boat.

    It was one of the most memorable journeys ever; Bruno took the scenic route, which was much longer than on the main roads. However, the views were incredible, passing through some wonderful looking small towns, such as Saint-Rapael, Frejus and Sainte-Maxime.

    Saint Tropez was completely jam packed with tourists of all descriptions, and the traffic was nose to tail, eventually Bruno pulled up at the bustling harbor area of Quai Jean Jaures, right opposite the famous café/bar Senequier. It was a bit embarrassing getting out of the limousine, as a small crowd gathered with cameras expecting to see some film star! We quickly followed Yves and were welcomed aboard a truly stunning luxury motor yacht. It was enormous and opulent, with all the crew in matching uniforms. Once everyone was on board we slowly cruised out of the harbor and around the coast a short way to the famous Pampelonne beach. Champagne was flowing freely and everyone was in party mood as we dropped anchor just off shore. We all swam off the boats rear platform and generally had "fun in the sun".

Mid-afternoon the small launch was lowered into the sea, and we were all ferried ashore to have cocktails with the "in crowd" at the Beach Club 55, whilst the chefs on board prepared our lunch. It was an idyllic setting, however, as it was August it was standing room only.... Until, Yves was greeted with great pomp and ceremony by the proprietor, who summoned an extra table and chairs for us all.... I felt a bit like Royalty, even the "in crowd" we craning their necks to see who we were, I felt like a real imposter, but managed to keep up the air of total nonchalance. It was all very hedonistic, but somewhat very false, and a great majority of the people were very transparent and insincere. A wonderful experience nonetheless.

Once back on board we were treated to a mouth-watering lunch of fresh lobster and a great variety of other shellfish, all accompanied by individual bowls of three different salads, with distinctly diverse dressings on each. The afternoon was spent very leisurely, with some couples adjourning to the stately cabins below deck for some intimate fun and games. I was just content lying on deck, catching the rays from the late afternoon sun and sipping on my drink, plus the fact I was totally stuffed from complete over indulgence on the never-ending variety of snacks and tidbits on offer. Also, whilst Paul was swimming, Yves wanted to hear all about my little interlude with Enrique the waiter. He also mentioned that he had a little surprise planned for me, mid October-ish, he wouldn't elaborate, but he said I was guaranteed to enjoy it! As ever, I trusted his judgment where it involved my sexual gameplay and my insatiable appetite for all things new.

After a wonderful day, we all arrived back in Valbonne late evening; everyone was exhausted, and after showering congregated around the pool, relaxing and chatting. One of the staff had gone out, and had returned with a huge selection of pizzas for everybody from the local pizzeria. Nice and simple and just what was needed, before having a nightcap and a good long revitalizing sleep.

After a day around the pool we skipped the dinner that the staff had prepared for everyone, as we needed to get ready for our evening at the Club 606 in Mougins. The theme on this Thursday evening was "Soiree Trio", for every couple they would allow entry to one select single male, this was strictly adhered to and all the males were well vetted and were put on a "guest list".

The ladies were encouraged to dress daringly, however, for those dining at the club there was a dressing room put aside, to enable you to change into more revealing attire after you'd eaten.

We arrived and were immediately greeted by the owner, who introduced us to his wife as they checked in my small bag, which had my outfit for later inside. Bruno told us that the club would organize our return transport as and when we required it.

We were shown to a table in the V.I.P area, over looking a small stage with pole and a larger dance area. Lionel, the owner came and joined us for a drink, and explained the basic layout of the club, and to simply forget the world outside and after dinner to go explore and enjoy all that the club had to offer…. which was everything one could possibly envisage and so much more.

The food was divine, but I was itching to get mingling and exploring. The table was exclusively ours for the duration. So without further ado I retired to the dressing room, to pop my "party" outfit on, it didn't take long, as it was just a tight white lycra micro skirt, which barely covered my bottom, and a tiny white string bikini top, which only just covered my nipples, but really enhanced the suntan, all topped off with a very high pair of vivid pink suede heels. On my way back to Paul several of the single men gave admiring and blatantly lustful glances, which immediately sent my body temperature soaring. Then, as I got closer to the table my senses went into overdrive, as there sat sharing a drink with Paul was Enrique the waiter, or as I had nicknamed him "Le Phenomena". He was more laid back than on our initial meeting at Yves, and charmingly said he'd come tonight, as he'd overheard us arranging it with the owner during the party. Swiftly another bottle of Champagne was brought to our table, by this time the club was very busy, but not in a claustrophobic way, there always seemed room to breath…. except around the large grope box!

Enrique offered to show us around the club, and we soon found ourselves in the thick of things as we climbed the stairs to the first level. It was like a maze, with many different themed rooms leading off the walkways. There was a very novel styled grope box, this design definitely had the ladies pleasure in mind, as it had a two circles cut out to put your breasts through and a larger cut out strategically placed below, on three sides. It was reverse engineering! as the man would be inside and ladies could press up to the sides offering the gentleman inside their bodies to fondle anonymously. It was good fun and I tried it several times, however, it was often very busy. It was certainly popular amongst the ladies that night!

I put it down to the heat and holiday spirit, as the club was a heaving mass of exhibitionists and the large group room was a "free for all" every time I wandered past it.

Enrique introduced us to a couple he knew from a party he'd attended the previous year, they had a holiday home close by, and were frequent visitors to the club. They refreshed our Champagne bucket and joined us. They were a fun couple, and it wasn't long before Enrique and the female of the couple (whose name I never quite worked out), joined the throng of semi-naked people gyrating provocatively to the music. It seemed that stroking and touching fellow dancers was fully encouraged by everyone and many people were caught up in the moment and openly making love whilst standing around the edge of the dance floor, I assumed this was the case, as I saw a multitude of women, whose legs were trembling wildly.

The three of us gravitated to a small, mirrored room, which thankfully was available; Enrique was very vocal in encouraging us to play with each other whilst we were kissing enthusiastically. She had a very tight body with natural breasts, which had large chocolate brown nipples, which were both pierced with small gold and turquoise crystal nipple bars. They were incredibly erotic to touch, even more so when I ran my tongue over them. Enrique's fingers were probing us simultaneously, and we both intermittently licked and sucked his fingers, tasting each other's juices. Soon, he had us both naked on the large bed, eating each other's pussies passionately, both on the edge of orgasm within seconds. I was carried away by the situation, and was rapidly climaxing forcefully into her receptive mouth, which was passionately sucking on my engorged clitoris, whilst her fingers were deftly fingering my anus. She was very skilled and was soon bringing me to yet another orgasm, while letting go with her own sexual apogee, squirting her juices up into my eager mouth. Enrique had meantime undressed fully, and was feasting on the sight before him, slowly stroking and flexing his immense penis. She didn't stop her fervent licking, even when he slowly penetrated me from behind, I heard her groan as she saw his immense thickness stretching my eager, wet vagina, slowly but very surely forcing its way inside me, again! I glanced down under my body, and watched her taking turns in licking my pussy lips and sucking on his heavy, smooth testicles. Soon it was her turn to take the beast. She came explosively as he slowly worked his penis into her. It was a very erotic image as I gazed into the mirrors and watched the spectacle from every angle. I adored seeing his colossal weapon sliding powerfully into her, she continued to feast on my labia with relish, and squealed her approval each time I squirted my climax into her mouth. Enrique was enjoying the intimate closeness, whilst I verbally encouraged him and lewdly sucked on his fingers. When, finally with a subtle gesture we took control of the situation and forcefully lay Enrique back on the bed. We both immediately shared the gratifying task of sucking him to a thunderous, fountain like climax, both avidly drinking the hot cum cascading in great thick torrents from his engorged penis. We were both deeply aroused by his copious ejaculation, and we wantonly licked his semen off each other's faces whilst he recovered from his exertions. It was a pure lust between three very liberated people, who simply wanted to bring pleasure to each other.

We eventually returned to Yves's, having enjoyed another wonderful evening of food and fun the French way!

We took brunch with Yves, and generally thanked him for all his generosity and kindness and all too soon it was time for Bruno to drop us back to the "Noga" to retrieve our car, and set of for Cap d'Adge.

We arrived back at "Les Chambres d'Andrea" late afternoon, in time to catch some sun around their lovely pool and enjoy a long cool, refreshing drink.

We'd telephone Elodie and Louis, the couple whom we'd met the previous weekend and arranged to meet up with them around eight at a local bar they knew well. Regarding the outfit for the evening, she told me to think "minimal". But after we'd eaten we would go to their apartment to get ready.

We had a lovely light supper in a small traditional tavern and sat in the tranquil courtyard, as a soft cooling breeze slowly replaced the heat of the day.

Once back at their apartment we all had a drink, whilst Elodie and I went to decide on what to wear. Paul and Louis were both wearing beach shorts and polo tops, as Louis explained that usually the dance area got showered with foam, so many people ended up wet and naked. Sounded like we were in for a fun evening!

At Elodie's suggestion, I wore one of her very small black stretch mini vest-dresses and my heels, whilst she wore a matching one in brilliant white.

The club was absolutely electric, from the moment we entered, the music was loud and an infectious beat was pumping all night, along with a fantastic light show. There were various naked or semi naked dancers, both professional and ordinary clubbers alike writhing on the raised pole areas. There was a cage on a podium, where couples could live out their exhibitionistic fantasies and make love, in full view of everyone. For a little more intimacy there is a large area upstairs, with many large sofas and quiet secluded areas for two or more couples to explore each other.

The area in which I had many exciting little encounters during the evening, was a small wooded zone outside, adjacent to the bar area. It had little walks ways and trails that were all seductively lit, with much furtive groping's and lovemaking occurring in every available nook and cranny. There were constant squeals reverberating from the bushes. It was very edgy, but in a safe and enticing environment. Many times when I'd wandered off to cool down and get some air, I would find myself engaged in a brief encounter with a complete stranger. Nothing long or drawn out, just simply, a quick and explosive orgasm with a "likeminded partygoer". Elodie seemed to love this area, as she was often to be seen emerging from behind a tree looking pleasantly flustered and contented.

When the activities were in full swing, several cannons covered the revelers with massive jets of foam, this only served to liberate people further, with a high proportion of party goers discarding their clothes completely, and participating in a decadent and hedonistic, mass dance floor orgy of gyrating slippery flesh. There was nothing elegant or sophisticated about it, when compared to the Parisian clubs. This was purely a liberated clubbers paradise. Certainly a fun evening, whilst holidaying on the Riviera, but not a place to wear ones finery! But nonetheless, a pleasurable and decadent experience.

The following morning we had a lovely breakfast in the Port prior to setting off to Paul's parents and having the final few days of the break with the children.

We spent the last remaining days relaxing and visiting local beaches and doing lots of family things. The children had really blossomed into adulthood, and thoroughly enjoyed the freedom their scooters had given them. They were sad to be leaving their friends and grandparents, but with "A" levels looming they had a busy six months ahead.

Chapter Thirty-Nine: A New Dawn Approaches

Back in Kew, all the talk was of the forthcoming Christmas and there was a much higher level of anticipation than usual, due in no small part to the impending "New Millennium"!

One major decision that had been made over the summer months was, that Paul and I were going to take an adult "Gap Year". We were going to take a step back and see what opportunities presented themselves during this period. It was going to be a key time in the children's education, with universities to look at, and establishing their three-year schedule (should they get the required exam grades).

Also, looming on the horizon was what was going to turn out to be an important milestone in our lives… my fortieth birthday! However, I wasn't giving much thought to this event, I simply had too much else going on over the forthcoming three months. One of them being a preplanned trip to Paris, which Yves had arranged, Antonia was going to accompany me, as she'd been promising to meet up with an old friend who was now living there! Plus I'd been threatening to show her the delights of Paris for quite a while, and this was the perfect opportunity.

Paul's parents were going to be with us over the festive period, as they desperately wanted for us all to be together and be back in the U.K for this once in a lifetime calendar event.

Paul had also agreed on his final leaving date, and was busy showing his replacement that had recently joined the company from a competitor the ropes. Paul wanted to ensure that everything ran smoothly up to, and to continue seamlessly after his departure.

Chapter Forty: Two Liberated Ladies

Antonia and I met at Waterloo on the Thursday morning, ready for our three-day trip to Paris. She was very excited and we immediately started discussing, what we could and should do, given the limited time available. She'd arranged to meet up with her friend on the Friday evening, which was appropriately planned, as this was the evening set aside by Yves, for one of my special" events!"

It was great to see Bruno again. He was waiting for us at my normal pick-up point, this really impressed Antonia, especially when he said, that the fridge at the apartment was already fully stocked in anticipation of our arrival.

As Bruno dropped us off at the apartment he informed me, that he'd return to pick us both up at eight sharp, to take us to the Ritz for cocktails, as Yves was going to be free for an hour.

There, hung waiting for me in the bedroom, was a stunning, vivid lilac Christian Lacroix silk cocktail dress, with a very high strappy pair of matching Manolo Blahniks. Antonia was now speechless and decidedly envious. Her eyes were a very vivid shade of green!

We went across to the bar, to an enthusiastic welcome from my old friends, and we took my customary table. Then between us we hatched a loose plan of attack for the next few days!

First on the agenda, was to spend some of Antonia's money and to kit her out with a cocktail dress and new shoes for her forthcoming introduction to Yves. We were like overgrown children, giggling and laughing as we shopped. Eventually settling on a very elegant and a little risqué black dress with a pair of killer heels to match.

We went wild in the lingerie department of Galeries Lafayette, buying several pairs of hold-ups each, and numerous pairs of tiny lace panties. A good hour later, and Antonia heavily laden with shopping bags, we found a bar and relaxed, sharing a gorgeous bottle of house red wine. She was very animated, when I told her that after we'd met Yves, that we'd get a bite to eat and then I'd let her experience the delights of L'Escapade (I'd spoken to Amanda and let her know we were coming!)

We returned to the apartment relaxed, and slowly got ready. I could sense she was falling in love with Paris already, in the few short hours we'd been here. I reined her in, and explained, that in all probability it would be a long night and not to peak early. I didn't want her crash and burn on her first day.

We met Yves as planned, and as ever he looked very suave and sophisticated, but always with that wicked twinkle in his eyes. Antonia was literally spellbound, by both Yves and the elegance of the hotel and its super wealthy patrons. We had two wonderful cocktails, then Yves had to go, he said he'd pick me up the following evening at eight sharp, and to wear the outfit that Bruno would deliver, sometime the following day. Throughout our conversation Antonia's eyes and ears were like a little cocker spaniel, I could see her mind racing!

We got a taxi to the restaurant I'd picked for us, which was a stroll away from the club, it was a very popular traditional French bistro called "Les Deux Magots" in Saint-Germain-des-Prés. It was first opened in 1933, and because of its location and keen prices, it had been popular with artists and writers, such as Elsa Triolet, André Gide, Jean Giraudoux, Picasso, Fernand Léger, Prévert, Hemingway, Sartre, Simone de Beauvoir, to name a few. The place was legendary, and full of charm and character. We both had the fillet of saddle of lamb, with herbs, ratatouille and thyme jus, and finished with an outstanding fresh fruit salad. We chatted continuously, with Antonia getting more and more horny as we sipped our brandies, as it would soon be time to hit "L'Escapade".

Eventually, around eleven-thirty we arrived to the normal flamboyant greeting from Amanda, who welcomed Antonia with open arms and called down to François for some drinks. He was shocked to see me, and told me with a grin, that I still must go with him to Le Chateau, as he remembered our afternoon fondly. Antonia wanted to know more… I laughed and told her, I'd explain all later if she behaved!

As always, I had to fill Amanda in on all my exploits since I'd last seen her. We had a constant stream of interruptions, as several couples and a number of handsome single men were arriving. By now Antonia was itching to go down into the club and party, so I told her to brace herself, and to be careful going down the marble stairs. I winked and told her to go slowly, as it always had a very positive effect on the men at the bar. She gripped the balustrade, and proceeded to descend with great style and panache, to the obvious appreciation of the men! Costas immediately greeted us and refreshed our drinks. She was silent for a few moments, mesmerized, soaking in the decadent and licentious atmosphere. Also enjoying the mental undressing she was getting from various men.

A short time later, after several men had given both of us their best chat up lines, and much chuckling at Antonia's limited French, I gave her a tour of the club, avoiding where possible groping hands. I pointed out the small area with the metal gate, this really piqued her interest, so I took the bull by the horns and led her inside, shutting and firmly bolting the door. I was suddenly in a very playful mood and asked one of the men, whom were by now staring intently in through the bars, in anticipation of what was going to happen, to fetch us both a glass of Champagne each. He was back in moments, drinks in hand, to reclaim his place by the bars of the gate. It was a real turn on, talking to the men in French, asking them what they wanted to see, whilst Antonia was clueless as to what was being discussed. After much suggestive banter, I stood her up and seductively removed her dress, until she was stood in just her heels, panties and hold- ups. There were several hands already reaching through the bars and playing with her breasts, tweaking her very responsive erect nipples. She was trembling with lust as I moved her closer, so one of the men could slide her panties down, to reveal her completely smooth pussy. There was much appreciative murmurings as I bent down to remove them completely, and put them in my purse for safekeeping. She was totally carried away as several anonymous fingers began to open and manipulate her eager wet sex. She soon climaxed impressively, several times in rapid succession. I soon turned her around and bent her over, so as a very eager young guy, with a very nice sized erection, could penetrate her from the other side of the bars. The other men verbally encouraged him, as he thrust himself vigorously inside her, until he couldn't hold back any longer and ejaculated into the condom that I'd discreetly handed him from the bowl. Gratefully, he blew me a kiss as another immediately replaced him. Antonia was vocal in her encouragement, eventually inviting two men to come inside and pleasure her from both ends. She simply adored being taken this way. After she'd disposed of the guys, I noticed an older guy with a very pretty young girl watching intently, and waiting to see if they could join our little scenario. I smiled and beckoned the girl over, and she swiftly knelt in between Antonia's legs and busily set about bringing on another climax with her tongue. Her partner was engrossed by what he was seeing and gently stroked himself whilst he simultaneously caressed his young lady friend's bottom from behind. I was fully enjoying my role of "ringmaster", as I let Antonia suck my fingers suggestively. As I directed the proceedings Antonia climaxed several times over the young girls willing and skilled tongue, much to the delight of her partner, who by now didn't know where to look, as now I was lewdly opening my legs, so he could also see my open pussy as I deftly pulled my panties to the side. He was rapidly at the point of no return and soon ejaculated all over his ladies bottom! After a while I suggested a bar break, so as Antonia could have a breather and reenergize! It was during this little rest that Amanda whispered to me that a couple of their regulars had just called and were on their way, and she was sure I'd be impressed. She wanted to know if it was okay to introduce us to them? Obviously I agreed in a positive manner?

Shortly, two very tall and powerfully built black men came down the marble stairway, my jaw dropped and Antonia's eyes popped out as if on stalks. Not only were they stunningly good looking, they were also both about six foot six tall. Amanda told me they were local celebrities and played for the French National Basketball team.

Amanda grinned at me and immediately introduced us, and they promptly had some drinks ordered for us all. The conversation flowed easily between the three of us, with me translating for Antonia. After a few more drinks and a few inappropriate dances they invited us back to their nearby apartment for some private debauchery. When I replied, and translated to Antonia, that they wanted to continue the evening at theirs, but I'd told them that she was too tired and maybe on another occasion, she went all animated saying "no, no, please tell them we'll go". We all fell about laughing, when I told her I'd already accepted, and was just winding her up!

Their apartment was a five-minute walk, very close to "Notre Dame", and once inside drinks of choice were served and some soft mood music was put on. These two huge guys wasted no time in removing our dresses as we stood admiring the Seine, from the large floor to ceiling windows! They were both so tall, Antonia and I looked like little dolls in between them. Subtlety was not on the menu this evening, as Antonia and I proceeded to rip off their clothes, to reveal two very muscular and awesomely endowed mahogany physiques. We both fell to our knees to worship these two ebony masterpieces! Antonia was gagging, trying to swallow as much of her mans cock as possible, where as I worked mine into a frenzy with my deft tongue technique. It wasn't long before we were both lifted up and unceremoniously impaled on their manhood's, both of us struggling to accommodate their size without screaming. Once we were in full flow Antonia and I were used and abused in every conceivable position, being tossed around like rag dolls! Eventually I gained a bit of control as we swapped men and pushed them both back onto the large sofa. Antonia followed my lead and we rode them in unison, stopping every once in a while to swap partners! We were both climaxing regularly, as these two skilled men pounded us hard and with great ferociousness. They seemed set for the long run, as they our pummeled our insatiable and very eager vaginas. I was impressed with the ease and flexibility of Antonia's pussy in accommodating her mans awesome girth. We were both wetter than an "English summer!"

They certainly worked us hard, eventually we could take no more and got on out knees and begged for their semen, in a mixture of French and English, but they certainly got the message, as they instantaneously began to feed our eager mouths with copious amounts of their hot and delectable cream. By the end I'd lost count of how many times I'd climaxed, but by the lack of feeling in my legs, I knew it was numerous. Eventually as dawn was breaking, we returned to the apartment well used and exhausted. We just about had the strength to collapse into bed for a well-deserved sleep.

We finally awoke at midday, feeling full of beans after a good seven hours slumber, refreshed and ready for another Parisian day. We gorged on crepes in the bar opposite the apartment, washed down with strong black coffee. We enjoyed a leisurely day shopping and popped in and took a drink with Michel, and said hello to all my old colleagues. Sadly, Frederic was away on a buying trip. Michel's eyes lit up when I introduced him to Antonia, and I grinned when he slipped her his telephone number incase she found her self with a few hours so spare! So predictable…. Not changed one bit in all the years I've known him, and he always reminds me about my first visit to the shop, way back when.

It was a beautiful Autumn day, so we played tourists, and walked along the left bank, taking in the atmosphere of all the street art and little stalls that were selling a wide variety of old books, magazines and general nic nacs. Stopping off every once in a while so I could introduce Antonia to the delights of "Pastis". Several times during the afternoon various Frenchmen chatted us up, which was a nice boost for our ego's, always gratefully accepting compliments from whence they came. Antonia was now completely and utterly enthralled with Paris and everything it had to offer, especially to an attractive single woman. She declared to me that she'd be living here within a year! (Actually it only took her nine months). She has always said since that, "She was born to live in Paris".

We strolled in the early evening sun back to the apartment to get ready for the evenings activities. She had the address of a bar near "Les Halles" where she was meeting her old friend, whom she knew when she was married and living in America. They were meeting at eight, so we had planned on her getting a cab, just prior to Bruno picking me up. I had previously arranged with Bruno to leave a spare key for her to use, in case she returned earlier than me. She told me that she expected to simply have a meal and a good old catch up, and maybe a few drinks afterwards, but that her friend was definitely not a "club" kind of girl.

Yves had bought me a very elegant white Thierry Mugler chiffon evening gown, slit to the hip and a pair of lilac and silver strappy heels. Obviously no hold-ups required, as chance would have it I'd bought a very tiny white lace thong the previous day, which would be a perfect compliment to the dress.

We took our time getting ready, and the subject kept coming back to how much fun she'd had the previous evening, she kept blaming me for leading her astray, as if?! But she said emphatically, that she wouldn't have had it any other way, and was already thinking about Saturday evening, and did I have anything in mind? I told her I'd give it some serious thought, and was sure that something risqué or down right depraved could be arranged! She said she'd be led by my expertise and greater knowledge.

Once she was safely in a cab and on her way, it was only minutes until Bruno collected me. Yves as ever complimented me on the way the dress suited me and explained that we would be going for a special dinner prior to my new unique "experience".

Bruno dropped us at the world famous "La Tour d'Argent", one of the oldest and most prestigious eateries in Paris. It is certainly a restaurant with a great history. Yves was full of knowledge, and got very animated, when telling me, that in was in 1867 during the Paris World Exhibition that the Cafe Anglais was at its peak, and one famous day Alexander II, Czar of the Russian Empire, the Czarevitch and future Alexander III, William I, King of Prussia and future Emperor and the Prince Otto von Bismarck sat down at the same table for a sumptuous banquet. Also, he went on to explain over an aperitif, that in 1582, during the reign of Henry III, an inn was built on a plot of land adjacent to a convent belonging to the Bernardin monks. It was given the name "Hostellerie de La Tour d'Argent". Next to the quay, this Renaissance-style structure would quickly start to draw an elegant clientele. The lords and ladies of the court would meet there to enjoy the view of the Seine, and sometimes of the boats kept at their disposal by the innkeeper. King Henry III himself would dine there on several occasions along with the lords of the Court after returning from a hunt. History lesson over!

The setting is absolutely breathtaking, with views over the Seine to the beautifully lit Cathedral "Notre Dame". We were presented with the finest foods and wines from the "Grand Menu Tour D'argent", finishing in spectacular style with Crêpes "Belle Epoque" flambéed at the table. It was and still is to this day, one of the finest and truly memorable dining experiences that I've been fortunate to have enjoyed.

Yves told me that my evening "fun" would commence at midnight and would last for approximately ninety minutes. We would arrive and take a drink prior to the event, which was being hosted by an elite group of high-ranking officers from the "Légion étrangère. Who met occasionally, after completing a foreign assignment. They always enjoyed a wind-down dinner, always with some form of "special" entertainment and…. I was to be it!!

Bruno drove us to an address in Western Paris, and a very distinguished man in military uniform saluted Yves with great ceremony as he greeted us at the large double entry doors. We were shown in to a large marble foyer, where our coats were taken.

The high walls were covered with Military portraits, going back to Napoleonic times; it was all very formal and quite imposing. We were led up the large marble stairs to the mezzanine level's balconied area, which had several passageways and imposing doors leading from it. At the far end of the main hallway was a very large imposing door, which when upon reaching our guide knocked twice in rapid succession.

As the door was opened and we entered the room, I was struck by, firstly the grandeur of it all, and secondly, with being confronted by a dozen gentlemen, all stood to attention saluting Yves and chanting some kind of ceremonial "Motto", which I didn't understand. Several of the men were in full Military regalia, with the remainder in full "black tie" evening dress. All very intimidating, but very exciting! However, the one defining feature that they all had in common, which was highly effective and thoroughly arousing, was that they were all wearing identical brilliant white "Phantom of The Opera" half masks. I assumed this was for security reasons, so I didn't question it. I was formally introduced, and each one bowed and kissed my hand. I was already in the first discernable stages of arousal; this just accelerated the process rapidly. I felt very self-conscious as they all slowly appraised me as my drink was being poured, and many made comments to Yves, such as…a true beauty…divine creature… built for pleasure, were among some of the more memorable phrases used.

After a while, a very effeminate looking gentleman came and led me away to be prepared! I followed him through in to a large dressing area, where he removed my dress and hung it neatly on a hangar in the corner. He then placed me on a large table, not unlike a massage bed. He appeared moments later, with a large porcelain bowl full of scented soapy water; which he started to wash me all over with using a large toweling mitten. Even though my body was hairless and only recently waxed he proceeded to gently shave my legs, under-arms and my vaginal area with great skill and attention to detail, until he was satisfied that I would pass even the most microscopic inspection! Once complete, he began to bathe my body in wonderful warm sandalwood oil. I simply couldn't help myself when he reached my pussy, I let go my first wet orgasm of the evening, soaking his arm in the process. He smiled and nodded his approval, saying that I was now ready for "use"! He helped me down off the table, where he handed me several pairs of incredibly high black patent shoes, luckily a pair fitted perfectly, they made my legs look never ending!

    I then followed him through a side door, into a very sensually lit room, with a door at one end, and what I guessed was a large one way viewing mirror at the other, with two smaller ones along the side wall. Positioned in the middle of the room, centre stage, as I liked to think of it, was a waist high plinth, that was padded in sumptuous black leather. There were two leg supports with ankle fastenings, thankfully my arms were free to reach and feel. I discreetly snuck into my purse, and took a huge hit of poppers before stepping up onto the plinth. Once in position, my helper produced, with great ceremony, an ornately embroidered, and obviously well used black and gold blindfold and fastened it securely in place. I was completely deprived of the merest glimmer of any light. He checked my ankles were secure, and told me he would be leaving now, but would occasionally return with a drink for me, at that point he disappeared, leaving me alone, trembling in anticipation, and unconstrained lust. I could feel my excitement leaking from me in readiness for what ever lay ahead!

    I lay prone and helpless, for what seemed like an eternity, sensing multiple pairs of eyes watching me from behind the mirrors. Eventually, I heard the door quietly opening and soft footsteps approaching. I flicked my hips, showing off my open and sodden vagina to the intruder. Suddenly, I felt a warm breath blowing on me, first on my neck, working its way over my breasts and downward to my wetness, the sensation was immeasurable. I could feel my juices streaming from me as he teased me with his breath, eventually as I felt I would explode, I felt his tongue gently start to suck on my labia and clitoris, skillfully probing my anus, instantly bringing me to a substantial squirting climax. I heard his distinct groan of approval. Immediately after my gushes had subsided, I felt his manhood rubbing up and down my pussy for several moments, spreading my lips with his helmet, until he expertly slid his length into me. I gasped in pure delight, and was totally shocked, when an unannounced, anonymous penis, gently pushed its way into my mouth, immediately without any encouragement my mouth went to work on it fervently, whilst my vagina was being pounded, with more and more powerful thrusts. They started to work as a team, rhythmically fucking my mouth and vagina in complete synchronization. I soon felt yet another hard penis rubbing against my cheek; my tongue and mouth went into overdrive, ensuring I pleased both with equal measure. Shortly the man inside me shuddered, and climaxed powerfully deep inside me, he was replaced by another in seconds. I was kept in raptures by all the attention and climaxed frequently as the two men who were using my mouth fed me their plentiful juices, which I lapped up eagerly, with my favourite words "grande salope"! being repeated several times. With my sense of sight totally denied, I remained clueless, as to who, or how many were in the room at any given time. After around forty-five minutes of constant and intensely enjoyable use, I was given a break, and my helper returned with a large brandy, and proceeded to cleanse me, with his trusty mitten and warm scented wash.

I felt I'd been freshly prepared for round two, as he helped me back on to the plinth, this time, however, positioning me on all fours, with my fully aroused wet, exposed vagina open and fully on show, to who ever entered the room next…. I couldn't wait, I wanted, and needed much more!

I didn't have long to wait, as the second half started with a flourish, as a large anonymous erection was placed at my mouth for me to suck on, whilst my bottom was being spanked. I wriggled and thrust it provocatively in the direction of their hands and busy fingers. I came forcefully several times, squirting my cum over their arms and wrists, to many appreciative utterances from the men that were using me.

A pair of hands suddenly spread my buttocks wide apart, I felt somebody start to rub a pleasantly cold jelly like substance over my anus, gently working it inside with his fingers. All the time I was concentrating on pleasing the various penises' that were offered to my mouth. After much anal stimulation, I felt the head of a large cock probe at my entrance, and slowly ease itself deep into my anus, until I could feel his testicles lying heavy against my butt cheeks. He began to fuck my anus with great urgent, powerful strokes, that had me climaxing furiously, as I felt him empty his hot semen deep inside, to be immediately replaced by another, and another, and so it went on. My anus was being given the workout of a lifetime, and I was taking it all with great indulgence. During the entire scenario, my mind was racing with the thought of all these very fit men naked, taking their pleasure, whilst still remaining completely anonymous, both due to the blindfold and their "Phantom of The Opera" masks…it was pure carnal eroticism at it best!

The final minutes were extreme and pure unadulterated wanton lust from both sides. Every one of my orifices was taken and pleasured and gave pleasure to the willing and ardent participants. My mouth, vagina and rectum, all working in perfect lustful harmony for these rampant men! After being fully cleansed of the vast amount of semen that had been deposited in and over me and appropriately redressed, I was returned to the main drawing room, to be greeted by a proud, smiling Yves, with a very much-needed tumbler of Jack Daniels in his hand for me.

As we were about to leave, all the men (still with masks in place) saluted and gave me a rousing three cheers, which made me blush, which was bizarre, seeing what I'd just experienced.

Yves escorted me to the car, but stayed with his comrades, as Bruno dropped me back at the apartment. Thankfully, Antonia had just returned and was still up, I poured us both a drink and proceeded to tell her in great detail about the evening, for once she was speechless and just sat open mouthed, finally saying "some girls have all the luck"…with that we both hit the sac. I needed some deep sleep and my body needed some serious recovery time.

I woke late morning parched and in much need of a strong coffee and a menthol cigarette, woke Antonia and we threw on some jeans and shirts and went across the road…they were well used to my morning after appearance and ensured much needed sustenance was quickly served. That first hit of strong French coffee coupled with a St Moritz never fails to hit the spot and reinvigorate an abused body.

We decided to take a slow walk through the wonderfully enchanting Parisian backstreets, stopping every now and again to take a coffee or a "Pastis". Eventually we felt sufficiently revitalized to find a small patisserie and re-energize further on a few large wedges of various cakes and gateau's, pure indulgence. Like a couple of teenagers on holiday for the first time; we giggled and dabbed each other's faces with cream and chocolate, much to the amusement of the staff and patrons alike. We decided we'd find a nice little bistro later, and just see where the evening took us... no firm plan in mind. And that's exactly what we did!

When we returned to the apartment, I could by this time sense intuitively that Bruno had popped in. How right I was, as on the table in the lounge was a gift-wrapped box, labeled "For Paul's eyes only, enjoy. Yves xxx". It didn't take a genius to work out what it was, and both Paul and myself had many a "naughty" hour or two, watching the DVD of my evening with the officers from the "Legion". Starring myself, and a multitude of fit French men, in glorious High Definition Technicolor. Paul christened it "A Masterpiece of Erotica".

That evening we ended up having huge juicy burgers and fries at the "Hard Rock Café", dressed simply in jeans and t-shirts, wonderfully dressed down and relaxed. However, after a few J.D's Antonia started to get horny and wanted to go clubbing. Even though I was physically wrecked, I couldn't deny her, especially as she was baron from her previous evening with her old friend, and also it was our last night.

So we dashed back to the apartment, where Antonia quickly slipped into a revealing "ravish me" dress, whilst I quickly had a chat with Paul, I slipped on a LBD and heels. Probably a speed record for getting ready for both of us! We took a cab to L'Escapade. Antonia's choice, as she wanted to revisit the "scene of the crime" of her decadent first night in Paris,

I was determined, or rather my muscles and limbs were determined, that my role tonight was simply as Antonia's "Chaperone". I spent most of the evening telling, and re-telling my previous nights tryst to Amanda and François, they were simply spellbound. I kept a close eye on Antonia, who was enjoying the attention of several different suitors, including a rather fine-looking middle-aged couple. It was a pleasant change to simply enjoy a drink and gossip at the bar…. my body was certainly grateful for the reprieve!

Chapter Forty-One: And There You Have it!

That was my last trip to Paris in the nineties, one that will live in my memory forever. The next escapade wouldn't be for a few months, four in fact, March of the year 2000, when unbeknownst to me Paul, Mike and Yves had colluded to throw me a party to end all parties, in honour of my Fortieth birthday, and yes, you guessed where.... In Paris! Where it all started, nearly ten years previously... more of that will feature prominently in the next installment of my memoirs, which after a brief break from writing, I will be starting to put together shortly.

I truly hope you have enjoyed reading some of the more explicit recollections, and sexual adventures, compiled from my diaries 1990-1999. There is certainly at lot more to divulge in my forthcoming "further exploits". Coming soon!

Emma Xxx